Dark Hearts in the Forest

Copyright 2017 Bruce A. Miles

All Rights Reserved

ISBN-13: 978-1974520497
ISBN-10: 1974520498

This book is a work of fiction and any resemblance to persons, living or dead, places, events, and situations is purely coincidental. The characters are productions of the author's imagination and are used fictitiously.

Also by Bruce A. Miles

The Shootings at Summerhill High School

The Greek Fire Killings

Teacher to Parent Confidential

Please visit Argentalit.com to learn more.

For

Kenny

Chuck

Mike

Cover Concept by
Donavon Thompson

Cover Design by
Jesse Burgener

Here's the hitch
Your horse is leaving
Don't miss your boat
It's leaving now
And as you go I will spread my wings
Yes I will call this home
I have no time to justify to you
Fool you're blind, move aside for me
All I can say to you my new neighbor
Is you must move on or I will bury you.

-The Dave Matthews Band

> He headed up the holler with everything he had
> It's before my time but I've been told
> He never came back from Copperhead Road
>
> -Steve Earle

    Legends of strange creatures roaming the ancient New World forests were shared among native peoples long before European settlers invaded their ancestral homes. Spanish and French explorers then carried the legends of feral forest men through the expanding frontier and across the ocean.

    The men at the root of the legends were the outcasts of their day; they were the psychopaths, the sociopaths, the diseased, the mentally retarded, and the physically malformed, who were driven from tribes, villages, settlements, and towns to live in the forests. Abandoned, the outcasts adapted to survive, and occasionally thrive, in the deep, unmapped wilderness where they had taken refuge. The pariahs had no laws, morals, culture, or imperatives other than to survive by any means necessary. Because of their secretive nature and frightening raids on travelers the outcasts were seen as demonic creatures ruling a no man's land. Half naked and raucous the mysterious savages were described as unholy feral creatures by native peoples. Often the reports were embellished in hope of scaring white trespassers away.

    Successive generations of explorers continued the reports of wild men in the forests and swamps attacking suddenly and fiercely when homesteading, hunting, or survey parties trespassed into their territory. Gruesome details of attacks horrified listeners as the news were spread. The world grew fascinated with the encounters coming out of the wild frontier, the ancient forests, and mysterious swamps.

    The legend continued from one century into the next century becoming established as truth through generations of retellings. As decades passed weaponry and technology improved, begetting countless groups and individuals mounting expeditions to capture one of the man-creatures. The best trackers of each era were hired by newspaper publishers to capture one of the fabled man-beasts. Carnivals and museums offered princely rewards for one taken alive. Every tracker and trapper boasted he would bring one of the creatures back. None succeeded.

Eventually, as growing settlements began to tame the wild lands, tales of feral beast-men roaming the uncut forests and strange swamps became scary campfire stories intended to keep children obedient through fear of dark forest monsters.

As the modern era began, sporadic reported sightings kept the creature in the newspapers even as the country's fascination turned to steam engines, coast-to-coast railroads, automobiles, and wars. Despite the lack of evidence, true believers, newspaper publishers, and dedicated searchers kept the legend alive.

Over time, the fabled creatures were given names of Bigfoot, Skunk Ape, Sasquatch, Yeti, and the Fouke Monster. Beginning in the mid twentieth century the ancient legends had a resurgence in popularity once again capturing the public's attention through reported sightings, movies, and television shows.

Throughout the latter part of the twentieth century a new breed of inquisitive souls embraced the Bigfoot legend and hunted for the creatures with all that modern technology had to offer. As technology advanced Bigfoot enthusiasts began using Forward Looking Infrared technology, state of the art night vision optics, high-definition, digital wild game trail cameras, and sophisticated audio software that could differentiate and isolate one insect from another insect out of a chorus of thousands. Yet, despite all of the technology in use, by hundreds of researchers, the mysterious Bigfoot remained elusive.

The elusive Bigfoot was seldom photographed, causing the legendary creature to remain an object of endless speculation. And, as with Unidentified Flying Objects, Bigfoot's popularity would come and go but it would not fade away.

Countless documentaries and television series following groups searching for Bigfoot in the American Northwest, the Deep South, and Middle America filled the cable TV channels' schedules. Most episodes were void of substance but sometimes elaborate hoaxes were exposed, occasionally intriguing evidence was discovered, and DNA samples were logged as unidentifiable. Although different shows yielded similar results, their loyal fan base persisted and decent ratings kept the programs on the air. Each season promised exciting news but no series provided proof or definitive DNA results, just renewed assurances an answer was coming soon.

Bigfoot had become one of the enduring mysteries of modern times; perhaps it is the grandfather of all mysteries born in the New World. It was certainly a mystery that could be used to keep trespassers away.

The LaHarpe clan did not start the Bigfoot legend but they gave their best collective effort to perpetuate, and embellish, the legend. At the start of the nineteenth century, the Louis Richard LaHarpe family used the legend, and some of the odder members of the clan, to drive trespassers and lost souls from the land they had carved out of the ancient forests near what would someday be the Louisiana and Arkansas borderlands. The ruse of the Forest Wild Men kept unwanted parties from accidently discovering the clan's illegal trading activities and moonshining operations while providing plausible explanations for the occasional soul who went missing.

The ruse worked efficiently, keeping trespassers away from LaHarpe moonshine stills and marijuana plots. For generations the LaHarpe family distilled moonshine and then grew marijuana with impunity in Chickasaw County. The LaHarpe's cattle ranch and timber sales provided perfect cover for laundering tax-free money and a way to distribute their products.

The late twentieth century spawned events that forced changes to the LaHarpe way of doing business. The first event was that the legend of the Skunk Ape experienced a new surge of popularity through television shows that increased the number of hunters armed with the latest technology and weapons; and rather than scaring people away, reported sightings drew Bigfoot enthusiasts to the area by the truck loads.

Occasionally a searcher would disappear or die mysteriously. Sometimes a death or disappearance would cause weekend Bigfoot hunters to flee the area, other times the death brought teams of law enforcement officers to the county to investigate the circumstances of the death. When careless interlopers crossed onto LaHarpe land they were taught a lesson about private property; usually only nearly frightened to death, but sometimes killed. The LaHarpe's were crafty in disposing of the bodies and crime scene investigators usually left Chickasaw County with an unsolved case. The fact that so many deaths and disappearances remained unsolved guaranteed the county a long shelf life in the annals of unsolved mysteries.

National television programs and news reports stated that over a one-hundred year period Chickasaw County led the region in missing person reports. When interviewed for documentaries about the number of missing souls, the local population's reaction was a disinterested shrug. To the residents of Chickasaw County, rural life was private life, and what happened on the other side of the fence was someone else's business. The sheriff's department did what they could, but evidence was scant and witnesses were nonexistent; it had been that way since frontier days.

Beginning in the 1800's, to perpetuate the Wild Man ruse as a way to keep interlopers away from their property, large members of the LaHarpe clan would wear a costume stitched together from rabbit, coyote, and bear hides to recreate the reported appearance of the Forest Wild Men.

The costume was a work of beauty and practicality. Four LaHarpe women spent two months crafting the suit. Leather boots that rose to the crotch, under the fur hide outerwear, helped the wearer of the suit bull his way through briars that would have shredded a conventionally dressed hiker. The heavy boots had a soul that was painstakingly carved to resemble a big, bare, human foot. Dressed in the impressively magnificent suit, a family member would scare away trespassers with blood curdling screams and thudding footsteps.

The family member chosen to wear the suit was always a man strong enough to hurl a large rock or tree limb at fear stricken trespassers. The LaHarpe clan men, in general, were large and strong people, a trait that had served them well in conquering the backwoods. Daily life and work around the compound kept the men fit and muscular while genetics did the rest.

During the latter part of the twentieth century people fancying themselves professional hunters and seeking their fifteen minutes of fame began arming themselves with semi-automatic weapons and cutting-edge technology; regardless of field experience, each man and woman was certain he or she would be rich and famous after being the first to take a Bigfoot, dead or alive. The dead or alive mentality of exuberant hunters added a level of danger for the LaHarpe man wearing the suit and a lottery was begun to determine who would wear the suit.

Many of the pseudo-hunters shot first and identified later; a ground check approach all ethical hunters denounced. But, Bigfoot was more than just an animal, it was a legendary animal with a bounty on its head; so caution and ethics were dismissed in the rush to be the first person to prove Bigfoot was real and collect the rewards and fame a body would bring to the lucky hunter.

Several times, in the heat of the moment, an inexperienced, panicked, hunter would shoot another hunter by accident, but most often it was small animals shuffling through the dry leaves littering the forest floor that ended up taking a bullet. With Bigfoot hunters routinely ignoring private property signs, the overworked county sheriff let Chickasaw County locals police their own lands.

Pierre Perseus LaHarpe was the unlucky LaHarpe to take a Bigfoot hunter's bullet while wearing the suit. Pierre's injury was a minor wound after which he chased the shooter for a quarter of a mile crashing over saplings and through briar thickets while roaring in pain and anger. After Perseus's brush with death the LaHarpe clan began to rethink their anti-trespassing deterrents.

A family meeting was convened and the incident was discussed at length. The men said the ruse was vital to protect the family's moonshining business but the women prevailed with the argument that the safety of family members was more important and demanded that a new plan be devised. By the end of the meeting it was consensus that the new breed of trigger happy bounty hunters and their use of technology put family members at too great of a risk; continuing the ruse of the Forest Wild Men was discontinued. The suit was retired with a ceremony then packed away with great care and respect.

A series of family meetings followed as the LaHarpe clan discussed how to keep trespassers away. No consensus was reached and any new incident of trespassing was dealt with in an individual manner. Three stagnant ponds on the property had long been the disposal sites for the bodies of trespassers and although the LaHarpe women were against murdering trespassers, for the most part, they did not protest the actions of the men. Life in the family compound continued as the world outside began to encroach ever closer to their private, isolated, lifestyle.

The War on Drugs was another event that forced the LaHarpe clan to rethink their businesses. The federal government's War on Drugs put helicopters with sophisticated detection devices into the air to search for marijuana patches and moonshine stills hidden in woody hollows. Locations of grow plots and distillery sites were marked from the air allowing heavily armed police units to march directly to the spot and eradicate the marijuana patch or destroy the still.

In Chickasaw County, on any given day, there would be a column of smoke rising into the sky from a still or a grow site that had been set ablaze by law enforcement. Other clever residents of Chickasaw County also devised ways to challenge the cops, but few were as successful as the members of the LaHarpe clan.

The government's use of military level technology had neutralized age old concealment practices and ground raids could occur with no recourse for the LaHarpe's other than to use expensive lawyers to claim the pot patch or moonshine still was the work of trespassers; after all, the LaHarpe patriarch stated, how could a family with so many acres be aware of what was happening on their property so far away from their living compound?

The anger the LaHarpe clan felt came not from the occasional raid that destroyed the still or burned the crop; that was a begrudged cost of doing illegal business. Their anger came from the fact that the government could just march onto their property and do what they wanted as the LaHarpes' watched with no recourse.

The LaHarpes came to realize that a different business plan had to be found. During one of the monthly family meetings, John Lee Sherman advocated a business idea to introduce a new profitable product. Sherman described the youth oriented product as a happy pill then explained how modern technology would help them manufacture the pill cheaply as well as effectively hide the lab where it would be manufactured.

Older clan members distrusted using new technology but were intrigued by John Lee's promise of a high profit margin. Several of the elders believed that the government had a way of spying whenever technology was used and were fearful of calling attention to the family. They feared their privacy and sovereignty would be compromised allowing the government access to their lives. John Lee Sherman persevered and slowly convinced the elders that a closed system bore the family no threat.

Slowly, over time, John Lee introduced wireless technology to receptive family members and demonstrated how technology could be their tool as much as it was the federal government's tool. Using the right sales pitch, framing technology as a tool to equalize the struggle between the family and the government, John Lee eventually had several of the older family members comfortable using an array of electronic, wireless, surveillance devices. He began by showing family elders trail camera photos of giant bucks roaming at night which slowly opened the door to acceptance. The door opened wider once trail camera photos allowed the family to see the animal activity that occurred in the gardens and when they were away from the compound.

After surveillance technology was embraced John Lee introduced cell phones to the elders. Cell phones suddenly made the LaHarpe clan's lives better; no family member disputed that. Livestock and produce coordination for trips to auction or the farmer's market in Tallyrand became more efficient and profitable. Occasional service outages, when thieves would steal copper wire from the cell tower, reminded the elders how much better portable phones were making life in Chickasaw County.

After overcoming all remaining resistance, wireless cameras, motion activated sensors, and early detection perimeter alert systems were installed around the LaHarpe compound. John Lee earned the respect of the elders and the admiration of the rest of the family for showing them an environment few knew existed. The hunters in the clan, having embraced trail camera use, kept the LaHarpe storehouses stocked year round with fresh meat that replaced salted and smoked cured meat that could be months old.

The gardeners were particularly grateful for the John Lee introducing technology to the family. Use of infrared cameras doubled harvest bounties as gardeners patterned then eliminated nighttime raiders. Fascination with seeing what occurred around the compound when no one was looking grew into understanding of how to eliminate pests and predators. Garden harvests grew to the best in decades once the plunderers were routed and the fruits, vegetables, and herbs were reclaimed by the family. John Lee had a plan and the first part, getting the elders to accept technology, had been very successful.

Once the older members of the clan came to recognize the usefulness of modern detection technology, John Lee was able to persuade them that similar technology could be used to protect a new business he proposed. John Lee assured the council that his venture, a pill, with the aid of technology, could be manufactured in a protected, concealed environment, was easy to transport, and, most importantly, had a large profit margin. The unexpected downturn in tax-free moonshine and marijuana markets forced the elders to consider John Lee's business proposal with an open mind.

The tribunal core of the council of elders stated emphatically that if John Lee's endeavor was approved, the entirety of the operation must remain within the family, from top to bottom. The fewer outsiders who knew about any LaHarpe family operation made it safer and kept all profits within the family. John Lee agreed calling the business philosophy Total Vertical Integration.

John Lee did not need to explain to the elders how outside market forces and the government were conspiring against the LaHarpes. Moonshine was now legally manufactured by craft distillers who added flavors and created a product with here-to-fore unknown smoothness. Marijuana was becoming legal and cities were awash in tax revenue collected from government certified dispensaries. The once lucrative market for moonshine and wild grown marijuana provided by the LaHarpes was shrinking by the day. It was a trying time calling for hard decisions as the family struggled with declining income and widespread, legal, competition.

The drop in moonshine sales forced the elders to take notice of legal competitors called micro-distilleries that were stealing their customers. The tax paying, modern, distillers made smooth, flavored, moonshine that could be purchased at any liquor store. The LaHarpes were forced to respond by lowering their moonshine prices to compete with legitimate outlets and their fancy, flavorful, offerings. The price war had reduced the LaHarpe's untaxed income to worrisome levels.

LaHarpe's primary clientele for white lightning were gambling houses, brothels, and bootlegger houses; and the business owners knew how to negotiate for a lower price, after all there were no taxes involved in the sale of LaHarpe moonshine and that held the prices down for both under the table sellers and drinkers.

In the end, the consumer's decision came down to price versus taste, and for the modern consumer taste was king. Faced with dire times, caused by changing clientele, the LaHarpe council of elders reluctantly agreed to allow John Lee an opportunity to proceed with his plan while the elders studied additional options. John Lee used the opportunity to establish his secret lab and guarantee the family that he would show a profit within one year.

John Lee thanked the elders by setting up one wireless camera security system overlooking the LaHarpe's single remaining still. The real time camera feed usually showed nothing but wildlife sniffing around the still, but the elders loved sitting in the shade of the porch watching the still from afar. The still was well hidden but there was always a chance of an accidental discovery by a very off road bicyclist, a tree hugger photographing the region's giant, old growth, hardwood trees, or competition looking to set up their own illicit still, meth lab, or marijuana grow site. The security system overlooking the still had alarms in five key homes, two barns, and on three cell phones. In six months of operation the system had gone off twice because of a human. Protocols were established for subsequent interlopers. John Lee Sherman became the clan's technological leader.

In early spring an unexpected event affected the LaHarpe family future again. Local Chickasaw High School football hero Tom Benson graduated from Wildlife Office Training School and was assigned to the county that was home to his family and the family he felt was his nemesis, the LaHarpe clan.

The animosity toward the LaHarpe family was born from the fact that Eli LaHarpe had raped two of Tom's love pursuits. He was as devastated as the women feeling he was somehow responsible.

Eli had gotten the girls drunk then raped them. Following the attacks the girls refused to testify out of fear of the LaHarpe clan. When confronted Eli smugly told Tom Benson, "You're welcome for having been saved the trouble of figuring out they weren't nothing but cold fish in the sack."

Benson finally convinced one girl to report the rape. Other victims came forward as news of Eli's arrest on rape charges spread through the county. Benson testified for the prosecution.

Seven women testified and Eli was convicted on six counts of rape and sentenced to prison. In prison, Eli himself was raped and subsequently hung himself. Eli's suicide was the beginning of the LaHarpe-Tom Benson feud. The LaHarpes vandalized Benson's car and property for months as Tom and his family waited in fear for the vendetta to run its course and stop.

Tom Benson knew the LaHarpe family routinely got away with illegal activities and he made it his personal mission to stop them all. Cops were limited in scope but a Wildlife Officer could surveille the LaHarpe holdings. So, now, Benson made it a point to patrol the LaHarpe lands every shift. As months passed with no observable infractions, Tom's impatience for payback on the LaHarpe's grew as frustration fueled an irrational drive for revenge.

Muscular, bald, heavily bearded, mountain sized, Preston LaHarpe enjoyed wandering the family's vast property at night; the nightly walks were more than relaxing, they were therapeutic. Preston, a combat veteran, could not sleep a full night after returning from Afghanistan. To keep his nightmares and thrashing in bed from disturbing his wife and children Preston prowled the old forest at night. Invariably he saw something interesting ranging from rarely seen animal behavior to spectacular meteor showers and stars that burned white holes in the dark heavens.

Preston especially enjoyed using customized night vision optics he frequently wore on night patrols. The big man loved to creep as close to an animal as he could before the animal sensed him. Stealth was more than a game to Preston as he crept like a wraith through the forest; stealth was a tactical skill that he honed nightly.

Preston loved the night and used the LaHarpe woodlands as his own personal playground. Tonight Preston was wearing custom designed night vision headgear he had constructed from a full coverage motorcycle helmet and state of the art night vision optics. Preston had an infrared component for the helmet but most nights he opted for night vision mode.

The modified motorcycle helmet wasn't well balanced because of the blocky battery, but Preston felt the exceptional optics was worth an achy neck the next day. The helmet had microphones embedded near the ears to pick up faint sounds. Preston was quite proud of his creation although the battery life was limited to about four hours with simultaneous use of optics and audio enhancers.

Preston enjoyed watching curious animals stop and stare at his hulking figure as he crept through the dark forest with the greatest of ease. At night, especially on a new moon night, the forest could be foreboding and dangerous, but not to Preston. The night vision edge allowed him to own the night. He could even use his riflescope while wearing the helmet and the microphones were sensitive enough to allow him to hear a bat flying above his head.

Sometimes during his nightly walkabouts Preston would wear body armor. The body armor was old, uncomfortable, and heavy from ballistic plates in Kevlar pockets. Preston had saved a fellow Ranger's life once and the grateful brother in arms would periodically send Preston items that had 'fallen off the truck'. The body armor was such a gift.

Preston felt confident about the old school body armor but hoped he would not have to test it under actual fire. He only wore it because he knew there were poachers and meth heads that would shoot first and never ask a question. It wasn't that Preston needed body armor; it was simply due diligence to wear and it was one more thing giving him a tactical advantage should he encounter a dangerous situation.

Most nights Preston was alone with nature but sometimes he discovered young lovers, teenage partiers, or more malicious minded intruders trespassing on LaHarpe land. Some nights Preston took action against the intruders, other nights he silently watched their activity. One of the benefits he enjoyed during his nightly patrols, other than avoiding the nightmares, was the excitement and anticipation of never knowing what he might discover.

Toward the end of spring, near dawn, at the end of one of his nightly patrols, Preston heard a man's voice coming from an old logging road so he crept toward the sound. The conversation was one sided indicating the man was either talking on a cell phone or radio. Preston attempted to adjust the microphone to focus on the speaker but the insects overwhelmed the helmet's audio enhancer.

Preston activated the visor and used his enhanced vision to creep toward the voice until he saw a Wildlife Enforcement Officer truck parked on an unused logging road separating the LaHarpe and the Carson properties. Preston crept close enough to see a male figure pacing on the dirt and rock logging road as he spoke into a cell phone.

The Wildlife Enforcement Officer reported he was going to take his break for breakfast then signed off and put the cell phone in his pocket. Preston watched from behind a tree and silently cursed as Tom Benson ignored the Carson property and crossed the rusty, barbwire fence onto LaHarpe land. Officer Benson moved his flashlight methodically right and left searching for something. Preston, intimately familiar with this section of the property, could not understand what Benson was doing.

After ten minutes of slowly searching through the forest Officer Benson found what he was looking for. He marked the spot with a handheld GPS unit then quickly returned to his truck. From the bed of the pickup truck Benson removed three steel leg traps and a camouflaged backpack displaying the Department of Wildlife logo. Preston LaHarpe watched in silent fascination as Officer Benson placed the three sawtooth steel leg traps, illegal in design, in the backpack.

Benson followed the GPS track back to the waypoint he had tagged and placed the three traps around a pond that held cool water at the edge of a grove of white oak trees. Benson methodically placed the traps leaving only the anchor chains visible over the leaves and sticks. Satisfied the steel traps were set just right Benson stood up, put his hands on his hips, and said aloud, smugness dripping off of every word, "Got you now, you sons of bitches."

Preston silently shadowed Benson, who was so pleased with himself that he whistled as he walked back to his truck. The big man closed the distance to Benson keeping one hand on his always present Colt Python revolver.

Back at his Department of Wildlife truck Benson dumped the empty backpack into the bed of the truck then turned and began to urinate as he looked up at the brightening sky. Benson began to whistle the Andy Griffith Show theme song as he urinated. Preston, gun in hand, silently crept to the front of Benson's truck, a soundless, flowing darkness in the pre-dawn dimness. Benson zipped his pants up but continued to look up at the last stars fading away in the pre-dawn sky. Preston holstered his Colt then quickly closed the gap between himself and Benson. He attacked the unsuspecting wildlife officer from behind. Benson fiercely fought to escape the vicious stranglehold but was no match for Preston's size, strength, ferocity, and element of surprise. After a brief struggle Preston snapped Benson's neck and dropped the man's body to the ground.

Preston effortlessly picked up Benson's body and slung it over his shoulder. He carried the dead wildlife officer's body to the rusted, barely visible, barbed wire fence that ran parallel to the old logging road separating the LaHarpe and the Carson properties. The LaHarpe clan and old man Carson had not been enemies but outside of countywide festivals and swap meets they did not socialize. In this part of the world social etiquette was to acknowledge but not engage unless conversation was necessary.

The Carson place had been abandoned for at least a year and hunting season was still months away. Staging Benson's body on the Carson property would ensure that investigators would not look at the LaHarpes. Preston rued bringing the authorities into the area for a death investigation but he felt confident he could make the death look like an accident diverting attention from his family.

Preston heaved Benson's limp form over the top wire where it landed on the leaf and stick covered forest floor on the Carson side of the fence. Preston crossed the fence easily and noiselessly and stood looking down at the body. He wondered briefly if any woman would miss Tom Benson before turning to wonder how the members of the LaHarpe family would celebrate Benson's death. Vengeance had been a long time coming, and Preston was proud he had been given the opportunity to correct a long standing wrong. Preston lamented Eli's death thinking if only Eli was still alive to hear the good news of Benson's death the murder would be even more satisfying.

Throwing Benson's body over his shoulder again, Preston walked toward an abandoned deer hunting box stand he had appropriated last hunting season. None of the Carson's had been in this part of their woods for years so Preston had taken over the elevated deer blind. It was an enclosed, plywood box stand, twenty feet tall, looking over a small spring fed watering hole circled by white oaks and a small stand of forage grass. The dark green stand was in good condition and had a wide field of view with multiple shooting lanes, so it seemed a shame for the spot to go to waste.

Preston realized that after tonight he probably would never have an opportunity to use the hunting blind ever again. He paused for a moment weighing the use of the stand now for his purpose against continuing to use it as a deer hunting stand; he had taken a nice twelve point buck from the stand last season and he rued giving it up. After a long pause Preston made his mind up.

Preston pulled Benson's body up the ladder to the floor of the plywood box stand and set him in the open doorway. Carefully the murderer grabbed one of Benson's boots and untied its laces one of which he securely snagged in a rough split on one of the ladder's aged wooden rungs. Preston next hooked the toe of the same boot behind the rung and shoved Benson's body out of the elevated box.

Benson's body fell, popping to a stop just above the ground, landing head down, booted foot twisted behind the rung of the ladder. Preston climbed past the body to the ground and checked out the scene from a few feet away. The accident scene would look exactly like he wanted to appear, the officer had climbed into the stand for some reason and a loose bootlace had become snagged causing the rookie officer to fall to his death. Just one of dozens of deer stand related accidents occurring in the county every year.

Preston had heard Benson tell dispatch he was taking a break for breakfast with no mention of where he was. When the officer failed to return following his duty shift a search party would be formed and the rookie officer would eventually be found. Looking at the staged scene the killer grinned from ear to ear; he had killed a family enemy and made it look like an accident. Preston had just committed a perfect murder, with the aid of a lie from the victim, and he was anxious to tell his family about it.

Preston carefully reviewed the crime scene under the beam of his halogen flashlight making sure he left no evidence behind. Carefully he re-crossed the rusty barbwire fence and scuffed the leafy ground roughly with his boots to indicate recent activity. Preston thought it best he steer the searchers to the abandoned hunting stand on the Carson land rather than giving the searchers a reason to come onto his land.

Next, Preston carefully collected the steel animal traps Officer Benson had planted. He laughed to himself that Benson would resort to such a ruse to bring trouble to the family. Preston noted the traps would make a fine addition to the traps he and his extended family already used regularly.

As Preston admired the animal traps, he wondered if Benson had purchased or confiscated the traps; either way Benson had been served his overdue justice. Preston began planning on how to announce to the family a long standing wrong had been finally righted. Preston carried the traps over his shoulder and smirked as he thought about karma.

As Preston made the long walk back to where his all-terrain-vehicle was parked he considered suggesting that the family look into buying the old Carson homestead; the selling price should be right for seemingly abandoned land following a tragedy. The Carson purchase would increase their vast land holdings by another two hundred and sixty acres.

Preston returned to the LaHarpe compound as the sun fully cleared the treetops and found the familiar sounds of milk cows, roosters, and gasoline engines soothing. He bounded up the steps to his small log cabin home sweeping up his wife, Eugenia, in a giant embrace.

Eugenia hugged his neck and asked, "What's gotten into you?"

Preston smiled, kissed her hard on the mouth, and said, "I'll tell everyone soon."

Eugenia looked curious but did not pry; Preston took her hand and led Eugenia into the bedroom.

2

> Do some down south jukin'
> Looking for a peace of mind
>
> -Lynyrd Skynyrd

As the summer season began James 'Kit' Carson received unexpected news. After Kit fully processed the news he called four of his closest friends with the same invitation. He was confident his friends would respond enthusiastically to his invitation; a chance to get away from the office to drink beer, grill burgers, fish, and shoot guns for a few days would be difficult to turn down.

Kit could barely contain his enthusiasm as he left voice mail messages. Kit said, "There's been an unexpected turn of events and Grandpa Ulysses' log cabin and acreage has come to me. And, get this, two different reality TV competition shows want to use the property as a location to shoot their series. Both production companies are waiting for me to email photos and details of the cabin and land before they send a crew down to scout it firsthand. I need to explore the property and make a photo file for them ASAP. Why don't you come down for a few days and help me explore? Bring your guns, food, sleeping bags, and favorite adult beverages and we can take some target practice and relax around a bonfire for a few nights. We can turn off the cell phones and chill. I'm staying for a week so you are welcome to stay as long as you want. I'll buy food and drinks but you should bring things to fill in the menu gaps and lots of ice and bottled water. I've got propane tanks for the cabin stove and I'll bring a grill and charcoal too. Call me back ASAP to let me know if you're in. You're not going to want to miss this opportunity to kick back in the woods. I'm going down next Thursday to get the cabin cleared out and check out the electrical and water status. When you guys arrive Friday, everything should be set. We can blow off some steam for a weekend! Call back ASAP."

The return calls came quickly with Kit's friends eagerly accepting the invitation to get away from the grind and spend time recharging with old friends in a bucolic setting. Kit smiled at the thought of the crew getting back together. He began to count the hours until he could leave town.

Kit stood in the middle of the century old log cabin admiring the craftsmanship visible in every detail. He could almost smell the meals Grandma Kellie once cooked in it. It was now his cabin; the same cabin he had spent many, many summers and weekends visiting while growing up. The twelve-hundred square foot log cabin had been lovingly cared for by his grandfather, a talented craftsman, and was still in remarkable condition for its age.

Kit turned and looked toward the rear of the cabin, the large open living room surrounding him. At the rear of the main room was a lone window next to a door leading out to a parking area and a nearby, well-constructed, outhouse. Turning to face the front of the cabin, to his left was the long narrow bunkroom, a tiny bathroom with a toilet and standup shower, a master bedroom, and kitchen area. The bunkroom and master bedroom each had a small pot-bellied wood burning stove in one corner of the room. The bunkroom, bathroom, and master bedroom had no windows. In the kitchen area, a large cast iron stove, once wood burning, now refitted for propane gas, dominated the space. An ancient refrigerator still kept food and drinks cold. The front of the cabin held one window to the left of the front door that served the kitchen area. It was the only window with a ledge on the outside. Kit recalled his grandmother setting pies on the wide ledge to cool.

A wide, covered porch ran the length of the front of the cabin. Wooden rocking chairs that usually lined the porch were currently stacked in a corner waiting to see the light of day once again. On Kit's right was a window that overlooked what once was a majestic vegetable garden, now overgrown with weeds. The long neglected plot was visible through the window and Kit envisioned fresh tomatoes and more growing tall and plentiful in the soil his grandparents had lovingly worked for years. The center of the wall featured a great stone fireplace that looked as if it should have been in a great king's hall rather than a rustic log cabin. Oversized wrought iron fireplace tools leaned on the stones waiting for a fire. The grate for holding the wood was thick iron and looked as if it could last another one-hundred years. A faint dusting of ashes littered the floor of the firebox.

Kit recalled playing in front of roaring fires as Grandma Kellie played the autoharp and family members sang gospel and county songs. He could almost smell chestnuts roasting on the open fire. Kit smiled as he recalled countless good times in the cabin.

Behind the cabin, near a parking area, was a well-constructed outhouse. Kit recalled being afraid of the outhouse as a child and being extremely happy when his grandfather installed the indoor toilet. Exceptionally well-constructed, the outhouse stood over a deep natural sinkhole, and young Kit feared angry Mole Men or other hellish creatures would emerge from the dark void below him angry over what he was dropping down into their realm.

Moving onto the porch Kit studied the area that passed for a yard surrounding the cabin hoping the lawn mower he had brought from home would survive the tall weeds. As he looked out over the weedy clearing he worried there might be snakes lurking in the thick growth. As Kit looked beyond the clearing his thoughts turned to the large barn past the old split rail horse corral on the bunkroom side of the cabin imagining what wonders, if any, the barn might hold.

Turning his attention back to the cabin's interior Kit marveled at the craftsmanship of the cabin and its furnishings; surely, living here had been heaven for a couple who had experienced a World War and the Great Depression. The furniture remaining inside the cabin consisted of a long, hand crafted, oak dining table with six hand-made dining chairs, a leather sofa, two reclining lounge chairs, and collection of rocking chairs.

No ceiling fans, wireless modem, or flat screen televisions were available. A wire net hanging a few feet over everyone's head stretched from side to side over the great room. From the wire netting hung ten bare incandescent light bulbs providing overhead light for the great room. The bunkroom, main bathroom, and master bedroom each had a single bulb hanging from the middle of their ceiling for illumination. The kitchen had two bare light bulbs, one hung over the cast iron stove while the second hung over a small cutting board island and trashcan.

Kit looked around the cabin overwhelmed by the reality that he now owned two very different homes. He made the most of his little house in the city, but this remote cabin felt like home; standing in the quiet cabin felt both like a return to the carefree days of his youth and a chance at finding some peace of mind during adulthood. Kit's mind raced searching for ideas to turn the extremely remote cabin into a money making venture and a chance to escape his current job. Kit opened a beer, took a sip, and walked out to his truck to begin unloading ice chests, grocery sacks, and liquor cases that would be key elements of making this weekend memorable.

Along the gravel drive leading from the county road to the parking area a Blue Jay harassed an unseen snake slithering through the tall weeds bordering the gravel drive. The bird finally drove the snake into the woods. Kit reminded himself to watch where he stepped. The image of his grandfather proudly showing off a rattlesnake skin belt he had made popped into Kit's mind. He looked down at his feet and considered his running shoes; Kit hurried to his truck to replace his shoes with knee-high hunting boots.

Kit spent the remainder of the day preparing the cabin and surrounding grounds for activities. Snakes and small animals fled to safer areas escaping the roaring mower's spinning blade. The mower struggled to cut the thick established weeds but succeeded in the end. Afterwards, admiring the freshly mowed clearing, Kit wondered which was more worn out, him or the lawn mower.

After mowing the area around the cabin and nearby structures Kit organized the fire pit to accommodate a large bonfire. As he piled kindling and pine needles into the fire pit Kit imagined his friends gathered around a roaring fire, drinking, catching up on recent events, and planning the future, much as they had done in college. Kit could almost feel the heat of the future bonfire as he sipped a cold beer.

Sitting around the fire drinking while telling tall tales was a time honored tradition Kit looked forward to enjoying. Afterwards, when the early birds had retired for the evening, the hard-core night owls would watch the flames die then embers pulsate until they finally cooled. Many nights the red of the dying embers had been gradually replaced with the red of the rising sun. Kit grew nostalgic as he thought of campfires gone by.

The old barn called out for exploration but Kit postponed that for a later time. He dragged a handcrafted rocking chair from the cabin out onto the shady porch and opened a new beer. Listening to the sounds of the forest and smelling freshly cut grass flushed the stress from his body and mind. Kit rocked slowly as he watched the woods and listened to the forest sounds. In the daylight, the forest looked bright and magical, but at night the dense forest could be menacing and spooky. In this part of the county there were no constant sirens, no chained up dogs incessantly barking, and no cars constantly honking or cranked up car stereos frightening dogs and annoying old women. Kit physically felt stress slipping away with each sip of cold beer.

The muscle soreness from yesterday's labors of mowing and cleaning melted away as Kit stood in the great room of his very own century old cabin studying the satellite photographs and maps covering the long, hand crafted, oak dining table. Kit had called the local power company before leaving home and had gotten the electricity turned on in hours; irritatingly, it took longer to get the water turned on. As he studied the maps, Kit let the faucet run wide open to purge the system. Having water and electricity provided a sense of comfort and security taken for granted in the city.

Used together, his grandfather's hand drawn maps, current satellite images, and county plat maps provided Kit with a thorough paper overview of his inherited property. The collection gave Kit a rudimentary understanding of the 240 acres, shaped like the state of Idaho, owned by his family since 1875. Now Kit just had to decide on what to do with the property from the several options he was considering. His mind swirled with possibilities, each promising an escape from his job. He hoped his friends would give him feedback and ideas he had yet to consider.

Despite the stewardship responsibility, and owed back taxes that came with the property, Kit felt the unexpected inheritance could be a Godsend enabling him to escape his job as a manager for a regional home appliance rent to own chain.

In a spiral bound notebook, bought at the county's only Dollar General store, Kit listed his ideas for the property. His ideas included a private hunting camp, a corporate retreat, a massive paintball game arena, and a dude ranch featuring horseback rides. He jotted down pros and cons for each idea. The cabin was a hundred yards plus away from a county highway and a forty-minute drive from the nearest town. The only hospital in the area was an hour's drive north. Kit wondered if the remoteness would be a positive or a negative as he pondered potential business ventures.

The only real businesses in Chickasaw County were cattle farming and cutting timber for lumber. Low wages and seasonal incomes for local produce kept the county's residents barely above poverty level. Years of tornadoes, floods, and droughts had devastated many farms and ranches in the county and a painfully slow recovery seemed to have ground to a halt. With only farming and no industry in the county, it remained one of the state's most undeveloped areas. Chickasaw County residents did whatever was needed to earn money.

Kit jotted down stream of consciousness outlines for each business idea growing increasingly anxious to discuss the ideas with his longtime friends. After two hours he felt mentally exhausted and pushed himself away from the spiral bound notebook. Kit left the notebook on the dining table with the maps using an old horseshoe as a paperweight. After opening a beer Kit dragged a rocking chair into a patch of sunlight near the bonfire pit. He stared into the thick forest and saw only thin shafts of sunlight were able to pierce the leafy forest canopy and reach the forest floor.

The interior of the forest seemed magical and mysterious with its areas of light and shadow. In the clearing butterflies flew through the sunny space searching for the wildflowers Kit had mowed down. Kit watched the butterflies search for the missing flowers and felt like an intruder in their sanctuary. One butterfly flew in close and checked out Kit's beer then flew away. Kit sat in the rocking chair putting his feet on a log next to the bonfire pit then closed his eyes and faced the sun.

As Kit relaxed in the warm sunshine he recalled driving along the two lane county road to the cabin. The asphalt road was in good condition and Kit knew that would be a plus for the television show people. He found it ironic that the producers and crews required comfortable accommodations and catered food even as their reality show contestants competed for rewards as simple as a taste of processed foods or a visit from a loved one. He hoped the producers would accept the limitations of the area.

The only problem Kit identified as a possible deal breaker was that thieves had stolen copper wire and electronics from the local cell phone tower shutting down service to the area. A public notice posted on the door of the local Dollar General store stated that repairs would take a while and that the tower company was sorry for the inconvenience. A second poster offered a $5,000 reward for information leading to the capture and conviction of the copper wire thieves. The clerk at the Dollar General store informed Kit that theft of electronics was a big problem in the area and that repairs to the tower usually took some weeks to be completed.

Kit took his purchases after thanking the clerk for the update. As he left the store he worried that his friends might be trying to contact him, and if unsuccessful might turn back. Or worse, the TV producers might back out due to unreliable cell service. Kit pushed the negative thoughts from his mind.

Yesterday, as Kit neared the gravel drive for the cabin he had been listening to one of Ted Nugent's hunting songs, Fred Bear. Nugent's lyrics, *'The spirit of the woods is like an old good friend, it makes me feel warm and good inside'*, spoke to Kit giving him a good feeling about repurposing the cabin and property. Still, a nagging worry about how the television show producers would react to someone ransacking the local cell phone tower dogged his thoughts. Kit prayed the cell tower would be repaired and working by the time the producers arrived for an on-site inspection of the cabin and property.

Kit's good feeling lessened for a moment as he neared the gravel driveway leading to the remote cabin. Ahead on the county road, coming toward Kit's vehicle, were two ATVs, each with a teen boy driving and a teen girl hanging onto the driver. The boys wore baseball caps, one a Dallas Cowboys cap and the other an NRA cap; the girls were letting their long hair flutter behind them.

The two ATVs slowed down and began to veer angling to turn onto the gravel drive leading to the cabin. Kit slowed his Trailblazer and put on his blinker to show he was turning onto the same gravel drive. He watched the ATV drivers react to the blinker.

The ATVs abruptly swerved and continued past the gravel drive roaring on down the county road. Kit studied the teens as they motored past him. The kid in the NRA cap stared at Kit as he drove past, a look of suspicion and possible loss narrowed the teen's eyes.

Kit turned onto the drive and disappeared from view hidden by trees. Twenty yards into the gravel drive Kit parked and exited his Trailblazer; he slowly walked back to the county road. At the tree nearest the paved highway he stopped and peeked down the road; the ATVs were idling a hundred yards further down and all four riders were looking back at the drive's entrance.

Kit emerged into the open and walked to the rusty, battered, mailbox at the head of the drive. He carefully opened the door and looked inside. Long abandoned wasp nests and spider webs filled the metal mailbox. Kit closed the mailbox and looked toward the ATVs. The drivers saw Kit look their way and with a roar sped away down the county road leaving Kit to worry what type of vandalism the cabin had endured during its unattended time. Kit returned to his Trailblazer and proceeded down the rough drive, his heart full of dread fearing the condition in which he might find his newly inherited cabin.

Kit fondly recalled visiting his grandparents as a child and thinking, as a child often does, that his grandparents lived in a magical forest. As Kit matured, the perceived magic of the forest grew into respect for the forest and its ecosystem. Ulysses had taught Kit outdoor skills from an early age that he honed as he worked his way to the rank of Eagle Scout.

After Kit turned fifteen he hunted the property with his grandfather nearly every season until Ulysses was forced to accept constant professional care in a nursing home. Kit continued to hunt the land to have fresh stories to tell his grandfather when visiting him, but after a while, seeing the look of loss and longing in Ulysses' eyes, telling stories saddened Kit so much he stopped hunting and never spoke of hunting with Ulysses again.

As the large cabin came into view at the end of the long gravel drive Kit pushed a hand through his thick black hair then wiped a tear from his eye. He vowed to honor his grandparents with whatever he did with the property.

Arriving at the cabin Kit found it to be very good condition. Exceptionally sturdy tornado shutters had protected the plastic windowpanes and the cabin's two doors of thick wood and sturdy iron fittings had kept the vandals at bay.

The worst evidence of trespassers were beer cans, fast food wrappers, and used condoms littering the covered front porch and tire tracks crisscrossing the tall, uncut, grass growing in the clearing between the cabin and the two story barn.

A fire pit ringed by rocks had been constructed between the cabin and the woods; the center of the shallow pit was filled with ash and beer cans indicating frequent use. Kit breathed a sigh of relief that, all-in-all, things were looking good so far, and the kids on the ATVs had not foreshadowed a wrecked cabin.

Moving past the fire pit Kit checked out what was left of an old horse corral. Two split-rail sides joined by a corner remained sturdy but the rest of the railings had collapsed. The bare earth inside the rails was compacted and barren from years of livestock use and horse training. Kit could almost smell the aroma of horse and cow patties in the air as he remembered being told countless times that the livestock were working animals and not pets.

Kit glanced at a large propane tank between the house and corral; a row of fifteen vertical railroad ties, buried in the ground, created a blast shield between the large capacity tank and the cabin. After testing the remaining corral rails Kit peeked into the two-story barn and found it in relatively good shape considering the main doors were off their hinges and leaning on the exterior wall exposing the barn's spacious interior to weather, wild animals, and trespassers.

Satisfied that the cabin and barn were in fair shape Kit began to consider which project to address first. All projects seemed equally urgent and Kit was uncertain where to start. He debated whether to mow the yard, clean the cabin, or take a discovery walk in the woods surrounding the cabin's clearing first. After watching a bird harass a snake along the edge of the drive, Kit decided mowing the field of weeds was priority number one. The remainder of the first day had gone smoothly.

Now, a day later, rocking in the sunshine, with a cold beer, a gentle breeze brushed his face and birdcalls were the only sounds he heard other than the breeze making the leaves sound as if they were whispering about the newcomer. Kit took a deep breath of the aromatic air and felt years of stress disappear with his exhalation. It was one of those rare moments when all seemed right with the world and Kit Carson was enjoying each rare second of the feeling.

In the serenity of the moment Kit envisioned the property as simply a private escape where he could leave the stress of his job behind. Calling the property Camp Nirvana passed through his mind reminding him he needed a catchy name for the property to help him market his new business venture.

Kit's thoughts turned to ideas of how he could live on site while making money from the property during different times of the year. He knew to be successful he had to provide activities year round because there would not be enough income to live on offering only warm season activities. However, first and foremost, he had to finish up the initial exploration of the acreage for the television show producers before any business plans could be made.

The TV show producers wanted dozens of photos, GPS coordinates, a list of interesting natural features on the property, and a utility location map of the property. To gather all of that information, and explore all of the acreage in a hurry, Kit needed help, and that's where his friends came in.

Kit knew his friends loved exploring and shooting guns as much as he did and would jump at the chance to blast targets in an unrestricted setting. Also, as often as his friends complained about work, Kit knew each man would relish a chance to get away and unwind for a few days in a remote, pastoral setting.

Kit looked forward to the first day of real exploration, which meant he could explore the forest nearest to the cabin, or lodge, as he had taken to thinking of it. As a child Kit knew every climbing tree, hidey-hole, and swinging vine, but time and weather changes everything leaving Kit to wonder how the passage of time had changed the forest and fields during his absence. He also wondered how the passage of time had changed his friends.

All but one of Kit's friends lived out of state and the long drive for them would be tedious as they each pulled a trailer loaded with an ATV and supplies. Despite the long drive, the promise of down time at the end of the journey filled the men's hearts with anticipation. Kit imagined them driving along singing to the radio as they had on so many previous road trips to concerts.

Kit paced the gravel drive next to the freshly mowed clearing, keeping a vigilant eye out for snakes, as he waited for his friends. He felt everything was in order for their arrival with the exception of the cell phone tower being off line. The disruption in service meant he had no way to contact his friends or knowing when they would arrive or if they needed additional directions to the cabin. The not knowing anyone's status was the hardest part of waiting and it added a taint of apprehension to Kit's anticipation. Kit's apprehension fell away as he heard the first sounds of tires on gravel coming toward the cabin.

To the men driving up to the rustic log cabin Kit Carson looked almost the same as he had in college. Thrice divorced Kit was five feet seven inches tall and weighed one hundred and ninety-five pounds. Kit's muscular, compact build earned him the name of The Fire Hydrant on the college intramural football and softball fields. Kit had campaigned to be called Hulk, but not even team all-stars got to pick their own nickname. Despite his short stature Kit's speed, strength, and relentless determination made him the one to account for on the playing field.

From puberty to present day, Kit's physique was genetically sculpted muscle. Gifted with such a build Kit had been a fan of the Hulk since childhood, but it was his junior year, high school, Halloween costume party that cemented his Hulk persona. All Kit had to do was paint his exposed skin green and commit to wearing ugly purple shorts to complete the character's look.

His jet-black hair, then long, not close cut as today, and penetrating green eyes had established the Hulk persona for him. After high school Kit transformed into the Hulk for college Halloween parties and became a fan favorite in costume contests. Today, Kit looked as athletic as he had in college; two changes were the flecks of gray hair making an appearance and worry lines etching his tanned face. But, to the men arriving at the cabin, it looked as if time had given Kit a pass on aging.

As the first vehicle neared the cabin Kit tried to think of a greeting other than, 'Welcome to the cabin'. That greeting seemed so dull to Kit. Camp Nirvana seemed like a fun name but it might not describe the resort properly. He briefly considered calling the property Camp Carson or The Resort at Camp Chickasaw. Then his mind flashed on what politically incorrect consequences he might encounter using the Native American name Chickasaw in the resort's name.

Mentally tabling the naming process until he could discuss it with everyone, Kit turned his attention to the amenities city folk would demand even though they were at a very rural resort attempting to get away from all the noise, relentless pace, media immersion, and concrete and glass that was every city's core identity. He imagined advertising the resort as an escape from the city allowing the visitor to experience the flip side of urban chaos. Thoughts of amenities and advertising budgets were disrupted as the first arrival came into view.

The first to arrive at the cabin was Charles Lee Denton. Charles crept along the dusty gravel drive in a freshly washed and waxed Escalade pulling a trailer hauling and an also freshly washed and waxed ATV. Charles had the driver's side window cracked and Kit heard raised voices competing, on some talk radio show, fighting for dominance. Charles sat in the Escalade until the talk show segment ended then waved at Kit and closed the window.

Ginger haired and bespectacled, Charles slowly exited the Escalade and stretched as he looked around. Kit immediately noticed his old friend was packing about fifteen extra pounds in what people commonly called a muffin top. Despite Charles's alarmingly bright Hawaiian print shirt, an affectation he maintained from his college days, and obviously brand new camouflage cargo pants, his weight gain was obvious as the extra girth stretched the bottom of the brightly colored shirt. Kit's face revealed his surprise at Charles's heavier look. Kit last visited him at Christmas two years ago and was astounded at how Charles had changed in the last years.

Soon after that visit Charles's wife had died in a texting while driving accident. She was at fault and had killed two people in the other car. The wrongful death lawsuit had nearly bankrupted Charles forcing him to move to a smaller house with his two teenage sons who dealt with the loss of their mother by writing emotionally heavy songs for their rock band.

After twenty years of marriage to the love of his life Charles found himself widowed with two teenage sons and a void in his heart. Charles filled the void by doting on his two sons, but he had let himself go in the meantime. Kit hoped the change was just his weight and did not indicate depression or worse.

Charles owned a well-regarded cyber-security firm and Kit wondered how he was balancing the business with being a single parent of twins following his wife's tragic and untimely death; Kit hoped Charles had not let the business slide as he had his weight.

Charles slowly made his way toward Kit admiring the tall trees surrounding the cabin as he took deep breaths of fresh country air. As he closed the distance to Kit an uncontrollable smile spread across his face. At that moment, seeing a spontaneous smile born from someone in Charles's situation, Kit knew most other people would have a similar reaction. Charles stuck his hand out for Kit to take. Kit smiled back at Charles.

As they shook hands and embraced Kit noticed deep worry lines etched into his widowed friend's forehead calling attention to his bloodshot eyes. Touches of grey were painting his temples trying to invade the rest of his short, dark ginger colored hair.

Charles said, "Damn cell service is out. Do you know anything about it?"

"Copper wire and technology thieves. It's a thing down here. It should be fixed soon."

The men continued talking enjoying the bright sunshine as Kit briefly outlined his plan for the weekend. Charles complained about the cell service again expressing his frustration at the situation. Charles explained the phone was his lifeline and emphatically stated his concern about being out of touch for an extended time period. Kit mentioned the reward offered for the thieves and tried to assure Charles that service would resume as quickly as possible. Charles expressed his skepticism over Kit's optimism in clear terms.

    Kit forcibly turned the conversation to other things until they heard a vehicle turn onto the gravel drive leading to the cabin. Charles excused himself, grabbed two heavy suitcases from his gleaming Escalade, and quickly headed into the cabin relishing the fact he was first in line to choose a bunkbed.

    Daniel Ethan Boone, Kit's cousin, arrived in a tricked out Avalanche with the Red Hot Chili Peppers blasting from the truck's audio system. Kit wondered how Ethan could still hear anything; he had been rocking loudly his whole life. Together they had spent years going to concerts and festivals, and although each event had been wild and memorable, their hearing was beginning to reveal the damage from years of listening to loud rock and roll.

    Ethan rolled down his windows so Kit could hear Anthony singing: '*Road tripping with my two favorite allies, we're fully loaded with snacks and supplies, it's time to leave this town, it's time to steal away, let's go get lost anywhere in the USA.*' Ethan turned the music off as the verse ended and smiled at Kit from behind the bug-splattered windshield. Ethan's loud rock and rolling arrival reminded Kit of the many concerts he and Ethan had attended; there were so many great memories from each event.

    Ethan's battered ATV was in the bed of the truck surrounded by coolers filled with food, beer, and more; the truck's cabin was packed with luggage. Ethan parked next to the Escalade, got out and immediately began stretching his back and legs.

    Kit noticed Ethan had not let himself go soft as Charles seemingly had done. Ethan wore faded denim jeans and a tight black tank top shirt exposing arms that were well toned and tanned. After stretching, Ethan gave Kit a quick wave then hoisted an ice chest from the back of his truck. The cooler had wheels and Ethan pulled it effortlessly over the rough ground.

Ethan greeted Kit then ceremoniously presented him a beer from the ice-filled cooler. Then he dug out a beer for himself. The men popped the pull-tabs together, touched cans as a salute, then took a deep drink before catching up on current events. As the men related what each had been doing the last few months Kit remembered Ethan as the fair-haired stud of the college dorm whose love life was the stuff of legends.

Ethan's icy blue eyes and dark blonde hair were as perfect as they had been in college. In addition to his handsome face Ethan had a silver tongue and a gift of gab that served him well then and in his current job as a Lexus salesman. Several times during college his mouth had gotten him into trouble, and nearly as often his gift of gab had gotten him out of the trouble as quickly as it had gotten him into it. Now, instead of talking himself into or out of trouble, he was talking customers into buying new cars so proficiently he had been named Salesman of the Month too often to count.

Kit noticed Ethan's gaudy gold wedding band gleaming on his tanned hand. Ethan had married an older woman seven years ago and had endured endless ribbing about marrying a 'cougar'. Kit asked Ethan how married life was only to have Ethan smile weakly and say they could talk about it later then assured Kit nothing bad was going on in response to Kit's quizzical and worried look. Kit pressed for details but Ethan said, "It's okay, but complicated. Life never really turns out like you plan. People never turn out like you anticipate they will. No one can escape the Law of Unintended Consequences. I know you know that!"

In the distance a new vehicle began creeping up the gravel drive; Ethan quickly grabbed a duffle bag from the cab of his truck and walked toward the cabin pulling the rolling ice chest behind him. Kit looked after Ethan watching him disappear into the cabin wondering what memories his cousin retained of visiting the cabin. He heard Ethan shout a greeting to Charles as he entered the cabin. As the crunching of tires on gravel grew louder Kit turned to look at who was arriving.

Kit couldn't contain a wide smile as he reminisced over some of the adventures he and his friends had shared in college. Kit knew their bodies were worn and older and life experiences had re-shaped the men since college, but he hoped everyone's spirits were still high, or at least could be rejuvenated by a weekend outing in the woods.

Alex Bobo arrived next and parked beside Ethan's Avalanche. Alex drove a battered Jeep outfitted with extra lights and a cargo carrier on the roof. The Jeep pulled a mud-splattered trailer carrying Alex's tarp covered ATV. Alex had been the gung-ho ROTC guy in college and had seen combat both in service to his country then with a private international security service. Currently unemployed, Alex relished the unexpected retreat in the woods. He had a twinkle in his eyes that called attention to a distinct Little Dipper pattern of freckles dotting his left temple.

Kit recalled that Alex had a knack for shrinking his shirts just enough to accentuate his lean, toned physique. Alex's civilian attire consisted of denim jeans, a T-shirt of a single color, and an ever present Boonie hat. Alex's collection of Boonie hats was a frequent topic of discussion often raised during the consumption of the second case of beer. Today Alex was wearing a green T-shirt and a desert camo patterned hat.

Alex's only concession to recently entered civilian life was to let his thick brown hair grow out an extra two inches. A close encounter with hot metal in Iraq had left Alex with a scalp scar above his left ear where hair would not grow. After the wound healed Alex had taken to constantly wearing a Boonie hat to cover the scar when his hair was short.

When his hair was cut to regulation the scar was visible and the Little Dipper pattern of freckles called additional attention to that area of his head. Both the scar and freckles were inevitable sources of questions Alex disliked answering. Alex still wore his trademark Boonie hat but at least when he had to remove the hat, the scar was partially hidden by hair.

Alex climbed out of the Jeep and stretched. Kit noted Alex still maintained both a residual military swagger and fitness. After loosening tight muscles Alex hugged Kit in a big bear hug. The lines around Alex's brown eyes showed years of combat stress, but those same eyes also showed delight and pure joy at being in the woods with his old friends. The men spent several minutes catching up on recent events before Alex unpacked two suitcases and carried them into the cabin. Kit noticed Alex had a bounce in his step as he walked away. Between Charles's spontaneous smile and Alex's demeanor Kit felt better about future reactions he might see from customers. Kit's thoughts were disrupted as the next arrival crunched on the gravel drive.

Last to arrive was Kit's neighbor Garrett Gardner. Garrett was the only non-college bonded man in the group. Kit and Garrett had bonded over beers shared across the chain link fence separating their lots back in the city.

Garrett had started his professional life as a police officer but nine years ago he had been forced to kill a fifteen-year-old boy. Garrett's actions were ruled justifiable as the boy had killed his aunt and her male friend at the end of a church service, and had shot another woman in the stomach during a carjacking in the church parking lot following the double murder. Despite the fact that Garrett's use of deadly force to neutralize the teen suspect had been ruled justifiable, the shooting haunted Garrett every time he went on patrol.

Two torturous years after killing the teenager Garrett had quit the police force and become a public school security officer hoping to give back to the community and perhaps prevent other youth from making wrong, life-ending decisions. In his school security officer position he felt he was making a difference until one day he realized that each new class of students were more disrespectful, selfish, and violent than the previous class of students. It seemed that parents had simply given up trying to be parents and that several generations of future citizens were going to be worthless or worse.

Two years ago, during an active shooter event, Garrett had taken two small caliber rounds to his lower back before a fellow security officer killed that teenage shooter. A moment of hesitation, born from the previous incident, had nearly cost Garrett his life. Garrett survived, recovered, and returned to work at the same school until retiring one year ago, disgusted by the state of public education and the disrespect the urban kids dished out to teachers, staff, and peers equally.

The accumulation of what he had witnessed on the police force and as a school resource officer had been too much to bear. Since the world was going to hell, Garrett wanted to enjoy his backyard sanctuary right up to the end.

Garrett had learned to work around the pain from the bullet wounds but occasionally the injury would flare up setting him down for an extended period of rest and recovery. It was during a forced rest while landscaping his back yard that Kit leaned on the chain link fence and asked if he needed anything; and thus a conversation and deep friendship had begun.

Expecting Garrett to arrive in his beloved Chevy Z 71 pickup truck, Kit was shocked as a large, garishly painted, food truck pulling a trailer with an ATV strapped to it lumbered down the gravel drive toward the cabin. The new food truck was painted sky blue over lemon yellow with flawless chrome bumpers and black plastic molding. The chrome trim was shiny, the paint unmarred, and the large windshield unchipped but covered in bug splatter. Kit shook his head at the sight of the behemoth crunching up the gravel drive.

Garrett's arrival in a food truck was something Kit would have never imagined in his wildest dreams. Kit watched as Garrett maneuvered the large truck into an open space at the end of the row of other vehicles. The truck dwarfed the other vehicles. Kit shook his head at the sight and wondered what a food truck might portend for the weekend.

Garrett waved at Kit from the driver's seat. Kit returned the wave and gave him a questioning look. The sixty-seven year old retired public servant stepped down from the cockpit and said, "Bet you're surprised," as he jabbed a thumb at the food truck.

Kit said "You betcha."

Garrett remained silent as he rubbed his lower back. He said, "That was a drive and a half."

Kit asked, "What's the story on this behemoth?"

Garrett grabbed an overnight bag and a hard shell archery case from inside the food truck. "I'll explain it all later. Now I just want to do anything but steer that stubborn beast of a dead horse."

Kit stared at the food truck, "Are you into catering now?"

"No. I'll explain later."

"Is there food in there?"

"No. I'll explain later."

Kit said, "Okay, the gang's all here. Let's get this party started!"

The early part of the evening was spent drinking, eating hastily made sandwiches, and catching up on recent events before the fatigue of the tedious drive caught up to the travelers. The mix of interstate highway and rural roads had worn the men out so they left the bulk of unloading for the morning unpacking only pillows, blankets, medicine, and toiletry kits.

Long after the sounds of the men settling into their creaky bunks quieted, Kit remained awake. He was far too excited to sleep and his mind raced with all of the possibilities before him.

At some point in the wee hours Kit realized that he was experiencing the same impatient anticipation now as he had waiting on the opening mornings of deer hunting seasons he had shared with Ulysses, in this very cabin, so many times before.

Kit quietly paced the cabin floor as the noise of a lone CPAP machine and snoring filled the long abandoned cabin with sounds of life. Eventually Kit settled into his sleeping bag lying atop the sofa in the spacious living room and began a fitful sleep.

3

> There ain't no moral to this story at all
> And anything I tell you very well could be a lie
> I'm just waiting for that cold black,
> Numb-inside, soul of mine,
> To come alive
>
>   - The Refreshments

    Saturday morning dawned cloudless and warm with the promise of more heat to come as the day grew older. Kit had planned a trip to the far northern section of the property where meandering, mostly clear water, Chickasaw Creek cut diagonally through the property. Over the years various Carson family members had pulled several respectable fish from deep holes scattered along the meandering stream. Beyond the creek, Kit planned to investigate an old stock pond located near the top of the Idaho shaped property. He remembered catching a few big bass and catfish out of the pond and wondered if any fish were left in it. Kit wanted to have a fish fry before starting the night's main event, a bonfire.

    As the others began to wake and stir about Kit sipped coffee and idly shuffled the maps and sheets of hastily written down business ideas as he waited. He silently nodded a greeting to each man as he emerged from the bunkroom.

    After the men took care of personal morning rituals they found their way to the coffee pot. The coffee's aroma filled the cabin and the hot black elixir began to chase the morning slows away as the men silently gathered around the cluttered dining table. Unwilling to break the silence Kit poured his second cup of coffee then turned his attention to an engraved walnut plank on the wall that read:

> General Malaise tried to rally the troops
> Colonel Cumulus forecast the weather
> Major Malfunction readied the armory
> Captain Confusion drew up the battle plan
> Sargent Snafu planned the logistics
> Corporal Cornucopia coordinated the mess hall
> Private Property was in charge of scouting

Kit smiled at his grandpa's wall plaque as his guests savored their hot coffee. With friends at hand and the aroma of coffee filling the cabin the space did not seem so large and empty this morning.

Kit watched in fascination as spiders, which had survived the bug bombs, crawled along the wire grid suspending the bulbs over the great room. The spiders were busy getting on with things while he had to wait. Kit was impatient to begin discussing ideas with the men, but knew to wait until the caffeine kicked in.

The men continued sipping their first cup of coffee in silence staring at the handcrafted dining table or glancing at the stack of papers and maps Kit had scattered along its length. Ethan picked up the horseshoe paperweight and looked around the cabin. The few items that remained exuded simple country charm. Hand crafted end tables accented the ancient leather sofa. A dusty autoharp rested on the lower shelf of one of the end tables. Copies of Guideposts magazines lay scattered under the other end table.

Kit had the tornado shutters open and natural light illuminated dust particles floating in the air below the network of bare incandescent light bulbs hanging from a wire grid. The windows were large single panes made of clear plastic rather than glass. The panes could be raised upward to allow airflow to cool the cabin; unfortunately there were no screens to keep the insects out of the cabin. The wooden plank tornado shutters on the outside of the windows could be pulled closed and locked from inside to offer protection from raging storms.

Garrett broke the extended silence by saying, "Those beds in the bunk room are long in the tooth. You need new ones."

Ethan said, "At least he doesn't have bedbugs!"

A few others muttered 'Amen' under their breath.

Kit said, "I'll add mattresses to the list."

After his first night in the cabin, Kit chose to sleep on the leather sofa preferring the openness of the great room to the claustrophobic size and mustiness of his grandparent's master bedroom. Kit had been relieved the beds had been left behind when the twins looted the cabin of the nicer things. His assessment was that the twins had taken everything that could be pawned or sold at a yard sale. He looked around wondering what all was missing, disappointed he would never know for certain. Despite the looted interior, Kit found the spaciousness appealing after living in his suburban, postage stamp sized, home and lot for the last nine years.

The cabin and large garden plot had been a joint labor of love shared by Kellie and Ulysses. A year after Kellie died Ulysses lost interest in caring for either and the property had taken on a forlorn look. Kit understood Ulysses' loss of interest and could have lived with the natural deterioration, but having the black sheep of the family loot all precious mementos was hard to bear. Especially now that he owned the cabin and the land!

Kit watched a red wasp circle the men at the table then move on. Not for the last time Kit wished there were mosquito screens on the windows and doors. Without a ceiling fan the cabin could grow quite warm and opening the doors and windows to facilitate a breeze allowed insects to invade the cabin. Kit leaned over the table and scribbled a reminder about pricing and sizing screens for the windows and doors onto a piece of notebook paper.

As the men drank coffee, Kit indulged himself in a little exercise he enjoyed now and again. In the exercise he would take a step back and look at his surroundings as if he were a Crime Scene Investigator. He believed re-examining familiar things with a fresh perspective strengthened his observational skills and kept complacency and mistakes at bay.

Kit imagined how the rustic cabin would appear to Hollywood television producers who were accustomed to luxury hotel rooms or lodges with room service and jetted spa tubs. Kit was sure only the camera crews were embedded with contestants.

To assess the property's future business possibilities in context Kit understood that he needed blunt input from objective eyes to get a clear idea of what needed improvement and what needed to be added. Kit glanced at the men sitting around the long table; they were all relaxed, smiling, and quiet; it was the cult of morning coffee enjoyed in silence with friends. Kit remained silent not wanting to tarnish the moment. Looking at the group his mind wandered back to when they met for the first time.

Kit, Ethan, Alex, and Charles had become great friends, or as referred to back then-drinking buddies, through intramural softball and football. Their softball team went undefeated for three years while their flag football team was less successful, but just as much fun. The friends had graduated college during a slow economic time and spent a year leisurely looking for post-graduation jobs.

The first year following college graduation the men had formed a softball team, mostly of local alumni, and competed in the city league. It was devastating to the men to disband the team when jobs in various cities sent each man on their individual career paths. The friends stayed in touch, frequently at first, then less frequently as job and family responsibilities grew.

Reunions became limited to summer holidays and special occasions. Looking around the table Kit saw maturity in his friends' faces and bodies; but it felt as if the group's heyday was not that far removed. The Thin Lizzy anthem 'The Boys Are Back in Town' played repeatedly in Kit's head, an innocuous earworm, as he waited for the day's activities to begin in earnest. Kit looked at the group wondering what each man was thinking.

Alexander Bobo, Alex to his friends, had recently left the security contractor Global Watchtower Worldwide "glad to be somewhere where you can tell the good guys from the bad guys." Alex's college ROTC training and math degree served him well as an Army Ranger. After leaving the Rangers, Global Watchtower Worldwide offered him a job paying good money and a guarantee his role would be advisory rather than boots on the ground.

That guarantee turned out to be a lie but the money was too good not to take so Alex stayed with the firm. Alex had left GWW six months ago, after a suicide bomber had infiltrated a scientific base camp where his detail was protecting a group of archeologists killing five of his brothers in arms in an insider attack. Alex had reached his limit of seeing blood covered sand and rocks so he resigned the day after the after incident inquiry was closed.

Currently unemployed, Alex was living off of a modest pension and was skilled enough, and healthy enough, to enjoy life while waiting for a new employment opportunity to arise. Unfortunately, Alex had entered the civilian world during a stagnant economy and could not find a job matching his skill set. The world was changing and for soldiers who had spent years in a seemingly parallel world, it was tough finding meaningful work.

Alex was elated to be out in the woods where he could enjoy beautiful scenery and peace of mind. He left the table, poured a fresh cup of coffee, then walked to each window looking out for several seconds before returning to the table and sitting down.

Kit started to speak to Alex but Alex's eyes said, 'Not until I finish my coffee.'

Kit turned his attention to Charles next. Charles Lee 'Chas', Denton was constantly checking his cell phone despite his repeated phrase of "I'm just glad to be away from my twin teenage sons and their rock band practice for a few days." Following the tragic and untimely death of his wife the suddenly single father had channeled all of his loneliness and grief into being a helicopter father to his twin sons, David and Daniel.

Tricia's life insurance policy would pay for the twins' college education, but the boys had other plans. And their plans disrupted Charles's life almost as much as the death of Trisha. The boys dreamed of being rock stars and delaying college until they found out if they would become stars or not.

Charles's biggest challenge, as a single parent, so far had been trying to balance leniency and discipline without alienating his sons. For the past month, every night as he waited for sleep to take him, he fretted about his decision allowing the boys to delay entering college for two years to give them a chance at getting a record deal for their band. Now, six months into the two-year grace period Charles worried that his sons and their band mates were making a mistake after a succession of demos were rejected by major record labels. In addition, the band could only play in under-twenty-one clubs barely earning enough to keep the band in guitar strings and the van gassed up. There were dark bags under Charles's eyes from lack of sleep and constant worry.

Charles stared at his cellphone's signal strength indicator while sipping coffee. He reached across the table grabbing a doughnut from a box he had brought in last night. He studied the cellphone he held in one hand while using his free hand to switch between the coffee cup and doughnut. Following Charles's lead, each man took a doughnut from the box to eat with his coffee. Alex cherished each bite of the doughnut as if he had been away from sweets for years. Kit ate a chocolate covered, cherry filled doughnut as he sipped coffee. Garrett ate a plain glazed doughnut in tiny bites.

Charles stood and stretched before taking another doughnut from the box; he lifted the box off the table and offered it to the others. Kit and Alex both shook their heads declining the offer and Charles returned the box to the table. Charles's obsession with his phone forced Kit to explain the copper wire and equipment theft to the others. The other men checked their cellphones but showed no stress over the service outage.

Ethan poured a cup of coffee then disappeared into the bunkroom limping lightly favoring his right leg. After a moment, Ethan exited the bunkroom with a slight grimace on his face until he noticed the others glance at him; then he smiled. A car accident during a test drive with a teen driver had left Ethan with injuries and chronic pain. Ethan grinned as he limped into the kitchen where he noisily rummaged through the liquor bottles looking for something to add flavor to his coffee.

Ethan was the top Lexus salesman in his city. His good looks and gift of gab were a perfect combination for a car salesman. Ethan's trip to the cabin was a source of joy for the other salesmen at the dealership. Every salesman with the exception of the sales manager suggested that Ethan extend his vacation.

Youngest of the group by thirty-four days, the thin, wiry, salesman prided himself on his appearance and charm. Ethan made a liquor selection then turned to the men sitting around the table and said, "It's a great day to be alive!"

Garrett said, "Isn't it a little early for an Irish coffee?"

"Not if it knocks the edge off of the pain. And I don't intend to operate any heavy machinery today."

Charles deadpanned, "Isn't everyday a great day to be alive?"

Kit said, "No. There are always exceptions. But the exceptions make you appreciate the great days even more."

Ethan poured fresh, coffee into a cup then topped it off with two fingers of Irish cream. He grabbed a doughnut and joined the group at the table watching Charles grow frustrated as he tried to will the distant cell phone tower to resume service.

Garrett Gardner pushed away from the table and limped into the kitchen toward the coffee pot for his third jolt of java. Ignoring the assortment of disposable coffee cups, Garrett drank from his own insulated thermos lid/cup combination. He stood looking out the window rubbing his lower back with one hand while sipping from the cup with the other hand. Feeling eyes upon him he turned and looked at the group lifting his cup in a silent salute.

Garrett was in good health except for the lingering effects of having been shot and was "looking forward to some challenging bow hunting." To Ethan he said, "The pain makes us appreciate the pain free days." The retired officer took a long draw from the cup and said to the entire group, "For those about to explore, I salute you."

Ethan said, "To pain free days!"

Kit smiled, wondering not for the first time, what the young Garrett Gardner had been like. The man Kit knew was stoic and levelheaded, but things he occasionally said gave Kit an impression Garrett had once been a wild youth and devious prankster. Garrett's prankster side emerged a little bit every Halloween giving the neighborhood something to talk about until Thanksgiving.

The Garrett Gardner Kit knew was one of the most community-oriented people Kit had ever met. Garrett's yard frequently won neighborhood 'Yard of the Year' honors and he volunteered as a member of the grounds crew for the neighborhood's single field, multi-use, sports complex. Garrett rejoined the others at the table where he gingerly sat on the wooden chair and rested his arms on the table.

Kit asked, "Back acting up?"

Garrett said, "Those bunks are a bit rough on a back like mine."

The men resumed drinking their coffee in silence until Garrett turned to Kit and used his thermos cup to point at the pile of maps and satellite images. Garrett asked, "Okay, where in the great unknown are we exploring today?" Kit pushed himself away from the table grabbing one of the eight by ten sized satellite view printouts from the table.

Facing the group, as if making a sales presentation, Kit said, "I thought today we'd go to the far north end of the property and check out Chickasaw Creek and an old stock pond. I don't know how long it will take to get there because I'm sure the trails have grown up over the last years. We might need to do some trail blazing. Bring your rifles because I remember Grandpa U telling stories of hunting feral hogs after they rooted up Grandma Kellie's garden, and, men, there is no limit on feral hogs."

"I hear they taste funky." Charles made a face and held his nose.

Garrett said, "Preparation prior to cooking is the secret to better tasting wild pork. That's the secret for all tasty wild game."

Kit said, "We're not required to eat them. There is no such thing as wanton waste on feral hogs. They are a menace to the environment! We can blast away!"

Charles muttered, "The real menace to society is the copper wire thieves."

Ethan asked, "Can we at least try some wild hog bacon?"

Kit shrugged, "I'd rather fry up some big old bream or whatever we might catch from the creek. But, I hear piglet is tender and doesn't taste gamey at all. But, if someone does take a piglet, I'm stocked with enough spices and sauces to whip up one hell of a marinade, and we can roast the little porker over hickory wood at the fire pit out front. But, as for me, I'd rather fry up some freshly caught fish. I'm just saying."

"Amen." Alex smiled at the thought of freshly fried bream.

Ethan said, "All this talk is making me hungry. I say we cook up a big breakfast if all we have to look forward to is a bankside lunch of granola bars and thin deli meat sandwiches. I'll get some bacon started."

Garrett said, "I'll scramble eggs once some bacon is cooked."

Kit said, "Go easy on the propane. The big propane tank is empty and I only brought two tanks with me. I've got one hooked up to the stove and the second one is our backup tank after we use it on the fish cooker."

Charles said, "Garrett, what are you going to make us in that food truck of yours?"

Garrett said, "It's empty."

Ethan said, "No! I was looking forward to tacos or whatever comes out of that truck."

Garrett offered no further comment.

Charles frowned and said, "I'll make some Texas toast after I answer the call of nature. This coffee runs right through me. But, I love the caffeine." He pushed away from the table and hurried into the bathroom.

Kit called after him, "Watch out for the Black Widows and Brown Recluses!"

Charles stuck his head out of the bathroom and stared at Kit with a concerned look. Kit laughed and said, "Just kidding!" The first thing I did was fumigate for bugs and sweep the corners."

Charles gave Kit the finger before slamming the door. Kit called after him, "Double check anyway. Just to be safe."

Alex said, "Man, I wish you had a TV. I need my sports fix."

Kit shrugged looking around the large open room, "Yeah, sorry about the spartan nature of things. The twins looted the place once Grandpa Ulysses went to the nursing home. I feel lucky they left any furniture and the stuff out in the barn."

Alex said, "How is it you got this place and not them?"

Kit looked into his coffee cup embarrassed about how he had come into his good fortune. After a long minute of silence, Kit began idly shuffling maps as he answered. "The twins were, apparently, passed out drunk when the infamous Mother's Day EF-5 tornado hit. The report said they probably never heard the warning siren or the tornado. Thankfully, I think, they died in their sleep. Their unexpected deaths pushed Ulysses to the end and the cabin to me."

Ethan said, "I thought the world of Ulysses but I really hated those twins. They were a dictionary definition of wasted lives."

Kit looked up, taking in his circle of friends, "I hate to think what those two would have done to or with this place."

Ethan turned thick slabs of bacon sizzling in a cast iron skillet then said, "So what are you going to do with this place?"

Garrett said, "What are the details about shooting television shows down here? And do you really want to give up the conveniences of the city for a forty-minute drive to the nearest store?"

Kit lightly tapped a satellite photo in the pile of maps and photos of the property. Staring at the image he said, "I won't really know what anyone wants until we survey and evaluate everything then send photos back to the producers. Two different outfits want to shoot a reality TV series here. One show is planning to pit youth organizations against each other in contests of skill and outdoorsmanship and the other show wants to put city slickers into the woods to learn outdoor skills. Plus, the state Natural Forest Conservation Society would like me to donate forty acres of old growth forest to them. I want to sell it to them to pay back taxes but they say they don't have the money to purchase the land. But, my other thoughts have included turning this place into a hunting lodge, corporate retreat, paintball course, an artist's retreat, honeymoon getaway, or just keep it all to myself. This place should have built in publicity if they shoot two reality shows here."

Ethan said, "You could turn that old barn into a recording studio and rent it to bands that need to get away from the distractions of the big city."

Kit said, "That's exactly why I need you guys to give me ideas."

"I'll send my kids to you first if you do that," Charles said as he returned from the bathroom looking more relaxed. He added, "But no one is going to come here if the cell service is so iffy."

Ethan said, "Part of coming down here was to get away for a few days. Getting away usually means going light on the cell phone and computer time."

Charles glared at Ethan but kept silent. Ethan winked at Charles. Charles continued glaring at Ethan who matched his glare.

"I couldn't get it done without you guys." Kit said, "That's what friends are for. And for the phone, I'm sure the cell tower company is working on repairs and that $5,000 reward should move things along on finding the thieves."

Ethan said, "Snitches end up in ditches."

Garrett said, "I thought we were coming down here to get away from it all for a while. Give your phone addiction a rest."

Charles snapped back, "You don't have two motherless teenage boys who dream of being the next Offspring or Green Day. Whoever the hell they are! Teenagers need constant monitoring. If it weren't for me they'd forget to eat and just practice until they starved to death in the garage. This is the first time I've left them alone for this long of a time since their mother died."

Ethan said, "Damn, cut the apron strings. Let the boys be boys. Some of us didn't have much adult supervision growing up and we turned out okay."

Kit said, "That's because we had friends, and some of us, church, if not parents, who kept us from going off the rails. Loyal and sensible friends are a valuable resource."

Garrett said, "True words there. Friendships are something that comes to be naturally; the best friendships are not forced but spontaneous. This weekend will be healthy for us all. We'll get to blow off steam and relax. And we are in the middle of nowhere, so it will be easy to unplug from all of our devices." He glanced at Charles.

Charles said, "Some of us need to remain connected for job and family no matter where we are. I own my own business!"

Ethan lifted a slab of bacon and toasted, "To friends."

Kit held up his coffee cup, "To friends, may the bond we've forged through happiness and sorrows never break."

Garrett said, "That was good. I'll drink to that."

Ethan said, "Garrett, you wouldn't believe some of the adventures we've had. Believe it or not Chas was right in the thick of it all with us."

"I can't say I'd do the same thing again." Charles sighed.

Alex said, "That reminds me of a comparison between civilian and military friends. I think it went something like this. Civilian friends tell you not to do something stupid when drunk off your ass, but military friends will post a 360-degree security perimeter so you don't get caught doing something stupid. Civilian friends will bail you out of jail and tell you what you did was wrong, but military friends will be sitting next to you in jail saying, 'Damn, we fucked up; but hey, that shit was fun.' Civilian friends will take your drink away when they think you've had enough, but military friends will look at you stumbling all over the place and say, 'Bitch, you better drink the rest of that shit, you know we don't waste a drop.' Civilian friends will tell you 'I'd take a bullet for you.', but military friends will actually take a bullet for you."

Garrett said, "Cops are the same way."

Ethan said, "I wish I had military friends."

Alex said, "You've got to give to get back. Friendship is not a one-way street."

Garrett lifted his coffee cup and said, "To friends."

Alex lifted his coffee cup. "Ditto."

Garrett set his coffee down and walked to the bathroom. He opened the door to the bathroom and paused in the doorway looking grim. "The toilet's backed up. Damn you Charles!"

As if on cue, in unison, the other men all said, "Oh, shit."

Charles snarled back, "Blame it on the plumbing, not the man. I saw a plunger in the corner."

Kit said, "Why didn't you use it?"

"I thought it might go down on its own."

Ethan shouted, "I call bullshit on that!"

Garrett said, "That plunger has your name on it! What the hell were you thinking? Get in here and unclog the toilet!"

Kit waved his hand, dismissively, "Don't worry; there's a real nice outhouse out back you can use until Charles unclogs the toilet." Kit glared at Charles before continuing, "The outhouse is only a dozen yards or so away, practically right out the back door. Apparently, an outhouse was needed often enough that Ulysses put some care into making it a comfortable destination. I suspect it was so he could sneak out and have a smoke without Grandma Kellie knowing. It's built over a natural sinkhole, so make sure you don't drop anything valuable into it. I dropped a rock into it the other day just to see how deep it is and it took a minute to hit bottom."

Charles said, "Really? We have to use an outhouse? That wasn't in the brochure."

Garrett said, "We only have to use the outhouse because you stopped up the only indoor toilet. I remember the brochure saying guests must pay for damages. Isn't that right, Kit?"

Charles shook his head looking away.

Kit said, "That's right. But, trust me the outhouse is not that bad. The seat is comfortable, there's an air hole near the ceiling and even a closeable cabinet built on the wall to hold supplies like toilet paper. There are even candles and waterproof matches if you think you need to burn off some gas."

Garrett said, "I can't wait, but I'm watching you."

"Great." Charles sulked as he grabbed his third doughnut of the morning. "I thought this was going to be a carefree weekend!"

Garrett said, "You can't use a plunger with a doughnut in your hand."

Ethan called out, "The weekend will be carefree once you've unstopped the toilet. Let's get this party started!"

The others glared at Charles who ignored everyone as he ate the doughnut. Garrett set his thermos down next to Charles giving him the evil eye then walked out the back door.

Kit glared at Charles as he ate his doughnut. Charles said, "I'll get to it. Stop giving me the evil eye."

"Sooner is better than later." Kit continued to glare at Charles.

Charles ate his doughnut staring at his cellphone.

Kit repeated, "Sooner is better than later," then began distributing paper plates and plastic utensils around the large dining table in preparation for breakfast.

Ethan said to Charles, "You'd better get a move on. That bathroom will be in demand after breakfast."

As Kit distributed paper plates he glanced out at what once had been Grandma Kellie's vegetable garden. The massive raised bed was overgrown with weeds and a tattered scarecrow's painted pail head and outstretched stick arms provided a perch for birds that searched for insects among the weeds. Kit imagined his grandparents eating breakfast looking out the window at butterflies and bees hovering around the flowers. He could see his grandparents clearly in his mind's eye. Kit smiled at the recollection.

Kellie and Ulysses Carson had been married for sixty-four years when Kellie fell ill and died suddenly. Ulysses carried on bravely but lonely after Kellie's death. He found temporary solace in frequent visits from the grandchildren but the joy in his eyes slowly dimmed as the ravages of age and isolation overtook him.

As the grandchildren grew older their visits to the remote, technology deficient cabin became much less frequent. As Ulysses grew older, travelling from the cabin to the city to visit them became increasingly difficult, and the inevitable, creeping estrangement took its toll on Ulysses.

Over solitary months and years, the rural land he and Kellie had inherited from Ulysses' father slowly lost its appeal to him. Ulysses spent his last good years visiting family for extended stays until a stroke required full-time professional care.

Hoping to keep the long-held property in the Carson family, Ulysses had promised the cabin and acreage to two troubled nephews, two drunken and meth using neer-do-wells, who Ulysses hoped would rise to the responsibility of owning property and ultimately make something of their lives with the gift of land. With the nephews dead, the deed to the remote ancestral land had eventually come to Kit. Kit was grateful for his unexpected good fortune; he looked at the overgrown garden and made a vow to grow tomatoes the way Kellie had grown them.

The hearty breakfast feast ended with everyone satiated and full of anticipation over what lay ahead. Following breakfast the men finished unpacking their trucks and prepared their all-terrain-vehicles for a ride through the forest.

As the others prepared for the day, Kit stared at Garrett's colorfully painted food truck sitting at the end of the row of vehicles and trailers. The automotive behemoth looked incongruous parked alongside the trucks, trailers, and ATVs. The food truck was longer than a truck and trailer combined and towered over Alex's light bar on the top of his Jeep.

As Kit watched the men retrieve gear and weapons from their vehicles he peppered Garrett with questions, "What is up with the food truck? You said it was empty? Is this a new business venture you're trying to get investors for? Why bring a food truck if there's no food?"

Garrett sighed and shook his head in resignation.

Alex tilted his head toward the brightly painted food truck and said, "Yeah. That truck is very conspicuous out here in the hinterlands. You must have enjoyed a fun drive down here. Especially while pulling a trailer with an ATV on it. That rig must have been a joy to drive on these roads."

Garrett nodded and smiled, "You have no idea."

Charles said, "Does that thing have a bathroom in it?"

Ethan snorted, "Not that you can use!"

Alex nodded, "Yeah, I always wondered about that. Do the cooks just pee in a can or do they make sure to park close to a public bathroom?"

Kit asked, "So, what is the deal with the food truck?"

Charles said, "Yeah, what is up with the food truck?"

Ethan pointed at the truck and said, "Why bring a food truck without food? It couldn't have been for the comfortable ride and state of the art sound system. Or, have food trucks improved their comfort levels?"

Alex said, "I've seen those TV food shows and those trucks look like they have precious little room inside. And they look hot."

Garrett sighed deeply before answering. Staring at the truck he explained, "My idiot son and his new wife got into a big fight over how to run the operation. They had seen all those shows on the cooking networks about owning a food truck and bought one without thinking everything through. Before they even bought supplies or developed a menu they got into a big fight with him threatening to burn the truck down to its chassis and her threatening to drive the truck into the river. Neither of them was thinking straight so I left them a note demanding they talk it out and have everything settled before I get back. I said they must have a business plan and menu on paper or else. I'm not sure what the 'or else' will be, but I'm tired of their constant dysfunction. I took the keys and drove off with the truck to keep their big investment out of harm's way. Maybe they will have their shit together by the time I get back."

Ethan said, "You don't think they'll report it as stolen?"

"No." The scorn in Garrett's voice was clear.

Kit said, "You could keep it and start selling snacks at the local park back home during ball games or soccer matches."

Garrett shook his head, "No thanks, I'm retired now. I've only got the thing to keep their investment from going up in flames."

Kit said, "Understood. Let's get back to prepping for our adventure."

The men drove their ATVs to the front of the cabin parking near the bonfire pit where they rechecked containers and bungee cords. The men concluded their preparations by spraying their clothes and exposed skin with insect repellant. Kit called the men over to form a huddle to go over the day's agenda one last time. They stood in a tight group near the brush pile that would provide kindling for an all-night bonfire Kit planned to ignite after the big fish fry.

4

> Can't you smell that smell?
> The smell of death surrounds you
>
> -Lynyrd Skynyrd

    For murdering Wildlife Officer Tom Benson without authorization, Preston Theodore LaHarpe had been banished from the family compound for thirty days. The honor Preston had expected to receive for righting a long standing wrong had instead been a public shaming. The image of the elders staring at him in tight lipped anger was burned into his memory. Instead of praise and love, Louis Lamoure LaHarpe brought his patriarchal wrath down upon Preston in front of the assembled family.

    Preston had chosen to announce his deed at the monthly family dinner believing everyone would burst into applause. Instead the room froze in shocked silence. Thunderously breaking the stunned silence Patriarch Louis lectured Preston at length on the scrutiny his action could bring upon the family.

    Louis stood at the head of the long table pounding its top to punctuate points, rattling plates and utensils, as he berated Preston. Louis reminded a red-faced Preston that Eli's suicide in prison had been tragic enough but Preston's unilateral act of an unsanctioned murder had been foolish and endangered the entire family.

    Eugenia wept as Preston was commanded to leave the table, pack a travel bag, and exit the family compound immediately to begin the punishment of a month long banishment with no contact with any family member permitted. Preston stormed out of the dining hall, stomped to his cabin, grabbed an always-packed go-bag, and left a cloud of dust hanging in the stagnant air as he sped away from the compound in his trusty Ford F-150.

    When Louis finally sat and resumed eating, the remaining family members kept their eyes on their plates finishing the meal silently. Eugenia would miss Preston terribly while he was away but she knew better than to intercede on her husband's behalf as angry as Louis was. Louis stared at Eugenia clearly believing she had known about the murder before Preston announced it at the dinner table. Holding an empty fork, afraid to move under Louis's gaze, she waited for his words. After several excruciating minutes of silence she found the strength to lift a roasted potato.

As the month dragged on Eugenia grew increasingly worried about herself and her family's place in the LaHarpe hierarchy as she found herself isolated from everyone but her sisters and her children. Eugenia missed Preston's presence and sense of stability he provided for the children.

Louis ordered one of the extended family members to assist Eugenia with garden chores and livestock care until Preston returned. The young man proved to be hard worker but he refused to talk to Eugenia making the days long and strained.

Preston's two young children did not understand where they father had gone and Eugenia failed to explain it to then in a way they understood. Her efforts were met with uncomprehending eyes and the repeated question of "Where is father?" Lying in bed each night Eugenia counted the days until Preston's exile ended, worrying and crying until exhaustion overtook her.

Preston's month of exile ended and he returned to the LaHarpe family compound. His homecoming was met with silent nods and an occasional handshake but there was no public acknowledgement of his return. His children climbed all over their dad and Eugenia hugged him for dear life. Eugenia and the kids presented him with a carrot cake and hand churned Orange Crush ice cream to welcome him home.

As time passed Preston settled back into compound life but Eugenia sensed her husband had changed during his exile. Preston's eyes still lit up when he saw his wife and children but Eugenia sensed darkness lurking, waiting for a chance to break free. She had sensed the same malevolent darkness when he had returned from 'over there'. Eugenia prayed nightly that the darkness would not overpower the light in her husband's eyes.

Even the children noticed that at inappropriate times Preston's voice took on a menacing tone. After an outburst he would gather the children and apologize. He told the children that the government had changed him but he would get better and keep himself under control because he was stronger than the government. Eugenia noted Preston began having more trouble sleeping than before his banishment and his nightly walk-abouts grew in duration. Preston also withdrew from socializing with extended family members during the day spending his newly found free time alone.

Eugenia knew better than to question Preston about his behavior; and she knew the penalty for discussing their personal matters with others. She focused on the children and the livestock to escape the stress.

Several times following his return to the family Preston petitioned for a private meeting with Louis but the patriarch refused to see him. Louis was cordial to Preston upon his return to the compound but he wanted no private audience with Preston or discussion of family business other than what related to Preston's crops or livestock. Preston watched helplessly as other members of the family grew closer to Louis further fueling his resentment and anger.

One morning, after completing chores, Eugenia was cramping badly and in a foul mood so Preston grabbed his favorite AR-15, pocketed a predator call and extra magazines, then went into the woods for a rare daylight walk-about. He loved his wife but her once a month transformation into a hell beast was something he had to escape to ensure his sanity and her safety.

This month's transformation coincided with a time when stress over the way Louis was treating him was peaking and all Preston could think of was getting some mind relief. And the best way to get relief was to shoot something. Preston knew an isolated spot where he could run through several magazines of ammo without being bothered. Desiring to burn off roiling emotions Preston ignored his ATV and exited the compound on foot.

Eugenia knew there was trouble simmering when Preston failed to turn and wave goodbye at the last moment before being swallowed by the forest. She returned to the bedroom, fell onto the bed and began to cry thankful her kids were at the compound's school.

In an isolated section of the large forest, near the western edge of LaHarpe's property, two of Chickasaw County's career criminals, Lonnie and Ronnie Lester, began their day of cooking methamphetamine. Their mobile drug lab was set up on a folding table crowded with supplies necessary to turn the lethal mixture of chemicals into the methamphetamine the men would later sell on the street. The two men had chosen this spot for its isolation without regard to whose land they were trespassing on.

Here, in the nearly inaccessible clearing, the fumes generated from processing their drugs were unlikely to be smelled by a casual passerby. Nor would there be a buildup of gases to cause an explosion as had happened in the camper truck the brothers once used as a mobile drug lab cruising rural highways. In this almost fairy tale woodland setting, the brothers had been cooking meth for three weeks; and here they planned to continue manufacturing meth for the foreseeable future. They had set up trail cameras to make sure there were no trespassers visiting the clearing. The cameras revealed that the clearing was isolated enough it was unlikely anyone would stumble onto their operation. The men barely even kept lookout anymore so secure they felt in their location.

Drinking beer as the noxious mixture cooked, the men discussed the most recent NASCAR news as Lonnie idly paced the edge of the clearing, beer in hand, and Ronnie made adjustments to his ATV's engine. The men rode ATVs to the clearing bringing in supplies for each day's cook and today Ronnie's engine had sputtered twice on the way in. Ronnie couldn't stand his engine acting up so he tinkered with it as Lonnie watched the batch cook. Ronnie gunned the engine and Lonnie attempted to shout over it unconcerned that anyone would hear them.

Preston discovered the Lester brothers when Ronnie revved his ATV's engine, the loud noise guiding Preston toward the men. Ronnie drove the ATV around the clearing before parking it and joining Lonnie by the folding table holding the paraphernalia. Satisfied the ATV's engine was properly tuned, Ronnie opened a cold beer.

Preston grew more incensed by the moment watching the men cavort as if they owned the land and had no worries in the world. Preston trembled as he pondered what to do; his anger growing from indecision keeping him from acting. Prior to his banishment he would have acted on instinct and the trespassers would be dead now; but Louis's public dressing down at the family dining table had fractured Preston's self-confidence.

Preston watched from behind a tree studying the men and their set up. Each man had a holstered sidearm but no rifle. Preston had his AR-15 which gave him the edge. The men were casually negligent with their chemicals and heat sources that Preston saw as a tactical advantage for him.

Lonnie, the thinner of the two men, tried to set his beer can on his ATV seat without looking. He missed. The beer can fell to the ground spilling its contents onto the dry grass. Both men looked at the fallen can then burst into laughter. The lighter man kicked the beer can sending it rolling along the ground.

Preston watched as the leaner of the two men walked to the folding table and checked the progress of the newest batch. After getting a replacement beer, the lighter man joined his companion and sampled some finished product. Words were exchanged and the two men began assaulting each other as if they were reenacting a Three Stooges slap-fest routine. After a few minutes the two men broke apart laughing hysterically. After catching their breath they gave each other a high five. Their actions told Preston all he needed to know.

After their silliness ended the brothers rested on their ATVs sipping beer waiting for the batch to finish cooking. Preston identified some of the chemicals on the table and pinpointed what he thought was the most explosive item. Fortunately it was close to an open flame. Preston smiled.

Next, he noted the men's sidearms were holstered; he was certain they did not even have a round chambered. Preston quieted his breathing and listened for distant sounds that might help disguise the noise that was about to erupt. The entire county seemed quiet; there were no log or cattle trucks rumbling on the distant county road, no timber company planes flying overhead, not even a distant train passing. Preston worried that the sound of gunfire might carry, but then no situation was ever perfect although he was far from inhabited areas.

The brothers sat on their ATVs, a cigarette in their left hand and a beer in their right hand. For a moment the brothers moved in sync as they took a drag off their cigarette then took a drink of beer. Preston stifled a laugh as he watched the men.

Preston began to finalize a plan of attack. He visualized each action he would take during his assault. First he would shoot a single shot along the length of the cookery table blowing up the chemicals and product. The unexpected explosion would disorient the men. Preston would then shoot the lighter man first. Based on their Three Stooges routine the lighter man seemed more agile so he needed to die first. The heavier man was slower and could be killed second. Each action he was about to take was clearly visualized.

Preston planned to spare the ATVs; by selling them in the adjacent county they would provide money he could use to purchase more ammunition. The folding table was fifteen feet from the parked ATVs and Preston calculated the all-terrain vehicles were out of danger. As long as he killed the second man before the man could take cover behind one of the ATVs and begin a firefight Preston felt comfortable he could neutralize the situation with a maximum of five shots; one shot to the cookery, and two shots each for the men.

Preston worried about such a brazen daylight attack but the urge to kill the men became an obsession as he continued to watch them disrespect LaHarpe property. One part of Preston warned him to wait and tell the family of the transgression; another part told him that waiting was weak and would allow the men to escape justice.

The Lester's continued to kill time sitting on their ATVs oblivious to the AR-15 pointed at them. The heavier man stood and began to urinate. The lighter man turned away and lit a fresh cigarette. Preston smiled and took the opportunity to creep closer to the men finding a prime vantage point behind a fallen tree. Preston readied his weapon and watched.

The heavier man returned to his seat on the ATV and pulled out a joint from a cigarette pack. He lit the joint, took a deep draw then handed it to his brother who tossed his cigarette to the ground. Preston watched the men pass the joint back and forth several times.

Preston took aim at the equipment and chemicals covering the folding table. He visualized the attack unfolding in his mind's eye. His plan was to shoot lengthwise along the table sending his bullet through everything, knowing at least one thing would explode to provide the initial diversion. Five shots and done. He also had the aftermath planned out; he knew where to dispose of the bodies so no one would ever find them. Preston told himself he was doing this for the family, even if they would never learn of it.

Preston looked through the AR-15's sights at the table full of drug making equipment. The men continued to share the joint unaware they were experiencing the final moments of their lives. Preston listened carefully for any sounds indicating they were not alone in the clearing. He heard nothing to concern him. The two men were now standing at the folding table staring at the table full of chemicals and paraphernalia watching their batch come to life. Preston exhaled and pulled the trigger.

5

> Rivers and rainbows, God's creations
> Out there waiting for you
> Get up on your feet, get 'em to move
> Take a holiday from the blues
> 					-A Group Called Smith

Kit sat on his ATV waiting for his GPS unit to lock onto satellites as his friends admired each other's collection of gear. Coolers of beer and food were fastened to cargo carriers next to fishing poles, tackle boxes, and tools. Kit had admitted he didn't know what to expect so he was packing for the unexpected, between them the expedition seemed well outfitted.

Buffalo gnats swarmed the men causing a comic display of swatting and cursing as the gnats flew up the men's nostrils. It was barely past ten o'clock in the morning and the temperature was pushing eighty-nine degrees. Adding to the misery factors, humidity was increasing by the minute as the jet stream drew moist air deep inland from the Gulf of Mexico and mixed it with heat moving in from the west to the east.

Kit marked the 'home' waypoint then fastened his GPS unit to the handlebars of his ATV before turning to address the group. Standing on the ATV's foot pegs, he said, "I think we can make decent time on the old four wheeler trail as far as Chickasaw Creek. North of the creek, toward the pond, I haven't a clue as to what the trail will be like. I'm mostly sure that Ulysses maintained the trail to the creek because I remember him talking about fishing it pretty regularly. I want to go directly to the creek, and afterwards, if we have time on the way back, we can detour and check out the old pasture plot where they want to tape the challenge shows. Oh, yeah, FYI, if you have to get off your four-wheeler to piss, especially once we get near water, be on the lookout for snakes."

Ethan said, "Hell, yeah. Maybe I'll get enough snakeskins to make a pair of boots."

Charles said, "I wish I had my knee high boots instead of these ankle high ones. I wonder if insect repellant will deter a snake. Don't they smell with their tongues?"

Ethan said, "Your Hawaiian shirt will scare them off."

Garrett said, "Kit, take the lead."

Kit nodded. He said, "North by northwest."

Garrett said, "Really?"

Kit smiled, winked at Garrett, then pointed at the trailhead and said, "That way."

Kit settled onto his ATV and started following the overgrown trail. The others formed a noisy convoy with Garrett bringing up the rear. The old trail was no longer tagged and months of neglect had allowed young branches to grow into the road forcing the men to bend low over the handlebars to avoid getting a face full of leaves. The first pit stop came five minutes in when the procession came to a deadfall blocking the road.

Garrett parked and opened a toolbox. Lifting out a chainsaw he walked to the head of the convoy whistling a lively tune.

Kit said, "I commend you on your preparedness."

"You don't get to be my age without learning a few tricks."

Kit said, "And I thought your tricks were limited to gardening and landscaping."

Garrett pulled the ripcord starting the chainsaw with the first try. He shouted over engine noise, "You told me we were surveying abandoned property. I thought a chainsaw might come in handy."

Kit smiled and shouted, "You're a great neighbor, I don't care what Mrs. Fields says."

Garret shook his head at the inside neighborhood joke and leaned into his task of cutting through the portion of the tree trunk blocking the trail. The chainsaw roared through the fallen tree blanketing the ground with sawdust. The other men found something to do far away from the noise while Garret worked.

Kit used the time to study Ulysses' hand drawn map of the property and try to decipher landmarks. Alex took the opportunity to investigate beyond a holly thicket not far from the trail. Charles wandered around, searching for an opening in the forest canopy where his cell phone might get a signal. Ethan pulled a beer out of a cooler and sat on his four-wheeler drinking watching the men go about their business.

Ethan yelled over the noise, "Even if you get a signal, no one will hear you over all that noise."

Charles shoved his cell phone back into his ATV's cargo box and complained, "No reception. I hate being out of contact with the boys too long. I could have sworn I saw more than one tower on the way in."

Kit said, "Don't you have a satellite computer? You run a cyber-security company, why don't you have a satellite computer link-up?"

Ethan said, "Yeah, I bet even Alex kept his super spy communications toys when he left the mercenaries."

Fortunately for Ethan, Alex was out of hearing range or he would have taken exception to being called a mercenary. Kit glared at Ethan then subtly shook his head.

Charles said, "I run a computer security company and what I need is cell service. Not having cell service is driving me to distraction. I heard the national news say that solar flares might disrupt satellite communication service for a few days, but I never thought about something like a cell tower being down being a problem. Damn copper thieves."

Kit said, "There are only a few thousand people living in this part of the county and the main telephone priority is 911 calls."

Ethan said, "What? They still use carrier pigeons down here?"

Kit glared at Ethan. "Not everyone who lives in the backwoods is backwards. This is a poor county and I think most people still do face to face communicating. Maybe talking face to face is what keeps these folks grounded and close-knit."

Ethan said, "I guess Kit's lucky to have any utility service at all. I'd hate to have to use an outhouse by candle light every single time. Besides, isn't one point of this rural adventure to get away, unwind, relax, and disconnect from the phone?"

Kit quipped, "Yeah, that and being sort of a shakedown cruise before I meet with the television producers."

Ethan shot back, "At least it doesn't sound like Hollywood is going to make us look like a bunch of hicks this time."

Kit said, "We can only hope."

Alex returned from his reconnoitering of the woods and said, "Kit, these woods look like you've got lots of critters roaming around. I saw all sorts of tracks and signs. It also looks like you might have a bear in the area. I found a ripped up log that looked like a bear had been going at it. I also found an old deer stand about a hundred yards in that direction with crime scene tape on it. I think you should put up some trail cams to see what you've got going on around here."

Ethan snapped his fingers, "Good call about the cameras."

Charles said, "Bears?"

Alex nodded.

Charles said, "Bears? Now we have to watch for bears?"

Ethan said, "I want a bear skin rug for my fireplace at home."

Kit said, "I wish I'd thought of cameras. Cameras are a great idea. I bet night vision goggles would be great out here too. I guess I need to think about a mix of rustic and modern. I patted myself on the back, for thinking to print out all of those satellite pics and topo maps. I've got to use modern technology more effectively."

Ethan snorted, "That's sounds like a good idea, doesn't it Charles?"

Charles ignored Ethan.

Garrett shut the chain saw down and called to the men standing by the ATVs, "I need some help rolling these pieces out of the way."

Alex, Kit, and Garrett laid hands on the larger sections of the fallen pine tree rolling two sections of trunk off the trail while Ethan watched from behind a second beer. Charles checked his cell phone one last time before climbing back onto his ATV. Once the trail was clear, the convoy resumed their ride to Chickasaw Creek.

After another few hundred yards of brush busting trail blazing, the men could see a change in the forest to their left. Trees were larger and less undergrowth cluttered the ground beneath the trees. The convoy slowed to admire magnificent old growth trees as they drove past. Century old trees supported a thick canopy of leaves that allowed only tiny slivers of sunlight to reach the ground. Every man shared an unspoken thought wondering what stories the trees would tell if they could talk.

As the men continued forward the edge of the old growth forest receded further away from the four-wheeler trail and Kit increased his speed. The thought of wading in a clear, cold creek after a hot stifling ride through the woods drove Kit, and the others, forward as fast the rough terrain would allow.

The forest was dense and healthy. Visibility was limited and the air mostly stagnant. Shrubs and saplings were reclaiming areas once cleared for uses long forgotten. Evidence of severe winters, tornadoes, and flash floods dotted the big woods reminding the men that storms were a force that held no compassion or regard for the works of man. Still, despite scarred areas of damage, the forest was beautiful and resilient despite the passage of time and storms.

The ATV trail came to a wooden crosstie bridge crossing the thigh deep creek. Kit parked and turned his ATV off. The others fanned out and parked as they arrived at the bridge. Kit sat on his ATV looking at the creek remembering fun times with his grandparents splashing and catching fish. Charles began scanning the nearby ground for snakes. Alex studied the opposite bank while Garrett rubbed his aching back. Ethan popped a fresh beer and asked who else wanted one. The others called for beer and Ethan tossed each man a cold one. The beers were opened and the men saluted the forest while taking in the beautiful creek side scene.

Kit studied Ulysses' hand drawn map. The trail crossed the creek on a rough wooden bridge, built from railroad track crossties. Kit dismounted and carefully walked to the bridge. He put one boot on the first tie testing its stability. The other men dismounted then gathered along the bank, watching for snakes while stretching and grousing about the hot, obstacle plagued, ride.

Assembled in a line along the bank, the men enjoyed cold beer in silence as they studied the mostly clear, slow moving water. As if on cue a fish broke the surface of the creek taking an insect for a bite of lunch. The men looked at each other with anticipation of an afternoon filled with cool water and hot fishing. Kit advanced several more testing steps onto the old bridge.

Garrett used his beer to point at a deep spot formed by the bridge supports and said, "I bet one of us will get a serious lunker out of that hole."

Alex seconded Garrett's prediction with a robust, "Copy that!"

Charles ventured out onto the rough bridge, stood beside Kit, and called back to the group, "Hey, this thing feels a lot sturdier than it looks." He took out his cellphone and held it above his head trying to find a signal.

Garrett said, "I'll stay on this side of the creek, but if you boys want to cross and explore what's on the other side of this creek I'll look forward to your report when you come back."

Ethan said, "I'm not leaving you alone with all these fish!"
Garrett said, "Damn. You're on to me!"
Ethan looked at the creek and said, "Let's catch dinner."
Charles left the bridge and said, "I'm ready to fish."
Alex nodded. "Me too. Beer and fishing."
Ethan said, "Hell, yeah. Beer and fishing."

Kit said softly, almost as if convincing himself, "Yeah, fish first, explore later." Reluctantly he left the bridge and joined the others by the ATVs.

Kit unloaded his fishing gear joining the others who were debating which lure to use. Kit interrupted the debate when he sprayed insect repellant on his clothes and the others followed suit. In short order the group was spread along forty yards of stream using every one of their fishing skills to best the others by landing the biggest fish; a feat that would guarantee ownership of the fishing bragging rights from this trip for the rest of their lives.

Whoops of joy and taunting shouts of "Fish on!" mixed with the splashing of fish fighting to stay in the creek filled the next two hours. The men paused only for lunch enjoyed in the cool, deep shade near the stream's bank.

After a relaxing lunch, Kit put his stringer of nine fat bream in a cooler on the back of Garrett's ATV then announced he was going to explore the other side of the creek for a while.

Kit asked, "Anyone coming with me?"

Garrett said, "I'm staying here."

The others just shook their heads and resumed fishing. Kit stowed his fishing gear and fired up his ATV. After marking the bridge waypoint on his GPS, he drove onto the bridge and idled. He looked back at his friends enjoying the shade along the creek bank.

Kit saw relaxation in each man's face and posture; each man seemed to have shed years from his countenance. Kit smiled in response believing then and there, that no matter what else happened, this weekend was already a success.

Ethan saw Kit pausing on the bridge and walked toward him. Kit waited for his cousin wondering what last words Ethan wanted to say before Kit disappeared into the forest beyond the creek.

Ethan walked onto the bridge and joined Kit summing up the men's thoughts by saying, "Thanks for the invite but it is so cool here in the shade with that, oh so gentle, breeze coming off the stream. I think I'll enjoy this little slice of Heaven rather than sitting with a hot engine under me and hot air blowing over me. Here's a beer for the road. Let us know what you find."

Kit took the beer and set it between his thighs then drove slowly across the crude crosstie bridge. The others watched his careful progress across the bridge. Kit remained in first gear as he disappeared into the forest on the other side of the creek.

Ethan returned to the group and said, "I would have bet ten bucks that the bridge wouldn't have held him."

Charles said, "And yet you let him go with no word of caution."

Ethan shot back, "You don't know what I said to him on the bridge. I accept your apology."

Alex said, "I can't believe you're stupid enough to bet against Kit."

Ethan laughed as he answered, "Hey, I'm not stupid. It's just that Kit's luck is bound to run out one day. And, I'd rather it run out on something we can all get a good laugh out of, rather than something serious. You know what I mean?"

Garrett said, "I do."

Piercing shafts of sunlight filtered through the trees highlighting different leaves and patches of ground and creek. The steady breeze carried the aroma of fresh greenery and decaying forest detritus. As Kit's motor noise receded the remaining sound seemed to be leaves whispering their discontent at the motorized intrusion. The men felt the weight of the world lift and float away on the breeze.

The men fanned out along the bank, fishing pole in hand and beer cooler centrally located. After an hour of fishing they found themselves drawn to the cooler for a beer break at roughly the same time. Alex moved fish from his stringer to Garrett's ice chest before getting a fresh beer. Charles walked onto the bridge and tried to call his sons again. Still, there was no reception.

As Charles packed his phone away he mused aloud, to no one in particular but to everyone within earshot in general, "Kit will have to do something about the lack of cell phone reception. Isolation will be a big drawback to any kind of retreat or corporate getaway."

Garrett nodded adding, "Yes, that's true, and I don't think he's thought about insurance, transportation, or medical issues."

Ethan said, "You're a buzz kill."

"Hey, I've got two nitwits trying to run a food truck without thinking anything through. Damn near anything you do has a better chance of success with planning. I'd love to see Kit turn this place into a successful resort."

Charles said, "I think the allure of getting away from it all has clouded Kit's judgment. I know he hates his job, but this will be twenty-four-seven, year round, work. I know about that."

Alex said, "You've got to utilize the strengths of your location. Turn potential disadvantage into useful advantage. Put a positive spin on the fact that when you're here, you are truly at a retreat away from the modern world. I'm all for Kit doing something great with this place. I will offer to help write a business plan for whatever he decides to do with the property."

Charles said, "Kit should turn that big old barn into a recording studio for bands who want to work in relative peace and quiet. I'd sign my kids up."

Ethan said, "I like Chas's suggestion of turning the place into a recording or rehearsal studio for bands. Being out here in BFE like this, where you're free to engage in all the debauchery, drugs, and sex you want with no one to be a buzz kill should be an inspirational gold mine for a band suffering from creative stagnation."

Charles said, "That's not what I had in mind. And not all bands are into drugs and debauchery."

Alex said, "He could turn this into a retreat for soldiers with PTSD or TBI."

Charles said, "Hey, I say if some of these modern rock bands got away from the concrete jungle for a while maybe there wouldn't be so many angst filled songs. I'm tired of growler and screamer bands bitching about how bad life is. And, whatever happened to vocalists who can actually sing?"

Garret said, "I know I'd like to hear rock and roll return to upbeat lyrics and singers who can sing."

Ethan shot back, "How old are you? There won't ever be another Beatles."

"Too bad." Alex said, "Maybe we need bands to sing about love and optimism at this time in our history."

"Copy that." Garrett opened another beer, "I'll drink to that. To the Beatles, and The Who, and Rolling Stones."

Ethan snorted and beer came through his nose. He wiped his face and said, "There are too many golden oldie stations as it is. Thank God for satellite radio and digital libraries."

Charles said, "Haven't any of you heard of Green Day or Offspring? My kids say they're the bomb."

Garrett said, "Don't know them."

Ethan turned toward Alex with a questioning look. Alex said, "Yeah, I know them. They're talented and have some not inane lyrics. Your kids could emulate worse or less talented bands."

Garrett said, "I'm fishing. You boys can discuss the sad state of modern music while I catch the rest of dinner."

The men fished silently for several minutes. After one particular cast toward the far bank Alex felt as if someone was watching him. Pretending to check his line, Alex surreptitiously scanned the brush bordering the far side of the wide creek and saw nothing amiss. Believing the moving shadows and whispering leaves had unnecessarily spooked him he shook the discomfort off, attributing the sensation to the ingrained habit of being watchful, suspicious, and tense every waking minute during deployments in Iraq and Afghanistan.

Alex relaxed after one final scan of the far bank remembering that trusting his gut and the hairs on the back of his neck had saved his life at least three times. Inhaling slowly, and then releasing a controlled exhale, Alex removed his hand from his Glock and relaxed a bit more. He didn't recall reaching for his sidearm, but then habits were mostly unconscious actions. He reminded himself he was far from suicide bombers, the Taliban, Al Qaida, and ISIS.

Alex slowly inhaled a second time, held the breath for a silent count of five, and then exhaled for a count of ten. He felt better and decided to get another beer. As he turned toward the beer cooler, he saw Garrett staring into the forest on the far side of the creek. Alex turned toward the shadowy area Garrett was focused on but saw nothing amiss in the mottled light and deep shadows. A moment later, Garrett relaxed and cast his lure toward the far side of the creek. Alex felt relieved that Garrett also seemed satisfied there was no imminent danger; he trusted the veteran cop and survival instinct that never dies. Despite a measure of reassurance there was no danger lurking across the creek, Alex wondered why the hairs on the back of his neck refused to lie down.

6

I'm gonna leave the city, got to get away
All this fussing and fighting, man, I just can't stay

-Canned Heat

Kit returned from his scouting mission to find his friends still enthusiastically catching fish. He parked his ATV near the others then sat on the side of the bridge, bare feet dangling just above the cool flowing water. He chatted with Charles and Alex who were fishing the pool created by the bridge supports. Further upstream Garrett noticed Kit had returned and slowly reeled in his ultralight line as he walked toward the bridge. Closing in on the men, Garrett lifted his stringer out of the water revealing half a dozen colorful bream.

A shout from downstream drew their attention and the group turned to look in the direction of the voice. Ethan was wading noisily toward the crosstie bridge and the group of men gathered there. He was hamming his effort to walk up stream, pretending to be struggling with the weight of the stringer trailing in the current behind him.

Charles said, "That boy drinks a bit, don't you think?"

Kit said, "Yeah. It's gotten worse over the last year or so. I'm more concerned over his use of pain pills. Mixing the two never turns out good. At least out here being drunk is safer than being drunk in town. Too many random elements have a chance of ruining a good time in the city. Plus, I've never seen him get belligerent, so in my book a happy drunk is always better than an angry drunk."

Charles said, "But sometimes that boy does get on my nerves."

Alex said, "Copy that."

When Ethan finally waded up to join his audience, he was grinning like a child on a Christmas morning. Pretending to strain under the weight of the catch, he slowly lifted his stringer out of the water revealing a mere four fish. Three of the fish were average size red eared bream, but one shell cracker bream was a monster. Ethan's audience applauded his catch.

Ethan bowed then lost his balance and tumbled into the cool stream. He sputtered and cursed but held his stringer of fish.

Charles said, sarcastically, "Nice."

Ethan stood up pushing wet hair out of his face. He saw the others laughing at him and tried to give them a withering angry glare but couldn't pull it off with a straight face. Ethan burst out laughing and joined the others in a long belly laugh.

Kit's return, and Ethan's dunking, prompted an end to the day of fishing. One by one, the anglers made their final cast of the day then put their stringers of fish on ice. As each man stowed his rod and tackle Kit handed him a cold beer. As the men refreshed themselves Kit related what he had seen on his trip, describing the pond located in the middle of a little finger of hardwoods separating a thick stand of pine trees and an unseen but heard cattle ranch. Kit estimated the pond was two acres in size but added it would be difficult to fish until some access lanes to the bank were opened up.

Kit concluded his report by saying, "The pond looks to be more work than any of us would want to do before we can fish it. Definitely more work than we want to do, or have time to do, this weekend. There is a fishing platform but it has seen better days and is listing badly. One corner is swamped. And, what looks to be a hand-carved dugout canoe is sunk next to the platform. But on the other hand, I think we can have some fun blasting feral hogs. There was hog sign everywhere. I know of at least two hog wallows Ulysses marked on his map."

"Hell, yeah!" The shout came from Ethan.

Charles said, in a questioning tone, "We don't have to get up at the crack of dawn tomorrow to do that, do we?"

Kit shook his head, "No we can make it a late afternoon hunt. You guys can sleep in tomorrow but I've got more scouting to do. Remember, this is a working weekend for me."

Garrett said, "I've got a predator call. We can take out some nuisance coyotes, too. They're bad for rabbits and ground nesting birds."

Kit said to Garrett, "I'm naming you as my information officer."

Garrett said, "Sorry, I must decline your generous offer. I'm retired and plan to stay that way. But, I have some new synthetic shafts I'm looking forward to seeing in action. These shafts are reported to be state of the art composite material. I'm ready to hunt nuisance animals!"

Ethan sneered, "I'm really waiting to see you take some big gnarly boar or a shaggy coyote with that bow and arrow set up you've got."

Garrett smiled, "If bow hunting is good enough for Uncle Ted, it is good enough for me. I've seen my share of modern weapons up close, personal, and in use. I'm sure Alex has too. It's not like wild game will be shooting back at you, so popping a deer or a bear from two hundred yards out with a high-powered rifle just doesn't hold much of a thrill for me anymore. Don't get me wrong, I admire marksmen but I enjoy a good stalk. And, as for me, at my age, I like to use stealth, deception, and skill to get in close and take my prey."

Alex said, "Don't forget the tracking. Ah, the thrill of picking up a trail and following it to the biggest buck you've ever seen. Or learning your prey's patterns as you plan and execute the perfect takedown."

Ethan said, "You talking ragheads or antler heads?"

Alex ignored him.

Kit said, "Tracking wasn't my thing; I hated following the blood trail trying to find some deer I shot before it gets too dark. At least with a rifle, at a moderate range, they pretty much drop dead in their tracks. Grandpa U always wanted to find the deer the same day he shot it; he didn't want to share his venison with the local wildlife overnight."

Garrett shot back, "But tracking is part of the fun. Didn't you guys play Daniel Boone or anything like that when you were kids?"

Kit said, "Westerns were my dad's thing so they were mine too."

Alex said, "No, sir, I played Army. I've bled Olive Drab since I can remember. It was a family expectation."

Ethan said, "I grew up in the city. I played video games."

Charles shrugged, "I think we just played touch football and shot hoops in the city park."

Garrett shrugged and addressed the group. "Okay. Just let me get the first shot tomorrow before you scare everything off with all of your cannon fire."

Kit waved his empty beer can at the assembled group, "Okay. We can plan all of this out tonight. Right now, I suggest, we head back to the lodge. We have a lot of fish to clean."

Ethan laughed, "What do you mean, 'we', Kemo Sabe?"

Kit said, "He who doesn't help, doesn't eat."

Ethan held up his hands, "Okay. I'm really good at frying up potatoes!"

Kit nodded, "That'll be your job."

Charles, sitting on his ATV, reminded Kit, "I thought we were going to check out that pasture you've been talking about on our way back."

Kit said, "Oh, yeah. I forgot about that. Everybody okay to take a side trip before we go back to the lodge?"

Garrett said, "I'll take the point and head on back to the cabin with the fish. But I'm not starting to clean them until you all get back."

Kit said, "Back to the lodge, you mean. I'd expect nothing less."

Garrett double-checked the straps securing the cooler of fish. The day's total catch were a dozen bass and a three dozen bream. The men finished their beers while policing the area for trash under Kit's relentless supervision. Satisfied the creek bank was thoroughly clean, Kit announced it was time to go.

Garrett maneuvered his ATV through a tight U-turn until he was facing the right direction to travel back to the cabin. Kit took second position and idled. The others lined up behind his ATV. Ethan gunned his motor until the others glared at him hard enough to make him stop.

The ATVs snaked through the forest until Kit signaled a right turn was coming up. Garrett continued toward the cabin as Kit led the others onto a questionable trail taking them deeper into the woods. He stopped often to refer to a hand drawn map while looking for decades old landmarks.

Under the canopy of the hardwood trees, the afternoon light faded far faster than in open country giving the men a false sense of time being later than it actually was. The trees grew close to the trail but fortunately no fallen timber blocked the narrow trail.

At the cabin, Garrett found the Chickasaw County Sheriff sitting on the hood of his cruiser smoking a cigarette. Garrett could tell by the sheriff's body language that there was no issue to be addressed; it was only a friendly get to know you visit. Garrett stopped his ATV and dismounted. With a wide smile and hand extended he approached the large black man.

Kit led the convoy of ATV's along the mere hint of a trail zigzagging around holes and fallen branches. The trip was slow and when Kit paused to check the map again the pause revealed how stagnant the air was among the close growing trees. Low branches and briars harassing the riders turned smiles into frowns as they forged onward. Kit made a mental note to look for another way into the clearing for future visits. His destination was a hay field once used to feed the cattle Ulysses and Kellie raised. Kit knew the field was the site where the scouts could camp and the producers could set up their obstacle courses and cooking challenges. The going was slow as the men ducked and dodged low branches and briar thickets.

Kit braked hard when he entered the clearing and saw the strange scene before him. Alarmed, Kit hurriedly tried to shift his ATV into reverse, but the other riders had come to a stop clustered behind him leaving him nowhere to go. He waved to the group to back up but instead they turned their ATV's off and dismounted unaware of what Kit had seen.

Once gathered around Kit the men saw what had alarmed him. Across the clearing were two abandoned ATVs, a large burned area, and a scattering of debris. Kit stood on his ATV's foot pegs hoping the slight elevation would provide him a better view of anyone, or any danger, that was hiding in the distant trees.

Alex instinctively put his hand on his Glock.

Kit called out, "Hello! Anybody here?"

Alex eased his Glock from its holster.

Kit called louder, "Hello! Anybody there?"

The men fanned out beside Kit's ATV waiting apprehensively for a reply to Kit's call. Kit dismounted and walked cautiously into the grassy clearing cupping his hands to shout hello again then waiting silently for a reply.

Alex flanked Kit with his Glock ready. Ethan and Charles stood behind their ATV watching Alex as he followed Kit. After a quick, nervous, look into the dark forest behind them Charles and Ethan joined the others.

Ethan whispered loudly to Alex, "You just can't shoot somebody for simple trespassing."

Alex ignored him.

Ethan said, "Don't start a feud with anyone."

Charles hurried forward and put his hand on Kit's shoulder slowing his advance toward the abandoned ATVs. He said, "Maybe we should come back in the morning. It's getting late."

Kit shrugged him off and continued walking toward the ATVs. He could see bullet holes in the ATVs from yards away.

Alex broke away from the group and walked toward the blackened earth where he knelt and began an examination of the burned area. Kit completed a cursory search of the field's interior area before rejoining the others. Ethan and Charles remained apart from Kit and Alex looking nervously at the forest surrounding the field.

Charles whispered, "This reminds me of that spooky forest in Lord of The Rings. Fangorn or Mirkwood, I forget which it was. I read the trilogy and The Hobbit over and over to my boys."

Ethan said, "Yet, you can't remember which forest was the spooky one."

Charles took a big, obvious step away from Ethan.

Standing next to the pair of ATVs Kit said, "The keys are in the ignition. And there are bullet holes."

Alex said, "Whoever was here fought back against whoever attacked them." He knelt, lifting a few spent shell casings littering the ground near one of the four wheelers. "Fifty caliber. And what looks to be a fatal amount of blood staining the ground."

Charles said, "What makes you think someone was attacked? Maybe this was drunks and target practice gone awry, maybe? Maybe one of them shot himself."

Ethan said, "You're not supposed to do that on other peoples' property."

Alex said, "Kit, come over here."

"What?"

"Over here."

Kit finished inspecting the ATVs and joined Alex. "What ya got?"

Alex said, "I've got a bad feeling about whatever it was that went down here."

Charles said, "Great."

Kit said, "Shootout between rival druggies?"

Charles groaned, "Not drug dealers too!"

Alex shrugged for an answer then stood and began a more systematic search of the grassy clearing.

As Alex searched the area, Kit unfolded Ulysses' map and studied it. "I'm not sure this is the hay field clearing noted on the map. Somewhere we got turned around."

Ethan said, "You were leading the way, with a map! Where the hell are we then?"

Kit stared at the map, "I'm not sure."

Alex returned and said, "All the action is confined to this small area."

Charles said, "Then we should leave this small area immediately."

Ethan said, "I wouldn't worry. If anyone was still here surely they would have shot at us by now."

Alex said, "All the signs are relatively recent."

Kit said, "I need to make sure we're actually on my land before we do anything about this."

Ethan said, "Hell yes! I've seen the movies; I know these backwoods southern folks don't take too kindly to trespassers."

Charles said, "If you think we are trespassing, we should leave now."

Kit turned to Alex and said, "Is it possible that there was a shootout between rivals and their drug lab took a stray bullet and exploded and burned? I know Ulysses said that sometimes some locals would cook up their meth in the woods. There was a big countywide brouhaha a few years back between the moonshiners and the meth heads. Ulysses turned in a meth site he found on his property once, and he went on an on over what a hazardous material removal nightmare the ordeal turned into. The HAZMAT people cordoned off the woods and brought in a front-end loader to scoop up the contaminated soil. Then they didn't even replace what they hauled off." Kit took a breath and looked around.

Kit sighed, then continued, "Plus, Ulysses had to pay for all of it himself. He was so pissed that he had to pay for cleaning up a trespasser's mess. He said he would never report a site again; he'd just clean it up himself. So, here, maybe some meth head got injured and it took two buddies to get him to a doctor or something. I see no bodies but blood. No bodies but shell casings. No bodies but evidence of a fast, hot, fire. Someone got shot or burned and that's why they left their ATVs behind. It'd take one guy to drive, and another to keep the injured guy from falling off the back of the ATV."

Alex said, "I don't know. Maybe. There is a lot of violence and scorched earth evident in this small area, as well as the shell casings around the abandoned ATVs. Something obviously went south for somebody. It looks like they were firing toward that section of the forest. They fired in a single direction." Alex pointed and everyone turned to look.

Charles shivered and asked, "Do you think someone is still here? Watching us from the cover of the trees?"

Ethan, who had returned from his four-wheeler with a beer said, "Maybe they had a big fire to cook rustled cows and it got out of hand. Or the cow's owner caught up to them. You know southern justice and all of that traditional old way of handling things."

"No." Alex cut Ethan a sideways glance of contempt.

Ethan said, "Okay. What do you think?" He sipped on the beer as he waited for Alex to respond.

"I'm not sure. It's a mystery to me. I've never seen anything burn this hot outside of a combat zone and I've seen ammo depots explode, IEDs explode, and I've seen oil and chemical fires. But this is unusual, especially being so tightly contained in a grassy clearing."

Kit said, "I'm going to write a note and put it on the four-wheeler telling them they are trespassing and this land is under new ownership."

"You don't know if it is them or us trespassing! They might come looking for you meaning to do you harm. Try to scare you off, or worse."

"That may not be a good idea. You just said you're not sure where we are. What if you're on the neighbor's land by mistake? Putting a note on their rigs might piss them off. At the very least cause an unnecessary misunderstanding. You know how territorial these country folk are. You don't want a Hatfield-McCoy feud starting."

Kit scratched his head and looked at the map again. "I think we're still on my land. I don't think Grandpa's map is to scale so I may have over or under estimated the distance. I know I was following more than a mere animal trail."

Alex said, "I saw the remains of some old road as we came in. It wasn't much of a road anymore. I'd barely call it an old logging road being generous. Maybe he didn't think it was enough of a landmark to put on the map."

Kit continued to scratch his head, "Surely we would have seen some posted signs if we had crossed into someone's land."

Charles said, "I don't want crazy neighbors or the local drug cartel coming after us."

Kit nodded, "I won't put anything threatening in the note. I just want them to know the old Carson place is about to become active. If it's not my land, then at least they will know the Carson property is inhabited again."

Charles said, "That sounds reasonable."

Kit walked back to his four-wheeler to get paper and pen out the cargo box to write the note. Alex moved slowly toward the two abandoned four wheelers studying the ground around the machines. Kit wrote an identical note for each of the four wheelers.

As Kit worked on his wording for the notes, Alex turned the first ATVs ignition key and the four-wheeler fired right up. He turned it off and tried the second one. It did not start. Alex left the four-wheelers and spent several minutes searching the area further away from the ATVs and burned area.

Alex rejoined Charles just as Ethan returned from the far side of the clearing after relieving himself. Kit took his time fastening a note to each of the ATVs. Charles continued to look around nervously.

Alex said, "I found a butt load of shell casings in the woods. I think these guys were ambushed. With all of the shell casings, blood soak, and fire scar, we need to report up the chain of command. I mean to the cops."

Charles said, "Remember, we got no cell phone service. Let's head back to the house and hash this out there."

Ethan said, "Yeah, I'm getting hungry".

Charles said, "I bet there are bears around here. I heard Alex say he found evidence of bears. Let's not meet one in the dark!"

Ethan said, "We're out of beer."

Charles said, "Plus, we don't have flashlights and not all of us brought guns to this fishing trip." He glanced at Alex.

Kit said, "Okay. Okay."

Ethan said, "Good. Let's go."

Kit turned to Alex "What do you think?"

Alex shrugged. "I don't want to jump to conclusions but we should definitely report this to the sheriff."

Charles said, "Remember, we don't have cell service."

Ethan said, "None of us has a satellite laptop? Alex?"

Alex said, "Those are only useful in certain situations. Granted this is one of those situations. But, no, I don't have a satellite laptop handy. We still need to report this even if we have to drive an hour to go into town or wherever the sheriff's office is located."

Kit said, "Okay. Let's pigeon hole that idea for latter. I don't want a big EPA or sheriff's investigation right off of the bat. Let's not make any unnecessary police reports to scare off the TV show producers. We'll come back and check it out tomorrow when we have more daylight to work with. If the ATVs are still here or if our mystery is not sorted out satisfactorily, I will report it to the proper authorities. I give my word of honor." Kit marked the spot on his GPS unit then took photographs of the ATVs to add to the photos he had been taking all day.

Alex looked at the sky and said, "We really do need better daylight to look around. We can come back tomorrow, like Kit said, and if the four wheelers are gone, then I'll buy into Kit's assessment that a drug lab blew up and two guys had to transport a badly injured third man out of here on a third four-wheeler. And, you can be sure that they will come back for these later. One of them looks nearly showroom new. Except for the bullet holes, of course."

Charles said, "And we can be sure we are on Kit's property before we start making waves."

An owl hooted somewhere from the dense leafy canopy above the men. Everyone jumped then looked around sheepishly. The owl hooted again and a distant coyote howled calling to his brothers and sisters. Ethan broke into a deep belly laugh that flowed from a sudden rush of relief. The others joined Ethan in a freeing laugh washing away a fear induced adrenaline surge, nervous suspense, and nagging anxiety. The men finally concluded laughing, wiped tears from their eyes, then looked at each other, a bit embarrassed they had spooked themselves.

Kit said, "Let's go fry some fish."

7

> I live back in the woods you see,
> A woman and the kids, and the dogs, and me
> I got a shotgun, a rifle, and a four-wheel drive
> And, a country boy can survive.
>
> -Hank Williams, Jr.

Sheriff Boscoe Washington Carver was a heavy-set, tall, black man. The decorated veteran was the first Black American elected sheriff in the history of Chickasaw County. Over the last four years Carver had laboriously worked at building a reputation of being fair but stern; he was a friend to law-abiding citizens but a fierce foe of scofflaws and relentless scourge of drug dealers and moonshiners. During the last election, no one even bothered to run against the much admired community leader and lawman.

When Carver slid off the hood of his dusty cruiser, the front of the car sprung upward. The main thing Garrett noted, besides the sheriff's bulk, was the large .50 caliber Desert Eagle sidearm holstered on his belt. The gun looked almost small on the uniformed officer. The sheriff tossed his cigarette butt onto the ground and waited for Garrett keeping one eye on Garrett's holstered sidearm.

Extending his hand Garrett said, "Hello. What can I do for you, sheriff?"

Carver's baritone voice was as impressive as his frame was large. "I'm Sheriff Carver. You the new owner here?"

"No, sir, James Carson should be rolling in just any time now. He and three other men stopped to checkout an old hay pasture near the edge of the property. For a TV show."

"That would be Kellie's hay field. It's gone to seed pretty badly from neglect."

Garrett said, "We just got here and Kit is checking the grounds out."

Carver eyed Garrett. "Yeah, we got a call from some TV types wanting to know if the area hospitals had medic-flight capabilities. Said they might be interested in filming a TV show down here. They got a tip from the state's film commission about Carson's property possibly being available for taping their show."

Garrett said, "Kit can fill you in on all of the details."

Carver nodded, "Word got out and people are already seeing dollar signs."

"Kit included. He's already talked about moving down here."

Carved glanced back at the cabin. "It'll be nice to have some activity here. I check on this place now and again just because it's such a nice cabin. After the twins died, I feared one of their yahoo buddies might burn it down or turn it into a drug house. Every now and again I run off some teenagers, but the really bad ones seem to leave it alone."

Garrett nodded and turned to look for Kit.

Carver folded his arms across his chest and stared at the trailhead where the ATV's would be entering the yard once they returned to the cabin. The men made small talk as they waited; Garrett let Carver know he was a retired police officer. Carver lit a fresh cigarette then offered one to Garrett who politely declined.

Then men shared service stories until Kit and the others returned parking in a semi-circle surrounding Garrett and Sheriff Carver. Kit looked at Garrett with a questioning glance.

Kit dismounted, striding directly to the sheriff. He offered his hand, "Hi. I'm Kit Carson. I'm the new owner here. What can I do for you, sheriff?" Kit noticed the name badge. "Sheriff Carver."

Sheriff Carver eyed the group, paying close attention to Alex and his Glock. "Well, first I'd like to see your ID. But other than that, I'm just stopping in to introduce myself."

Kit said, "Great. It's good to know you pop in now and then. I was pleasantly surprised to find the lodge hadn't been destroyed or vandalized." Kit fished his ID out of the cargo tote on his ATV and handed it to the sheriff.

Carver said, "Lodge?" He looked back at the cabin.

Kit tilted his head toward the cabin. "Cabin."

Carver smiled as he studied Kit's ID before handing it back. He studied the other men for a long moment. Carver said, "Yeah, that's as much luck as anything. Most of the young kids in this area all leave the county ASAP. Still, we get our fair share of poachers and vandals. We've got our share of survivalists, too. And, we've got some folks who like to cook up methamphetamine out in the woods. Hell, we have a thriving meth business that is rather sophisticated, at least for country boys. I'd advise you to be careful and take everything you hear with a grain of salt, being outsiders and newcomers and all that."

Kit glanced at the others, most of whom averted their eyes. He turned back to the sheriff, "Yeah. We came across something weird in a big clearing near an overgrown logging road. There's a badly burned area that looks like something exploded. And, there's two ATV's just sitting there, keys in the ignitions, but no sign of the owners. We think maybe they blew their drug lab up by accident and it took two of them to transport a third to get some help."

Kit glanced at Charles and Alex who nodded their approval of Kit coming clean about the mysterious scene in the clearing.

"Where is this you say?" The sheriff leaned toward Kit towering over the much shorter man.

"Inside of a clearing ringed by some of the biggest trees I've ever seen. I don't know what you might call the spot, but it's between a cattle ranch and a long unused logging road. You can hear cows but you can't see them. We might have veered off of my property-by accident; Ulysses did not make his hand drawn map to scale. I've got the coordinates on my GPS unit."

Carver said, "You should have your property properly surveyed. Just to make sure you stay on your property. And take No Trespassing signs seriously. There are several families around here that shoot first and ask questions never. Some of our locals believe trespassing is a death penalty offense."

Kit said, "We didn't mean to trespass. If we did."

"I believe you. But remember you can't argue with a bullet once it's been fired."

Charles said, "How dangerous are these people?"

Carver said, "Hard to say. The Charolais cattle folks are good people. But, your neighbors to the north, the LaHarpes, are sketchy at best. They like their privacy and defend it strongly. I'd not want to get on their bad side. We suspect them of lots of things, but no one has been able to shut them down. They are very good at being discreet and have been established in this county forever."

Charles paled, "You think we were on their property? Now we've started a feud?"

"We don't have feuds anymore. That's a stereotype."

Ethan said, "Stereotypes are real because the repeated activity is quantifiable and documented."

Charles groaned softly. Kit shot Ethan a dirty look.

Kit said, "I don't want any trouble with the neighbors."

Charles said, "Kit left notes on the ATVs."

The sheriff returned to sit on the hood of his cruiser. The car's suspension groaned under his weight. Carver tossed the cigarette butt down and sighed before continuing. With a serious and frustrated look, Carver said, "I think I know the field you mentioned. We've had some local career criminals set up their drug labs in that clearing before. There's a logging road that comes off County Road 61 giving all manner of yahoos access to that spot. It sounds like it is on LaHarpe land. They own over two thousand acres.

"There is a trail that skirts the cattle farm and leads straight into that area you're talking about. I'll check it out later. You didn't touch anything did you? Since you said you found unattended ATVs, the LaHarpe boys may have dealt with the situation themselves. If it's a meth lab operation we'll have to call a cleanup crew. The LaHarpes will not like that."

Charles said, "Kit." Charles looked pale and scared.

Carver glanced toward Charles then looked at Kit. "What?"

Kit looked worried. "Well, I left notes on the ATVs telling the owners the Carson place was becoming active again. But I didn't move anything and I didn't accuse anyone of trespassing."

Charles said, "What if we were the trespassers? Will they come looking for us?"

Sheriff Carver stood and wiped one giant hand across his brow. Carver said, "Doubt it. But you never know. I'll check it out." Carver looked each man in the eye and shook his hand. Each man knew he was being evaluated. The sheriff held Kit's eyes as he said, "I'm glad you ended up with this place rather than Ulysses' twin nephews. I don't understand why Ulysses liked those two slackers so much. I just never understood what he saw in them two boys. There's no telling what they would have done to this place. What are you planning to do with this place? Our office had a call from some TV types asking questions and asking for statistics about the county."

Kit spread his arms, "Yeah, reality show producers want to tape a youth competition and then some other show, kinda like Fat Guys in the Woods, if you've ever seen that on the Weather Channel. That's part of why we're all here this week. The TV producers want photos and maps and county stats. They are thorough. This is a working weekend. We're collecting on-site information to seal the deal."

Ethan said, "Welcome to Camp Carson."

Carver turned and walked to the door of his cruiser. He opened the door and started to get in, then paused. He glanced at the men finally fixing his gaze on Kit.

"Mr. Carson, by the way, did you or any of your friends notice any other signs of trespassing or recently used trails today?"

Kit looked at his friends, his expression showing confusion at the odd question. They shook their heads no.

Kit said, "No. Why do you ask?"

Charles took a step closer to hear the sheriff's answer.

Alex looked around, peering at the shadows under the trees.

Carver leaned heavily on the car's open door. "We had a tragedy near your property line not too long ago. A local boy, a Wildlife Officer, new to the job, seemed to be in one of your grandpa's deer stands and had a fatal accident. No one believes that the young man could have been that careless so suspicions remain surrounding his death. The case is closed as an accident but it just doesn't sit right with folks who knew young Benson. We think some bad blood or family history between him and a LaHarpe came into play, but we can't prove anything. Just, if you see something strange, give me a call. Please."

Kit said, "Will do."

Charles said, "Any word on the cell tower being fixed?

Carver shook his head, "I'm just glad the county has a good radio system for us."

Charles said, "Are there land lines anywhere?"

"There's a phone booth on the town square in Tallyrand. Don't know if it works or not."

Charles said, "Okay." Resignation dripped from the word.

The sheriff handed Kit a business card before continuing. "I'll drop in on you in a day or two to give you a report on what I find out concerning your burned area and abandoned ATVs. If I may make a suggestion, you might think about getting an iron gate for the start of your driveway at the county road. Around here, a road just standing open like that is an invitation for all matter of trespassers.

"Have a good day, gentlemen. And, I honestly don't think you have anything to worry about but since you left a note on the ATVs you might be extra cautious for the next day or so." Carver pointedly glanced at Alex's sidearm then slid into his cruiser. The car sank under his weight. Carver turned the cruiser around then slowly drove down the gravel driveway.

Ethan let out an explosive breath, "Well, talking to the local cop was a buzz kill. At least he didn't breathalyze us for driving drunk in the woods."

Garrett shot Ethan a glance that clearly said, 'Show some respect.'

Kit said, "I think we made a good impression and I think we're off to a good start."

Charles, worry in his voice, said, "I wonder if we need to be concerned about starting a feud?" He looked at the dark woods surrounding them. "Maybe leaving notes was a bad idea."

Alex said, "I thought that feuds were a thing of the past unless you live in Kentucky or Tennessee or Alabama. Or, the Middle East. Or, any country in Africa. Or, in any American inner city. I guess feuds and tribal warfare are in mankind's DNA."

Garrett said, "Anytime you have people who disagree there will be a chance for a feud. Modern versions of tribal warfare have taken root in American inner cities."

Kit looked around at the woods surrounding the cabin and said, "I think I'll need an iron gate and a big dog if I'm going to live here full time."

"You might need more than one dog."

"You need more than an iron gate."

Garrett, standing by the cooler of fish said, "Hey, how about some help with these fish. They're not getting any fresher!"

The men moved as one toward Garrett and the cooler. In the distance, a train blew its whistle and coyotes began howling. Alex searched the darkness under the trees for movement and saw none. He felt a tinge of anxiety rise but forced what he was feeling to subside. Garrett kept an eye on Alex as he scanned the forest surrounding them. Once Alex's posture relaxed Garrett turned his attention to the fish.

Kit and Garrett lugged the heavy cooler into the cabin. Ethan went to his truck returning carrying an impressive selection of mixers and liquor. Ethan stumbled up to Charles and pushed some of his armload of liquor into Charles's arms then continued into the cabin. Charles hesitated for one last look at Alex. The veteran seemed relaxed. Charles breathed a sigh of relief then followed Ethan into the cabin. Alex took one last slow look around the area before walking into the cabin. The sense of anxiety he felt earlier diminished as the smell of hot cooking oil filled the cabin.

Billy Jo Thurber and Jo Buck Thurber leaned on a muddy, king cab pickup truck as their buddy, Peanut Willis, loaded hunting dogs into wire cages secured in the bed of the battered truck. The hounds were excited, barking, and playfully nipping at one another, knowing that the cages meant they would get to hunt tonight. Billy Jo turned his attention to gear piled in the back seat of the truck. Methodically he made sure each of the powerful flashlights had good batteries, as did the lone pair of night vision goggles that the UPS driver had delivered just yesterday.

From the other side of the cab, Jo Buck dumped extra boxes of shells for the shotguns and a .22-caliber rifle into the back seat of the four-wheel drive truck. Peanut talked softly to the dogs calming them a bit. Billy Jo and Jo Buck finished stowing their gear then ambled up onto the creaky front porch of a plywood shack to kiss their voluptuous wives goodbye.

Peanut watched the couples kiss, wishing he had as much luck with women as he did with dogs. Peanut sighed, as he leaned on the truck, coveting the passionate French kisses his hunting buddies were getting from their wives

After a long minute, Peanut used a tattered red rag to wipe sweat from his face as he continued watching the Thurber brothers kiss their wives goodbye. The longer Peanut watched the two couples kiss the hotter the night seemed to grow.

Peanut swatted mosquitos wishing he had brought insect repellant spray. The mosquitos and gnats seemed drawn to him, ignoring the four people on the shack's sagging porch. He absently swatted mosquitos as he watched the make-out session on the porch continue.

The summer had seemed unusually hot; Peanut had heard something on the radio about solar flares making it hotter than normal and affecting orbiting communications satellites, but scientific talk like that was beyond his understanding and interest. Still dabbing the sweat beads streaming into his eyes, Peanut felt, despite the heat, tonight was going to be a good night for raccoon hunting. Times were tough all over and coon meat ate as good as store bought meat and, being free, it tasted even better than store bought meat.

Overhead fluffy white clouds dotted the night sky. The stars reigned supreme as the moon waited to rise. Bats flew above the truck snatching insects out of the night sky.

Peanut, standing by the closed tailgate, began bouncing on the balls of his feet as he watched the make-out session on the porch of the shack drag on. The women, braless, in their sweat soaked tank tops made Peanut wonder if he had enough cash to visit the local house of pleasure after tonight's hunt. He felt his loins stir but pushed the thought way, saving it until after the hunt.

Tired of the show on the porch Peanut called out to the brothers, "We need to get a move on now. These dogs are gonna get hard to handle if we keep 'em caged up for long."

Sallie Thurber called out, "Peanut, you just keep your head on straight and don't shoot my man. We don't need no hunting accidents."

Mollie Thurber whispered to Jo Buck, "Honey, you and BJ just stay behind him if you go and give that fool a gun. You know he gets as excited as those dogs of his once they tree something. I don't want you coming home with a bullet hole in you."

Jo Buck kissed her again and said, "We got a single shot .22 for him. He might be a retard but I ain't never seen anybody as good at working hunting dogs as him. We'll let him think he's one of us. Don't worry. We'll all be back after sunup."

Peanut ignored being called a retard. He knew he wasn't book smart, but few people could match his hunting and fishing skills. Peanut was aware of his limitations and his strengths and being called names, even to his face, no longer bothered him.

The Thurber brothers joined Peanut at the truck, each brother slapping him on the back in a gesture of comradery. Peanut scrambled into the littered back seat while the brothers took the front. With a last wave to the big women standing on the sagging porch, the men drove off. The women watched until the truck's tail lights disappeared. They looked up as a large thick cloud passed overhead. Wiping sweat from their face they waddled into the dilapidated shack to watch their TV shows hoping the passing clouds wouldn't affect the satellite signal.

Kit and his friends were relaxing around the fire pit as the dinner of fresh, fried fish, beans, sliced white onions, tomato slices, fried potatoes, corn on the cob, and ice cold beer settled in their bulging stomachs. Sitting in a wide circle the men enjoyed music coming from a wireless speaker Ethan had set up on the porch.

The campfire grew larger with each piece of wood gleefully added to it. Empty beer cans formed a shiny square pyramid base next to the flames. Coyotes, owls, tree frogs, and a multitude of insects could barely be heard above the crackling of the burning logs. Smoke rose lazily toward the heavens mingling with a few low hanging drifting clouds. The men marveled silently at the sight.

A slap broke the silence. Charles said, "I think I just got bit by a mosquito! Do these mosquitoes carry that West Nile Virus or Zika around here?"

Ethan chuckled, "That'll be one drunk skeeter. I think alcohol is an antidote for West Nile."

Charles persisted, turning directly to Kit, "Do they have West Nile out here?"

Ethan said, "I think West Nile is passé. Zika is the new threat. And don't forget the ticks that have Rocky Mountain Spotted Fever or that newly discovered disease that makes you allergic to mammal meat. I'm just waiting to hear that biting gnats carry some new found disease too."

Alex said, "It's hard to say if Mother Nature or Man will cause the end of the world as we know it first."

Kit said, "Think about this: the summer season used to end with Labor Day but now the weather extends it to Halloween. It frustrates me that the politicians and scientists focus on reversing climate change rather than developing ways to adapt to the inevitable. Climate change cannot be stopped; politicians and scientists need to admit that to the public and work on adapting to the new normal. Think of all the industry addressing the issue of adaptation would create. The climate change train has left the station; let's focus on adapting to the change for the rest of the ride."

Alex said, "Mother Nature will beat humans with critters or weather or tectonics, but she will get the better of man."

Charles said, "Great. I'm going to get another can of insect repellant out of my truck."

Ethan said, "That stuff will kill you quicker than the mosquitoes."

Charles shot back, "They wouldn't sell it if kills people and not pests."

Kit watched Charles pull out his cell phone and try to connect as he walked to his truck for more insect repellant.

Alex produced a Rocky Patel cigar from his shirt pocket.

Garrett pointed at the cigar. "Those are what will kill you."

Kit asked, "When did you start smoking cigars?"

Ethan pointed to the cigar, "That is the best bug repellant."

Garrett said, "It's a people repellant too."

Alex lit the cigar before replying. He savored the first wonderful taste of all natural tobacco then exhaled slowly. Alex said, "I had assignments in Iraq and in Afghanistan. When you're stationed in the fucking middle of nothing but sand, desert, and mountains, you tend to think a lot about water and fishing. If you're not dreaming of a woman you dream of lakes, ponds, streams, rivers, or the ocean. Even a nice big washtub full of clean water is a common fantasy when you're in country. Anyway, some corporal had a box of donated books sent over by the library in his hometown and there was a series of paperback books about a government outfit called NUMA that dealt with ocean related tales. In the book the admiral in charge of the fictional federal agency smoked Rocky's. So, when I had the chance, I bought a couple and tried them out. I liked them. I've got some more in the cabin if any of you want to give one a try."

Kit said, "Lodge. They won't make me turn green will they?"

"A smooth smoke by any standard." Alex took a draw, exhaled, and smiled.

Kit said, "Okay, I'm in. I'll try one."

Garrett said, "Mouth cancer and smoky bug repellant. That's the only thing cigars are good for."

Alex stood and walked to the cabin to get Kit a cigar.

Ethan said, "I'd take a big fat blunt of good Kush or Bruce Banner Number Three if anyone had one."

Garrett snorted, "I'd have to leave."

Ethan said, "It's legal in lots of places."

"Doesn't mean I have to approve of it."

Kit said, "Well, it's a good thing we don't have any weed since the local sheriff seems to be the type who likes to pop in unannounced. Surely he doesn't think we had anything to do with the meth lab?"

Ethan staggered to the beer cooler, opened the lid with some difficultly then pulled out a quart jar of clear liquid. He tapped the jar's label and said, "I brought some craft moonshine. This one is apple pie flavored. I have another one that is blackberry flavored. Anyone interested?"

The men nodded and smiled. In unison the men said, "Pass it around!"

The men took long drinks from the moonshine jar and nodded their appreciation of the smoothness and taste. Alex returned to the group and handed Kit a cigar. Kit studied the cigar's ring then smelled the tobacco.

Kit lit the cigar using a burning twig taken from the growing bonfire. Alex took the moonshine jar from Ethan and took a long pull. He wiped his mouth and gave the jar back to Ethan. The quart jar made one more round before being drained. The empty jar was passed back to Ethan. He said, "Keep open flames away from this."

Ethan gingerly placed the jar back in the cooler and pulled out the blackberry flavored moonshine. He took the first sip then passed it around. The men drank a little slower from the second jar.

Charles returned to the group complaining about the lack of cell phone reception to the empty air. As Charles neared the bonfire he cried out, "Hey! Look up there. I just saw something fly by!"

Ethan looked up nearly stumbling into the growing empty beer can pyramid. He said, "It was a UFO no doubt. I bet it was an alien trolling for a nice, juicy, rare, free-range, Angus cow burger!"

Garrett snorted, "It was probably an owl."

Ethan said, "It was a bat."

Alex said, "Or a whip-poor-will."

Kit spoke from around the cigar in this mouth, "You'll see lots of things down here. Mostly, stars. There's no light pollution for miles around. The nearest town of any size is a forty-minute drive. The nearest hospital is at least an hour away, so it pays to be careful out here." The last statement was blatantly directed at Ethan who ignored it.

Charles stared at the roaring fire and said, "Snakes, spiders, bears, feuding families, and no medical help for sixty miles. Maybe, listening to teenagers practicing their rock music isn't so bad, after all. I'm going to have to drink till I pass out or I'll stay awake worrying all night."

Ethan said, "You're a born worrier. Somebody give that man another drink."

Garrett said, "Worrying won't keep you awake. It's Alex's snoring that you've got to worry about."

Alex laughed, "It can't be that bad, it doesn't wake me up".

Charles said, "Oh, it is bad. Trust me on that one."

Kit said, "I seem to remember you telling me you slept through a mortar attack once."

Alex nodded, "The United States Army is fond of reminding you that you never know when you'll get a chance to sleep or eat again, so do both when you can. Sometimes you just have to trust your buddies to take up the slack while you get some needed sleep."

Charles said, "Somebody toss me a new beer."

Kit said, "I'll take another shot of moonshine!"

"Tell that to Ethan!"

Ethan farted as he wobbled toward the ice chest where he had set the blackberry moonshine. At the ice chest he stopped to analyze the situation momentarily forgetting what his goal was.

Kit sighed. He looked around at the others but no one wanted to intervene. Kit asked, "Having a senior moment, are we?"

Ethan turned and looked at his friends then slowly raised his middle finger. "Not in this lifetime you bunch of lazy assed sots!" He turned quickly toward the ice chest nearly losing his balance. Steadying himself he lifted the quart jar then opened the ice chest and cursed. "Damn. There are only two cold beers left in this chest. And one of them is mine!"

Kit called, "I want the 'shine."

Garrett snorted, "I guess it's time to break out more liquor."

Charles said, "What the hell do you think moonshine is, if it ain't liquor?"

Ethan lifted his beer, "I'll drink to that." He tossed the moonshine jar to Kit.

Charles leaned forward in his chair, "Do you guys hear that?"

Alex leaned forward tilting his head. "Just somebody hunting with dogs. Probably coon hunting. Or blasting coyotes. Poachers."

Charles strained to hear the distant hounds. "How do you know they're not the ATV owners? Are they on your property?"

Kit said, "I'm guess I'm gonna have to put up some 'No Trespassing' signs."

Garrett stood, "I'm going to get some more liquor."

Ethan said, "I've got more moonshine and beer."

Alex said, "How about some different music?"

Ethan nodded enthusiastically. 'Right on, dude. There's only so much rural tranquility, crackling fire, and animal noise a man can take. Let's rip the volume knob off some up tempo rock!"

Charles said, "What you got?"

Alex said, "I got some old Allman Brothers Band and Little Feat. I've got like three thousand songs on my iPod."

Ethan said, "I've got five days and seven hours' worth of music on mine."

Kit said, "I've got some Dylan and Tom Petty."

"Don't you have anything from this century?"

Charles interjected, "Hey that is some good stuff. I've got some Coldplay on my iPod but most of my music is on CDs."

Garrett said, "I bet none of you have any Sinatra or Martin or Tennessee Ernie Ford or Johnny Cash for that matter."

Alex said, "No rap or growler or death metal!"

Ethan said, "Damn, there goes half of everybody's collection."

Alex felt the need to explain his music preferences. "Listen up, I was stuck listening to rap or country or speed metal on several deployments. All the young guns like that rap shit or speed metal bands. The old farts listen to country. I just don't want to hear any of that anymore."

Ethan said, "You know what you get when you play country music backwards, right?"

Charles said, "I'll bite. What do you get?"

"You get your wife, dog, and house trailer back."

Alex said, "You remind me of this grunt who said he used to go to Thailand for sex. He said he found this great whorehouse that specialized in exotic sex. It was said that the women could make a dead man come they were so sexy. So, one day this guy goes in and notices there's new menu board up over the welcome counter. There at the bottom of the list of services was something called a 'wax job'. Well, he'd had blowjobs, rim jobs, and hand jobs, so he thought he'd try the wax job.

"Well, this cute little troll takes him up to the room and has him undress. She undresses and he gets all worked up looking at her tight little body. His prick is hard and begging for attention. He tells the girl that he wants one of those wax jobs. She nods and winks at him. Well, she kneels in front of him working on his cock with her mouth for a while before slowly leading him over to a table.

"The table looks something like a massage table except hard, not soft. Then she wrangles his big, swollen, cock onto the table then, without warning, she whacks his cock with a knife edge karate chop."

Alex paused, looking around at the men and their puzzled and pained expressions. "When she whacked his rock hard dick-wax shot out of both of his ears. She looks at him and says, 'You like wax job?'"

Kit spewed the last swallow of blackberry flavored moonshine out of his mouth as he exploded in a fit of laughter. The rest of the group groaned at the joke. Alex laughed even harder at his friends' reactions.

Garrett said, "Now, I'm really going to get the liquor. I've got to drink the sound of that joke out of my ears."

Charles said, "I need a cotton ear swab after that joke."

Ethan said, "Or a wax job!"

Garrett returned with two bottles of bourbon and a case of cold beer. He dumped all of the liquor into the ice chest. He poured two fingers of bourbon, neat, and took his seat. The men grabbed beers or mixed a drink while Kit added wood to the bonfire.

8

> Well, I know just what you need
> I might just have the thing
> I know what you'd pay to see
> We could build a factory and make misery
> We'll create the cure; we made the disease
> Frustrated Incorporated
>
>   - Soul Asylum

  After replenishing the cooler, the conversation ebbed and flowed competing with the roar of the raging bonfire, the nocturnal sounds of the forest, and leaves rustling just beyond the bonfire's bright glow. As the music's volume inched upward the sounds of nature receded. In a moment of silence between songs Ethan slapped his cheek. He cursed and looked at his hand then rubbed the dead mosquito onto his pants. Ethan swatted his cheek again just to be certain there wasn't another mosquito sneaking in a bite.

  Charles said, "I've got spray."

  Ethan swatted his cheek again. He looked at his palm.

  A voice from around the fire said, "We got ourselves a fight club!"

  A different voice replied, "What a great movie."

  "Yeah, too bad most everyone missed the point of the movie." The sentence ended with a dismissive snort.

  "Which was?" The question sounded challenging.

  "Their goal was to reset everyone's credit history and give people a fresh start. The buildings they blew up at the end were the credit reporting agency buildings."

  "Bullshit. The whole point of the movie was the scene with the convenience store clerk. Something he said indicated he wasn't doing anything with his life so they pretended they were going to kill him but instead took his ID and said if he wasn't in college or doing something better with his life than being a clerk in a year they'd come back and kill him. The message to do something with our lives was the point of the movie."

  "I thought it was just about dysfunctional people doing crazy things."

  "It was so much more than that."

  "Whatever. I can watch it over and over."

"I like the resetting of everyone's credit history theory. What a great idea. Why hasn't some hacker group like Anonymous done that? Or the Russians? They could erase student loan debt or home mortgages and be heroes. That'd sure as hell win them more fans than releasing government info or hacking some retail chain."

"Because Anonymous knows that would be pointless. Everyone would return exactly to where he or she had been in six months or less because they'd immediately buy all the shit they couldn't buy previously when their credit sucked. It's human nature not to learn from our mistakes."

"That is why we will always have government intrusion. Individuals rarely make selfless decisions. Politicians rarely ever make wise decisions. Neither group seems to make noble decisions. Politicians are supposed to represent us not lobbyists. But now and then, a bill gets passed that actually benefits the public."

"It's all bread and circuses anyway. Look at the groups who riot and burn their own community at the least provocation. That accomplishes nothing and only turns the rest of the country against them. The government understands it has to keep various groups pacified or it would be constant rioting. The government's use of entitlements to control groups ranges from total tax breaks for corporations to incomes for those people who don't really want to be a part of our society but demand other people's tax money to live on. The people who feel alienated or are sociopathic turn to crime whether it's white collar or common street level thuggery. And there are a majority of people that will never be happy no matter what you do. Our politicians may be greedy, self-centered, clueless, bought and paid-for idiots, but they are intelligent enough to know you got to keep the masses distracted or they pay attention to details and start to turn against the politicians. Thus it becomes all about bread and circuses to keep the population orderly."

"That's why inner cities are such problem areas. Whether it is DNA or something else, the fact remains many people just don't want to be part of the solution. It is easier to bitch and loot than work, or change, to help yourself. Those folks don't want to follow societal rules because they feel alienated; they want more bread and bigger circuses. The government in its attempt to pacify certain demographic groups always alienates other demographic groups. The government has taken away the incentive for many groups of folks to work or participate in making our country better."

"Those people need to understand to get respect they must give respect. Act like you want to be a part of society to be accepted by society. When you act like a violent mob you will be treated like you are a violent mob. Parents have relinquished control over their children, or worse, set very poor examples for their children to follow. Bread is entitlements and circuses are whatever diversion the government or media creates. America is on cruise control riding a highway to hell."

"It's not really those people's fault. Our own government set the system up to fail them because politicians didn't know any better or to think fifty years ahead. Think about the Selma protesters. They were well dressed, peaceful, orderly, unified, and had a plan. Our government handled that all wrong creating today's thugs who just want to burn it all down. There's no order or unity or incentive or common sense in how hoodlums try to change the system now; so call their actions what it is: vandalism, looting, and impotent rage."

"Hey, freed slaves had a chance to go to Liberia and run their own country their own way but they chose to stay here and seek guilt based entitlements instead of saying 'Goodbye, thanks for the fresh start. We can handle our affairs from here on without you white folks telling us how to do things.'"

"Damn, that's racist; it isn't just those folks in the inner city. Look at all of the white kids running away from home, often affluent homes, to be domestic terrorists or to join ISIS. There are more disenfranchised people out there than you realize including thousands from every race on the planet. Hell, if ISIS only had a charismatic leader we'd have ourselves a bona fide James Bond level global villain. ISIS has money, weapons, recruitment, and media savvy; if that's not a James Bond franchise villain, I don't know what is."

"Of course there are disillusioned people in every country in the world. Not just America, the Middle East, or Africa. You can't make everyone in your country happy. Humans are selfish asses."

"Alex fought for America. He's happy with his country."

"I'm happy with the concept of America, not the way it actually works most of the time. But I'm proud enough of it to defend it. I wish politicians were proud enough to do right by it."

"I think every soldier would agree with you. It has been the same with every war, except for the Vietnam War. It is a shame the government doesn't treat its veterans any better than it does."

"Amen."

"Providing soldiers state of the art war machines is great, but state of the art after service care and support would be great too."

"This country has been having problems for a very long time. It's inevitable for a nation with this population mix. Think back to the year 1969 and there was a song by the group Steppenwolf called Monster and the chorus was 'America, where are you now? Don't you care about your sons and daughters? We can't fight alone against the Monster.' That was 1969.

"Then there's the classic Ball of Confusion from 1970 and so much of Bob Dylan's early stuff. The songs we hear on the radio or even this mix we're listening to reminds us that things have been screwed up for a long time.

"Hell, since the public, voters, taxpayers, concerned citizens, none of us, didn't riot or actually challenge Congress during any of the years of mortgage and banking and legislative grid lock disasters, that seems to indicate the bread and circuses approach is working. And, working quite well it seems. That is all the evidence you need to realize that whichever political party is pulling the strings, the diversions are working."

"Hey, at least we don't riot and burn our own neighborhoods down to the ground and loot the place. What kind of message does that send out? Don't people know that hurts their cause more than anything? There's got to be an effective method somewhere between the old civil disobedience route and today's senseless violent riots in the streets."

"So, neither petitions, nor riots, nor voting works?"

"Do you feel represented by your politician?"

"Mostly."

"Then you must feel just like those special interest folks."

"Why do you continue to vote if you never feel represented by who you vote for?"

"Hope springs eternal. All we need is a charismatic Jimmy Stewart, Mr. Smith, type to lead the way. All we need is a fearless man, of and for the people, willing to gamble his political career on doing the right thing. We need one good man who bucks the special interest groups and their money."

"It's the special interest strangle hold that causes gridlock. There are no altruistic politicians anymore. Money talks."

"As for me, I'd rather have gridlock than new taxes any day."

"Amen!"

"The tax fix is simple, but like everything else, and I mean everyone else, no person, no generation, no group wants to be the first one to suffer the unpleasantness that the amount of necessary change needed requires. That's why public schools and Congress are disasters and why they are a microcosm of the whole of society.

"No person or group wants to be the person or group to go through the very painful, very life disrupting, very comfort zone destroying, but very necessary upheaval of everything they know. No public school student wants to be in the first class where discipline suddenly carries some weight and consequences are more than a slap on the hand, or where they are measured against peers around the country using a common benchmark, or where extra-curricular activity is second to grades, or where parents are required to be active in the education process until their kid graduates or drops out. If citizens cared about educating kids then there wouldn't be such a backlash against successful charter schools and discipline. We'll be playing catchup no matter what anyone does at this point.

"No corporation or bank or billionaire wants to be the first to pay their fair share. Think of the level of peer pressure at that level of commerce, power, governance, and thinking. No politician wants to be the first one to turn down lobby money and just simply work for his constituents. One term of fifty Mr. Smith's going to Washington or one Congress who en masse refuse to bow down to lobbyists or special interests until the infrastructure and campaign reform is fixed is all we need. Peer pressure and greed assures that change will not happen. But no one, I bet none of us here right now, want to be in the group that suffers through the first round of real change."

"What the hell does that have to do with credit history erasure?"

"I forget."

"Jeez, that's some good moonshine."

"Pass that jug back this way!"

A night bird flew above the group causing the men to look skyward. There was a moment of silence as the men gazed at the starry sky.

"Does anybody think we'll see an actual UFO?"

"You mean some light we cannot identify?"

"I bet we see some shooting stars. There are no UFOs."

"I've seen plenty of strange shit in the sky. It is a UFO if you can't identify it."

"So, you think God made ETs that come and abduct humans or make crazy crop circles in fields and tease us with mysterious light shows in the sky? Why? What would His purpose be in constantly having ETs teasing humans?"

"Who made God?"

"The Big Bang?"

"Some of you are going to hell!"

"Aren't those the questions that get answered once you die and go to Heaven?

"The Lord works in mysterious ways."

"I think God was a benevolent alien that tried to set early man on the right path for a sustainable civilization."

"Are you saying God made everything but turned guiding early man over to aliens rather than angels? Or God was a passing ET who decided to tamper with life on earth?"

"Could it be that the aliens and angels from history were simply the crazy people of that time? No one knew about psychology back then. Crazy people were either revered or banished."

"Look around you. The diversity of plants, humans, and animals makes you think there was intelligent design in all of this. Animals and plants are constantly evolving to meet the changes our planet is undergoing. I don't understand why God would start everything up then let religion devolve into bloody chaos. I would think He would remind us He is around or at least visit and see how His master plan was working out. Something obvious. On the other hand The Big Bang theory sounds preposterous as well. I mean all the material we know of came from nothing? Nothing exploded and everything was created? Obviously, we are here so there is that. I think there is a third option we aren't smart enough to think of yet.

"I'm not saying God made man or aliens. I'm not saying we evolved from some marine critter either. I'm not saying we didn't either, but I am saying there is probably something we just haven't discovered yet. Scientists discover new things by accident or emerging technology. There are a lot of questions with answers just waiting out there. Something our science hasn't discovered because it ain't got the technology to see it or the knowledge to even consider looking for it.

Think about it. On one hand you have the belief that everything we see and know was created by a benevolent supreme being who gave the first few generations of man instructions on how to survive and thrive but then washed his hands of his pet project saying he'd come back someday to reward everyone who kept this teachings. On the other hand you have the Big Bang Theory which proposes that everything we see and know began from nothing. So a spontaneous explosion from nothing that generated the entire known cosmos of material and life is our origin story. Both of those sound pretty damn far-fetched if you look at them closely. Yet, here we are, so, there's that."

"Everybody's got to believe in something. I believe I'll have another drink and try not to think about how all of this might have gotten started."

"Maybe the science fiction writers are right and there is a multi-verse and a giant other dimensional universe swallowing black hole sucked all the matter from one universe through it and spewed it out on this side transforming it into the material that makes ups our universe. We could be the cosmos-formed landfill of an extra dimensional universe's refuse. Either that or Earth is the Botany Bay of some galaxy. That sounds as plausible as the Big Bang's all from nothing or God making the universe in six days."

"Dude! That's not right! If there's a Hell you're on the A-list."

"At least the Bible has sound philosophy to live by. The Ten Commandments, The Golden Rule, and some other nuggets I can't name right now. But no sane person can say those are bad ideas. Those are basic life guides and shouldn't offend anyone."

Kit sensed the mood turn. Ulysses always said religion and government were touchy subjects and formally forbidden topics at family gatherings. Attempting to reign in the conversations Kit stood and accidentally knocked the beer can pyramid over in a loud clanging racket. The conversation stopped. Everyone looked at Kit.

Kit said, "My bad. I was getting up to pee. But since there's a lull in the conversation, let's change the subject to hunting or anything else but politics or religion. Just to something we can all agree on. I hear enough bitching in my daily work life; I really don't want to hear it here."

A voice said, "You work in collections. You know what I mean about a credit history reboot."

"Yes, I hear all of the sob stories. But, in the end, their problems are self-made because most humans put possessions over people. I just have one of those jobs where I see the worst of people. I've got no sympathy for those parents who must have a giant flat screen TV or the newest iPhone or a tricked out Cadillac while their children wear dirty rags and live on unhealthy dollar meals. Those kids are doomed because of their selfish, stupid, parents."

"Okay, let's talk hunting and turning his place into a money maker."

Kit said, "Yes, let's do that!"

Ethan said, "Yeah, let's talk about Camp Carson!"

Kit said, "I haven't settled on that name."

Ethan said, "It has a nice ring to it."

Charles stood and moved away from the fire to check his phone. After a futile attempt to connect he rejoined the others reluctantly putting his phone back into a cargo pocket.

Ethan said, "I'm putting on a different playlist. It's a mix so I don't want to hear any bitchin' about song selection." Ethan got up and fumbled in his pants pocket. Finding the player's remote he pulled it from his pocket with great fanfare. Winking at no one in particular Ethan pressed a button and, after a moment of silence as the mix changed, music from wireless speakers sitting on the porch filled the yard.

Kit took a few steps toward the dark woods then turned back to the group. The bonfire had not been fed recently and the flames were less than five feet high. Kit pointed to the bonfire and said, "Someone stoke that fire, I don't think the space station can see it anymore." He disappeared into the darkness beyond of the fire's glow to pee hoping the conversation would change topic by the time he returned.

Billy Jo and Jo Buck shouldered their shotguns and waited for Peanut to release the dogs from their travel cages. Peanut slung a single shot Ithaca .22 over his shoulder before attaching leather leads to the hounds' collars as he let each dog out of its cage. Once on the ground, the hounds tugged and pulled on the leashes nearly pulling the diminutive Peanut off his feet. Straining against the pull of the dogs Peanut got the pack under control then looked at the other men.

Jo Buck opened a bottle of cinnamon flavored moonshine and took a long drink before passing the bottle around. Each man took a long pull from the plastic flask. Jo Buck took a second swig before capping the bottle and shoving it into his coverall's back pocket.

The dogs continued to strain at the end of their leashes. It was clear that the dogs were more than ready to hit the woods. A whip-poor-will called from somewhere overhead. In the distance a train whistle aggravated a pack of coyotes. The night was hot, and relief came only from an occasional passing breeze.

Peanut said, "It's gonna be a good night."

Billy Jo said, "Let the hunt begin."

Jo Buck adjusted his new night vision goggles surveying the area. "I'm set. Let's go."

Peanut said, "I want to try those out later on."

Jo Buck said, "Maybe."

Peanut said, "Okay. Just remember I let you try out my steady stick last hunt."

Jo Buck snorted, "Peanut, it ain't the same thing. You bought your stick at Wal-Mart for a few bucks. These are state of the art and cost two-thousand dollars. You have a knack for breaking things."

Peanut nodded and knelt to pet his lead dog. The brothers looked at Peanut and shook their heads. Peanut said, "Well, I'll be extra careful this time."

The three men walked into the dark woods with Peanut's dogs leading the way. It was thirty minutes of carefully stepping over fallen timber, dodging limbs, keeping their guns from becoming tangled in vines and branches, and swatting mosquitoes before the hounds found a scent, then another ten minutes until Jo Buck spotlighted a big coon the dogs had run up an old hickory tree. Billy Jo fired one shot and the men had their first kill of the night.

Keeping with tradition the three men took a hearty shot of moonshine after each kill. Five hours later the men had four coons in the bag. Their journey had taken them over several fences and roads and only their GPS path and Jo Buck's night vision goggles could lead them back to their truck.

When the GPS unit showed forty minutes until dawn the men started the return walk to their truck. While bypassing a thicket of privet bushes the dogs began acting oddly, reluctantly moving forward only under Peanut's constant urging.

Billy Jo and Jo Buck attributed the hounds' skittishness to being young; after all, this was only the dogs' third nighttime hunt. Billy Jo checked his GPS pointing his finger in the general direction they needed to travel. He was concerned as the night vision goggles' battery indicator showed only ten percent power left. He hoped the goggle's battery would last until the sky became lighter.

The dogs were staying closer to the men now, no longer tugging and straining at their leads in the excited way coon dogs are wont to do. After another twenty yards of winding through close growing trees, the dogs were becoming a nuisance, underfoot, and skittish to the point of Peanut almost having to drag the youngest hound along. The Thurber brothers' amusement with the situation grew as Peanut's frustration with the dogs grew. The Thurber brothers sipped moonshine as Peanut tried to wrangle his dogs.

Peanut began cursing the dogs. The dogs barked back. Peanut kicked the youngest cur.

Billy Jo called for a stop so he could urinate. The elder Buck brother leaned his shotgun against the trunk of a large tree relieving his bladder with an exaggerated sigh. Peanut and Jo Buck shared a drink. The moonshine was smooth and for a moment made the men forget about the heat.

Suddenly the dogs bristled and started a low, guttural growl signifying something was near they did not care for. Peanut instantly thought 'black bear' and bent down to release his dogs if necessary. Peanut Willis loved his dogs but he was not above sacrificing his dogs if it meant he would escape a bear's claws and teeth.

Billy Jo startled the other two men by quickly zipping up his pants and shouldering his shotgun. "We've got company." He took cover next to a tree. Jo Buck adjusted his night vision goggles and began to scan the darkness.

Peanut tried to calm the dogs. "What is it BJ?"

"I don't know. I just saw a shape. Shine your light over that direction."

Peanut said, "I'm gonna spotlight them."

"Wait!" Jo Buck turned off his night vision goggles. "Go!"

Peanut thumbed the 'On' button activating the one million-candle power beam of his flashlight. He slowly panned it back and forth across the trees. Strange shadows came and went as the beam highlighted the trees before being absorbed by the black empty spaces between them.

The Thurber's were breathing hard hoping it wasn't a game warden. Peanut was praying it was not a black bear with cubs nearby.

The dogs fidgeted and pawed at the ground with a low growl. Peanut wasn't sure what to make of the dog's actions. He knew they were young, but this was very strange behavior.

From the blackness came a voice. "You, who goes there?" The voice was deep and guttural, adversarial; there was a distinct tone of challenge behind the words.

Jo Buck shouted into the darkness, "Identify yourself!"

Peanut tried to help by calling out, his voice unsteady but loud, "We got dogs here!"

Jo Buck panned the darkness with his shotgun.

Peanut nervously fingered the quick release clasp on the lead dog's collar. Without warning the skittish dogs bolted yanking Peanut to the ground as they struggled against their leashes straining to flee in the opposite direction.

Peanut's heart pounded as he yelled, "Bear!" at the top of his lungs forgetting a concealed man had just spoken to them. He had not seen a bear but knew of nothing else that would make the dogs act so spooked.

Spooked by Peanut's shout and the sudden retreat of the dogs, the Thurber brothers opened fired into the dense woods spreading out before them. Peanut dropped the leashes to cover his ears as the men emptied their shotguns into the darkness. The hounds bolted into the forest trailing their leashes behind them.

The men's ears rang from the shotgun blasts long after the last shell was fired. The Thurber brothers quickly reloaded barely taking their eyes off the dark woods surrounding them. Peanut slowly got to his feet, so pale with fear he practically glowed in the dark. Shaking with fear he raised the .22 to his shoulder.

Peanut whispered loudly, "Oh, God, please, God, don't let that be a game warden." The Thurber brothers turned and scowled at Peanut.

Jo Buck growled, "You shouted, 'Bear!'"

Peanut lowered his gun then his eyes; he picked up his flashlight, then turned and pretended to look for his dogs. He used the light to illuminate the dark forest.

Jo Buck shouted softly with a barely controlled rage, "Peanut, turn that damn light off!"

To the men's left low lying branches of a holly tree shook. Peanut dropped the flashlight and swung his rifle toward the movement as the others dropped shells and raised their shotguns. Suddenly a muzzle flash of bright fire and dark thunder erupted from the darkness. Half of Peanut's head disintegrated in a bloody cloud. His body collapsed to the ground with a soft thud. The flashlight landed illuminating his disfigured head.

There was a moment of stunned silence as the two men looked down at Peanut's body in disbelief. The disbelief gave way to fear and disgust as their hearts tried to explode through their chests. Their eyes and minds were momentarily disconnected. In the light, Peanut's one remaining eye looked up at them.

The Thurber brothers cursed and fired the few shells they had been able to reload in the direction the muzzle flash had come from. In a moment their shotguns were empty again. The two poachers dove for cover behind a tree. They reloaded quickly, ignoring the grisly corpse of Peanut.

Eerily, the guttural voice called out to the men from the dark woods. "Identify yourself."

Billy Jo quietly whispered, "I don't think a game warden would shoot first then ask questions."

Jo Buck shot back, "No shit".

"Who is that?"

"How would I know, dipshit?"

"Identify yourself." Billy Jo shouted into the darkness.

There was no answer.

"Okay, what now?"

"Shit."

"No shit, shit."

The guttural voice seemed to come from behind the men now. The voice was menacing as it repeated, "Identify yourself."

Jo Buck replied, "Hey, who goes there?"

A fallen limb cracked behind them.

The brothers spun toward the sound, their backs pressed tightly to the trunk of the large tree, hearts beating wildly, as they searched the darkness in vain for their attacker. The cold chill of fear tap dancing down their spines gave each man's trigger finger a tremor. Billy Jo raised his shotgun firing blindly toward the dark. Jo Buck emptied his shotgun, firing in a wide arc, and then started to reload.

The dark night was terrifying for the brothers as they tried to reload with shaking hands and unresponsive fingers. Anger tempered their fear further reducing their motor skills.

Without warning, the unseen attacker's weapon fired again flashing in the darkness. Billy Jo died instantly as dozens of tiny razor sharp flechettes tore into head and torso. Billy Jo was dead before his body slid to rest at the base of the tree.

Jo Buck screamed in rage and fired, counting his shots this time, stopping with one last shell left in the gun. The woods grew quiet as his ears returned to normal. There were no insects, tree frogs, or any other noise. All Jo Buck Thurber could hear was his heart pounding in his ears and his breath coming in short, ragged gasps. Then, twenty feet in front of him, his adversary stepped into a spot of filtered moonlight. The figure seemed to fade in and out of sight as it moved, almost as if cloaked by a dark shadow. Demonic eyes seemed to glow from deep within a dark, painted, human face.

The fearful apparition raised a common military tactical style shotgun. Facing the incongruous sight, Jo Buck wondered, despite his fear, why a demon would need a gun. Jo Buck was sure it was a demon; maybe even one of the legendary Forest Wild Men. He had heard the tales as a child but in all of his years in the forest, he had never encountered one of them-until now. The demonic Wild Man took a long stride forward as he shouldered the shotgun and aimed it at the fear stricken man.

Jo Buck shifted his shotgun with terribly trembling hands and fired his last shell. The shot missed the dark hulking figure because of his trembling. The large menacing figure closed to fifteen feet as Jo Buck grabbed his shotgun's hot barrel intending to use the gun as a club. The figure stopped, his shotgun aiming squarely at Jo Buck's head. Jo Buck took a breath, knowing it was his next to last breath. He wanted to face death like a man so he tried to stand tall but his body would not obey his command. His last thought was that he did not like to lose. The towering figure fired and Jo Buck joined his brother and Peanut Willis in death.

Preston slung his shotgun his shoulder. He removed the hood of his camouflage suit and shined a flashlight on the three dead men. He recognized the Thurber brothers from the monthly county flea market and swap meet at the Tallyrand Municipal Fairgrounds.

Preston did not know the men personally but had heard through wide spread gossip that the men liked to ingratiate themselves to people by doing favors or dirty jobs no one else wanted to do. He had never heard anyone say they liked the men, only tolerated them; and that was only because their services came cheap.

Local gossip said if you invited them into your home you would need to use a crowbar to get them to leave and, like a stray dog you fed once, they kept returning. Preston rationalized he had done the community a service by killing them; next he then turned his attention to eliminating the bodies and the men's truck. He was disappointed the dogs had escaped but then, dogs couldn't testify.

Preston knew a deep, murky, pond where he would dump the bodies. The truck was another matter; he could sell the truck for scrap to a black market chop shop in the next county. Dawn was coming and Preston would have to move fast; he only had half an hour of darkness left to sink the bodies, collect their guns to add to his collection, and hide their truck until he could move it safely to the chop shop.

As Preston dragged the three bodies into one pile he realized he did not feel as satisfied as he once did following dealing with interlopers. His demotion in the family hierarchy dogged him constantly, fueling a sense of righteous indignation over being treated in such a manner. Preston grew irritated as he knew he had to keep these deaths secret from the family as well.

It was clear he was on his own; no one in the upper hierarchy would provide him any comfort or hope for a quick return to the family's graces. Angry at the family's reluctance to forgive him, he kicked one of the Thurber brothers in the ribs. Preston looked at the three bodies, took a breath to steady his hands, and then proceeded with the task of disposing of the bodies and the other evidence.

The bonfire blazed away lighting up everything nearby. The beer can pyramid was repaired, towering next to the fire as the music played on. Garrett learned more about Kit as Kit and his friends reminisced about concerts from their younger days.

Several stories of Kit's attempts to sneak backstage would provide Garrett source material for playfully digging at Kit for months to come. Songs were applauded or scorned as time passed.

The next song in the mix started and Alex groaned theatrically. Garrett heard the exaggerated groan and looked at Alex who shook his head in resignation of what was coming. He then looked at Kit, Ethan, and Charles who were grinning madly.

Alex pleaded to the trio, "Don't."

Ethan smiled at Alex and said, "You know you want to sing along too."

Garrett focused on the song, a country song, and thought he remembered it, vaguely. The song was a classic and often played in bars. Garrett looked at Alex who simply shrugged in silent resignation.

Kit, Ethan, and Charles leaned toward each other as the song neared its climax. The singer paused singing to relate a story and the three men took a drink getting ready to sing along with the next verse.

The next verse began and Kit, Ethan, and Charles sang along:

"Well, I was drunk the day my mom got out of prison,
And I went to pick her up in the rain,
But before I could get to the station in my pickup truck
She got run over by a damned old train."

Alex looked at Garrett as the others finished singing the song, out of tune and at the top of their lungs. Garrett grimaced and shook his head while rolling his eyes. Alex said, "Yeah, that happened."

9

> I love the way you wear your trees
> And I swear all my thoughts are about you
> The most beautiful world in the world
>
> -Harry Nilsson

    Kit and the others continued to stoke the bonfire and add empties to the beer can pyramid. A series of live performance songs ended and Dobie Gray's classic Drift Away came through the speakers. The men grew quiet as some stared at the starry sky while others stared into the bonfire. Slowly the fire's outermost edges formed a ring of embers encircling the tall, dancing, flames.

    The firelight reflected off the nearby trees and even illuminated the cabin's face many yards away. The scent of burning pine and oak filled the air. The heat rising from the fire seemed to carry stress and worries skyward with it.

    Kit and his friends remained by the fire drinking and talking until the remaining embers had turned grey and safely cooled. Retiring to the cabin closer to dawn than midnight the men fell asleep the instant their heads hit their pillows. On the porch, the wireless speaker continued to play music for the creatures of the forest until its batteries failed and natural sounds returned for the nocturnal creatures roaming the forest.

    It was ten o'clock in the morning and the sun was shining brightly, well above the trees, when Kit rolled off the sofa and began brewing a pot of coffee. As Kit waited for the coffee to make he searched the refrigerator for any kind of food that did not require an effort beyond warming to prepare. Unable to find an easy snack to quiet his growling stomach, Kit stared at the coffee maker thinking of all the things that he would need to turn the property into a moneymaking enterprise.

    Kit tried to itemize the big picture. There would be ongoing maintenance of the lodge and grounds. Insurance. Food. Consistently working bathrooms. Designing safe but interesting trails for horseback rides and hikes. Veterinarian bills for a stable of horses. Reliable utilities. Reliable cell phone service. He would need fences and gates to keep out riff-raff. The list grew longer and more costly the more Kit thought about what was needed.

And he needed a name for the venture. Green Acres Resort sounded family friendly and had name recognition. He put Green Acres on the short list. A good name, familiar, friendly, and happy sounding, would go a long way toward selling the place as a resort.

Kit's head began to hurt as he calculated the amount of startup money he would need to launch a business in such a rural area. He folded his arms on the long oak table and rested his head. In a moment, he was deep asleep.

It was high noon before anyone else moseyed into the kitchen. Garrett woke first, getting his coffee as quietly as possible so not to wake Kit who was still sleeping with his head on the table.

Kit sensed movement and stirred, nodding a silent greeting to his neighbor. The two men talked quietly until the others were awake and gathered around the cluttered table. The five men sat silently around the table for several minutes sipping coffee and ignoring rumbling stomachs. No one admitted to being hung over but their faces revealed their unspoken burden. Multiple cups of coffee were poured and consumed with little conversation. Once the caffeine took effect, talk turned to food.

Kit said, "There is bread and bacon and eggs in the fridge."

Alex, who had moved to the garden window, laughed, "Don't sound so unexcited. Anything you've got has to be way better than MREs". Alex peered out the window watching the garden weeds sway from a light breeze.

Ethan said, "I thought these fancy lodges served three banquets a day."

Kit called out in reply, "Not for the hired help. Especially not for the hired help that drinks on the job!"

Garrett added, "I need a Bloody Mary."

Ethan said, "I feel like I could eat a bear."

Charles said, "Why don't you go get one?"

Ethan said, "Maybe I will. After I join Garrett for a Bloody Mary."

Garrett said, "Okay, then, if you two ladies are done bickering, why don't you whip up some sandwiches and chips for lunch while breakfast cooks."

Ethan said, "This is noon. This is lunch. We missed breakfast."

Charles said, "This is going to throw my pill schedule off."

Ethan said, "Too bad the food truck isn't operational."

Garrett snapped back, "It is operational, it just isn't stocked."

Ethan said, "Too bad the food truck isn't stocked. I think it has more room to work in than this kitchen does."

Kit said, "Any meal can be breakfast. You are simply breaking your overnight fast when you eat the first meal of the day. It does not matter what time the meal happens. Break-fast. Get it?"

Ethan said, "Ooh that never gets old, Kit."

Garrett snorted derisively.

Charles left the table and began gathering sandwich-making supplies. Garrett sat the coffee pot on the table after filling his thermos. Kit started bacon frying in a cast iron skillet. Once he transferred some bacon grease he began frying eggs in a second skillet. Garrett toasted bread and passed out plastic picnic style plates and plastic knives and sporks. The men eagerly piled bacon, eggs, and toast onto their plates.

Alex took his plate and ate on the front porch.

After the meal Kit said, "So, today we hunt feral hogs."

Garrett said, "Another day in paradise".

Charles held up a piece of bacon as he said, "There's your name for this place. Kit's Paradise Resort."

Kit said, "I'll take that under consideration."

Ethan said, "Hey, hold on there." He pointed at Garrett, "You're bow hunting, right? Of course, it is all so clear to me now. You bow hunt so that no matter how bad of a hangover you have, you can still hunt quietly."

Garrett said, "I've never thought of it that way before."

Alex entered the cabin and said, "Silent and deadly."

"That's not really why I bow hunt. But it does give a whole new meaning to 'silent but deadly'."

Ethan snorted, "I thought that only applied to farts."

Charles said, "Garrett, you haven't smelled a bad fart until you've smelled one of Ethan's farts after a night of drinking dark beer!"

Kit stretched, pushing away from the table. "I think I'll explore the barn while the meal settles. Anyone want to join me for a little treasure hunt before we pig hunt?"

Ethan perked up. "Treasure?" He was stirring a two finger shot of vodka into a new Bloody Mary using a plastic knife. "I'd love to find some Confederate gold!"

Charles said, "You've got enough liquor in there to melt that knife."

Ethan glared at Charles but remained silent.

Kit shook his head, "Treasure was just a figure of speech".

Ethan shook his head. "Damn. I thought maybe you were looking for Confederate gold or rare antiques."

Charles was hesitant, "I don't know about poking around in that old barn. There's got to be a million spiders and God knows what else creeping around in there. I bet you've got snakes and rats."

Kit said, "Look. I'm not stupid. I nuked the cabin, the outhouse, and barn with multiple bug bombs each. I'm sure the biggest bugs are dead or at least run off for a while."

Charles asked, "Multiple bombs each? That's not very eco-friendly for someone who is considering living out here in the wilderness among God's creatures. How many did you use?"

"Dude! At least one in the outhouse, two in here, maybe three or four in the barn."

Charles looked skeptical. "Really?"

"Hey, I'm not a fan of getting spider or snake bit. The nearest hospital is over an hour away. I've got no problem using modern technology against venomous pests."

Alex said, "I saw bugs over there that could eat bug bombs for breakfast."

Garrett said, "It's the little things that kill you. Spiders. Snakes. Ticks. Viruses. Bacteria."

Charles said, "Big things with teeth and claws can kill you too. Cougars. Gators. Wolves. Bears."

Ethan chimed in, "Bees and mosquitos."

Alex said, "Don't forget gun toting thieves. Drive-by shootings. Inattentive drivers. Drunk drivers. Drivers yakking on cell phones. Salmonella. E-Coli. Faulty manufacturing processes."

Ethan said, "It's not safe to leave the house to hear you guys talk."

Kit said, "That's why I'm moving down here."

Garrett said, "You pay your money and you take your chances."

Kit sighed, "At least we have countermeasures for most of your death dealing list of threats. And despite all of your gloomy talk, I'm off to the barn for at least a quick look-see before we go hunting this afternoon."

Alex and Garrett said they were coming with him; both men were excited about the wonders the old barn might hold. Ulysses' collection of oddities and antiques were legendary by Kit's telling; the question on Kit's mind was, 'What had the twins left behind?'.

The paper trash was dumped on top of fresh kindling to be used for starting the next bonfire. The previous bonfire had used up a good amount of wood but a moderate pile remained for one more big fire before the group returned home. A lone wisp of smoke curled up from the pile of ashes.

Kit rummaged around in a suitcase until he found a flashlight. "I'm off to the barn."

Ethan said, "I'm mixing up a little of the hair of the dog, then I'm right behind you."

Charles said, "I'm going to the bathroom. If I'm not at the barn in fifteen minutes, come and look for me."

"Don't stop up another toilet!"

Charles said, "The outhouse is over a giant hole. Thanks."

Ethan said under his breath, "You're a piece of shit."

Kit said, "Take a can of bug spray and spray the place first if you're that worried."

"Where is the bug spray?"

"Wherever it ended up last night."

Charles said, "Oh, right. I think I had it last."

Ethan said, "I think you took it to bed with you."

Kit checked the batteries in the flashlight and said, "I'm off."

The cedar plank barn was much nicer on the inside than the outside suggested it would be. The cans of fogger spray were strategically placed throughout the structure, right where Kit had left them. Telling the others to wait, Kit pushed the lever on the fuse box to the 'On' position sending power to the fluorescent lights running the length of the barn. The long rows of glowing tubes filled the barn with their full spectrum light.

Garrett whistled and said, "Nice place. I can tell Ulysses spent a good amount of time in here."

Alex said, "Good lighting in here. I wouldn't have guessed it from the way this place looks from the outside. I would have expected kerosene lamps or candles."

Garrett said, "Is the hayloft secure enough to walk on?"

Kit said, "I didn't go up there, but the ladder seems solid."

Garrett looked up and surveyed the hayloft's floor.

Kit said, "I was surprised everything still worked. Ulysses mostly kept up maintenance right up to when he went into the home. I admired his fortitude. I hope I am that spry when I'm that old."

Alex said, "None of us will live that long. You know that. We've all known that since college. We just don't know how we're going out."

Kit said, "This property is full of surprises. I think U had more than a tiny bit of survivalist in him. I just wish he hadn't disconnected the landline. At least the power and water people hooked me up quickly. The barn has electrical power but no water. But, Ulysses also installed a nice gasoline generator for backup when the power line is down. The generator is in the large pump-house structure beside the lodge past the propane tank. The corral is obvious. But this barn is unexplored territory."

Alex put his hand on Kit's shoulder and said, "Aww, you can be Lewis and I'll be Clark."

Ethan walked into the barn at that moment. "You two look sweet together."

Kit glared at him while Alex gave him the finger.

Ethan sat drinks on a shelf and asked, "What have I missed?"

Garrett called from another area of the barn, "Hey I found a pool table".

The rest turned toward him saying, "What?" in unison.

Garrett threw back a heavy canvas tarp weighted down by years of accumulated dust. Under the canvas tarp was a massive, old, slate top billiards table with badly faded green felt. Cue sticks, balls, and two racks lay askew on rippled felt.

Kit whistled, "Now, that's sweet. I'd call that a treasure. Let's see what other surprises wait for us."

The men split up to explore the aged two-story barn. One side of the ground level held horse stalls and well used riding tack. An old, dusty, tarp covered Farmall tractor was parked in one of the stalls. At the end of the stalls, a work area strewn with tools and spare parts filled the only space on that side of the barn that wasn't built to be a stall. An empty hayloft stretched over the work area and horse stalls. The floor of the barn was a mix of hard, bare, earth, and dried spilled chemicals compressed by years of foot traffic. One corner of the barn, across from the stalls, was taken up by a large, windowless, room secured with a pad locked wooden door.

Kit felt like he was inside of a well preserved time capsule. Suddenly he felt like a man-child who had rediscovered a magical place that made him forget the drudge of adulthood. Kit looked around at his friends and saw the same look of wonderment and anticipation on their faces as he had on his face. For a moment all the turmoil and stress of the outside world fell away replaced by a childlike sense of adventure. The barn smelled musty but it was a smell that took Kit's memories back to when he was a child.

The remaining area of that side of the barn was open space containing the pool table and a folded up table tennis table that bore the signs of many years of hard use. The painted plywood playing surface was warped and cracked in places. There was a box of sandpaper paddles and dirty white balls on the floor under the table. Badminton and Horseshoes equipment was piled in a heap in a corner. Kit remembered playing games as a young child visiting Ulysses and Kellie. He smiled at the memories as his buddies explored all the wonders lying around in the old barn.

Of course, it was the pad locked room that drew everyone's attention. Unable to find a key to the locked room in the barn, Kit returned to the cabin to search for the key to the mysterious room. Garrett and Alex continued searching the barn for a hidden key, double-checking every nook and cranny, sifting through cans of nails and jars of screws, and looking under any surface a key could be hidden.

Unable to find the key, and impatient for Kit to return from the cabin, Alex fashioned lock picking tools from the pile of spare parts lying around and set to work attempting to open the lock.

Fifteen minutes later Kit returned to the barn empty handed in time to see Alex gently pulling the door open and step back with a wide smile of satisfaction.

Kit shook his head approvingly, "Nicely done. Your talents have been honed while you were abroad, I see."

Alex displayed his homemade lock pick and said, "Just one of the many skills needed by a successful contractor.

Ethan said, "I need you to teach me that trick."

Alex said, "Sorry, it's a need to know skill. Don't you have a slim stick or something to pop open car doors and such?"

"That's a need to know trade secret."

Kit stepped up to the door pulling it fully open revealing his great grandfather's private workshop. Several large sets of buck antlers were hanging on the wall mounted high near a plywood sheet drop ceiling. Faded black and white photographs of Ulysses holding huge fish dotted the lower wall below the antlers. There was one picture of a nine-year-old Kit holding a stringer of fat bream.

Kit stared at the picture, his mind flooded with fond memories of visiting the cabin as a child. The smells and sounds of his time spent in the country made him smile. The others looked at the photographs wondering how people seemed to live so happily in the time before air-conditioning and satellite TV.

A narrow workbench, running the width of the back wall was littered with hand tools, tackle boxes, folding pocketknives, and a vast array of black powder hunting and cartridge ammunition reloading supplies. But, there were no guns. After seeing all of the reloading supplies Kit had hoped to find an antique rifle hanging on the wall.

Ethan picked up a five-gallon plastic bucket with a label that read: Beaver Dam and Stump Buster. He turned the label so Kit could see it and said, "What the hell is this?"

Kit said, "Oh. That could be fun later on. It is a binary mix that separately are inert but when combined form an explosive combination that can be set off from a distance by a bullet."

Ethan said, "Bullshit."

Garrett said, "Most sporting goods stores have something similar for target practice. It makes target practice a little more fun."

Kit said, "I've seen Ulysses use it. He said it was safer and cheaper than TNT. I never saw him bust a beaver dam but I have seen some stumps blown to pieces. I never saw him use if for target practice. Soda jugs full of water were fine for him."

Ethan said, "We definitely need to try this out."

Alex came moved closer for a better look at the label and contents. Ethan watched over his shoulder. Kit took a quick glance to see how much of the compound was left in the bucket. Both sealed packets were full.

Alex said, "I'd leave it alone, if I were you."

Garrett whistled low and said, "I bet that gets used in some IED overseas. I don't know if making that available to the public is such a good idea. I wonder if the maker exports it overseas."

"Let's hope not!"

Alex looked at Garrett then back at the five-gallon buck of unmixed compound. Ethan said, "Hey, Alex, you should know all about that kind of stuff. You can get us the biggest bang for our buck, right?"

Alex looked at Ethan without speaking. After a long moment Alex turned to Kit and said, "This stuff is dangerous. I say leave it alone." Alex held Kit's eyes for a moment longer before turning and walking away.

Ethan called out, "Don't be a buzz kill."

Garrett added, "Maybe Alex is right. This is old and could be unstable."

Ethan snorted, "Christ, where is everyone's balls?"

The men watched Alex leave then turned their attention to stacks of old issues of Field and Stream and Argosy magazines that were lovingly stored in clear plastic boxes filling a low shelf under a long, well-worn workbench.

A naked incandescent light bulb hung from the center of the plywood ceiling covering the top of the workroom. Kit dusted off a battered tackle box and moved to the more spacious floor area of the barn to examine its antique contents. Garrett was soon lost in another world while admiring Ulysses' collection of knives and old magazines. Ethan labored to clean the pool table the best he could.

Charles finally returned from the outhouse, waving his cell phone in one hand, voicing his frustration at the lingering lack of cell phone service. Charles assured everyone that the outhouse was uncloggable then immediately returned to complaining about the delay in getting the cell phone tower repaired.

Ethan took Charles' mind off the phone by talking him into a game of nine-ball while the others busied themselves exploring the barn. A round robin tournament was on!

The balls rolled unevenly and the games started slowly as the men learned the non-subtle nuances of the old table; after a game or two each man had a feel for the lay of the long neglected table and thought that he alone had discovered the secret to get the balls to roll as intended.

Ethan took a break at the end of one game, surrendering his cue stick to Kit, and went to the cabin returning with his arms filled bottles of tequila and mixer, a bag of limes, a box of salt and five plastic cups. He sat everything on the ping-pong table.

Alex and Garrett joined the others as Ethan shouted, "The barn's bar is now open!"

Alex looked around the dusty barn and said, "With some TLC, I can see this barn becoming an ultimate man cave."

Kit said, "I need this to be family friendly if I want to make money."

With the group reassembled and drinks flowing freely, a rotating nine-ball tournament was full on. No one could take any game seriously as the balls rolled with the warp of the table. Laughter mixed easily with the clack of balls and shouted advice.

While Kit waited for his turn to play a winner he examined a boxed collection of antique colored glass bottles Ulysses had accumulated during his lifetime. Sipping on a margarita, Kit moved from the box of colored glass to the horse stalls where he ran his hand over an old saddle resting on wooden sawhorses in the center stall. Kit's mind wandered to images of children on ponies and adults on horses enjoying sixty-minute trail rides for seventy-five dollars each.

As Kit continued to explore the barn, his thoughts settled on the ramifications of living so far out in the woods, away from all of the conveniences he had grown up with and took for granted on a daily basis. He feared most tourists would expect more from a rural resort than he could ever offer. The fact that the nearest hospital was over an hour away had seemed inconsequential when he visited his grandparents; after all, no one really ever expected to be injured badly enough to need emergency medical help.

But, out here, well, 'out here' was a phrase that was finally sinking in the more Kit thought about the property's remote location and the logistics of successfully managing a rural based business. He wondered what kind of moneymaking venture he could realistically expect to turn the place into, so far from an airport or major interstate highway, so far from safety, so far from modern conveniences. The heavy thoughts began to drag his mood down, so he mixed himself a stronger drink as he watched his friends having fun.

Kit sipped his margarita staring out the door taking in the cabin, the corral, the fire pit, and woods surrounding it all. He listened to the birds. He watched squirrels jump from limb to limb. Wind shook small branches making the trees seem to dance with joy.

Kit realized that all of this activity would be occurring even if he were not here to witness it. Here was unmodified reality and what he experienced back in the city was merely mankind's self-indulgent pursuits in a manufactured world while trying to be an overlord of the natural world.

Tree limbs fell to the earth bouncing and crashing down from tall treetops whether a human was there to see them fall or not. At night the coyotes sang and the whip-poor-wills called and the bats flew whether they had a human audience or not. Out here, animals were unconcerned about the tribulations of humans; out here in the country, it was an endless cycle of eat, sleep, and reproduce for the fauna and grow then go dormant for the flora. It was at that moment Kit realized his role would be that of a shepherd for the land, not the role of a terraformer attempting to remake nature.

And the darkness! Kit had enjoyed the darkness of his grandpa's place every time he visited. The brightness of the stars had been amazing and the unseen creatures making sounds in the dark were both terrifying and intriguing. In the city there were streetlights, security lights, car lights, house lights, shopping mall lights, all manner of lights washing out the stars and sky. But now, immersed in the darkness of the country with a new perspective, the darkness took on a slightly ominous feel. Kit knew every creature moving in the night could see far better than he could. Man was far more vulnerable in the animal's domain at night than in daylight. Maybe, Kit thought, city people would pay good money to experience that feeling of borderline danger. In the meantime, Kit was happy he had a flashlight and weapons to face any danger that might be real.

Caught up in the billiards competition, the men did not realize how late the day had become until their stomachs growled from hunger. Outside the barn, the sky was growing darker. A single star was visible in the early evening sky, bright and awe inspiring so far from any light pollution. An owl hooted nearby and a pack of coyotes howled in the distance as a train whistle roused them for the night.

Charles loitered by the barn's door-less front opening looking into the growing darkness and said, "It's kinda creepy out there. It looks like a long way to the cabin. I guess we missed our chance to hunt today. We should get back to the cabin before it gets too dark."

Kit corrected him. "We're calling it a lodge."

Charles said, "Why don't you call it The Lodge at Chickasaw Creek?"

Garrett said, "Too many politically correct ramifications if you call it anything related to Native Americans."

"It's the name of a creek not a people, for God's sake!"

"Whatever. We've lost a day of hunting."

Kit said, "I wouldn't call today a loss."

Ethan said, "That's okay we're just luring those hogs into a false sense of security. We'll nail them tomorrow."

Charles said, "We need a flashlight to get back to the cabin."

Kit corrected him, "It's a lodge."

Garrett scoffed. "We don't need flashlights. The lodge is right there."

Kit turned to Garrett, "Thank you, neighbor."

"That's a lot of ground to cover in the dark." Charles peered around the edge of the barn's door as if he were afraid of the dark.

"What are you scared of?" Kit's question had a sharp edge to it.

Charles bristled, "I'm not scared. I'm cautious. I've got two boys depending on me. I don't want to step in a hole and break an ankle, or get bitten by a snake, and be out of commission for them. Those two boys are handfuls. Plus, I have a company to run. A company with my name on it. That means something!"

Ethan said, "I hope your pussification isn't tainting your boys during their formative years. Besides, a guy like you surely has a life insurance policy on yourself. Don't you?"

Charles bristled. "It's not always about money. Sometimes it is about responsibility. Sometimes it's about love and putting other people ahead of yourself. You wouldn't know about that would you? You are a salesman. I hear they don't have souls."

Alex said in a commanding voice, "You two chill."

Ethan and Charles looked at each other for a long moment then did a half-hearted fist bump before walking to opposite sides of the opening.

Kit walked to the work area retrieving a large hurricane lantern he had seen earlier in the day. He returned to the group and looked at Alex.

Alex looked back blankly.

Kit lifted the lantern a little higher.

Alex shrugged.

Kit said, "Your cigar lighter."

Alex coughed a rib-rattling cough, spitting a large hocker onto the packed dirt, "Oh, yeah." He produced the Zippo lighter he had used earlier to light his cigar tossing it to Kit.

Kit nodded. "You should get that cough looked at."

Alex sighed, "Been looked at. Nothing anyone can do so say the docs at two hospitals. As long as I don't cough up blood, they aren't going to worry so I'm not going to worry."

The lantern glowed as the wick caught fire under the Zippo's flame. Kit ceremoniously offered the glowing lantern to Charles who cautiously led the way back to the cabin. Once inside the cabin the men washed up and made their way to the kitchen area. The five friends made a dinner of what should have been the day's lunch then turned in early, determined not to waste the next day's chance to hunt.

Kit lay on the sofa listening to the men's breathing change as each man drifted off to sleep. He wondered if the men felt as rejuvenated as he did. As Kit stared at the dark ceiling he felt as if the cabin was coming out of a long hibernation, awakened by the activity, energy, and excitement the men emitted. Kit finally drifted off to sleep but tossed and turned as dreams took over.

Strange dreams filled Kit's REM stage sleep. One dream involved Clydesdale horses, ridden bareback by diapered toddlers in ten gallon cowboy hats, galloping through the lodge scattering guests and poker tables alike as if a scene from a rowdy western movie. In the dream Kit chased the horses out of the cabin across an extremely long wicker porch. Brandishing a straw broom Kit chased the fire snorting steeds across a flowery plain into the barn where he found, instead of the troublesome horses and babies, white linen clad bikers cooking meth and teaching pole dancing to bikini clad pigs. The bikers and the pigs all stopped and turned to look at Kit. Kit found the broom had morphed into a microphone. He brought the microphone up to his mouth wanting to tell the odd assembly to get out of his barn. But when he spoke into the broom-microphone there was no sound, only text that immediately fell to the filthy barn floor where the letters transformed into worms and burrowed into the oil stained earth. That was when Kit woke from the dream drenched in sweat. It was half an hour before he fell back to sleep.

10

> Oh, I was born six-gun in my hand
> Behind the gun I'll make my final stand
> That's why they call me, Bad Company
>
>   -Bad Company

  Following the principle, 'Leave no stone unturned', Sheriff Boscoe Carver followed up on the report Kit had given him regarding the unattended ATVs. Carver meticulously searched the edges of the abandoned logging road separating Kit's property and the LaHarpe's land until he found tire tracks veering off into the forest through a break in the fence line. The tire tracks were near the opposite end of the logging road where Wildlife Officer Tom Benson's official truck had been found and hundreds of yards beyond the deer stand where Benson's body had been discovered. Even with the distance involved, Carver thought it odd that two events, in such a relatively short time frame, would occur in such a localized area. He was drawn to mysteries that seemed coincidental; particularly events that he could investigate in an official capacity. It was a characteristic that made him a good cop.

  Sheriff Carver examined the ground where grass and dry leaves had been compressed. The scene seemed to indicate that a truck and trailer had been parked in the spot recently. Motor oil soiled the ground and scuffed earth indicated some kind of vehicle had been rolled off a trailer.

  Carver took a step into the leaves and knew whom the leaky truck belonged to as he kicked an Old Milwaukee beer can from beneath windblown leaves. Carver visualized the suspected truck; the Confederate flag front license plate and the deer, turkey, and NASCAR decals covering the back window would confirm the owner of the truck as Ratchet Ronnie Lester.

  Carver left the road and followed the ATV tracks a short distance into the forest. He paused and thought of calling backup.

  Staring at tire tracks that only hinted at misdeeds Carver recalled the only time the drug dealing Lester brothers had nearly been apprehended red-handed. The men had managed to evade the raid with only minutes to spare causing Carver and his trusted deputies to believe the Lester brothers had been warned of the raid at the last moment.

Any evidence against Ronnie and his brother had to be rock solid or their uncle, the county judge, would find a reason to dismiss the case in a heartbeat. Sheriff Carver patted his Desert Eagle sidearm as he thought maybe this would be the time Ronnie Lester's luck would run out causing a Lester to face criminal charges that would finally stick.

With kinfolk in high judicial positions, rued Carver, you had to have solid evidence to make charges stick in Chickasaw County. The only other county in the state with a more rigged legal system was Johnston County. The sheriff shook his head in frustration but continued deeper into the forest.

Carver hesitated as he looked at the barely visible, weed and stick littered path he would have to travel to get to the clearing Kit had described. Resigned to the unpleasant task ahead of him, he returned to his cruiser and began digging in the packed trunk, where he found knee high rubber boots to pull over his shoes. Next, he made sure he had two sets of handcuffs clipped to his belt.

After spraying down with insect repellant he grabbed his shotgun from the front seat and locked the door. With a sigh of resignation, the sheriff began following the path, struggling to keep his balance as he traversed the uneven terrain and holes hidden by weeds and years of leaf fall. The weeds growing in the wheel tracks were flattened, confirming there had been recent vehicular activity. Carver walked in the right wheel path where he could see the ground a little better.

Twenty minutes of difficult walking later, Sheriff Carver wondered if he would ever arrive at the clearing. Covered by a sheet of sweat, Carver grew increasingly irritated at the workout the two scofflaws were putting him through. Twenty-five minutes into the walk, he decided that if Ronnie or his brother tried to make a run to escape he would just shoot them instead of giving chase.

The trees were larger and the canopy denser as Carver progressed deeper into the forest. The tracks eventually merged with a four-wheeler trail weaving a circuitous path through the trees switching back sharply several times. Following the winding path was tedious and Carver's uniform was saturated with sweat.

Carver stopped frequently, searching for a more direct route to the clearing, but the thick stand of trees prevented him from seeing far enough ahead to find a shortcut. This part of the LaHarpe land was untended and the brush was thick and clingy.

After several more minutes of careful walking, the four-wheeler trail straightened out and Carver quickened his pace. Ahead Carver noted a break in the forest, a lighter spot glimpsed through thinning trees, and he hoped it was his destination. Finally, as if magically appearing before him he saw the field. The sheriff paused at the tree line surrounding the open area, and there, parked just as Kit had described, were the four wheelers and large burned area scarring the ground. Sheriff Carver carefully studied the scene from behind a wide-trunked oak tree.

Carver cautiously broke cover and made his way to the ATVs. He stood still listening for any sounds that seemed unnatural. After listening carefully for several minutes, Carver took note of the bullet holes in the ATVs and took pictures with his cell phone's camera.

The notes Kit had written were still on the machines, and the keys were still in the ignitions. Slowly Sheriff Carver approached the burned area. It was obvious there had been an explosion and a fast, hot, fire. He doubted that a meth lab going up in flames would be enough to vaporize a man let alone all of the equipment; yet, the men weren't to be found nor was there much evidence to collect other than a lot of spent shell casings littering the scorched earth among fused and blackened debris.

Intrigued by the clues, the sheriff made a methodical search of the area double-checking the scorched earth and abandoned four wheelers. He collected the keys from the ATVs and with a smirk, removed the notes Kit had written. Smiling, devilishly, the sheriff crossed out Kit's words and wrote his own message on the other side of the paper. Pocketing one note, he re-secured his new note, which read, 'If you want your keys come see Sheriff Carver,' onto the handlebars.

Whistling the Andy Griffith Show theme song Carver began walking back to his cruiser. The sheriff had a mystery on his hands, but on the upside, there had been no confrontation or drama to deal with; and as a bonus, he would have a little fun with the Lester boys by taking their ATV keys. Whoever came to collect the keys would be arrested immediately and held until the mystery was solved or someone at least confessed to trespassing. Carver was certain someone was going to pay for making him sweat so much.

The walk back to the cruiser did not seem as arduous now that the 'hard part' was over. Pausing to enjoy fresh berries that were growing alongside the path Carver let the sun shine on his face as he ate. A whiff of an unpleasant odor drifting on a slight breeze brought the big man out of his reverie. The odor was a mix of death and filth. Instincts caused Carver to raise his tactical shotgun and pump a shell into the chamber. The smell, faint and indistinct, caused his thoughts to flash back to old cases of cattle mutilation he had seen as a young man. Taking up a position next to the trunk of an oak tree Carver carefully scanned the direction from which the wind was blowing.

Voices, as well as the smell, were carried on the wind. Carver looked in the direction of the voices and caught movement on the far side of a cedar grove. Two figures, thirty yards away, were slowly meandering through the woods unaware of him. He remained hidden watching until the two men passed into thicker cover. The larger man was armed with a sidearm. The thin man had a large knife on his belt, but Carver could not see a sidearm. Sheriff Carver began following the two men, moving quietly. He silently closed the distance between himself and the two men who were engaged in an intense debate and never looked around. Their intense focus on each other was Carver's advantage.

The two men crunched through the forest, talking, without care. The smaller man, John Lee Sherman, listened as Preston rambled. Despite killing the Lester brothers and prepping their truck and trailer for sale to a chop shop for a tidy profit Preston's mood remained foul as the two ATVs remained loose ends.

Preston could not stop talking about the indignities of his demotion and treatment upon his return from banishment. Despite his wife's obedience and willingness to do what Preston asked he constantly felt tense and filled with rage. Neither murder, sex, nor the meditation techniques he learned in his PTSD class succeeded in calming mind. He felt overwhelmed by changes passing him by while he sat on the sidelines rejected by the elders of the family. The news he was hearing from John Lee added to the pent up and growing stress that troubled his mind.

Carver followed as close as he dared without giving himself away. He only caught an occasional word from the men's conversation but the tone was clear: the big man was angry and the small man was trying to make the best of a bad situation.

One of the things Preston was just hearing about was the new business venture the family was implementing. Preston was walking with his third cousin, John Lee Sherman, and Preston was not happy with what he was learning. John Lee spoke in a lowered voice, a natural habit born from years in the woods as a hunter, poacher, and drug manufacturer. Preston's voice would rise until John Lee gently reminded the big man to be quieter. Preston, angry over the reprimand, fumed as he listened to John Lee, ten years younger than him, talk to him like a novice. Worse still, Preston had to submit to the younger man's lead until he earned the family's respect and trust back.

Carver maintained his distance as he pursued the two figures, stealthily moving from tree to tree, still straining to hear their conversation. The sheriff studied the men as they stopped so the thin man could urinate. One man was bulky and muscular and the other was thin and twitchy. Both moved through the woods with ease and familiarity indicating they knew the area intimately. Carver recognized the giant camouflaged man as a family member of the LaHarpe clan.

Carver grew certain that the LaHarpe clan had some connection to the shot up ATVs and scorched earth. He wondered if the LaHarpe's had taken out the Lester brothers over a drug or turf dispute. Unconsciously the sheriff thumbed the shotgun's safety off. Ahead the men had stopped by a towering pine tree. Carver closed the distance between himself and the two men as they examined a fresh lightning scar on the tree.

After spending several minutes examining the wide scar running down the trunk, the two men began walking again. Reluctant to use the radio to call for backup, for fear of giving himself away, Carver resumed stalking the two men as they leisurely moved through the thick forest. The sheriff maintained his concealment using large trees as cover but the men he was following never looked back.

Preston and John Lee would stop and engage in an animated, face-to-face conversation occasionally. Now, as their voices rose in a heated exchange, Carver strained to overhear their conversation praying he would hear something incriminating that he could use to place the men behind bars.

The two men stood facing each other using their hands to emphasize what they were saying. After a moment the conversation ended and the two men resumed walking. Sheriff Carver hurried to gain ground on the men. His pursuit remained stealthy until he stepped in a deep hole, hidden by leaves, and fell awkwardly, snapping his fibula. The sheriff fell forward with a cry of agony, eyes blinded by tears of pain from a compound fracture, his shotgun flew from his hands landing just out of reach. Carver's involuntary scream of pain would be his undoing as Preston and John Lee turned back to investigate the shriek.

11

> Hey man, nice shot
> What a good shot man.
> That's why I say
> Hey man, nice shot
> What a good shot man
>
> — Filter

No country morning had ever felt so good to any man, Kit was sure of that. Coffee mug in hand, Kit wandered the mowed area surrounding the cabin, idly meandering between the parked trucks, the barn, and the bonfire pit waiting for the others to wake up. A king snake searched for prey in the weedy garden plot. Squirrels scampered from branch to branch overhead. Birds searched the recently mowed areas chirping and calling in the morning sun.

Kit had spent a long night tossing and turning on the leather sofa in the great room and had been awake to watch the sun rise above the trees. He had been awake when Alex stole out to the front porch just after midnight to smoke one of his cigars and stare at the starry sky.

Kit had also been awake when Garrett and Ethan made their separate trips outside to pee and look at the stars. Drifting in and out of sleep all night revealed that his friends were all afflicted by various sleep disorders ranging from apnea to Periodic Limb Movement Disorder to nightmares. Kit experienced a series of dreams and power naps; but mostly he thought of his plans.

Once dawn had broken, Kit felt no need to confine himself to the sofa. Nursing a cup of hot, black, coffee he listened as the daytime sounds of the forest replaced the nighttime sounds. Under the cloudless, dawn sky, Kit knew, in his heart, that this property could be a godsend if business plans were properly detailed and executed. As with everything in life, money was the sticking point.

Then, as voices of his friends, finally awake, floated out through the cabin's open doorway, the weight of the logistics of transportation, amenities, medical needs, insurance, security, and everything else required to run a business receded from Kit's mind. He took a seat in one of the rocking chairs on the front porch, sipped hot coffee, and waited for someone to join him.

Alex was the first to join Kit on the porch. After a mutual nod of silent greeting the men sat drinking their coffee. Charles came out next carrying a mug of coffee and his cell phone as he made a beeline to the outhouse.

Kit called out after him, "I thought you fixed the inside toilet!"

Charles never looked back as he called out, "I'm not taking a second chance. I know I won't stop up the outhouse."

Alex turned to Kit and said, "That man just won't give up on the cell phone. I'm happy to be incommunicado."

Kit nodded. "He's just worried about his boys. Who knew a copper theft would become such a big deal?"

Ethan joined the men on the porch; the aroma of more than a shot of whiskey mixed with his coffee drifted from his cup.

Kit said, "Morning."

Ethan said, "I guess we'll get to hunt today? Garrett 'Hawkeye' Gardner is already checking over his bow and arrows." It was difficult to tell if it was playfulness or disdain in Ethan's voice.

Kit said, "Sure. We can start out looking for feral hogs. Remember, there is no limit on feral hogs or coyotes. I've got the hunting regulation book to check it for the rules if any of you want to hunt anything else. I don't think any wild game is in season yet."

Alex said, "It's definitely not rabbit season. They carry Tularemia during the hot season. You've got to wait until after the first frost to eat wild rabbit."

Ethan said, "I don't know what that is but that's okay with me if we don't waste time on rabbits. I want something big so people don't confuse me with that dimwitted Elmer Fudd guy. I want a hide or tusks to take home."

Alex said, "I'd like a boar tusk to take home. Since my wife left me while I was in Afghanistan, I've got the whole house to myself, and I can fix it up any damn way I please. Maybe put a bear skin rug on the floor in front of my fireplace."

Kit said, "It is not deer season or bear season."

Alex said, "What about found antler sheds?"

Ethan lifted his coffee mug in mock exasperation, "I was expecting to east wild game this week!"

Garrett joined the men carrying his archery case and a huge thermos full of coffee. He sat the case on the porch and stretched.

Ethan said, "Morning, Mr. William Tell. Going to shoot an apple off of one our head's today, are we?"

Garrett smelled Ethan's spiked coffee replying. "I can shoot an apple off of your head if you want to be my son's stand-in today."

"I would never think I could replace your son. But thanks for asking." Ethan eyed Garrett as he took a long slow drink. Garret winked at Ethan.

Kit said, "You know, neighbor, I've seen all of your trophies and photographs but I've never seen you use that thing."

"I have to go to a public range to practice. You know my backyard just isn't large enough. You'd be okay with me practicing there, but Ms. Fields might not be so good with me practicing so near to her cats."

Kit laughed, "Yeah. Ms. Fields is the mother of all cat ladies isn't she?"

"And somewhat of a 'The sky is falling type' as well."

Kit and Garrett exchanged knowing glances and a smile over their shared experiences with the neighborhood busybody.

Charles returned from the outhouse. "I guess we're going hunting today?" He eyed the camo patterned bow case sitting on the floor of the porch.

Ethan used his coffee cup to indicate he was addressing Charles. "Yep. And Robin Hood here is going to show us how good he is by shooting an apple off of your head."

"Bullshit. Not my head."

Ethan persisted. "Yep. You know how it works. Those people not present for the meeting are selected for the shit jobs and boring committee work. You weren't here for the meeting so you got picked to be Garrett's lovely assistant."

Charles said, "I resign. Effectively immediately."

Kit laughed, "Don't worry. There's all sorts of stuff we could use to hold an apple. But, we don't have an apple. Sorry. I don't think any of us planned the fruit and vegetable side of our meals too well. My bad on that."

Charles added, "Or planned to have a salad."

Ethan said, "Yep. We even have an empty food truck just parked there taunting us."

Kit said, "Leave the food truck alone."

"And you brought a bow and arrow to a gunfight. What were you thinking?"

Garrett placed his cup of coffee on the porch's railing and walked off toward the remains of the bonfire carrying his bow case. Searching the ground around the fire pit he found a large, intact pinecone. As the men watched from the porch, Garrett constructed a tall base of empty beer cans then gently placed the pinecone the topmost can.

Turning, Garrett smiled at the men watching him, and then, aloud, counted off fifty paces as he moved away from the target. Garrett set his bow case down, turned, and faced the pinecone target. Methodically he prepared his bow and mounted an arrow. No one spoke. Slowly, Garrett sighted in and let the arrow fly. The broad head blade shattered the pinecone as it made contact. Only the top beer can wobbled then fell. The arrow buried itself in the earth a dozen yards beyond the stack of empty beer cans. Garrett turned to look at the group.

Kit, Alex, and Ethan all raised their coffee cups and mugs in salute to the shot.

Charles whistled in admiration. "Let me get a video of you doing that so I can send it to the boys."

Kit said, "Uncle Ted would be proud".

Garrett nodded and smiled.

Ethan and Charles looked at Kit and simultaneously said, "Who?" The two men looked at each other wondering to whom Kit was referring. Neither man recalled Kit having any Uncle Ted.

Garrett carefully replaced the fallen beer can then set a new pinecone on top of the tower so Charles could make a video for his sons. Ethan watched Charles's cell phone screen over his shoulder as he recorded video of Garrett's feat. Garrett performed a second flawless shot.

Alex said, "Well, I guess I'll check my rifle scope before we head out. Kit, have you got something I can use as a target? I mean, something bigger than a pine cone!"

"You bet. There's a big sheet of plywood for the backboard in the barn and we've got paper plates we can use for targets."

"Great. I'll help you get the plywood and plates. Where can we set it up?" Alex looked around the open area then toward the barn.

"Over there should be okay." Kit pointed toward the old horse corral. The others doubted the old corral would support a piece of plywood leaning against it.

Alex stood, "Let's get going before it gets much hotter." Kit agreed and the two men walked off toward the barn. Alex adjusted his Boonie hat, which today was a black and white camo pattern.

The sky was cloudless and the barely noticeable breeze promised a hot day ahead. Under the dark edge of the forest two squirrels began fussing at each other breaking the otherwise peaceful quietness of the setting.

Ethan and Charles watched Alex and Kit walk away. Garrett retrieved his arrow, checked its fletching, then placed it lovingly into the quiver, and returned to the porch to finish his coffee.

Ethan pulled a pill bottle out of his pocket, popped one pill into his mouth and washed it down with a long drink of spiked coffee. Garrett looked at Ethan questioningly.

Ethan said, "Back pain. Chronic. Only way to beat it back."

"How did it happen?"

Ethan's face clouded as he said, "A test drive went bad. Some kid test driving a new car got distracted and ran a red light. We got T-boned on my side of the car. That was one of my worst days and some of the worst months as the lawsuits and insurance issues got resolved. No amount of money is worth the pain and annoyance chronic pain presents. These pills are the only thing that knocks it down for me."

Garrett nodded, "You know there are other ways to ease the pain besides pills."

Ethan said, "Yeah, tried them all, pills work the best."

"Don't let them get the better of you."

"Never."

After finishing his coffee Charles disappeared into the lodge and began preparing breakfast while Ethan and Garrett remained on the porch listening to Charles banging pots and pans as he assembled the utensils he would use to cook a hearty breakfast. Kit and Alex busied themselves in the barn as Ethan and Garrett enjoyed their coffee without speaking.

After breakfast, Kit and Alex leaned the warped sheet of dirty plywood against the one corner of the horse corral that was still standing. While the other men spent time admiring each other's guns Alex marked half a dozen paper plates with a vertical and horizontal line meeting in the middle of the plate.

Using tacks and a hammer from the barn, Kit attached four paper plates to the sheet of plywood. Satisfied the plates were securely attached to the plywood; he nodded to Alex who counted off one hundred paces from the target. Using the heel of his combat boot he dug a line in the dirt. Kit and Alex retrieved their guns from the cabin joining the rest of the men as Ethan finished repositioning his truck so the men could use the truck's hood as a bench rest from which to check the accuracy of their weapon's scopes.

Kit took his Winchester Model 94 30/30 out of its hard plastic carrying case. Ethan looked at the Winchester. "Kit, my man, you need to come into the modern area. All I see are regular guns, where the hell is our tactical weapons? Why do you insist on using that cowboy rifle?"

Kit held the gun up. "Why? This caliber gun has taken more deer than any other rifle. I don't see a need to use a cannon to kill a deer or a wild hog. It'll kill most anything I shoot. I'm shooting one hundred and fifty grain hollow points. I've loved this style gun since I saw my first cowboy movie, the classic Winchester 73."

Alex opened his gun case to reveal a .308 caliber rifle. It had a large scope. Alex placed a laser boresighter into his gun's muzzle and pointed it downrange looking through the scope. Alex looked through the scope and seemed satisfied.

Kit said, "Let me borrow that for a minute. It's been three years since I've shot Killer here. I bet my scope needs some adjusting."

"You named your gun Killer?"

"I didn't name it. Ulysses named it for me after I made a memorable shot on a running eight-point buck through a thick pine grove. He said the shot was amazing so he dubbed me and the gun the Killer Twins. I was young and impressionable so the name stuck. It was a special moment between Grandpa U and me."

Ethan pulled a shotgun from a camouflage pattern soft-sided carrying case. Then from a different bag he pulled out two very thick leather shotgun shell belts that had been sewn together to make an X shape creating a heavy, thick, bandoleer that he lowered over his head. Ethan adjusted the buckle and straps until the bandoleer fit comfortably despite the weight and thickness of the shell belts.

The bandoleer's padded leather straps and shell holders covered Ethan's torso. A huge shiny Professional Bull Riders trophy belt buckle he had discovered at a swap meet gleamed at the point the two leather straps crossed his chest. Another large buckle secured the belt of the bandoleer around his waist. Thick cotton padding under the leather straps cushioned the wearer's shoulders protecting them from chaffing. Kit estimated the bandoleer must have weighed thirty pounds between the thick leather straps, ostentatious buckles, and rows of shells.

Garrett said, "It's no wonder you have back troubles."

Ethan said, "It's not the weight, it's the restricted movement."

Kit said, "Where is your sombrero?"

Ethan ignored Kit making final adjustments on the bandoleer. "It is well constructed and built with care. Someone's heirloom."

Garrett said, "A tourist gimmick. Too heavy for me."

Ethan nodded, "Your issues are from being shot, right?"

Garrett nodded.

Charles opened his gun's hard travel case and revealed a .22 for all to see. The gun had no scope but had a twenty round magazine. As everyone checked his gun Charles snuck a quick peek at his cell phone.

Ethan looked around at the group and nodded. "Well, it looks like we've got all of our bases covered. At least in regard to caliber variety. Those feral hogs had best look out; the camouflaged Wild Bunch is in town!"

Kit said, "That was a good movie! Lots of good westerns back in the day."

Garrett said, "I hope Westerns make a TV comeback before I die. I miss Matt Dillion and Miss Kitty."

Charles said, "All Ethan needs is a giant sombrero to go with that bandoleer thing. And a Mexican accent wouldn't be out of character. And a big, bushy, droopy mustache. Kit, why don't you turn this place into a western theme retreat? You've got the barn, the corral, plenty of acreage for riding trails, and you've always been infatuated with cowboy stuff."

Ethan said, "You can call this place Kit's OK Corral."

Kit said, "That name has a bad connotation to it."

Garrett said, "Except for that fact that's a great name!"

Ethan said, "Not until cowboy movies make a comeback. I think you should have the word resort in the name."

Kit said, "I'll accept input on naming this place. But since I got here, the reality of the expenses of keeping horses, a veterinarian, insurance, and the time and expense to train horses hit me like a brick. I need to come up with an idea with low startup costs."

Ethan said, "There ain't no such thing as low startup costs."

Garrett nodded toward the food truck, "Just don't let it become Camp Moneypit."

Alex had been arranging a pile of well-used shop towels on the hood of Ethan's truck to use as a soft base while firing the rifles. He finished positioning the towels then sat on the open tailgate of the truck watching and listening to the conversations in silence as he finished his morning coffee.

Kit noticed Alex waiting and said, "Proceed."

Alex positioned his rifle and peered through the scope. He adjusted his body's position several times while the other men continued to talk quietly. Minutes passed as Alex fidgeted. Kit wondered if looking through the scope was dredging up unpleasant combat memories. He took a step, intending to speak to Alex, when Alex straightened up and looked around at the men.

Alex said, "Fire in the hole. You guys ready? Got your ear plugs in?"

The men nodded silently.

Kit said, "Wait!" He hurriedly put earplugs in his ears. Glancing around he noticed only he, Garrett, and Alex wore ear protection. "Ethan and Charles just put your fingers in your ears when the rest of us shoot."

Charles said, "This can't be louder than listening to my boy's band practice."

Ethan shook his head, "Nobody said anything about needing ear protection."

Alex returned his attention to his Browning rifle. He flicked off the safety. "Weapon hot!"

Mentally Alex counted off five seconds then squeezed the trigger. The bullet hit dead center on the black lines marking the center of the white paper plate. Alex chambered a second round and fired again. The second bullet's impact was only a fraction of an inch different away from the first hole. The two shots together made a small, connected figure eight.

Alex straightened up lifting his weapon from the pile of clothing and towels. "I'm good. Who's next?"

Kit settled in next. He took aim at a different plate and fired. The first shot was a quarter of an inch high and to the right of the intersecting lines. A second shot put a hole to the left of the first one. Both holes could be covered by a quarter.

Kit said, "I'm in the kill zone. Good enough for government work." Alex winced at the comment but remained silent.

Charles settled in to position after Kit moved out of the way. His first shot was high and clipped the edge of the plate. He looked around at his friends clearly embarrassed. No one said anything. Turning back to his rifle, Charles took aim and fired his second shot. It, too, hit high but was roughly in line under the first shot. A third shot was wildly off the paper plate.

Alex said, "Mind if I take a shot with your gun? I might be able to help."

Charles said, "Okay." He handed his rifle to Alex.

Alex fluffed the pile of rags. "I noticed that you flinched when you pulled the trigger. If that's the case then you just need to learn not to be afraid of the tiny bit of recoil. But on the outside chance your iron sights are off, I should be able to tell with this shot."

Alex took a firing stance and said, "Gun hot. In five."

He squeezed the trigger and the bullet struck high but in line with the other two shot holes. Alex looked at Charles, "You really need a scope."

"Yeah, I haven't gotten around to that yet."

Alex adjusted the gun's iron sight then looked downrange after settling into a shooting stance over the hood of the truck. "Gun hot."

The former military contractor pulled the trigger. The shot hit dead center on the crossed lines. Alex fired another round. The next bullet hit so close to the other one that it simply enlarged the hole. Alex smiled then handed the gun back to Charles.

Charles said, "Thanks."

Alex smiled, "My pleasure. Don't flinch. Lean into the gun. You'll be fine. And thanks for cooking breakfast!"

Kit said, "Ditto."

Ethan said, "Well, I guess since I don't have a scope I don't need to waste a shell."

Kit said, "You can see what your shot pattern looks like."

Ethan said, "My what?"

Kit asked, "What kind of choke are you using?"

Ethan said, "My what?"

Alex said, "Never mind. You can't really miss with a shotgun."

Ethan said, "That's why I use one."

Garrett said, "Don't you want to know what your pattern will look like? What kind of choke do you have in?"

"I don't know what a choke is. I've got buckshot and slugs. I believe I'm ready for anything that comes our way."

Kit looked at the men then turned to look at the plywood sheet holding their paper plate targets. "If you guys don't mind wasting some ammo, I like us to do the gun orgy from Predator."

Charles said, "What is that?"

Ethan perked up, "Oh, hell, yes!"

Charles looked around the group, "What?"

Kit said, "Haven't you ever seen the movie Predator?"

"No."

Ethan said, "He's never seen Fight Club either."

Kit said, "Predator is this great sci-fi movie where there is a scene where this commando unit unloads their weapons at an unseen enemy. It's a gunfire orgy. They decimate a patch of jungle. It is an awesome scene."

Charles asked, "How do we do this?"

Kit said, "We all just shoot at the plywood at the same time. Full magazines and shoot until you're empty. Feel free to reload."

Ethan said to no one in particular, "Shot or slugs?"

Kit said, "Whatever you feel like wasting."

Charles said, "I guess that sounds like fun."

Ethan said, "Oh, it will be."

Kit said, "Okay we all load up, move in, and do this from about thirty feet out. I love the smell of gunpowder in the morning! It smells like, men doing manly things. Someone needs to video this."

Garrett said, "Since I don't have a rifle, I'll record it."

Charles said, "I'll record it and send it to the boys. They'll know what movie you're talking about."

Ethan said, "I'm recording it too."

Alex said, "Might as well record it too."

The men set their cell phones along Ethan's truck's hood to record the mayhem. Garrett stood off to one side cell phone camera at ready.

The shooters loaded their weapons and moved to within thirty feet of the plywood. They formed a picket line facing the plywood target. Kit smiled and said, "Everyone good to go?"

The men nodded affirmative and shouldered their weapons.

Kit said, "I'll count us down to 'Go'."

The men nodded they understood. Charles looked around sheepishly while feeling a bit out of the loop never having seen the movie or the scene everyone else was talking about. But, he knew his sons would love to see the videos he was collecting.

After a last quick glance at the row of cell phones Kit said, "Three, two, one. Go!"

The men emptied their magazines sending dozens of rounds into the sheet of plywood which disintegrated under the onslaught of bullets. The split rail corral holding the plywood also collapsed as various caliber bullets tore through the ancient wood. Splinters and sawdust floated on gentle air currents before falling to the bare dirt ground below.

When the guns ran out of ammunition the men lowered their weapons and looked at each other. The smell of gunpowder filled the air. Kit and Ethan exchanged a high five.

Ethan said, "We have got to try that explosive stuff we found in the barn yesterday."

Kit said, "Hell yeah!"

Charles was overwhelmed, "That was the most thrilling thing I've done in a long time."

Ethan snorted but didn't say a word.

Garrett said, "It didn't seem to last very long."

Ethan said, "Let's blow something up!"

Alex said, "Because we didn't have high capacity mags. But for being as brief as it was, it was pretty damn fun."

Ethan said, "I'll drink to that!"

Kit said, "I've always wanted to do that. I'm glad you guys agreed."

Alex said, "I'm glad we thought to record it."

Ethan said, "I can't wait to see the video. We busted the holy shit out of that piece of plywood."

Charles said, "Looks like a pile of kindling for tonight's big bonfire."

Ethan crooned, "Burn, baby, burn. Bonfire inferno. Burn this mother down!"

Kit said, "Well, we got a big day ahead of us. Let's go to the porch while we look at the video. I've got a good feeling about today."

12

> My daddy he made whiskey,
> My granddaddy he did too
> We ain't paid no whiskey tax since 1792
>
> -Bob Dylan

After murdering Sheriff Carver in front of John Lee, Preston had been forced to show the younger man where he disposed of bodies. Preston did not reveal how many bodies were in the bottom of the pond already but he did tell John Lee about a different, deeper, pond where he dumped vehicles, like the sheriff's cruiser, that couldn't be taken to a chop shop.

Preston, hoping to ingratiate himself, decided to reward John Lee for helping him. Preston had found the Lester's ATV keys in the dead lawman's pocket. Leading John Lee through the forest to where the Lester's ATVs were parked Preston pointed to the least damaged one and tossed John Lee its key.

While John Lee admired his gift, Preston read the sheriff's note. Preston also read Kit's note on the flip side of the paper and made a mental note to check out the Carson place later on. He did not reveal the note's message to John Lee; enough had happened already and Preston did not trust forced alliances.

Preston realized that for every problem he solved, a new one popped up right away. He had never killed a man in front of any civilian; and for what he actually knew about John Lee, he could have been a passing acquaintance.

John Lee said he would come back later to retrieve his new ATV, but in the meantime, he wanted to show Preston how much he appreciated the gift. Out of a sense of gratitude John Lee told Preston he had a secret to share with him. Preston groaned inwardly, apprehensive about just what he had gotten himself involved with. He could not seem to control his own fate and now he had a partner in crime that knew too much.

On the positive side of today's events Preston noted that John Lee had shown no emotion when Sheriff Carver had been killed, nor had he shown any emotion during the disposal of the evidence. Preston had been forced to take John Lee into his confidence; as a show of solidarity, and to reciprocate Preston's trust, John Lee was willingly showing Preston his secret drug lab.

John Lee led Preston through a relatively unfamiliar part of the forest guiding him to a secluded, natural clearing in a little visited section of the property. The two men were standing on the edge of a large sinkhole hidden in a grassy glade encircled by a dense stand of tall oak trees. The fact that during all of his time wandering the forest he had never discovered this place was difficult to accept. Preston began to wonder about what else he might be missing. The sinkhole was in a section of old growth forest that had been spared cutting but largely overlooked by LaHarpe hunters.

The roughly circular sinkhole opening was dark and its mouth was only twelve feet around. Preston grew a bit queasy looking down into the dark void. The tall grass hid the gaping hole in the ground making it all the more dangerous. Looking into the abyss he wondered how many animals had fallen into the concealed hole and died while looking up at the sky and unobtainable escape.

John Lee looked around the glade then glanced at Preston. He smiled at Preston's look of amazement but remained silent allowing the sinkhole to speak for it. Preston turned and gave John Lee a look of, 'So?'

John Lee began babbling on about the wonders of the find, but Preston resisted becoming caught up in the thin man's excitement. Preston was concentrating on not falling into the abyss when he felt pressure on his arm and looked at John Lee.

Preston said, "What?"

John Lee held Preston's arm and said, "Now let me show you the power source." John Lee guided Preston to a device located on the southwest edge of the clearing fifty yards from the hidden sinkhole. The device was white and orange, shaped roughly like an overly large fire hydrant, with five large solar panels on its arms and top. An antenna rose from the top most part of the device.

Preston shook his head and said, "What the hell?"

John Lee used his hand to point to the device as he explained the device to his cousin. "Those are solar panels to provide solar energy for the equipment. No energy is taken from the power grid to give us away. There is nothing above ground to draw anyone's attention. The cables are buried. This is a solar power converter made to look like a government seismograph."

Preston could not hide his surprise, "A seismograph?"

"It seemed like a device no one would really want to fuck with. No copper wire, no high tech electronics." Preston nodded.

John Lee tapped the odd-looking device with his fist. "This is just a shell. But we painted it to look like an official United States Geological Service thingamabob. It's a beauty. It's supposed to look like an earthquake monitor. Ain't going to raise no suspicion if anyone stumbles across it. The phone number printed on it calls Dixie Jean's cell phone and she has the patter written down on a notepad to answer any questions any caller may have about it. The cables from the power unit to the equipment in the sinkhole are buried underground. There's nothing suspicious that an aircraft might spot from above."

Preston looked around searching for a telltale sign of the underground cable run. Even his trained eyes couldn't find a trace of the buried cables. He wondered how long it had taken the area to return to a natural looking state. Preston silently, and grudgingly, admitted John Lee had done an excellent job of hiding his setup.

John Lee guided Preston back to the sinkhole. "Now, see if you can see any sign of using the sink hole."

Preston looked around and again could find no sign. "It looks unused to me."

John Lee said, "No smoke, no smell, no drain on the power grid to give us away. We've come a long, long, way from brewing moonshine in the hollow. And, no pot patches for the helicopters to find. This is literally as undercover as you can get. Sweet, right?"

Preston said, "You seem to have thought it out."

John Lee smiled and offered up a palm for a high five. Preston shook his head 'no' and kept his hand by his side. John Lee shrugged the disrespect off.

John Lee said, "I can't believe you left me hanging."

Preston asked, "How do you get in and out?" The hole in the ground looked menacing and eerie.

"Let me show you. We've thought it all out."

"Okay. Show me."

John Lee left Preston's side and ran to the edge of the forest where he knelt behind a tree. He dug an object out from behind the tree and returned to where Preston stood. John Lee held a chain ladder in his arms. It was the kind of ladder that could be rolled up for storage and kept in the second floor bedroom of a house to use as an emergency window exit fire escape device. The U-hooks on the top of the ladder could be hung over a window ledge allowing the user to climb down and escape a fire.

John Lee took the ladder and knelt by a large flat rock at the lip of the sinkhole. "We just hook the ladder over this rock and let the rungs drop down into the hole. We've been doing this for months and there aren't no wear marks on the rocks to give us away. We hide the ladder in the trunk hole on that old tree and toss brush on top of it. Someone would have to be looking for it to find it."

"How did you find this sink hole?" Preston emphasized the word 'you'.

John Lee smiled, "We were tracking a wounded deer and followed the blood trail to this. The deer fell right in. Man, I shit you not. There were dozens of bones and skulls from dozens of animals scattered down there. It's deeper than you think. And it goes back, like a cave, a few dozen yards. I guess critters running along don't see the hole till it's too late to stop. Then whoops, splat, game over. At least we haven't had an animal drop in on us yet since we've been up and running. The only thing we worry about is a cop or forest plane flying over while we are moving the equipment or product but we've got camo netting and tarps to throw over stuff if we hear a plane coming."

Preston begrudgingly said, "I guess this is pretty clever."

John Lee smiled. "Thanks. That means something coming from you. Want to see the operation up close?"

"Sure." Preston was not sure if John Lee's flattery was sincere or not. The anxiety and frustration Preston constantly felt was growing and conversing with John Lee revealed that Preston had been left out of the family loop more than he had realized.

"Great. Follow me down. The ladder may seem iffy at first but, trust me; it's secure and well tested."

John Lee eased over the edge of the sinkhole and began to climb down into the darkness. Preston looked around the clearing pausing to gaze at the distant solar panels.

John Lee called up from the depths of the sinkhole, "You coming or what?"

"I'm right behind you." Preston took a breath and started to descend the chain ladder into the dark sinkhole. A déjà vu feeling of cave combat encounters overwhelmed Preston with anxiety. He fought the feelings off telling himself he was at home and master of his domain. Still, gazing down into the dark void stirred up chilling memories, and his growing apprehension was difficult to quell. John Lee called again and Preston resumed his descent.

Kit and his friends had watched everyone's videos several times until Kit said, "Okay, then. Let's pack the drinks and snacks and be on our way. We'll need to park far enough away not to spook the hogs with our four-wheelers."

Alex said, "Seeing all of us standing around with our guns reminds me of a list of rules for a gunfight I heard."

Charles said, "Yeah, I recall something like that from my kid's combat simulator video game."

Kit said, "At least they're not playing Grand Theft Auto."

Charles asked, "What's that?"

Ethan said, "I thought the only rule was 'Don't bring a knife to a gunfight'."

Garrett said, "The rule is to avoid gunfights if at all possible."

Ethan said, "That sounds odd coming from a cop."

Garrett said, "Not all cops are like the ones that seem to make the bad national news headlines!"

Alex said, "If I remember correctly the rules of a gunfight went something like this. Bring all of your friends and ten times the amount of ammunition you think you'll need. If you get to choose what you get to bring to a gunfight, bring a fully automatic long gun and all of your friends who also have fully automatic weapons. After a gunfight no one will remember the details, only who lived and died. If someone ever kills you with your own weapon, it should be by beating you to death because your gun was empty. In a gunfight, the only unfair fight is the one you lose. Regardless of the reason for the conflict you will feel bad about killing another human but it is better to feel sad than be on a morgue slab."

Garrett said, "True. So true."

Kit said, "At least the animals don't shoot back."

Charles said, "Speaking of insect repellant, I'm out of spray. Anyone got any to spare? Does anyone have bear spray?"

Ethan mugged, "What? No one said anything about bear spray. All I heard about was ticks, chiggers, and skeeters."

The men looked at Charles who looked back at them, not the least bit concerned that the others thought he was overly cautious.

Garrett said, "I've got some on my ATV. I'll share."

"Thanks."

"Just pass it around to everyone when you finish, and the last man to use it put it back in my cargo bag."

Each man used the insect repellant saturating their camo clothes, boots, hats, and exposed arms. The smell of the repellant filled the air.

Charles, waving the cloud of repellant away from his face, said, "As much as I hate the smell of this stuff it is necessary. Soon the insects will carry enough disease to keep us indoors all of the time. I just hope my kids enjoy some of the world before climate change changes everything we all grew up with."

Alex said, "It's bad enough people kill each other with wild abandon; but to have the planet pull the rug out from under you is adding insult to injury. It's almost like the planet cannot wait for man to eradicate himself from the world soon enough."

Garrett said, "The planet carries on doing its natural thing; we are merely observers. The planet is fighting back against our relentless efforts to terraform the place. We are alive during one of the planet's natural cycles. Changes are measurable and obvious but still no one had moved the focus to adaptation. Russia, China, India and the U.S. still talk about stopping or slowing it but the planet is doing what it does, we may be accelerating the change, but that train has left the station. We need to adapt to it on a day to day level and stop wasting time trying to assure the people we can stop it. The emerging industrial nations aren't going to stop polluting. It is frustrating to know we elect these idiots to positions of power and they keep disappointing us. We are sheeple."

Charles said, "Yeah, but I'd rather be alive now than at any other time in the history of the planet."

"What about your kids?"

"Technology will emerge to fix things sooner than later."

"It is already later, later than we want to accept."

"We don't have a choice as to when we are here, but we do have a choice about how we live while we are here."

"Okay, time to move on to another subject."

Kit and Garrett packed a cooler full of drinks and trail mix bars. Ethan loaded a second cooler with a thirty pack of beer, a liter of cola, and a gallon bottle of Mellow Bourbon.

All of the coolers were fastened to ATVs. All of the long gun cases were secured next. The men checked each other's gear as Garrett filled the chainsaw with gas from a gas can then secured it to his ATV. Everyone doubled checked his gear then mounted up and waited.

Kit noticed that Alex had his holstered Glock on his belt. For the second time in as many days, he wished he had brought his Smith and Wesson .38 from home. Walking around armed seemed foreign to Kit, but then he wasn't in his postage stamp sized suburban landscaped backyard where the only wild animals were squirrels, raccoons, and opossums.

Out here, a creature with teeth, fangs, and claws could be lurking behind the next tree, not necessarily meaning to do harm but simply acting on instinct when encountering a human intrusion. He wondered how the animals would react to a resurgence of humans.

As Kit thought of animal encounters it was then he realized an outdoor themed attraction might be a hard setting to control especially with the explosion in the population of feral hogs and relocated bears only thirty miles away. Plus, the fear of Zika, West Nile, and tick borne diseases might keep tourists away in droves or relegate his business months to the cold, winter months only. Kit suddenly had a nauseating wave of panic from the reality of the complexity of his dreams. The fear of uncertainty caused an involuntary shiver to chill him despite the heat.

Kit pushed the fear aside as he spread several PDF maps across his ATV's seat. Leaving their engines running, the men gathered around Kit as he pointed out where he thought the hog wallow was located and where he thought the best place to kill coyotes would be as the day got closer to dusk. Kit made it clear he was going on the stories Ulysses had repeated over and over, and warned the men he had no first-hand experience in regard to the hog wallow.

Satisfied everything was in order the men drove into the woods after Kit reminded everyone that he was using this time to scout the land for the television producers and he would be taking photos and marking sites on his GPS unit. As Kit thought about the television show producers, dollar signs overpowered his apprehension of repurposing such a remote location.

Riding their ATVs in a single file convoy the men crept along the overgrown trail leading from the cabin into the forest. Visions of tanned animal hides, European skull mounts, and fresh wild game roasting over an open fire filled the men's minds. To a man, each shared the unsaid thought that today was going to be a great day for adults to play in the woods.

Kit steered his four-wheeler up to a large fallen oak tree blocking the trail and stopped. The column of ATVs had been slowly following a trail marked with faded blaze orange vinyl strips tied to the lowest limbs of trees. The faded vinyl strips marked a long, winding path leading toward the edge of Kit's property. The bordering section of a neighboring forest had been recently selectively cut for particularly valuable hardwoods. Treetops and ugly broken stumps made it look post-apocalyptic. Kit vowed never to do that to his property.

Kit stood on his ATV's footrests looking for snakes, then dismounted and stretched as the others stopped their engines and dismounted as well. Kit unfolded the map and spread it out on the seat of his ATV. The rest of the men gathered around stretching and warily looking for snakes and ticks. After a moment of stillness the men began swatting at gnats and biting flies.

Kit said, "Okay, I think our destination is about a dozen or so yards past this tree, give or take, straight ahead of us. I hope there are markers taking us right to where Ulysses had an old hunting blind. We should be able to mow hogs down in relative comfort; I just don't know what time of day they come out to feed. I say we just creep in to the spot and figure out a game plan once we get there."

Alex sighed, "You mean hurry and wait, don't you?"

"What do you mean you don't know when they come out?" This was from Charles who was obsessively checking himself and his clothes for ticks. "What if they don't come out?"

Kit tapped a sheet of paper and said, "Ulysses left instructions and hand drawn maps for the twins on different things they needed to do once the place was theirs. One of the things he covered was telling them the locations they needed to go to if they wanted to have some fun shooting up nuisance animals. He even left the contact info for his favorite taxidermist. Anyway, that's how I have directions to his hunting hot spots. Ulysses never took advantage of satellite and topo maps available on the internet but he sure was an avid amateur cartographer. And his hand drawn map has been useful."

Charles said, "What about deer ticks? Lyme disease? Snake bites? Poison Ivy? Poison Oak? Does he have those hot spots marked? I don't want to get bitten by a tick and never be able to eat red meat again!"

Ethan said, "Christ, give it a rest, why don't you?"

Garrett said, "What about moonshine stills? Any of those hidden around here? All of this riding has made me thirsty." He walked to Ethan's ATV and took a cold beer out of the cooler.

Ethan said, "Anyone else thirsty?"

Alex and Kit said, "Yeah." Ethan tossed the men a beer each.

Charles said, "Look you've got enough alcohol in you to incapacitate any tick before they can infect you. As for me, I don't have a problem erring on the side of caution. And I don't want to run into any moonshiners; I hear they shoot first and don't ask questions."

Kit said, "When I talked to you about coming down here this week, I made it very clear we would be roughing it. I told you to bring everything you thought you'd need to make a week of roughing it in Bum Fuck Egypt tolerable. I didn't sugar coat any of this. So shut up about the allergies and creepy crawlies, and just watch what you sit on and where you step."

Ethan said, "Ooh, Kit's got an attitude." He drained a beer tossing the empty can into the carrier on the back of his ATV.

Garrett patted Kit on the shoulder, "You know you will probably hear the same from your future paying guests no matter how clearly you print out warnings on the advertising brochure."

"Thanks for that, neighbor."

"No problem, neighbor."

Alex walked up to stand beside Kit, "Hey, if you turn this place into some kind of hunting retreat I'll tell the guys in my old unit and have them get the word out. You can cater to soldiers like me who don't put too much stock in amenities as long as no one is trying to kill you. Maybe you can get a government contract, somehow. You know you could open a retreat for recovering wounded soldiers and soldiers suffering from Post-Traumatic Stress Disorder or Traumatic Brain Injury. Private organizations have been far better at serving our men after discharge than our own government."

Garrett said, "That would be very good."

Kit said, "Okay. I'll give that some thought."

Alex nodded, "Yeah, you should. There are many good resources for disabled kids but too few for soldiers suffering from PTSD or TBI or missing limbs. It is a shame there are better private organizations to help vets than the government who puts them in harm's way. But it could be a great opportunity for you."

Charles said, "That's good, come way out here to recover from the horrors of war only to catch Lyme disease or Rocky Mountain Spotted Fever or Zika."

Garrett snapped back, "You sound like you could use a little relaxation yourself."

Charles said, "My idea of relaxation is a hotel stay in a suite with a spa tub and room service." Turning his back to the others he checked his cell phone for reception. Service had not been restored.

Charles fumed aloud, "I'd like to kick those copper thieves in the mouth. Don't they know they affect people's lives when they destroy a communications tower? Don't they have a conscience?"

Ethan said, "Okay. We agree Chas is a bit paranoid and a worrywart. And he's addicted to his cell phone. And that he is probably going to die from insect repellant overdose. Let's go kill some hogs to get our minds off of Charles."

Charles said, "Okay. Okay. Give me a break. I just can't get sick or hurt. My boys depend on me."

Ethan said, "Okay. Okay. We see you're a good father. There is no need to be a martyr."

Kit said, "Hey, Chas is a good dad. I'll vouch for him; he's just a bit more citified than the rest of us."

"Is citified code for pussified?" Ethan looked around for support.

Charles snapped, "It's not a contest about who can rough it the best! It's just that I'm having second thoughts about letting my boys waste a year or two trying to get a recording contract before starting college. I need to be available to guide the boys. Excuse me because I care!"

Kit said, "Okay, everybody off of Chas's ass. Let's just go blast some nuisance animals."

Charles glared at Ethan. "Yes, let's go blast some nuisance animals."

Garrett lifted his bow case from the back of the ATV.

Ethan eyed the bow and asked, "So, how do you plan to use that thing?"

"Effectively."

"No. Wise-ass. I mean are you going to stay with us on the ground or climb up a tree?"

Garrett looked past the fallen tree as he answered. "I won't know until I get there."

Alex said, "Silent but deadly. And I'm not talking farts!"
Garrett winked at Alex in reply. Alex nodded and smiled.

Kit led the group over the fallen tree toward the location marked on Ulysses' map. He pushed past low branches and through thorny vines progressing from one faded vinyl marking strip to the next. The men kept a short distance between them so flailing branches would not slap them as it rebounded from the fore man's passing. The path was far more overgrown than Kit had estimated causing Charles and Ethan to grumble about the laborious walk. Kit was amused the two had finally found a topic to agree on.

Breathing hard and sweating profusely, the men navigated their way through undergrowth that thwarted any breeze from penetrating into the interior of the forest. The men passed through a large cloud of gnats that went up their noses and hovered around their eyes. The trail finally opened up and made walking easier. Ahead it was lighter and Kit when spied a break in the trees he quickened his pace.

Moments later, the woods opened up revealing a sizable clearing. Twenty yards inside of Kit's barbwire fence line a spring fed, muddy hog wallow filled an oval shaped clearing. Kit noted that a small trickle of overflow seeped from the wallow allowing woodland weeds to bring a little color to the grassy clearing.

After a quick search, the men found a dilapidated, two by four framed, plywood covered, ground hunting blind. The weathered blind was placed a dozen yards from the muddy wallow. The five men stood around the blind, reluctant to barge inside fearing they would disturb wasps or a venomous snake.

Kit took the initiative peering into the rectangular structure through the gun openings running the lengths of the blind's front and sides. A quick inspection revealed no wasp's nests on the ceiling or snakes on the earthen floor. For good measure, Kit kicked the blind three times, breathing a sigh of relief when no horde of insects exploded from an unseen nesting place. Charles breathed an audible sighed of relief.

Alex used his binoculars to scan the mud wallow and distant tree line. He stated, "There's fresh mud out there. The hogs are definitely using this place. We might make contact today."

Kit said, "I think it'll be damn stuffy in that blind. Why don't we just fan out and wait for them to come in."

Garrett said, "I brought a predator call. If the hogs don't show soon I could try to call in some coyotes."

Ethan said, "Is there a call for hogs?"

Charles said, "Sooey-Pig, Sooey, Sooey."

Ethan said, "That's a football chant."

Charles replied, "I've seen people use that on TV shows."

Ethan said, "Yeah, Green Acres, maybe."

Charles said to Kit, "There you have your name for your resort. Green Acres. It's friendly, it's got name recognition, and it's established as a fun place to be."

Alex said, "Yeah, name recognition among Baby Boomers only. I think you need something original and seductive for a name."

"Seductive?"

"Alluring is a better word."

Ethan said, "I didn't come out all this way just to waste a day waiting and sweating in this God-awful heat. Let's lure the porkers in."

Charles said, "Yeah, before it gets any hotter."

Ethan pulled a plastic liquor flask from a cargo pocket and sniffed the bourbon in it. He offered the flask to the rest of the party who took long drinks hoping bourbon scented sweat might keep the gnats and mosquitos away. Shaking his head as the drained flask returned to him, Ethan revealed a second flask, took a long sip, and then slid it into a cargo pocket of his camouflaged pants.

Garrett eyed a big, squatty tree with low strong branches and said, "I think I'll go off in that direction and look for a comfortable limb to settle in on. It looks like it was grown for someone my age to use."

Kit said, "Okay. Let's give the hogs an hour or so to come in and if we don't see them Garrett can go to town on the predator call and try to lure in some coyotes. Don't shot any bobcats. I don't want them gone."

Charles said, "An hour! Don't we need a license or something to shoot some kinds of animals?"

Kit said, "Oh, right. Okay, let's just stick to hogs and 'yotes."

"Chas, you are one big buzz kill." Ethan adjusted his heavy bandoleer.

Charles said, "What about game wardens?"

Kit said, "Okay. Keep an eye out for the game warden, too. Try not to shoot the game warden or the sheriff."

Charles reluctantly moved into the blind. He noticed there was no chair or bench to sit on, just three overturned five-gallon plastic buckets. "Hey, where am I supposed to sit?"

Kit said, "Don't know. There's nothing about chairs in Ulysses notes. Use the buckets."

Charles said, "Damn."

Ethan said, "Your ass ain't that tender."

"Says you!"

"You can take a bucket; there's more than enough to share."

Alex said, "We should have brought some folding camp chairs. No matter how well you plan, something always comes up that you just have simply forgotten to bring. So it goes."

Ethan groaned, "Yeah this isn't going to be good for my back." He took out a pill bottle, popped a pill and chased it with another shot of bourbon. The others looked on but said nothing.

Kit said, "Pick your spots to set up."

Ethan yelled, "I call the shadiest spot!"

The others turned their backs on the plywood hunting blind and the sour look Charles was giving the situation. Charles slowly settled into the old blind and picked a bucket to sit on as the others moved away searching for a comfortable spot to hunt from.

Fanning out along the tree line bordering the clearing the hunters took positions concealing themselves in a spot offering either a good shooting lane or a steady branch to use as a gun rest. The one common factor each man sought was shade. Five minutes into the wait, the men were frantically swatting gnats and biting horseflies.

Ethan squirmed trying to find a comfortable position as the heavy bandoleer kept rubbing his shoulders. The weight from the shotgun shells and heavy belt buckle pulled down on Ethan even as he sat leaning against a tree. The cotton shoulder padding was soon sweat soaked.

Kit softly called out to Ethan, "Ethan, everything okay over there?"

Ethan replied, "No worse than usual. I didn't think this bandoleer would be so heavy. I guess weight means quality!"

Alex called out, "Not always."

Kit said, "It's the case of shells you're toting around."

"I'm okay. Just a little out of shape for carrying half a cow on my back."

"Your pills aren't helping? You've taken a few already today."

Ethan said loudly, "It's like the Guns and Roses song, *'I used to do a little, but the little wouldn't do it, so the little got more and more. I just kept trying to get a little better, say a little better than before.'*"

Ethan's harsh imitation of the singer's distinctive vocal style filled the clearing. The birds grew silent at the sound.

Alex used a shouted whisper to say, "That should draw some type of predator or scare every living thing away."

The conversation ended and the clearing remained silent giving it an eerie feel. Wind dropped down into the clearing rustling the taller grass and stirring the potpourri scent of natural decay and fresh green growth.

Ethan squirmed under the heavy bandoleer. "I think I should have used some kind of oil on this leather to soften it up."

Kit cautioned Ethan, "Don't throw your back out."

Ethan whispered, "I got it under control."

"The pills too?"

Ethan said, "Thanks for thinking of my health."

"I got your back, cuz." Then silence fell across the clearing as another round of waiting began.

Thirty minutes into the wait the men no longer cared if their swatting movements scared away any game; the swatting was forceful and, at times, loud. Butterflies and birds returned and drank from the spring fed wallow.

An hour into the tedious wait for feral hogs to appear the men began running low on patience. The remaining bottled water, now air temperature warm, tasted like the plastic bottles it was contained in. No one wanted to walk all the way back to the coolers to get more water or liquor, so they all suffered in silence, waiting for someone to break first and make the trek back to the coolers.

Kit thought he heard snoring coming from the blind Charles was in. He loudly called to Charles but got no reply.

Kit assumed most of the other men had fallen asleep as well. He wished Garrett would use his predator call just to liven things up. Then, as Kit was considering breaking cover and calling everyone together to formulate a new plan, he heard the distinctive sound of the electronic predator call.

The squeal was designed to mimic a wounded rabbit. Kit knew from previous hunting trips with Ulysses that if you used an owl call, turkeys would often respond, so it seemed logical that an injured rabbit crying would lure an animal seeking an easy meal.

Kit hoped the electronic lure would not bring in a bear; the fact that the state wildlife agency relocated nuisance bears, rescued from urban population centers, only thirty miles from his property worried him as he pondered how to present his location to the television show producers.

A shadow flickered across the sunny ground, capturing Kit's attention. Looking up he watched a turkey vulture alight in a dead tree on the far side of the wallow. A murder of crows filling the treetops surrounding the clearing started a racket that quickly grated on the men's nerves more than the haunting cry of the electronic rabbit. A second turkey vulture landed in the dead tree towering over the fence line. More vultures landed on exposed branches as Kit and the others continued to slap at gnats and flies.

After leaving John Lee at the sinkhole Preston chose to take the long way home giving him time to clear his head and digest the surprising discovery. John Lee's operation, anger, alienation, and his diminished position in the family troubled his mind. Preston wandered aimlessly letting his thoughts flow from one problem to the next hoping solutions would also pop into his head. He could not believe that righting a long standing wrong had taken such an unexpected, and undeserved, turn. He held the truth 'no good deed goes unpunished' to be self-evident and proven by his current predicament. Tom Benson's name always arose at family gatherings cursing his role for Eli's absences at Christmas and birthday parties. How could the family be mad at him for avenging Eli?

Preston reluctantly had to admit that John Lee had replaced the reduction in moonshining and pot growing with a solid operation and that made Preston jealous of the younger man. John Lee was manufacturing a new drug, a combination of methamphetamine and ecstasy that provided a larger profit margin, a guaranteed repeat user's market, and a discreet manufacturing process. Preston wanted to be angry with John Lee but he grudgingly admitted to himself the younger man seemed savvy.

Preston had mistakenly thought that avenging a festering family dishonor would have been better received; he had not expected to be so wrong and it ate at him constantly. Preston despaired over what had happened to the family's mettle while he had been overseas learning tactical skills to help the family survive.

All of the unanswered questions, the public humiliation, and nagging frustration boiled incessantly tormenting Preston's thoughts. Then, over the loud angry voices arguing in his mind, an external sound cut through the internal din. Carried to his ears on a breeze Preston heard an electronic game call in the distance.

Preston cleared his mind of the voices by focusing on the sound. John Lee had brought the enormity of his fall from grace to the forefront of all his thoughts, but now he had a distraction to focus on. Preston intended to take his anger out on the brazen poachers.

Preston zeroed in on the predator call and moved toward the sound with renewed vigor and purpose as curiosity competed with caution. Preston paused as he calculated the distance to the sound. His ears told him the call was fifty yards or so to the west. It wasn't on LaHarpe property but that did not mean he couldn't investigate the source. He carefully climbed over a sagging barbwire fence and crept toward a distant clearing using trees and shrubs as cover. The sound definitely was coming from somewhere on the old Carson spread and he wanted, no, needed, a look at the noisemakers.

Preston was surprised, then outraged, that poachers would be so bold to set up in broad daylight. If the user was a poacher he could not let that transgression stand, no matter whose land they were on. Preston grew certain that the county had gone crazy while he was away serving it and felt it was up to him to restore order and reclaim his rightful position in the LaHarpe family hierarchy and Chickasaw County. Preston stopped near the edge of the hog wallow clearing and knelt behind a tree trunk searching for the source of the sound. He heard voices and began looking for the speakers.

The way the men spoke to one another made it was obvious they were not poachers nor did they seem comfortable in the forest. Preston assessed the conversation and concluded that the men were part of the Carson group. He wished they had been common poachers. Although he felt like killing them all and burning the bodies, just to relieve his stress, he made a rational decision and waited, listening, and evaluating the unseen men. He was certain he could learn much from eavesdropping on the group.

Preston listened as he sought to pinpoint the men's locations. After several minutes of careful observation he spotted the speakers. The way the men were positioned, their setup around the hog wallow, and the predator call clearly indicated what the men were at the clearing to do.

Preston wondered which one of the men was, Kit, the man who had left the note on the ATVs. Preston saw the interlopers as unwelcomed city slickers who would ruin everything with whatever nefarious plans they were bringing in from the city. As he spied on the men hidden in the shade Preston felt a burning anxiety grow in his chest. He saw the men as one more problem dealt him by the hand of fate. An impotent rage boiled in his stomach as he listened to the three men talk.

As the men's conversation continued Preston's indignation grew until he began to tremble. The men were bitching about the heat, the wait, their thirst, and insects, and the crows, as if they hadn't expected such nuisances in the great outdoors. Their whining caused Preston's anger to grow and he struggled to ignore an onslaught of murderous impulses and calm his mind.

A sudden outburst from the murder of crows brought Preston back from the brink of a void. As he regained composure and assessed his situation Preston realized he was gripping his Python with white knuckles. Seeing his hand gripping the weapon in such a manner snapped Preston back into full control of his thoughts and emotions. The big man exhaled slowly and carefully holstered his gun then moved to an easily climbable tree that would provide a better vantage point. He skillfully climbed the tree barely moving limbs or shaking leaves despite his size.

Assuming that the men would be shooting at hogs or coyotes, based on the predator call and their set up around the wallow, Preston stealthily climbed the large gnarled oak tree seeking high ground out of any stray bullet's path. He carefully chose sturdy limbs keeping one eye, and ear, on the men across the clearing. Preston realized he was having fun; he was climbing a tree fifty yards from obtuse city boys who had no idea he could take each one of them out before any of them ever thought to look up into the trees. A smile crossed Preston's face as he found a large limb that could easily hold his weight. Preston settled comfortably on the thick limb to watch the men and listen hoping to learn what these interlopers were planning and how it could affect the LaHarpe holdings.

Far across the clearing, on the ground thirty-feet below him, the men continued to talk loudly to each other. Preston could hear the slap of hand on skin as the men killed horseflies and fought off gnats. The men's discussion focused on the heat, the humidity, and the agonizingly long, boring, wait for something to happen.

Effectively concealed by the leafy canopy Preston relaxed on the large limb analyzing the men while watching and listening for anything that would alert him to other men he had not seen yet. The constant whining led him to believe that Mother Nature would drive the city slickers back to the city without him needing to intervene. He suddenly felt as if luck was about to swing back his way. It was a nice feeling and Preston allowed a smile to form under his bushy beard.

Resting against the tree's trunk, spying on the men, Preston felt alive. He felt strong and invincible. He remembered the thrill of offensive combat while ignoring the terror of being on defense; he remembered doing what had to be done while rationalizing the manner in which it was done because he was still alive.

The green leaves whispered as a breeze found a way through the forest. The air movement was refreshing and Preston refocused on the men below. He continued the waiting game with the men; a game that only he knew was in progress.

Eventually Preston became bored. Fidgeting as time crept on Preston sighted down the barrel of his Colt Python methodically moving its muzzle from man to man. The distance was a challenge for a handgun, and his aim would be critical if he were forced to take a shot from his elevated hide. Not for the first time, Preston wished he had a rifle instead of a revolver.

The men's conversation died out and the glade became quiet. Time passed slowly until one of the men below shouted, breaking the ambience of the clearing, and another answered. Preston used the distraction to adjust his position on the wide, thick limb giving his back and butt a break. He moved ever so carefully; practiced movements kept the branches from giving him away. Preston strained to listen but the whispering leaves distorted their words.

The men were now fidgeting and moving without caution. Preston guessed they had enjoyed enough of Mother Nature for the day and were about to pull up stakes and high tail it for air conditioning and soft chairs. He waited for the men to stand up so he could identify them.

Ethan took another drink from his second flask while looking at his wristwatch. He lightly tapped the face of his watch which seemed, to him, to be moving in agonizingly slow motion. Sighing none too subtly, Ethan drained the last drop of bourbon from the flask then shoved it back into a cargo pocket. Feeling good and feeling bored warred within him. The waiting had been tedious and hot and he was anxious for something to happen. He was so antsy for anything to happen that he began considering making something happen.

Ethan called out, "I'm bored! Let's call it a day."

Kit raised his voice and answered, saying, "Just a little while longer. Be quiet, don't scare them off now. It's late enough in the day for activity to start."

Ethan shouted back, "Then why the hell did we get out here in the damn heat of the afternoon? There's nothing here to scare!" Kit held his reply and the glade's natural sounds returned as the men resumed waiting. Garrett had stopped using the predator call moments before Preston had arrived. The others wondered why he had stopped, but secretly were glad the annoying sound had ended.

The only animals moving in the clearing were birds. Several turkey vultures sat in high tree branches sunning themselves with their wings unfurled. Ethan wondered if the big, ugly birds could smell that he was nearly dead from boredom. Taking it upon himself to liven things up, Ethan stood, shouldered his shotgun and took aim at a lone vulture sunning itself exposed on the end of a limb of a towering dead tree.

The sudden movement of Ethan rising to his feet and shouldering his shotgun caught Alex's attention. Alex quickly looked up to see what Ethan was aiming at. The only creatures visible were the large black vultures sunning themselves high above the wallow.

Alex glanced around to see if the others had their weapons ready as well. Kit failed to notice Ethan's actions; he was distracted swatting insects and wiping sweat out of his eyes. Garrett was hidden in a tree several yards away and Charles was snoring loudly in the ground blind.

Alex hesitated then opened his mouth to shout at Ethan not to shoot but his shout came out too slowly. The shotgun's sudden, unexpected, blast got everyone's attention while overpowering Alex's warning Ethan not to fire.

Kit jumped up and looked toward Ethan then out at the clearing. Charles stuck his head out of the ground blind wiping sleep from his eyes. Kit saw nothing in the clearing. He listened for the sounds of an animal's mad flight through the forest's leaves and shrubs. A shadow crossed the ground. Kit looked up.

The buckshot from Ethan's shotgun tore into the big, black, bird causing an explosion of feathers to cloud the air where the bird had been roosting. The bird dropped to the earth followed by dozens of feathers slowly floating earthward behind it. The crows took flight fleeing the explosive sound. The other vultures shifted nervously on the sun drenched limbs but did not take flight.

Kit was shocked and angry and the combination made him unable to speak to Ethan. As Kit fumed, trying to control his anger, Ethan ejected the spent shell and looked down the barrel of the shotgun for his next target. Alex started to callout Ethan but deferred to Kit who was closer to him.

Ethan let out a rebel yell then drew a bead on a second vulture as it flapped its wings preparing to launch itself from its lofty perch. The vulture spread its wings then dropped from its perch trying to catch an updraft. Ethan's second shot shredded the bird's left wing and the bird spiraled downward. Ethan fired a follow-up shot as the bird spiraled toward the ground but the shot missed the descending bird harmlessly shredding leaves and peppering limbs in an adjacent tree. A third shot missed the bird as well.

The wounded bird crashed to the clearing floor with a heavy thud. After a moment of hesitation the bird slowly tried to rise. Unable to take flight it wobbled on unsteady legs before sitting down and looking at its destroyed wing. Ethan finished the maimed bird off with an easy shot once it was sitting on the ground. The other men were too dumbfounded to speak. Ethan looked around for applause but found none.

Alex broke the awkward silence and began berating Ethan for his recklessness. Alex's words came out in a mostly unintelligible roaring stream of consciousness scream; and while his words may not have been intelligible his anger at Ethan was unmistakable. Ethan turned, smiled at Alex, ignoring Alex's anger, and pumped his shotgun up and down in a sign of victory.

Kit waited for Alex so stop yelling at Ethan so he could start. He could not believe that Ethan had just blasted a bird that no one could eat and that might even be a protected species.

Preston steadied his Colt Python and aimed at the man wearing the ostentatious bandoleer as he fought off the shock of having pellets come so close to his hiding spot. He struggled to regain control of his breathing so that he could take a shot. Ethan's shotgun blast had shredded the canopy beside Preston. Preston felt he might have taken a little buckshot in his shoulder, but he was too outraged to look for blood. Preston knew the man in the silly bandoleer must die. It was not a smart thing Preston was about to do, he knew that, but it was the only thing to do. Such a transgression must not go unanswered.

Preston's camo clothing blended in well with the leafy canopy but now he wished he had his body armor; they might not be able to see him, but a careless shot by an idiot could still kill or wound him. He thought that if he killed the shotgunner then the others would panic and run away. He would be long gone before the sheriff was notified. Preston didn't want to start a turf war; he just wanted payback on the careless ass with the shotgun.

Charles stuck his head out of the blind shouting questions that no one answered. Kit shouted over the others for everyone to shut up. The shouting slowly died out leaving Alex and Ethan standing and staring at each other.

Alex fumed as he said through clenched teeth, "That was stupid."

Kit said, "Man, I think those things are a protected species."

Ethan said, "No way! Those big ugly pterodactyls are protected? No way something like that is protected!"

Kit said, "Plus you probably scared off anything that was headed this way."

Charles called out from the old box blind, "If he scared everything off, let's call it a day."

Kit said, "It's a little early to call it. People shoot guns around here all of the time. It's one of the perks of living in the country. Animals get used to it as long as you don't scare them off with a near miss; they'll come back around."

Charles said, "We gave the hogs a fair chance to show up. Let's try another time."

Alex said, "Ethan, you can be an ass hat sometimes."

Kit said, "Let's give it a few more minutes."

Charles called over to the men, "This doesn't feel like fun anymore."

Ethan adjusted his bandoleer and said, "Yeah, let's get the hell out here now since Charles thinks it's not fun anymore. Let's go back and shoot up some more plywood; I hear it grills up pretty good if you put enough butter on it." Ethan leaned on a tree trunk eyeing the dead tree where the birds had been roosting. The birds were gone and the tree looked lonely and barren. With no more targets to offer Ethan turned his gaze to the tops of the distant green trees where squirrels scampered and small birds flitted from limb to limb.

Kit shouted, "All right then. Let's call it a day. Saddle up boys."

Ethan shouted, "I was kidding! It's just now going to get good. We've got live bait, not some electronic call. And it's just now getting cool enough to breathe easy."

Charles said, "No! Let's go. I've been sitting in this sweatbox all day and I'm ready to go. It's so damn hot in here, even the insects stay out of this thing."

Kit said, "Charles, you slept in the hot box all day. You snore funny."

Ethan shouted to all, "Stay under cover. There's blood in the mud and that will surely bring in some predators. I want to kill something more than ancient plywood and paper plates!"

Charles shouted, "You just killed two birds." Charles began walking toward the far side of the clearing heading to where the ATVs were parked.

Alex, through clenched teeth, slowly said, "You shot helpless birds. It was not part of the plan. I should kick your ass."

Charles said, "Do it at the cabin. I'm out of here." Charles continued to stomp toward his ATV ignoring the looks of the others.

Kit yelled to Charles, "At least have dinner ready when we get back."

Ethan said, "Yeah. Burgers with all the fixings tonight."

Charles never looked back and remained silent as he stomped down the path back to his ATV. The men heard the ATV's engine start and turned back to look at one another wondering what to do. Alex shrugged and Kit shook his head debating what to do.

Alex glared at Ethan as Ethan shook his head in disgust.

Ethan said, "He'll never make it back to the cabin on his own."

Kit said, "Damn it Ethan, why did you have to do that?"

"Because, I was fucking bored out of my mind."

"Not the correct answer."

Alex said, "What you did was wrong. Period. That kind of shit betrays the whole code of honor you have with nature!"

"What?"

"Ethics! Fair chase. Code of honor."

Alex glared at Ethan hoping Kit would intervene. Ethan adjusted his bandoleer. Kit stared at Ethan wondering if there was anything he could say to get the point across to him.

Preston smiled at the dissent he was hearing among the men. It seemed that country life was not for these city slickers. Their own bickering and softness would drive them from the property with no effort required from him. He decided to let the shotgunner live.

Kit rubbed a hand over his eyes shaking his head at the situation. Then he looked around at the others seeing they were looking to him to intervene. Kit turned and glared at Ethan who simply smiled back at him and raised his shotgun.

Both Kit and Alex knew from Ethan's body language that he was about to unload his shotgun into the air just to make a point. Alex knew the sensation of unloading a magazine just to feel the recoil, smell the powder, and feel the power of the gun intimately. Ethan had that look in his eyes and from the fully loaded bandoleer it was clear Ethan had been anticipating an opportunity to send quite a bit of heavy steel shot down range.

Alex debated intervening; he knew Kit was going to let Ethan do his thing just to deescalate the confrontation. Alex made the decision to let Ethan burn through some shells and calm down without interference.

Alex made a bet with himself that Ethan would burn out before he went through a dozen shells. Exhaling deeply Alex relaxed preparing to watch the show. Kit glanced at Alex who shrugged in reply. Kit and Alex watched Ethan fire into the air like a crazed duck hunter sky-busting cloud level mallards.

Ethan wanted to see leaves and limbs falling like rain so he began firing a sweeping arc of pointless shots at the top of the distant trees. Two shells worth of buckshot again peppered the leaves near Preston. Instinctively Preston compressed himself into as small of a target as he could and waited for the fool to run out of shells while his finger pressed ever so lightly on the trigger of his Colt Python.

Preston waited until the man had emptied his shotgun and stood with his arms wide open waiting for applause or admiration from the two other men. Ethan frowned and looked hurt by the angry reaction from his friends.

Preston decided the shotgunner needed to die so he aimed and squeezed the trigger. The thick canopy of hardwood tree leaves dispersed the sound of the shot making it seem to come from everywhere. The bullet hit Ethan solidly spinning and knocking him backward to collapse out of sight.

Kit reacted and returned fire in the general direction from which he thought the shot had come. Kit fired three quick rounds from his lever action rifle then ducked behind a tree trying to make sense of what had just happened. Two of Kit's bullets hit the tree trunk well below Preston who remained motionless evaluating the weaponry of the group.

Alex took cover behind a tree and held his fire searching for the sniper. He was sure the shot came from above, but the forest canopy hid the shooter well. The glade grew eerily silent.

In the distance, Charles's four-wheeler could be heard racing its engine. Over the distant motor noise, Alex heard Ethan groan. Kit heard Ethan groan as well and breathed a sigh of relief that his friend was alive. The ATV engine continued to rev in the background. Alex eyed the distant trees trying to locate the sniper.

Alex next looked in Ethan's direction and saw Kit hugging the forest floor as he crawled toward his wounded cousin. Alex repositioned himself to provide cover if Kit and Ethan began taking fire. Kit crawled over leaves and sticks until he was beside Ethan and tried to assess where and how badly Ethan had been shot. The thick bandoleer prevented Kit from assessing the shoulder wound. There was a bullet hole in the bandoleer with blood oozing through the hole. Kit took off his shirt and jammed it between the bandoleer and the bullet hole. Ethan was groaning, dazed, and in obvious shock; he looked at Kit without speaking.

Kit scanned the forest until he spotted Alex; Kit gave Alex an 'oh shit' look. The bullet had penetrated the thick leather bandoleer and embedded in Ethan's shoulder. Kit could not tell how bad the wound was but it appeared the bandoleer had reduced the damage from the bullet somewhat. Blood saturated Kit's shirt as Ethan groaned in pain.

Alex silently mouthed, "How bad?"

Kit shrugged in response and tilted his head toward the ATVs. Ethan patted at his shoulder and grimaced.

Alex nodded his head affirming Kit's plan to move Ethan to the four-wheelers. Kit acknowledged Alex then began dragging Ethan along the forest floor. Ethan moaned and grimaced as he was dragged over every leaf covered limb, root, and hole. Alex remained hidden providing cover and watching for their assailant to show himself.

Preston remained motionless on the tree limb watching the panic around the glade unfold. He evaluated the men as they reacted to the situation. Preston watched and patiently waited feeling confident the group could be easily taken out should the need arise. He believed they would turn tail and head for home back in the city as soon as they could.

It took Kit a long time to drag Ethan to where the four-wheelers were parked. He was breathing heavily by the time he got Ethan to the parking area. Kit propped Ethan against the fallen tree then crept back to the clearing to retrieve his and Ethan's guns.

Kit rested against a tree trying to steady his breathing. Alex emerged from a thicket and knelt next to Kit. Kit said, "Did you see anyone? What about Garrett?"

Alex said, "No and don't know. Head back to Ethan and I'll join you soon."

"Just shoot or shout if you need help." Kit crawled away.

Preston remained motionless watching the glade for several minutes after Kit disappeared. The glade grew eerily quiet.

Garrett remained hidden, a dozen trees over from Preston's perch-though he didn't realize it. Preston continued to wait long after the activity of the men ended before climbing down the tree.

Garrett was more patient determined to see who had shot Ethan. Time seemed to have stopped until Garrett sensed the sniper's movement. He shifted slightly to try and get a better view of their attacker. Unfortunately for Garrett, Preston climbed down the far side of the tree and disappeared into the forest moving like a wraith using trees and bushes as cover. Garrett waited looking for any other men to reveal themselves. The glade grew quiet. Once Garrett was sure he was alone he climbed out of the tree.

13

> She's got a 3D Jesus in a picture frame
> Got a child she's never named
> She shakes a snake above her hair
> Talks in tongues when there's no one there
>
> -Tom Petty

Alex tossed Kit's blood soaked shirt and Ethan's bandoleer to the side then examined Ethan's bullet wound. Kit stood over the men looking between Ethan's wound and at the trail hoping he would see Garrett but fearing he would see their attacker instead. The sound of the ATV engine revving madly further down the trail was loud enough to cover any noise from someone coming for them.

Charles had not traveled thirty yards before driving over a hidden tree stump and becoming high centered. Alex and Kit glanced toward the noise and watched Charles bouncing on the ATV's foot pegs rocking it side to side shaking his head in frustration unaware of what was happening behind him.

Alex said, "Go deal with that idiot and I'll deal with this one."

Kit said, "Well, this went south in a hurry."

Alex said, "In the blink of an eye."

Kit patted Ethan on his good shoulder then walked away to deal with Charles. Kit found Charles, red faced, soaked with sweat, cursing aloud, and red-lining the ATV's engine while bouncing on the foot pegs desperately attempting to escape the stump. Kit yelled twice but had to walk in front of the ATV to get Charles's attention.

Charles turned the ATV off, "You scared me!" Charles looked defiant and frustrated at the same time.

Kit, exasperation evident in his tone, said, "You could have just stayed on the trail we made."

Charles said, "I turned around to see if you guys were following me and I drifted."

"Yeah, trying to save your own ass, you left us high and dry. This kind of serves you right for bugging out and being an idiot."

"Look, I can't live the carefree life you do. I don't care what you think but my children are my top priority."

"Charles, I know what you say is heartfelt and true. But it is getting old."

Charles's complexion changed from red to white when he glanced past Kit and noticed Alex bandaging Ethan with gauze from a first-aid kit. Kit looked at the stump and ATV while Charles tried to come to grips with what he was seeing.

Charles said, "What happened?"

Kit took two long slow breaths before motioning for Charles to follow him as they walked back to Ethan and Alex. Charles looked at Ethan. Ethan winked at Charles as Alex stood.

Ethan looked at Kit and said, "Aw, man, you didn't have to ruin your shirt for me. You got a nice tan for a city boy."

Kit shook his head and said, "Be quiet."

Alex crept back down the trail disappearing into the under growth. He was away several minutes returning just before Charles gave into overwhelming anxiety over the length of time he had been gone. Alex smiled and said, "I don't think anyone is coming after us."

Charles asked again, "What happened?

Alex said, "Talk later. Help us secure Ethan to Kit's ATV."

Charles looked past Alex's shoulder and asked, "Where's Garrett?"

Kit began rearranging cargo to form a backrest for Ethan during the ride back to the cabin. Alex kept an eye on the trail. Ethan groaned.

Charles said, "Where's Garrett? Is he injured too?"

Alex said, "He was cut off from us. I'm sure he's fine."

Charles said, again, "What happened?"

Kit looked at Alex and said, "What the hell happened back there?"

Alex shook his head. "I'm not sure."

Alex and Kit worked together to place Ethan on the ATV. Ethan groaned with pain from the jostling movement. Kit wiped his bloody hands on Ethan's pants. Ethan frowned but said nothing about it.

Ethan clenched his teeth and said through the pain he was feeling, "Don't leave my bandoleer behind. I mustn't lose that!"

Charles said, "Where's Garrett?"

"I'm not sure. We couldn't communicate."

Kit looked at Alex who tossed the first aid kit into Kit's pile of discarded cargo. Alex took Ethan's pulse as Charles paced around the men.

Kit stared into the dense forest watching the path he had beaten down by dragging Ethan from the hog wallow clearing.

Charles said, "Do you see Garrett?"

"I'm not watching for Garrett."

Charles shouted, "God damn it, tell me what the fuck went on back there!"

Ethan pushed at Alex's hand, "What are you doing?"

Alex ignored him and continued to monitor his pulse.

Ethan said, "It hurts like fuck. How bad is it?"

Alex said, "You'll live. Just let me do my thing."

Charles said, "What is happening? What about Garrett? I wasn't gone but a minute."

Alex said, "Let's secure Ethan to the ATV and get back to the cabin."

Kit said, "It is a lodge."

Ethan said, "Yeah, it's a lodge."

Charles said, "Whatever! Ethan needs a hospital."

Kit looked over at Charles who ignored him and turned his attention back to Ethan and Alex.

Alex barked, clearly frustrated, "He needs good first aid. Then we'll decide what's next."

Kit said, "Triage?"

Alex nodded. Charles snorted in derision.

Kit stared back down the trail. "I'm open for suggestions."

Alex assessed the situation shaking his head in frustration. "We need to get to the cabin and regroup."

Kit said, "Lodge."

Charles said, "Give it a rest."

A crow cawed from somewhere high above causing the men to jump. The crow's call spurred Alex to action. Alex grabbed one of Ethan's arms and Kit took the other arm. Together they bungeed him to the backrest Kit had fashioned from ice chests.

Kit told Ethan there was no padding so brace for what would be a long and jarring ride; a factor that would have been more satisfying if only Kit knew his friend's condition more clearly. After making final adjustments Kit settled onto the driver's seat.

Charles said, "What about my ride?"

Kit looked at Alex and rolled his eyes.

Ethan said, slurring his words, "I told you guys he wouldn't make it back to the cabin by himself. Told you so."

Alex grabbed Charles by the arm and pulled him to his ATV. Together they wrestled Charles's ATV off of the stump. Charles wiped sweat from his face with the hem of his brightly colored tropical print shirt. Alex removed his Boonie hat and ran a hand through his sweaty hair.

Charles began to wipe a little tickle that he thought was sweat running down his arm but found a tick instead. He shouted, "Tick!"

Alex said, "They are the last things you need to worry about right now."

Kit said, "Shut up about ticks. Just knock it off before it digs in! We need to go now!"

Alex said, "Go. Get back to the cabin and tend to Ethan. I'll wait for Garrett. I'll search for him if he isn't here in fifteen."

Charles needed no more encouragement and mounted his four-wheeler. He started it and began driving away without looking back. After one last look at Alex, Kit followed Charles who kept to the established trail. The journey was jolting but the men did not stop until they were back at the cabin.

Garrett waited until he was certain the mysterious shooter had left the area then slowly climbed out of the tree. Once on the ground Garrett skirting inside the edge of the clearing keeping one eye on the direction he had seen the gunman leaving. Trying to move quietly was difficult as his back had yet to loosen up. Cautiously and painfully Garrett wove a circuitous path through the trees until he returned to the ATVs.

Preston, keeping to thick cover, crept toward where the sound of the ATV's revving engine had come from. He stopped and listened frequently as he silently made his way from tree to tree. Preston discovered the ATV parking site before Garrett returned. He concealed himself behind a large pine tree trunk and waited.

Garrett finally reached the ATVs and assessed the situation from behind a thick privet patch. It seemed clear until Alex stepped out from behind a tree and waved to Garrett. Alex's sudden emergence from behind a tree only a few yards away from Garrett nearly gave the older man a heart attack.

Garrett glared at Alex, "You nearly gave me a heart attack!"
"Sorry."
"Don't do it again."
Alex nodded then asked, "Were you followed?"
Garrett shook his head then turned and looked back at his path as if to make sure he was correct.

Preston LaHarpe watched from behind a tree but held his fire as he spied on the two men. He struggled to overhear the conversation as the men spoke softly. Preston noted one man was older and the other lanky and fit. Preston cupped his hand behind his ear to try to better hear the conversation and learn what was going on.

Alex's thoughts were troubled by the incongruous situation he found himself in; he had believed he had left life and death situations behind but he now found himself in a situation with untrained men that were dependent upon him and his skills for survival. Sure, Kit had hunting skills and Garrett had a law enforcement background, but only he and Garrett had ever been in actual life or death situations. And that fact worried Alex greatly.

Preston raised his Colt and took aim at the lanky man. Both men's exposed backs were toward him and with his finger on the trigger he waited them to start their machine so the noise of the engine would provide cover noise for his first shot. Target number one would be the lanky man with the rifle. The archer, target two, would be slow getting an arrow ready so he was a minimal threat.

Alex waved off Garrett's questions saying only that he would update Garrett once they were safely at the cabin. Garrett agreed and stowed his archery equipment. He kept an eye on the trail as Alex mounted his ATV. Alex kept watch as Garrett straddled his ATV. Alex motioned for Garrett to take point. Garrett put his ATV into gear and slowly aligned his ATV with the established path.

Preston reasoned that two easy kills now meant less work later. The man with the silly bandoleer might already be dead so that left only two more, the man in the Hawaiian shirt and the stocky little guy.

The ATVs idled as the men took one last look around the area. Alex was concerned about the litter they were leaving behind, worried that if their attacker rummaged through it he would have a lot of information to work with; but time was of the essence and he felt they needed to get moving now. Once they had time to regroup they could return to retrieve the abandoned items. He looked at Garrett and mouthed, 'Let's go!'

Preston braced against the tree and aimed wishing he had a rifle instead of a pistol. He was confident he could take both men with a single shot each. Preston applied a tiny bit of pressure to the trigger then felt something strike his combat boot. It was a hard tap that he couldn't ignore. Instinctively, he looked down and saw a copperhead snake preparing for a second strike. Annoyed at the interruption, he used one boot to hold the snake in place while stomping on its head with his other boot's heel. The distraction allowed Alex and Garrett to escape.

Alex and Garrett began their journey back to the cabin with frequent glances over their shoulders. The two men were blissfully unaware of how lucky they had just been. Preston, on the other hand, was fully aware of how lucky the men had been. He looked down at the mangled snake and cursed it before turning his attention to the remaining ATV and scattered contents the men had left behind.

Preston wasted no time or thoroughness rummaging through the maps and satellite photos Kit had discarded to make room for Ethan. The intrusive plans Kit had for the property became clear. Ethan's ATV was a wreck of empty bottles and jumbled fishing tackle providing no useful information for Preston.

Preston's findings disturbed him greatly. Suddenly, an unknown branch of the Carson clan was planning to turn the property into a sideshow attraction attracting unwanted scrutiny and visitors to the land bordering LaHarpe property.

Preston looked at the beaten down ATV trail and cursed the damn city folk who he regarded less highly than the traveling carneys that invaded the county seat every fall with their gypsy infested carnival nonsense and petty crime. Nuisances that came once a year could be tolerated but a year-round tourist presence would increase police patrols and surveillance making the family's tax-free income pursuits more difficult.

Preston's mind reeled under the possibilities of what else could go wrong. No matter what he did, it seemed Fate made sure his decisions and actions broke badly.

Staring at the materials littering the ground Preston debated bringing this newly discovered information, and evidence, to the family. He simply was not sure how the family would react to the news, let alone his involvement; it was a chance he was not willing to take considering what he had just learned.

It was obvious to Preston that something must be done to derail Carson's plans for turning this part of Chickasaw County into a tourist destination, but Preston feared the family would not make the obvious and necessary decision about how to handle the invading troublemakers. Preston's head began to ache as he longed for the simpler times, times that seemed to be only a few months removed.

John Lee returned to the sinkhole after watching Preston walk away. The sinkhole was cool and dark, a refuge, providing a respite from the sun and heat above ground. The air was cool, slightly dank, and smelled of earth and chemicals.

John Lee had not shown Preston how far back the sinkhole went beyond the main chamber because he didn't quite trust Preston with all of the details of his operation. As much as John Lee admired Preston's reputation, John Lee understood that Preston had been demoted, so publicly he had to go along with the family sanctioned shunning. Privately, John Lee was certain Preston had some tricks to teach him if John Lee could ingratiate himself with Preston without the family finding out about their alliance. Still, admiring the man, and learning from the man, was not the same as trusting the man.

The sinkhole was John Lee's kingdom and what he created in the sinkhole would assure his ascension in the family hierarchy. John Lee put his hands on his hips and looked around the underground laboratory imagining seeing it the first time through Preston's eyes. Looking at the setup from that perspective brought a smile of satisfaction to John Lee's face. Marketing the drug and creating a distribution method for it was John Lee's final test before being considered for promotion. Everything had been going so smoothly he could barely believe it. By secretly befriending Preston, he hoped he would learn something from Preston that would elevate his acumen and solidify his dependable and competent reputation.

John Lee knew he had a well-oiled operation in play and he felt the sinkhole was the perfect clandestine drug laboratory location. The main chamber was lit by electric lanterns placed throughout the room. Laboratory equipment and sealable tubs covered plastic folding tables and wood shelves resting on cinder block supports. The main chamber was crowded with equipment and product but allowed easy movement between the cookery and shelving. There were even beanbag chairs to provide comfortable seats while waiting on a batch to cook.

The sinkhole was twenty feet deep with a chamber off the main cavern. The depth kept the odor of chemicals and human activity from drifting up and out into the clearing. The sinkhole wasn't home, but John Lee had made it comfortable enough for long periods of cooking product while remaining out of sight. John Lee moved a plywood sheet covering an opening to a low ceilinged tunnel leading into a rear chamber of the sinkhole. John Lee smiled and turned his attention to who waited at the far end of the tunnel. Sounds of two people talking softly, with music playing in the background, drifted from the back of the short natural tunnel.

The passageway leading to the secret chamber was not lit. A single battery powered LED lantern lit a small natural chamber at the end of the rock walled tunnel. Fastened to the chamber's wall by heavy chains with comfortably padded ankle shackles were a young man and woman. The two twenty-somethings were well fed and hydrated. A twin mattress filled one side of the chamber while a five-gallon plastic bucket toilet and water bottles filled the other side. Crumpled, stained, and smelly fast food bags littered the earthen floor. A cell phone played music at a moderate volume from a small speaker on the floor next to the mattress.

As John Lee entered the chamber the pair rose to face him. The young couple was smiling with expectation. The man and woman were not fearful to see John Lee, in fact they were excited. They moved to greet him with smiles, outstretched arms. and expectant looks.

John Lee smiled back. He hugged each of the captives.

The longhaired young man said, "I'm ready for my next dose. Man, I am so ready to be your prophet. I feel elevated!"

The couple held hands as they spoke to John Lee. Their eyes were alight with anticipation of beginning a new phase of their lives as dealers of the new wonder drug John Lee had introduced them to.

The young woman bounced on the balls of her shoeless feet. Her short black hair bounced even as she ran a hand through it. "Me too. I can't wait to spread the word. Are we going to get another dose now?"

John Lee smiled and said, "Glad to see you again, too."

He was elated his experiment was going so well and that his subjects were still enthusiastic. The man and woman had been chained to the wall of the sinkhole chamber for over a week but neither asked to be freed.

The couple had been hitchhiking when John Lee had offered them a ride. During the ride John Lee learned the two wild and crazy kids loved to smoke pot and pop pills that allowed them to party all night. John Lee also learned the two travelers had a specific dream in mind and were open to making tax-free money to finance their long held dream.

After a long night of partying, the couple agreed to an offer they did not want to refuse. They agreed to become dealers for John Lee even after he warned them that being outsiders in Chickasaw County their new life would likely have a rough start. John Lee explained they would have to prove themselves first but they willingly agreed to his terms. The pair even agreed when John Lee told them he couldn't let them leave the lab while they got to learn the nuances of the product. He explained, in a matter of fact way, that he expected them to know the drug inside and out and that would make them better sales persons.

Between John Lee's sales pitch and his charm the two young lovers were sold on the idea. As young lovers hurling themselves into the great wide open they were fearless and trusting of a seemingly fantastic opportunity to pocket tax-free cash to finance their plan of opening a pot shop in Colorado. The two free spirits took being chained to the wall well; the long chains gave them enough slack to move around the chamber freely. They could use the toilet, eat, sleep, and make love without feeling restricted. Their freedom ended two feet short of the plywood sheet that served as the door of their underground chamber.

To perpetuate the ruse, John Lee had bought them new clothes for their introduction to the users in Chickasaw County. He brought them food, water, and sodas on a daily basis. All in all the two young lovers were happy and content, already under the sway of John Lee's happy pills.

John Lee smiled broadly as he said, "Yes, you can have another dose and we'll discuss getting you cleaned up and into action to promote our product in the next few days. We can't make any money without moving product, and I think you know everything about our product by now. I'll introduce you into the right people, but it is up to you to make your own connections. You could have a stash of cash within a couple of weeks."

John Lee reached into a pocket and pulled out two of the off-white pills. He held them in the palm of his hand. The young couple could not take their eyes off of the pills but they refrained from just grabbing them out of his hand. "Here take your doses and have some fun."

John Lee ceremoniously presented the young man and woman one pill each. The couple received the pills swallowing them immediately. Afterwards they thanked John Lee profusely with hugs and teary eyes. As the kids returned to sit on the mattress John Lee checked the chamber's slim amenities. The five-gallon plastic toilet bucket was only half full so he put the cover back on it and left it alone. Four rolls of toilet paper remained in the plastic wrapper. After a wink at the young lovers, John Lee left them alone. He re-secured the plywood door to cover the secret chamber entrance.

Back in the underground lab's main chamber he checked on the chemicals and equipment used to make the profitable little pills. His plan was to freely distribute the pills for two weeks then start selling them. Summer was in full swing and pasture parties and river parties were popping up every weekend giving John Lee ample opportunities to introduce his product. Time passed while John Lee checked production logs and on how well the stored product was holding up in sealed plastic tubs stockpiled in the dank sinkhole lair. All seemed right with the world.

John Lee grabbed a different legal pad and began adding names for the drug to the list he had begun weeks ago. The current list began with fun names then moved on to discreet names before ending with a few inside joke related names. John Lee wanted a name that was not on the cop's known drugs list, but at the same time would catch on fast and could be talked about freely without revealing the subject was a drug. So far he had two dozen names on the legal pad to choose from. Tabling the naming decision, again, he decided to check on his two young captives.

John Lee silently crept down the earthen tunnel to the chamber holding his test subjects. Sometimes, he would check on them and find them having sex; sometimes he would watch and record their lovemaking on his phone's camera. The two were so into each other that he believed he could just walk in and have a seat next to the bed where they were fucking and never be noticed. For now John Lee quietly watched from the darkness of the tunnel. He wondered if he could sell the recordings; everyone seemed to have a sex tape, and these two were not an eyesore, and definitely enthusiastic enough to make watching a sex tape enjoyable.

The two lovers were having sex now, unaware of anything but their own passions. John Lee smiled as he watched, he smiled for several reasons, one of which was if the drug made people fuck like wild animals, then demand for it would surely be phenomenal and the money would come pouring in far beyond his wildest dreams. John Lee watched until the man and woman both climaxed.

John Lee was constantly amazed at what people would do in the names of love and money. Watching the two young lovers cuddle after having wild, animalistic sex, despite being chained to a wall in a strange sinkhole, made John Lee feel oddly empty inside. For a moment all he wanted was someone to love him like that; he felt a wave of jealousy overcome him before turning away from the chamber.

John Lee silently returned to the main chamber and froze in his tracks at an unexpected, alarming, and disturbing sight. In the main chamber he discovered his current dealer, Billy Joe LaHarpe, and a barely dressed, buxom, blonde, teen girl in the lab. Worse yet, Preston had caught Billy Joe with his hand in yesterday's production run of the drug. John Lee froze at the sight, standing at the entrance to the low tunnel that led to the secret chamber. John Lee cleared his throat alerting the two to his arrival.

Billy Joe turned and said, "Hey, Johnnie Reb, I didn't know there was another room back there."

John Lee concealed his overwhelming feeling of anger and betrayal. Nodding at the pair he asked, "What are you doing here, Billy?" John Lee nonchalantly grabbed a sheet of plywood sliding it across the passageway's entrance. "It's the bathroom and, trust me, you don't want to go back there now."

The big-eyed girl said, "Gross." She made a disgusted face and turned away.

Billy's face reddened. At a loss for words he pulled on the woman's arm pulling her to his side. He said, "This here is Polly Ann. She's my girl."

Polly Ann nodded and stared John Lee down with that look of contempt young people so often give older people; especially before they get to know them. Her eyes returned to the tub of pills.

John Lee ignored the girl and pressed his cousin for an answer, "Billy, what are you and Polly Ann doing here? Why is your hand in my cookie jar? You didn't think I was here, did you?"

Billy looked at the tub of pills he had been caught raiding. He looked back at John Lee. His face grew red under his unruly fine, peach-fuzz soft, brown facial hair.

Polly Ann broke the awkward silence. "Billy and I are together and I just wanted to see where the magic happens. I wanted to try the new stuff ahead of everyone else. I ain't never seen a real drug lab before, excepting on TV. Don't be mad at Billy, he's in love with me. I wanted to see the lab and he just wanted to show you his new tat. He got one with different colored inks. Ain't no harm meant Mr. Sherman."

John Lee smiled and relaxed his posture although inside he was enraged by the trespass violation. Billy, his dealer to the county's teens, had grown sloppy from youthful arrogance; he had been arrested only two weeks ago for possession at a music concert. Fortunately for Billy he had only been caught with a well-resinated pipe so he had been simply fined and released.

John Lee choked back what he really wanted to say, "Okay, since you're here take a dose and kick back for a while. I've got some paperwork to finish up. But, let me see your new ink first." John Lee's mind was in turmoil over what to do about security; he knew he couldn't put a door on the sinkhole and suddenly he wondered what happened when he was away.

Billy said, "Johnny Reb, you are the best."

Polly Ann said, "Thanks. Billy always says you're the best."

John Lee smiled shyly and dug the toe of his work boot into the dirt floor of the sinkhole. He looked up at Polly and winked. "Hey, you know it's nothing. Family gotta stick together. United we stand, divided we fall, and all that. Loyalty."

Polly Ann said, "Hell, I wish I had a family like yours. Billy Joe, you got good people in your bloodline."

Billy said, "That's the truth."

Billy motioned for Polly to take a seat on one of the beanbag chairs scattered around the lab area. He pulled off his NASCAR T-shirt revealing a tattoo of a demon biker with a grinning skull and red flaming eyes. A large diamond sparkled under its right eye socket. The skull had all of its teeth and its left front tooth was shiny gold. The tattoo covered Billy's back. John Lee nodded and said that he admired it. Smiling at the compliment Billy put his shirt back on.

Polly Ann said, "It's a shame to cover it up."

Billy said, "It's a little cool down here."

Polly shrugged then turned to study the beanbag chairs. Billy looked at John Lee and winked. He nodded toward Polly Ann's ass as she bent to test the chair.

Both men watched Polly touch and evaluate each beanbag chair before deciding on which one to choose. Billy winked at John Lee knowing his cousin had admired the way Polly's young, firm, ass packed her faded, tight, denim shorts.

As Polly slowly tested the bags John Lee wondered if she was consciously showing off or simply being oblivious. After Billy's wink, John Lee felt uncomfortable and averted his eyes. Billy continued to stare at Polly's ass.

John Lee said, "Nice art work. Why did you pick that design?"

Billy said, "I don't know. Polly and me got drunk one night. I decided I wanted new ink. I picked it out of a book. She wanted me to get a Ghost Rider head but I wanted something original."

Polly plopped down into a beanbag chair then chimed in, "We picked it out of a book." She used a dirty hand to brush back her greasy bottle blonde hair.

"Yeah, we chose it together." Billy leaned over and gave Polly a kiss on the top of her head.

Polly Ann rubbed the kiss in, smiling at Billy Joe.

John Lee said, "I've got paperwork to finish. You two kick back. There's a boom box behind Polly's beanbag." John Lee smiled and winked at Billy.

Billy said, "We got our own playlist," then grabbed the nearest beanbag chair and moved it next to Polly. Polly removed an iPod from a pocket and gave one side of the earbud to Billy then put the other one in her ear. They held hands as their heads rested on each other. John Lee picked up a clipboard, pretended to look at the papers on it, and paced while he evaluated the situation.

Preston LaHarpe wandered the woods in a daze clutching one of Kit's documents in a sweaty hand. His headache grew more intense as the events of the past two months replayed in an endless loop in his mind. Preston could not stop the indignation, self-recriminations, and second guessing from swirling like a tornado in his troubled mind. Desperate for relief Preston leaned against a pine tree and quietly recited mantras he had learned in therapy. When the mantras failed to calm his mind he recited the Lord's Prayer, but nothing could dissipate the whirlwind of dark chaotic thoughts.

Continuing on Preston came across a wind downed tree and sat on its trunk re-reading the document. The document represented, to him, the end of his world planned out by someone he had not known existed. He felt a tick crawling on his arm and flicked it off with a finger wishing he could get rid of all his problems so easily.

The practical voice in Preston's mind told him the family should deal with this new threat to their way of life through conventional means like legal negotiations. But, the only thing more distasteful to the LaHarpe family than paying taxes was using a lawyer. The LaHarpe clan believed that in America's legal system the Golden Rule meant that he who had the gold made the rules. Because of the rigged system, it always proved best, so the LaHarpe's believed, to take matters into their own hands and confront the problem directly, quickly, and with finality.

But, Kit Carson's plan was already underway and soon out-of-state parties would be involved. Preston was certain that Hollywood lawyers would eat up and shit out even the most expensive Chickasaw County lawyer the LaHarpe family could hire. If a judge thought Carson's plan would bring revenue to the county nothing would stop the judge from approving Carson's plan. He thought of the adage, 'Money talks and bullshit walks'. Preston fumed.

The primal voice of Preston's mind told him to kill them all and burn their bodies by torching old man Carson's cabin. Killing the remaining Carson clan survivors would surely stop the impending invasion of big city pains-in-the-ass types.

The practical part of Preston's mind reminded him that the body count was already alarmingly high for such a short period of time and that he was pushing his luck. Future deaths must look like an accident; like city slickers let the woods beat them; at least deaths when there were bodies meant to be discovered.

House fires were common in the county and would not draw too much scrutiny; the problem was that it was summer and few house fires happened in the summer. Preston considered planting meth making evidence at the scene of the fire to mislead investigators. Law enforcement didn't mourn or dig too deep into drug related fatalities in Chickasaw County.

Benson and Carver's death investigations were still active but the scant amount of evidence had stalled all progress. Sheriff Carver's body and car had been sent to the bottom of a pond, far from his murder site, where water, catfish, and turtles would destroy most evidence in time. Carver's clothes had been burned and the ashes scattered throughout the woods. Preston took Carver's gun and sunk it in a different pond on the property without telling John Lee which one. A beautiful Desert Eagle like Carver's would be too tempting to show off or sell. Keeping the gun was too dangerous of a chance to take; it was an invitation to be caught. 'Best not to fall into temptation and betray yourself', Preston thought as he had watched the beautiful gun sink into the murky water.

Preston had told no one about killing the Thurber brothers. He had dumped their bodies in the same pond where he and John Lee had dumped Carver's body. Surely their wives were wondering where they were; but Preston doubted the widows would make much of a fuss until more time passed. The catfish and turtles would consume the fleshy evidence and their bones would sink into the muck on the bottom of the pond. Preston had also burned their clothes and scattered the ashes throughout the forest.

The Lester's would surely be missed by their clients by now. Preston wasn't sure what response drug addicts' missing persons' reports would get from the sheriff's office.

John Lee witnessed Sheriff Carver's death but Preston felt confident that John Lee could keep the murder a secret; John Lee had said nothing as Preston shot Carver in the head. John Lee was a good soldier.

Sitting alone on the tree trunk in the serene beauty of the hardwood forest Preston weighed killing the Carson group against the likelihood of local cops bringing in an outside agency, mostly likely a team of Feds, to look into a sudden surge of deaths and missing people in Chickasaw County. Preston's heart began to race and his head pounded with each heartbeat. He wasn't sure he was thinking correctly, but he was sure he was thinking determinedly.

After several long agonizing minutes the pounding in his temples and stabbing pain behind his eyes ebbed. Preston made a decision; a decision he hoped would distract and frustrate investigators. Preston would visit the Phil Coulson Charolais Farm and mutilate several head of cattle at the first sign of outside investigators. Chickasaw County had seen several instances of cattle mutilation during the 1970's which had generated sensational national headlines and a horde of curiosity seekers flooding the county and trespassing on multiple private farms.

Preston was a toddler at the height of the cattle mutilation era but he remembered people debating whether the cows were killed by aliens from outer space or by hippies in a LSD fueled ritual. Ranchers hid in trees with guns waiting to confront those responsible for butchering their cows; but no one was ever caught and eventually the mutilations ended. Preston imagined a re-emergence of cattle mutilations would generate a social media frenzy flooding the county with people that would impede the investigation. Then he recalled hearing old family tales of using the ruse of Bigfoot sightings and how that had gone almost fatally wrong; and that was long before automatic weapons and today's hunting technology.

Certain the distraction of a new round of cattle mutilations would impede any investigation Preston decided to reconnoiter the Coulson Farm the next day. Even if the mutilations themselves did not disrupt the investigators surely the crowds drawn by the sensational reports, would interfere and impede the investigation. But first, he had to kill some cows and make it look satanic or alien related somehow. Ideas swirled uncontrollably in Preston's mind.

Preston grew thirsty as his headache returned becoming a constant, disturbing, low level thumping behind his temples and ears. His mouth felt like it was coated with sand and his throat grew more constricted by the moment. His vision dimmed but it was the pounding drumbeat in his temples that distracted him the most. The unknown element at this moment was how Carson would react to the attack earlier in the day. City slickers were notoriously hard to decode especially when they were in a foreign environment.

Preston rued firing on the group, and in hindsight, he couldn't remember pulling the trigger. A rival drug gang would never go to the sheriff; but city slickers were a different breed. They may have already called the sheriff. Preston wondered if the man he had shot was dead or merely wounded.

Suddenly overcome with thirst, Preston wished he had brought bottled water with him. He folded the Carson document and stuffed it in a cargo pocket. Seeing another tick crawling on his pant leg Preston casually flicked it away. Determining his location after orienting himself, Preston realized he was closer to the sinkhole lab than the family compound. He licked his lips as he visualized the two large coolers full of drinks and snacks in the cool sinkhole. As he concentrated on ignoring his thirst, the turmoil in his mind faded. Forcing himself to focus on one thing, satisfying his thirst, Preston stood and began to walk back toward the sinkhole.

John Lee paced the hard packed earthen floor as he shuffled papers on the clipboard while one pair of young lovers enjoyed their plush captivity and another pair listened to music while relaxing on beanbag chairs in the main chamber.

Billy and Polly Ann acted as if they had no cares in the world. It seemed that the only person in the sinkhole who did have a worry was John Lee. The fact that his main dealer had thrown a monkey wrench into his plans at this stage enraged him.

The hitchhikers in the secret chamber did not know they would die sooner than later. Killing them after testing the drug had been John Lee's plan from the beginning; the hitchhikers were merely lab rats. The reality was the hitchhikers were test subjects for evaluating the drug's strength, purity, and addictive nature. John Lee thought of it as a clinical trial prior to launching a new product line.

John Lee fumed at the obstacle he was encountering here at the end of run up to release. Everything had been going so smoothly and now in one day he had revealed the lab to Preston and been betrayed by his cousin.

As for Billy and Polly Ann in the main chamber, John Lee was uncertain how to address Billy's betrayal. Billy needed to be replaced now that he had revealed he could not be trusted; but how to fire Billy without him reacting childishly and giving the operation away was the great unknown. Polly was even a greater unknown and that worried John Lee to his core. Grooming a replacement to take Billy's place would cause resentment and jealousy from within the family; but this was business, not personal; it was also his future on the line. The conundrum with finding a replacement was that all of Billy's friends were idiots just like Billy.

A commotion in the lab area slowly penetrated through John Lee's concentration drawing him back to the seating area. He hoped his secret captives were too busy and too isolated to hear the shouting and cursing coming from the main chamber. John Lee placed the clipboard on a shelf and entered the main chamber.

Billy and Polly Ann were squared off, facing each other, fists raised like bare knuckle brawlers in a fight club. Billy had a bright red hand slap impression on his cheek. Polly Ann had a swollen, bleeding, lower lip. Billy's knuckles bled. They warily circled each other, slowly, mimicking professional boxers looking for an opening. Rap music blared from the dropped earbuds. The two had yet to notice John Lee's return to the main chamber.

John Lee shouted, "What the hell are you two doing?"

The two young lovers ignored him continuing to focus only on each other. Their unblinking eyes were locked on the other person with their jaws set in grim determination and unrestrained anger.

John Lee repeated even louder than the first time, "What the hell are you two doing?"

The two youths remained focused only on each other blocking the rest of the world out. John Lee took a few steps forward but did not step between them.

He shouted again, "What the hell are you two doing?"

Billy and Polly Ann continued to ignore John Lee. His shout filled the chamber but fell on deaf ears. He shouted again, louder, and then thought about the captives in the hidden chamber.

John Lee grabbed an empty glass lab beaker and hurled it at Billy. The glass beaker hit him in the shoulder then crashed onto the hard packed floor shattering into multiple pieces. Billy shrugged at the impact of the beaker on his shoulder but never took his eyes off of Polly Ann. Polly Ann never looked away from Billy. John Lee put his hands on his hips and sighed wondering what to do next.

John Lee turned away from the pair moving toward a two-by-four piece of wood left over from constructing the shelves that supported equipment and held tubs of stored product. As John Lee took a second step toward the two-by-four he was intending to use on the back of Billy's head, he stepped on Polly's iPod and broke it. The music stopped.

Polly Ann screamed, "My iPod!" She turned toward John Lee and glared at him.

John Lee said, "Finally."

Billy said, "Oh, shit." Billy uttered the statement with unabashed fear and dread. John Lee felt the unbridled panic behind the utterance. John Lee glanced at Billy and saw soul shaking alarm on his face. John Lee experienced a moment of spine chilling fear.

John Lee turned toward Polly Ann as she unleashed a banshee scream and launched herself toward John Lee. Polly Ann's arms were fully extended in front of her and her fingers were splayed open revealing long, dirty, unpolished, jagged fingernails, that were coming straight for John Lee's face.

Billy knew the look all too well. Polly Ann's face was contorted by single-minded blind rage and that rage was focused solely on John Lee. Billy dove for Polly Ann's legs as she launched herself toward John Lee hoping to tackle Polly before she reached her target, but his out stretched hands only grazed her ankle as she raced past him.

John Lee was shocked at the consuming anger and murderous rage on the girl's face. Polly Ann was nearly upon him. Billy lay on the sinkhole floor looking terror stricken. Reacting to the crazed girl, John Lee grabbed the two-by-four in his right hand and swung with all of his might. The board caught Polly Ann on the side of the head above her ear. The blow staggered her sideways but the girl remained on her feet, blood spurting from the head wound.

Billy looked at the blood and said, "Oh, shit!"

John Lee waited for the girl to go down.

Polly Ann was dazed but not out. The men watched her green eyes slowly regain their focus. She ignored the blood gushing from the side of her head. Polly Ann stared at John Lee as he watched her lips slowly form into a snarl as she prepared for another charge at him.

John Lee held a palm out and shouted, "Stop!"

Polly Ann ignored the shout.

Billy, still lying on the dirt and rock floor, shouted at the top of his lungs, "Whack her again!"

Polly sprung forward beginning her second charge toward John Lee. She screamed a banshee wail of hate. John Lee held the board like a baseball bat and swung for the fences as Polly Ann entered the strike zone. This time the girl's head snapped hard sideways and she collapsed to the ground.

Billy rose from the dirt floor and said matter-of-factly, emotionlessly, "She has a temper. And she loved that iPod."

John Lee looked from the fallen girl to his cousin and said, "What was all of that about?"

Billy stared down at Polly Ann. He said, "She has a temper."

"No shit, bro'."

"She has a temper."

"You already said that. Why did she go crazy?" John Lee silently prayed her outburst was not a bad reaction to the drug. He hadn't seen any results like this from the pair chained in the chamber; but then the two captives were a small test sample to rely on.

Billy continued to stare at Polly Ann. "I told her that temper of hers was gonna get her in trouble someday."

John Lee shouted, "What the hell is going on?"

Billy said, "Well, we had a disagreement about rappers. Polly Ann loves rap music but I think most rap and hip-hop is shit. The lyrics are repetitious and they disrespect women and white people. I just can't take most of it. But I like the beats, mostly. Anyway, Polly Ann couldn't understand why I am okay with some white rappers but not the nigger rappers. She didn't take too kindly to me saying nigger, she kept telling me not to use the N word. She said the word hurt her ears when I said it. I told her all the rappers say it and it's a double standard that regular folks can't say nigger too. People call us white trash, trailer trash, crackers, rednecks, and all other vile names. Honky. White Bread. The police hate us as much as they do the niggers. I said it was a bullshit double standard that we can't say the same words they use all of the fucking time. That's when she went crazy on me."

John Lee shook his head as he looked at Polly. All he saw was a ninety-eight pound problem. "Billy Joe you took up with the wrong girl. You've got to be able to have a conversation with them if you want to keep a girlfriend. Jeeze."

Billy said, "We talk. You just got to know what sets her off and avoid it."

John Lee heard Billy's voice but not the words as he ran a hand through his sweaty hair and stared at Polly. John Lee's mind tried to grasp the fact that his entire operation may have just gone down the toilet because of his idiot cousin's girlfriend. Billy Joe droned on as John Lee stared at the fallen teen. Billy sensed John Lee losing focus and tapped him on his arm. John Lee returned to the moment with a startled jump.

Billy continued talking, "You remember Uncle Cletus saying that the best lovers were women who had strong periods or bad tempers? Well he was right. Polly is a wildcat in the sack. But the downside is she is prone to snap at the slightest provocation; and believe me, no one wants to be on her bad side. As you just saw for yourself."

John Lee said, "No shit."

Billy Joe looked down at Polly Ann lying on the ground and nudged her with the toe of his cowboy boot. Looking at her he said, "Thanks for saving my ass before I had to punch her good."

John Lee said, "What the fuck! Why did she turn on me?"

Billy said, "Besides her being bat shit crazy? You stepped on her iPod and broke it. She loved that thing. It is one of the few things she has left to remind her of her mom. Her mom died in the big ass Mother's Day tornado." Billy toed Polly Ann again. "Man, you knocked her out cold."

John Lee said, "You need to break it off with her."

"Can't. She too good in the hay."

John Lee said, "Got to. After this especially. But you can't let her get mad and rat us out! You can deal with angry people but you can't deal with crazy people. You've got to learn how business operates. Keep business and personal separate. So you've got to break it off with her. I know this will be hard but you've got to man up and take care of this. And you can't let her rat out the lab. Buy her off if you have to. This is your mess for bringing her here."

Billy looked at Polly Ann and said, "Can't. She knows too much. If I make her mad she's liable to bust us all as revenge now that she knows where the lab is. I told you she is crazy."

"So you say. And yet, you brought her here. Maybe I should kick your ass with this two-by-four."

Billy said, "Plus, I love her and we've been through a lot together. We're what she calls 'soulmates'."

"Billy, listen to me, if she goes nuclear over any little thing you've got a ticking time bomb on your hands. Why the hell did you even bring her to the lab if she is capable of ratting the family out?"

"I told you we're in love."

"Bullshit. You're in lust. You're not even eighteen yet. How much can you two have been through together? I can't believe you brought a crazy bitch to the lab. You are a fucking moron." John Lee enunciated each word of his last sentence with an angry tone.

Billy bowed up facing his larger cousin. "Hey you don't know anything about us. We have lives you know. Just like you and all of the other adults."

"Really?" The word was tinged with skepticism and arrogance. John Lee raised one of his thick, dark eyebrows.

"Dude, okay. But this stays between you and me. Don't ever tell Polly Ann I told you all of this. But we've had an abortion, gave each other a STD, she lost her mother and I lost my brother in the big tornado, and our lovemaking is extraordinary. We are soul mates." Billy looked down and nudged Polly with the toe of his boot trying to rouse her. "Put all that together and you got yourself a soul mate. Soul mates are for life." Billy used his booted toe on the girl again. He nudged her a little harder this time. Polly Ann gave no response.

John Lee said, "Okay, you've had a life together up to now. What happens when she wakes up? Am I going to have to look over my shoulder for her, waiting for the monthly crazies to make her come after me, just because I stepped on an iPod? What if I buy her a new iPod?"

Billy looked sheepish, "Maybe. Hard to say. That iPod was her connection to her dead mama. She took losing her mama pretty hard. Still feels the loss. Maybe a board up side her head is exactly what she needed. We won't know till she wakes up." Billy toed the girl again. Polly didn't move. "I hope you didn't put her in a coma. She ain't got no insurance."

John Lee said, "When she wakes up, can you restrain or contain her. I do not want another fight in this lab. Do you understand me?"

"Yeah, I do."

John Lee took a bottle of water and poured half of the bottle onto the girl's face. Polly Ann did not react. John Lee poured the remainder of the bottled water onto the girl. There was still no reaction from the girl.

John Lee felt panic rise like the first taste of vomit when you know you can't hold it back. Everything was falling apart. Billy just was slow getting to the truth; John Lee wondered how he would react.

Billy looked down at the girl and shouted, "Polly Ann! Wake up!" Polly remained motionless, lying on the floor, between the two men.

Billy knelt down next to the girl and shouted again.

Polly Ann made no reply. Billy looked up at John Lee then wiped wet hair away from her face. He looked at the head wounds and called to her again. Polly remained still; Billy stared at her as he touched her hand.

John Lee realized what had happened and his heart sank. He was surprised the younger man hadn't caught on yet. John Lee wondered how Billy would react when he realized his soulmate was dead. John Lee adjusted his grip on the two-by-four board in case Billy took her death badly.

The splashing water had soaked Polly's Duck Dynasty middrift cut T-shirt and her firm braless breasts were clearly visible through the wet, thin, cotton fabric. John Lee couldn't help but wonder what the girl was like in bed. He tried to turn away but couldn't. Still kneeling beside Polly Ann, Billy looked up at John Lee and said, "Dude, I think she's dead." Billy began to cry.

14

> Now I'm reliving my whole damn life
> And it's a shame that I can't remember
> And now I'm living the same damn lie
> It's a shame, but nothing's forever
>
> -Seether

Ethan was lying on the oak dining table, bandaged, staring at the ceiling of the cabin. He ignored the huddle of people staring at him while they spoke in whispers about him. The heavy, thick leather, bandoleer he had been wearing, the subject of so much ridicule, rested on the floor next to the table. Alex had removed the bullet with hemostats taken from the first-aid kit then expertly stitched the wound closed because no one could find any super strong glue to use. Bandages from the cabin's first aid kit covered the grisly wound.

Ethan used his good arm to adjust the pillow for his head as he listened to the men discuss the situation. Ethan had taken several pain pills Alex had found in the first-aid kit, chasing them down with a bottle of water. When no one was looking at him Ethan took two of his own prescription pills and chased them with a beer. Finally, the pain was lessening and Ethan smiled at the ceiling as the others conversed nearby.

Alex pointed at Ethan, "One very lucky idiot there. Ethan is very lucky that god-awful shell belt and the distance of the shot minimized the damage. That and the fact it was a long range pistol shot, not a rifle shot."

Ethan said, "Who shot me?"

The men all turned as one to look at Ethan. Ethan smiled at them.

Kit said, "Don't know. Yet."

Ethan mumbled, "Well, this will change everything now that the animals are shooting back. "

Alex shook his head in despair and said, "Yeah."

Charles interrupted with urgency, "We need to contact the sheriff now! Whoever shot at us can follow our path back here and do God only knows what next! We almost lost a friend out there today and whoever shot Ethan knows where we are."

Ethan cooed, "That's sweet."

Alex said, "We did not lose a man! There's no need to panic. They didn't fire again once we started moving. They're not insurgents and they didn't seem intent on following up."

Garrett eyed Alex, "Insurgents?"

Alex shrugged it off, "Old habits die hard."

Kit said, "Friendly folks don't usually shoot at strangers. And even folks down here usually shout at trespassers before shooting at them."

Garrett countered, "He was obscured but I saw the shooter leave. He was an agile mountain sized man who didn't seem interested in following up by chasing us down. I'd give him props for his woods skills. I don't know how he moved in that tree without shaking it like King Kong. I couldn't ID him in a lineup but he has skills. I think he just reacted to Ethan shooting into the trees near him."

Charles nearly screamed, "Why was there a man hiding in the trees watching us?"

Kit shrugged, "Probably a poacher waiting by the wallow and we blew his setup."

Garrett said, "A poacher probably would have a rifle, not a pistol."

Ethan said, "So, we're sure it wasn't a bird that shot me?"

Kit ignored Ethan and said, "Yeah, that sounds right."

Charles said, "Ethan has a bullet wound in his shoulder. We need to report that. We need to get him to a hospital."

Kit started to speak but Ethan interrupted before Kit could begin. "No, we do not. We don't need to do neither of them. No."

Kit looked at Ethan.

Charles looked at Ethan.

Alex and Garrett looked at Kit.

Charles looked around the assembly searching for support.

Ethan struggled to sit up, grimaced then said, "I don't have health insurance." The pain pills made him unable to lie with a straight face.

Kit snorted in disbelief and said, "Dude, your cougar wife wouldn't let you go golfing without health insurance. She's got health and life insurance policies on your sorry ass. What gives, really? Does Martha think you're somewhere else?"

"No.'

Ethan struggled to maneuver into a sitting position with his legs dangling off the table. Once positioned Ethan said, "See, Alex stitched me up just fine. I'd rather Martha not know about this until she absolutely has to know. What happens in Chickasaw County stays in Chickasaw County." He lifted a half-full warm beer from the table and offered the raised can as a toast. No one reacted to his gesture.

Charles said, "You can't hide a bullet wound forever. Unless, that is, you two live separate lives under a shared roof. Has it come to that?"

Ethan stared at Charles as he said, "No."

Kit looked around the room and saw no resistance in any of the men's faces save Charles who put on his most displeased look and crossed his arms. All of the men except Charles were obviously ready to leave Ethan to his own devices and consequences.

Kit stared at Ethan debating what to do. Ethan was smiling but none of the men were sure what he was smiling about. Kit wondered why so many people got lucky breaks but so many more deserving people never got that one lucky break allowing them to change the direction of their lives. Kit felt he was witnessing his one lucky break, courtesy of Grandpa Ulysses, slip from his grasp.

Charles knocked on the table, "Hey. We still haven't determined why a guy with a pistol was in a tree watching us."

Kit said, "Okay, first things first. The reason we were sniped will come next. As for Ethan's situation the story is simple. When Martha asks what happened you say it was a ricochet. We don't talk about this unless we have to, and by have to I mean whoever shot at us comes here and tries something or ambushes us in the woods again. I don't want to put a damper on any kind of business deal with a report of trigger happy survivalists living around here. It's best we let Hollywood think what it wants of southerners without confirming it."

Charles said, "I can't believe you're saying that. I thought we were supposed to get wiser as we get older."

Kit said, "Wiser in the things we keep encountering. We can only adapt what we know to new situations. In this case Ethan learned the lesson and we benefit from it."

Ethan said, "What lesson? That birds shoot back now?"

Charles shook his head and walked away to begin staring out the kitchen window worrying about possible attackers.

Garrett walked to the back door to take a look at their vehicles. He scanned the area and breathed a sigh of relief the food truck appeared untouched.

Alex gathered the blood stained rags, bandages, and Ethan's bloody shirt dumping the pile into the kitchen garbage. After washing his hands twice he walked to the front door and paused. The men looked after him. Alex turned and said, "We may have unfriendlies looking to do us harm. I'm checking the perimeter. It is the prudent thing to do." Alex patted his sidearm and pointedly stared at Garrett's sidearm. "Keep alert. Situational awareness at all times. United we stand strong, divided we fall." He turned and left the cabin.

Garrett leaned in close to Kit and whispered, "We need to watch him. PTSD."

Charles paced the cabin floor shaking his head and wiping sweat from his brow. "Look this isn't right. We need to get the hell out of here before somebody actually dies. Right now! I've got two kids who depend on me. I can't be the guy we actually lose today!"

Ethan said, "And I thought you thought we were all equally un-expendable."

Kit said, "Maybe they thought we were trespassing on their side of the line and what happened was a warning shot gone wrong."

Charles nearly shouted, "What does that matter? They shot first and asked no questions. Haven't you ever heard of the Hatfield and McCoy feud? That shit is real. Even today. Some people are just born wired wrong and operate in a way we'll never understand. You encounter crazy people dozens of times every day!"

Kit said, "You're over reacting."

Charles pointed at Ethan's wound and said, "Ask Ethan if he thinks I'm over reacting."

Ethan said, "I do think he's over-reacting. I'm the one with a bullet hole in my shoulder. I might not be thinking clearly but I definitely say no hospital!"

Garrett spoke, sounding grandfatherly, "Kit, you still see dollar signs from the TV show projects and that is clouding your judgement. Remember, the man shot without warning. It doesn't matter if they can aim or not, the shot proved they are dangerous. And have little regard for life or honor. You're walking into unknown territory and today should make it clear that there is violence down here just like back in the city."

Garrett took a breath before continuing, "If this is a drug outfit you absolutely must get local cops involved and the situation under control before a TV show will even think of taping anything way out here. This is Deep South backwoods terra incognito to those Hollywood people. The remoteness is a lure and a detriment at the same time. Those kinds of people believe the movies Southern Comfort and Deliverance are documentaries."

Kit looked at his neighbor, "You are right, dollar signs and an escape sign are coloring my decisions."

Ethan said, "If you get cops involved we'll have to tell the truth about how I got shot. I don't want Martha to find out. Period."

Charles stopped pacing and folded his arms across his chest. "I can't stay here while you guys debate what to do."

Kit said, "Look, stop panicking. If Garrett is right, as he frequently is, and they are drug dealers they made their point. If they wanted one of us dead they wouldn't have shot Ethan with a pistol from fifty yards plus away. And, if they only wanted to scare us off, they made their point. Following us back here and attacking us here would be overkill and necessitate an appropriate response from us. A response that could involve the sheriff or another kind of attention they do not want."

Garrett looked at Kit. "You are knee deep in bullshit rationalization. You like that position because it favors your purpose."

Ethan said, "Garrett, you sound like my wife. Always has to have the last word including a dissertation on why I'm wrong and why I need to come around to her correct way of thinking."

Garrett and Charles said in unison, "Sometimes the wife is right."

Ethan snorted wincing from the pain of movement. "Yeah, that's a given. Even when they're wrong, they're still right. But I think the combination of hormones, menopause, and insomnia has replaced the woman I knew with a pod person. I don't think a Dr. Phil and Dr. Oz super team-up intervention could fix her at this point."

Charles snorted, "You mean to say you didn't think about menopause when you married a cougar?"

Kit added his thoughts to the conversation, "It doesn't matter what age you marry them; all of those issues come with time if they weren't part of the deal from the beginning."

Charles said, "You haven't been married long enough to anyone to reach the so-called Golden Years."

Ethan said, "Not everybody gets a good woman the first time." He looked pointedly at Kit.

Kit showed Ethan his middle finger and said, "Hey, we were young and neither of us were really ready for adulthood."

Charles said, "For you it was always the thrill of the chase not the end game. You were too much of a player to convince the one you really loved that you really loved her. You are a slave to psychologically driven karma."

Kit held up his other middle finger and glared at Charles but refrained from adding words. Charles nodded in silent victory.

Ethan brought the conversation back to him. "Too bad the shooter didn't get me in the head. I'll have hell to pay to from Martha for God knows how long over how this outing turned out. I think she is expecting a Hangover type weekend, but this is party out of bounds by her standards. Probably by most people's standards. I went to play in the woods with my bros and got shot. Kit, maybe we should just say I got abducted by aliens then I can stay down here and be your on-site manager. I'd rather shit in the outhouse year round than listen to the list of everything I did wrong and have Martha try to ground me. She's got a memory like a fucking elephant for every bad decision she thinks I've made."

Kit said, "Jesus, Ethan, I didn't know it was that bad at home."

Ethan said, "Only for the last year and a half. I thought I had the Law of Unintended Consequences beat. I saw signs of the change coming on, but I thought her hormone pills would keep her emotions level. But I was oh so wrong. She doesn't even realize that she has changed and won't listen to me when I try to show her. I just don't know what to do anymore. I'm damned if I do and damned if I don't. So I just keep my head down and power through the difficult times."

Kit shook his head and said, "Hmm."

Charles said, "There is no way this is going to end well. I'm going to take a shit and think this through. I hate to leave you guys but my boys depend on me. I'm no good to them dead. Once I get to cell service again, I will call the sheriff for you." Charles turned on his heel and disappeared into the cabin's bathroom.

Ethan asked no one in particular, "Someone bring me my toiletry kit and three fingers of bourbon."

Kit turned to Garrett said, "What do you suggest we do?"

Garrett said, "You need to call the sheriff. But, first, we need to fortify the cabin more if we are staying. I mean it was only one guy that I saw and he looked to be acting unilaterally. He made his point, scared the shit out of us, and he wins. Isn't that what you want me to say?"

Ethan said more forcefully, "Would someone please bring me my toiletry kit and a glass with three fingers of bourbon in it?"

Kit looked at Garrett, "I'll be right back to talk about that. Ethan, chill, I'll do it."

Kit entered the narrow bunkroom, found Ethan's bunk, and then rummaged through the messy pile erupting from haphazardly unpacked luggage until he found the toiletry kit. Garrett had poured Ethan's drink and gotten a beer for himself and Kit by the time Kit returned with Ethan's toiletry kit.

Kit tossed the kit to Ethan and took his beer from Garrett.

Garrett said, "I'm just providing a sounding board. I see the different points of view to cover all of our bases. No hard feelings. As the old guy I felt like I should be the voice of reason."

Kit took a long drink then nodded his head.

Ethan said, "Thanks, both of you."

Kit and Garrett turned away from Ethan and walked to the open front door of the cabin. Alone, Ethan removed a bottle of pills from his toiletry kit. He took a pill then washed it down with a shot of whiskey. As he tried to return the bottle to his toiletry kit he dropped it and the bottle landed with a thud on the hardwood floor.

Garrett turned and frowned at the dropped bottle. Ethan waved off help with his good arm, "No help needed. But, thanks. You've heard the expression, 'death by a thousand cuts', this is a slow soul crushing death by a thousand cuts, or in terminology from Garrett's era, a thousand nags. Martha doesn't hear it so there's no talking to her about it. So get off of my ass about pills, they're the least of my problems, and not one of your problems!"

Garrett held his hands up, palms facing Ethan, and backed away. Ethan nodded signifying his appreciation while looking embarrassed over having blurted out his home life situation to them.

Kit glanced at the bottle that Ethan had dropped wondering if he had dropped it before or after getting a pill. Ethan stared at the bottle then said, "Well, I guess that shows I need to wait a minute before my next dose."

Kit said, "Aren't you a little frequent on those pills?"

"Don't worry, Mother, I'm not a member of the Hemlock Society. The pills are mine, prescription, and legal in the United States of America. I'm going to bed now. I'll see you in the A.M."

Ethan wobbled as he bent to pick up the bottle. He put the bottle in a pocket and grabbed his drink. Kit nodded as Ethan staggered toward the bunkroom. Garrett watched Ethan use the wall for support as he disappeared through the bunkroom door.

Garrett turned to Kit, "We need to watch him."

Charles emerged from the bathroom. "I think you should have forced him to show you the pills."

"Not worth the effort. I know he used to know his limits; I'm trusting he still does."

Charles snapped, "Damn it, Kit. We aren't the same people we were back then. Yes, our core might be the same but we, our beliefs, our personalities, are different now. We. Are. Older. Now. You may not have anyone depending on you but I do. I'll stay tonight but I think we should all take turns standing guard, just in case whoever shot Ethan is OCD or a true psychopath and feels compelled to finish us off and not just scare us off. I'm sleeping with my gun in my bunk so I suggest no one startle me."

Kit said, "Good idea. Garrett and I will set a watch schedule and wake you when it is your turn to stand guard. Remember, Alex is out there scouting and he did this shit for a living. I feel safe."

Charles said, "Okay. I'm going to have nightmares over this."

Kit said, "Take a chill pill." Charles glared at Kit and turned red.

Garrett said, "Go to bed. Rest. You will feel better, clearer, in the morning."

Charles nodded, "Okay." He sounded defeated. "Just wake me up when it's my turn to stand watch."

Garrett said, "Will do."

Kit said, "Don't get into it with Ethan. You both need rest and no more arguing."

Charles snorted in reply.

Kit watched Charles disappear into the dark bunkroom. The atmosphere in the cabin lightened, despite the dire situation, once Ethan and Charles had disappeared into the dark bunkroom.

Garrett repeated, "We need to fortify the cabin more."

Kit looked around the cabin's interior; yesterday the hand crafted cabin seemed formidable, but today, the eighteen inch thick log walls didn't feel so substantial and the tornado shutters protecting the windows seemed inadequate. The stone chimney looked large enough to let two Santa's in at a time and even with a metal roof, the log sides could be made to burn.

Kit said, "Tell me what you're thinking regarding fortifying this place and then we'll see what Alex has to add when he returns."

The living room grew silent with only the noises of Charles and Ethan getting their bunks organized rising over the insects outside the windows. Charles grunted and Ethan began singing a Jimmy Buffett song to annoy Charles. Charles told Ethan to shut up but he only sang louder, *"This storm may pass, it was too late. Hey, we ain't the kind to evacuate. The impact zone is callin' out my name. Sea monster night pulling nothing but pride and fear, St. Christopher may not get our asses outta here, flooded roads, trailer parks, maybe a tornado lurkin' in the dark, the perfect life, riding to eternity."*

Eventually the commotion in the bunkroom settled. Garrett shook his head at Kit then turned to look out the window into the darkness. Kit quietly walked to the bunkroom and closed the door. He returned to stand beside Garrett and said, "Sometimes I wonder what I've done to deserve all this this. I must have really shit on someone once and forgot to make amends."

15

> I'm like a mad dog; I'm on a short leash
> I'm on a tight rope, hanging by a thread
> I'm on some thin ice, you push me too far
> Aw, it's just the little things that drive me wild
>
> - Alice Cooper

Billy Joe looked up at John Lee, tears flooding his eyes, and wailed, "She's dead! You killed her! I'll kill you!"

John Lee took a step back as Billy stood to confront him with clenched his fists. John Lee raised the board and said, "You said 'whack her again'. I thought you knew what you were doing."

Billy wiped tears from his eyes as John Lee looked for any sign of Billy calming down. John Lee planted his feet and tensed up, preparing for whatever Billy might do.

Billy was cycling between sad and angry rants toward John Lee as he stared at Polly Ann's body lying on the dirt floor. John Lee hoped his cousin would calm down; a prolonged fight in the lab would ruin everything forcing downtime in production. Downtime in production when launching the new drug was this close was not acceptable. John Lee would see to it that there would be no production delays no matter what it took to accomplish his goal.

Billy suddenly grabbed a large glass beaker and lunged forward swinging the beaker at John Lee. John Lee blocked the brunt of the attack with his forearm but a shard of glass gouged a long gash in his arm. The blocking move redirected Billy's momentum causing the youth to stumble past John Lee. John Lee's arm went numb and dropped to his side as blood gushed from the cut. Billy regained his balance and grabbed another beaker for a second attack.

John Lee screamed, "For God's sake, Billy, calm down! This isn't going to make anything better!"

"You killed my girlfriend!" John Lee watched the look on Billy's face as the sorrow and anger over losing Polly hit home releasing an explosion of rage.

Billy rushed forward swinging the glass beaker at John Lee's face. John Lee deflected and shattered the beaker with the board sending broken glass flying in all directions. Flying glass shards ripped gashes in John Lee's left cheek just under his eye.

John Lee screamed in pain. Billy prepared to charge again.

John Lee dropped the two-by-four onto the dirt floor stunned by the pain and shocked by closeness of the wounds to his eye. He doubled over in pain, hands to his face, and Billy took the unguarded moment to land a kick to John Lee's chin. The punt like kick flipped John Lee backwards onto his back. He was conscious, barely, but too stunned to move. Billy lifted the two-by-four with both hands and prepared to smash the piece of lumber down on John Lee's head.

As Billy took a deep breath and started his downward swing, a gunshot rang out. The gunshot was deafening in the rocky sinkhole. Billy lurched grotesquely forward as the bullet shattered his spine and exploded his heart. Blood and tissue covered John Lee as Billy collapsed face down on top of him. Blood from the hole in Billy's chest flowed over John Lee. John Lee, barely conscious, remained motionless under Billy's body. Preston wondered if John Lee was still alive.

Preston thought he heard screams cutting through the gunshot report ringing in his ears. He looked around and saw only the dead girl, Billy Joe, and John Lee. The sinkhole smelled of blood, urine, sweat, and chemicals. Preston marveled at how much had changed in the short time since he had left the sinkhole.

Preston LaHarpe stood perfectly still, gun in hand, surveying the sinkhole. The scene around him was unexpected carnage and it made his head hurt even more. All he had returned to the sinkhole for was a bottle of water from the ice chest. What he had found was chaos and death and a cave full of questions.

After quietly climbing down the metal ladder Preston discovered the body of a teen girl. Next he came upon John Lee incapacitated and about to miss what was to be his last moment of life before his skull was bashed in like the dead girl. One body and a homicidal male still wielding the apparent murder weapon, preparing to use said lumber on John Lee was all Preston needed to see to end the rampage. Preston had pulled his Colt and fired into the board wielding man's back.

Holstering his Colt Preston noted that John Lee was alive enough to explain what had happened. Preston's ears rang but he still thought he heard voices and screams through the aural fog. He considered that the screams could be coming from the voices shouting in his head as it became increasingly difficult to quiet the mental chaos. Answers were all that Preston wanted and getting answers meant getting John Lee functional as soon as possible.

Preston stood perfectly still in the center of an enigma. He glanced behind him for another intruder before realizing anyone lurking would have surely made his move by now. Preston gathered his thoughts and opened the cooler; he grabbed two cold bottled waters then plopped down into a beanbag chair. Preston drank the first bottle of water in one long gulp. He savored the second water, sipping it slowly as he surveyed the underground laboratory. He admired the laboratory setup but would never tell John Lee; but he hoped aiding and abetting the younger man would send a message to the family that he had learned his lesson and was a team player.

In the back of the sinkhole the two runaways had heard raised voices then the single gunshot. Then all was silent. After their initial calls for John Lee went unanswered they grew terrified. Briefly, the two captives desperately looked for a place hide before realizing the chains that bound them would lead straight to their hiding place, even if there had been cover to hide behind or under.

Minutes passed with no other sounds besides their staccato breathing. The sinkhole was eerily quiet to the young lovers, suddenly feeling more like a dungeon than a secret drug lab. The lovers, hand in hand, crept forward, toward the plywood sheet covering the chamber's entrance. They stopped short of the plywood, stymied at the end of their chains, feeling like prisoners and for the first time fearful for their futures. Together they strained to hear any sounds coming from beyond the plywood door but their fearful hearts pounded in their ears muting all other sounds.

Preston grabbed John Lee's attacker's arm pulling the body off of John Lee. Preston looked at the attacker's face and felt his legs grow weak. The body was that of a distant cousin. Preston recalled the kid's name was Billy. He thought he had heard the boy called Billy the Kid because during the winter months he favored wearing a black duster resembling a long rider cowboy. Preston backed away from the body and rubbed his dirty hands through his hair and over his face. Preston felt everything he had worked for, all he had accomplished, spiraling away into a void. The air left Preston's stomach. He glanced at John Lee and felt to urge to stomp him to death, after he explained everything, of course.

Preston collapsed back into a beanbag chair. There was no way this was going to end well, he was sure of that. He had killed a family member, an extended family member, not a member of the LaHarpe compound proper, but a family member all the same. And this was happening so soon after his banishment. And the body count was growing so fast Preston felt he was an instrument of some power greater than himself pulling strings he had no power to cut.

Preston gathered his composure and opened two bottles of cold water. He poured both bottles simultaneously onto John Lee's face. John Lee regained consciousness, sputtering through an aching jaw that Billy's kick had nearly broken. After a few moments John Lee sat up feeling the cut under his eye and examining the deep gash on his forearm.

Preston stared at John Lee without speaking. John Lee struggled to his feet and opened one of the coolers. He pulled out a can of beer that he opened with difficulty as Preston silently watched. After drinking half the can in one draw, he sat in a beanbag across from Preston.

John Lee said, "This looks bad. I know."

"It is bad."

"Yes. It is bad."

"What happened?"

John Lee stood, "I'll tell you in a second." He walked into the lab area. John Lee began searching around the floor and behind beanbag chairs loudly mumbling toward the dirt floor.

Preston said, "What happened here? I wasn't gone that long." Preston could not believe he had been away that long, but evidence on the floor of the dirty hole skewed his recollection of the day's passage of time and brought the ache back to his head.

John Lee continued searching without talking. He rolled Polly's body over and found what he was looking for. John Lee sat on the dirt floor and rummaged through Polly Ann's purse discarding things onto the floor with abandon. After the main section had been thoroughly searched he began exploring the smaller pockets.

Preston said, "What are you doing?"

"The crazy bitch has a purse. I'm going to see if she has some pain meds. My jaw is killing me."

"Did he kill the girl too?"

"No."

"Then who did?"

"I did."

"Sit down and explain all of this to me."

John Lee ignored Preston as he used one hand to rummage through the Polly Ann's purse. Frustrated by the clutter in the handbag he dumped the remaining contents onto the floor of the sinkhole. A bottle rolled off to the side of the main pile. A felt tip pen had been used to write 'For Cramps' on the side of the bottle. John Lee opened the bottle and looked at the pills. They looked like common pain killers produced as a generic store brand. He took four pills and chased them down with the remaining beer. John Lee pulled two cans of beer from the cooler then tossed one to Preston.

Preston said, "Did you find your pain killers?"

"Yes. I'm hoping they are pretty strong since they are for menstrual cramps and the like."

Preston said, "Yeah? Give me some."

John Lee tossed Preston the bottle. Preston took four pills and chased them with the first half of the cold beer. Afterwards he stared at John Lee, waiting for an explanation.

John Lee stared at Preston as he rubbed his injured cheek with the cold can. "I guess you want to hear the story?"

"What do you think, you dumb fucker?"

"I'll tell you what I think." John Lee unleashed a loud scream of frustration and threw the half-full beer can into a table holding glass beakers and burners causing a loud commotion of breaking glass and clanging metal. His sudden scream followed by the sounds of breakage seemed unnaturally loud in the rock walled chamber.

Startled by the new sounds in the main chamber the runaways locked in the secret chamber began screaming for help. Their voices were muted by the plywood sheet acting as the door, but there was no denying others were present in the sinkhole. The captives rattled their chains and screamed at the plywood sheet.

Preston cocked his head and looked at John Lee. John Lee tried to look innocent ignoring the screams. Preston made a subtle head movement that shouted 'What now?'

John Lee looked thoroughly defeated as he unsuccessfully fought back tears of pain, frustration, and looming failure. Preston could not tell what John Lee was experiencing, something emotional, physical, or other. But something damn powerful was causing man tears to well up.

John Lee wiped his face, then got a new beer from the cooler. He looked at Preston who nodded, hoping a second beer would clear his muddled mind. Preston opened the beer feeling confused and uncertain as to what was real and what was not. He felt he had fallen down Alice's rabbit hole where John Lee was a southern Mad Hatter in a surreal Quinton Terratino directed movie written by LSD inspired monkeys fueled by energy drinks. Several of the voices in his head laughed at the imagery. Preston put a hand on his head; it hurt even in the cool air of the sinkhole. John Lee seemed to be ignoring the muted screams, but Preston was sure the sounds were real.

John Lee grimaced as he struggled to open his beer can. "I hope the pain meds kick in soon."

"John Lee Sherman, who is that screaming and raising a ruckus back there?"

John Lee took a long drink of cold beer. "You still got some bullets in that big hog leg revolver of yours?"

"Yes. Why do you want to know?"

"Come with me. I have two people I need you to kill. After that I'll explain everything."

16

> Trust yourself to do the things that only you know best
> Trust yourself
> Trust yourself to do what's right and not be seconded guessed
> -Bob Dylan

Garrett and Kit grew more concerned about Alex's absence as the night dragged on. Alex's extended absence left the two men imagining the worst had happened. They had taken turns standing watch, and waiting, wondering if they should go search for Alex.

Now, as dawn brightened the sky, Kit and Garrett stood by the windows watching the forest ecosystem change from the night shift to the day shift. The sun was peeking over the treetops when the men heard engine noise from the forest. They listened to the sound as it slowly grew louder. The motorized vehicle was slowly coming toward the cabin.

Kit grabbed his rifle and braced it on the windowsill. A smothering blanket of dread enveloped Kit as he imagined the unknown assailant boldly driving into the clearing with a dead Alex slung over the cargo rack of an ATV. Kit had protective cover and a wide field of fire overlooking the clearing; none of which meant a thing if Alex was a hostage or dead.

Garrett took up an offensive position beside the front door. He checked his handgun then returned it to its holster.

Kit said, "No arrows?"

Garrett said, "Time for more than a single shot weapon."

Kit was happy the bunkroom had no windows which meant only three sides of the cabin were vulnerable. The front had one window, the garden side had one window, and the rear had a single window next to the back door. Kit felt the cabin was as secure as they could make it. The motor noise was closer now.

Garrett said, "Stay sharp."

Soon an ATV emerged from the thick forest and entered the clearing. Kit and Garrett breathed an audible sigh of relief. Alex drove Ethan's ATV looking solemn and focused. All of Kit's cargo that had been discarded to make room for Ethan was piled onto the back of the ATV and secured with bungee cords. The pile swayed as the ATV bumped over the rough terrain.

Kit and Garrett exited the cabin relief obvious on their faces. Alex parked Ethan's ATV next to the others. Kit and Garrett walked toward Alex with obvious relief showing on their faces.

As Kit and Garrett neared, Alex asked, "How's my patient?"

Garrett said, "Breathing but still sound asleep."

Alex said, "Where's Chas?"

Garrett said, "Still sound asleep."

Kit said, "Where were you all night?"

Alex turned toward the forest, "Keeping watch. Garrett said he only saw one guy and I think whoever shot Ethan is long gone. I'm thinking it was an unfortunate isolated incident. But, you've got a lot of animal movement at night in your woods by the way." Alex emphasized the words 'a lot'.

Alex continued, "Whoever shot Ethan knows the animal trails and uses them to disguise their own travel movement. I don't think they planned to ambush us because their weapon was a handgun. If they had shot Ethan with a rifle, he'd be dead or more badly injured. So, the encounter was either unlucky happenstance or it was local meth heads trying to scare off rivals. Maybe once the county knows about the television shows and potential revenue coming to town the local drug groups may chill so they don't bring undue attention to themselves. But you never really know."

Kit said, "I said that last night but Garrett said I was rationalizing."

Alex said, "You were. I'm basing my report on solid reconnaissance."

Kit said, "Garrett said we should fortify the cabin. What do you think?"

Alex said, "Not a bad idea. I think we can modify it without making fortifications permanent or making it look like a last stand."

Kit looked around the grounds as his vision of an enjoyable profitable business dissolved. He slung his rifle over his shoulder and let the weight of it rest on the shoulder sling as he sighed.

"So, what's next?"

Alex said, "I'm not sure. Keep an eye out while I check on Ethan. I'll evaluate the cabin and report back with my recommendations. We can see if they match up with Garrett's. One of you can keep watch while the other one cooks up a breakfast for the group. An army moves on its stomach and hungry soldiers are a nasty lot."

Kit said, "Okay. I'll keep watch and let Garrett cook. I really need to learn the lay of the land."

Garrett said, "Bacon and eggs and fried potatoes and hot coffee for all coming up."

Alex nodded then walked toward the cabin to check on Ethan. Garrett and Kit looked at each other. Garrett winked at Kit then followed Alex. Kit unslung his beloved Winchester and crept toward the tree line. Even with the sun rising Kit could not see more than twenty feet into the forest. The dense shadows and breeze shaken limbs made the forest appear ominous and danger filled. Kit thumbed the Winchester's safety off and entered the dark forest.

Dawn. John Lee and Preston had spent the entire night talking, planning, and, surprisingly, bonding. John Lee was grateful for Preston's help and told the older man everything. Preston was taking it hard that there were so many family activities going on that he was unaware of, but he maintained a stoic face as John Lee elaborated. Preston realized his place in the family was not exactly what he thought it was; and that had been true, although kept secret from him, even prior to his banishment.

There was no sense of time down in the bowels of the sinkhole as all above ground sounds were muted and the temperature stayed consistent around the clock. Limited natural light came through the opening in the ground, but interior light in the chambers came from LED bulbs, strung along the natural ceiling and walls, powered by the solar energy system,.

The men had piled the bodies of Polly Ann and Billy in the deeper, recessed, chamber with the bodies of the two hitchhikers. The chamber was cool so the bodies would keep for a while. Preston wondered what four more bodies would do to the murky ponds that were his body dumpsites.

The men had consumed beer and pills through the night and were feeling no pain by dawn. Sunlight finally began to brighten the bottom of the sinkhole.

Overnight Preston had discovered that he enjoyed the effects of John Lee's pills. They found themselves idly cleaning the laboratory area as they talked and moved around the sinkhole. The fresh blood had soaked into the dirt floor and the glass and broken equipment was swept into an out of the way corner. A mix of left over lumber was stacked next to the traffic path.

Beads of sweat soaked Preston's and John Lee's faces and pooled under their armpits and their hearts raced, but the men paid no heed to the accelerated rate because they felt good, they felt alive, but above all else, they felt energized. They spoke rapidly, often over each other's words. The laboratory was mostly restored to its pre-fight condition and Preston was pacing as John Lee sat in a beanbag worrying over the remains of Polly Ann's iPod trying to piece the device back together so he could hear what was on the playlist that made the crazy girl go homicidal.

Preston opened one of the ice chests and said, "Damn, we're out of beer, water, and soda."

John Lee said, "Check the cooler from the other room. And double check the girl's purse to see if I missed any loose pain pills. I kinda like 'em."

Preston rummaged through the contents of Polly Ann's purse but found nothing useful. He shook his head at John Lee.

John Lee said, "At least we have an endless supply of my product. I need a name for it. It needs to be something catchy. You got any ideas?"

"You want to name it?" Preston snorted in derision.

Preston moved toward the second ice chest and noticed the growing light of dawn brightening the sky above the gaping mouth of the sinkhole. He grabbed the last two beers from the cooler and walked back to John Lee handing him a beer.

Preston said, "It's a new day. The first day of the rest of our lives."

John Lee said, "We're gonna do this?"

"Do what?"

John Lee said, "What we talked about."

"Yeah, I think it's the only way. We can't let Carson bring a bunch of outsiders down here. They'll make the cops work harder. There'll be yahoos trespassing and spooking the animals and just too much activity. We've got to sour the deal so much that no one will even think about coming down here and disrupting our lives and business again."

John Lee looked up at Preston and said, "Just run it by me once again. I know we worked it out but my memory is a bit fuzzy."

"You'll need to have your shit together when we do this."

"Yeah, yeah. Just remind me of what we discussed. We covered a lot of ground last night."

Preston grew suddenly irritated at John Lee but needed his help to pull the planned attack off. Preston silently studied John Lee for a long moment as the smaller man grew increasingly uncomfortable under Preston's withering glare.

John Lee, feeling the need to speak to break the spell, said, "I just want to be clear."

Preston sat in a beanbag chair next to John Lee. "Okay, since we have four bodies to account for we must shift the blame to someone else, somewhere else. This is an opportunity to take care of two problems at one time. We go take care of this Kit Carson fellow, and all of his friends, so they can take the blame for these bodies and keep attention off of us.

"You scratch my back and I scratch your back. After Carson's group is dead we move the kids' bodies to the cabin then burn the cabin and everybody inside to the ground. Ashes to ashes and our sins are absolved and evidence destroyed. It should look like a drug operation by reckless city boys gone horribly wrong and focus the investigation on Carson. Even if the scene doesn't make sense it will give the cops a fit trying to figure it out. And we aren't involved at all."

John Lee said, "Yeah, I remember now." He rubbed his jaw where Billy had kicked him. He wiggled two loose teeth with a dirty finger but felt no pain.

Preston asked, "Are you okay?"

"Hell, no! What do you think? I'll have to go to a dentist for this. That'll cost a fortune without no insurance."

Preston said, "I've got to go back to the compound and get weapons for the Carson job. And I've got to do my chores so no one notices anything unusual. I'm already late."

"How are you going to do that without talking to anyone? This is supposed to be our secret. And what about your wife? You've been gone all night."

Preston thought aloud, "Eugenia won't ask and I won't tell. She knows the score. What day is this? Oh yeah! Look, it's a sign for us. Today is when most everyone takes produce or livestock to the Farmer's Market in Tallyrand. They'll be gone when I get back to the compound. I'll do my chores then pack and leave before anyone comes back. Shouldn't be nobody in the house. Eugenia and the kids are all at the Farmer's Market. In and out. Easy peezey."

"Bring back beer, too. And water!"

"Of course!"

John Lee said, "Since we're outta Polly Ann's cramp meds see if you can find some at the compound or I'll start using our product up."

Preston said, "You're sure about the safety of your pills."

John Lee smiled, "Absolutely. Those runaways had been taking them for two weeks straight and they were fine right up to the moment you shot them. Anyway, it's a little late now to worry about taking strange shit. We both took Polly's pills already and we were only guessing what they might turn out to be. Remember?"

Preston said, "Because you said it would clear my mind and make my head feel better."

"Hey, I was desperate for pain relief. I didn't want to share the girl's pills but I did for the greater good."

Preston balled up a fist as if he was going to punch John Lee in the face. John Lee cowered.

Preston opened his fist and laughed. "I hate it when someone out thinks me. Let me have one of your pills."

John Lee took two pills from one of the large plastic tubs. He tossed one to Preston and swallowed his pill with the remaining beer in his can. Preston followed suit.

Preston said, "I'll be back as quickly as I can."

John Lee, "Yes! Make it quick as you can, I need a new beer already."

"I've got your back. Don't go anywhere today. Stay here until I get back. Do you understand me?"

John Lee nodded that he understood. Without further ado Preston turned and climbed up the long chain ladder into the morning sun.

John Lee watched Preston ascend the chain ladder wondering if he could even climb out of the sinkhole with his injured arm. Preston disappeared over the rim. Alone in the sinkhole, John Lee turned his thoughts back to naming his new drug.

When Kit returned to the cabin after patrolling the surrounding woods, Alex was changing Ethan's bandage. Ethan was sitting on one of the dining chairs this time rather than lying on the tabletop. The smells of breakfast foods filled the cabin.

Alex was lecturing Ethan as Kit walked in the cabin. "You were lucky, but you are still wounded."

"Yeah, a bad flesh wound as they say. But let us get in the habit of calling it a ricochet so we keep our stories straight. Just like Kit wanting us to call this a lodge not a cabin. We all need to be on the same page."

Kit sighed loudly but said nothing.

Alex pulled off his latex gloves tossing the gloves and bloody bandages into the trash. He addressed Ethan using his best field medic imitation. "Your wound can still get infected. If the shooter had been closer or the bullet had hit you anywhere other than your ostentatious bandoleer we wouldn't be having this conversation."

Ethan looked at the ceiling of the log cabin and shouted to no one in particular, "I'm a lucky man! Somebody bring me a beer. Or, better, a Bloody Mary! Or a Powerball ticket!"

Alex said, "You'll heal faster without alcohol."

"Yes, mother."

Garrett said, "Tread carefully, Alex. Ethan has issues with being overly mothered."

Alex said, "I'm not mothering you. I'm trying to talk to you as a doctor would. You need rest. Don't move your shoulder or arm too much. My stitching is field triage at best. Man up and don't be a pain in everyone's ass."

Garrett mumbled softly, "Too late for that."

Ethan yelled, "Someone bring me a fucking alcoholic drink!"

Kit said, "Ethan, it's barely ten in the morning."

"Then Bloody Mary it is!" No one moved to make Ethan a drink. Ethan started to rise but Alex put his hand on Ethan's wounded shoulder and roughly sat him back down into the chair with a thud.

"Hey! That hurt!"

"My point. You're not ready to return to duty. Now eat breakfast then take a load off on the couch or back in your bunk. We've got work to do and you have healing to let happen."

Ethan knew better than to confront Alex. He turned to look at Kit for support but Kit stared him down wordlessly. Ethan slowly stood up and looked around the room. Everyone was staring at him. Ethan grabbed a warm bottle of water someone had left on the table the night before and turned toward the bunkroom. After one last glance back at the men, Ethan stomped toward the bunkroom.

Ethan passed Charles who groggily wandered into the main room. Ethan glared at Charles but said nothing. He vanished into the darkness of the bunkroom as Charles entered the lighted great room. Alone in the bunkroom Ethan took a pill and washed it down with warm bottled water wishing he hadn't stomped off before eating breakfast.

Charles said, "What was all the shouting about? And why didn't anyone wake me up for my turn at watching the woods?"

Garrett said, "Breakfast is ready. Buffet style. And, Charles, we did try to wake you up but even with shaking you around we couldn't rouse you."

"My bad. I took a sleeping pill because I knew I would be too worried to sleep. Sleep doesn't come easily anymore. I'm sorry. At least we lived through the night."

Kit said, "Alex thinks it was an isolated incident. A freak incident of bad luck."

Alex said, "And we are going to continue living."

Charles looked at Alex, "You're certain they're not going to come after us? Here at the cabin? We're safe?"

Alex said, "That is not what I said."

Garrett said, "You can never predict what a crazy person, an evil person, or an intoxicated person will do. I've seen people with tunnel vision so acute that in their mind there is no outside world, only the world of thoughts inside their mind that is controlling them. You can never prepare for psychologically troubled people. Some turn into lone wolf predators, others simply disappear inward."

Kit was piling bacon, scrambled eggs, and fried potatoes onto his paper plate. He took his plate and utensils to the table and began eating. Garrett, Charles, and Alex followed. Five minutes later Ethan returned and used his good hand to scoop up the remaining food. He joined the men at the long table but distanced himself from the others by a keeping an empty chair between them and himself.

The men ate in silence. Kit finished his breakfast first, he was a fast eater, and dropped his plates and plastic utensils into the trash. He wandered to one of the cabin's front windows and leaned against the thick wall peering cautiously through the window at the forest outside. One by one the other men finished breakfast and dumped their paper plates and plastic utensils into the trash. Ethan waited until the others were busy with after breakfast activities before he took time to mix a Bloody Mary. No one tried to stop him.

Kit turned toward Alex and said, "Well, I know what Garrett suggested to fortify this place. What are your suggestions, Alex?"

Charles said, with alarm in his voice, "Fortify! You're going to stay and wait for whoever shot Ethan to come here? I thought you just said it was an isolated incident!"

Kit said, "Chas, you can leave now. We'll cover your exit. But, I'd really appreciate you helping us get this lodge ready, in case, just in case, they do decide to do something stupid and attack us. Something would have happened by now if anything was going to happen. They had all night to attack us or work themselves into a murderous frenzy and they just haven't made it here yet, or they decided to cut their losses and move on."

Alex said, "Or they are waiting on reinforcements. But, my best guess is nothing is going to happen. I bet some poacher was hiding in the trees and when Ethan blasted away, some shot struck close by him and scared the guy and he fired back from instinct."

Charles said, "So we scared him as much as he scared us?"

Kit said, "This is my place and I'm not taking chances. I'm not going to cut and run after one incident. This is more than a mere cabin in the woods; this is my best chance for a better future, a future that doesn't include listening to people whine over losing their fifty-seven inch high definition television or recliner or washer or dryer to repossession or trying to justify why their children go hungry when they choose bling and luxury items instead of good food for their own children. Selfishness is ruining generation after generation."

Charles asked, "So, everyone is in agreement with Kit?"

Kit folded his arms across his chest and looked adamant.

Charles looked at Garrett, whom he saw as the voice of reason in the group. Garrett nodded.

Charles looked at Alex who nodded as well.

Charles said, "Damn."

Kit said, "Charles, we all know you have two boys who need you. You can leave and no one will think any less of you. I know you must be going through withdrawals from not having your phone work."

Charles took his cell phone and looked at the signal strength bars. There was still no service. "Shit. I've never felt so isolated."

Garrett said, "Charles, go. Get a signal and call in the cavalry for us. That is the best way you can help us and help your boys. You can be the hero here if you can get through to the sheriff."

Alex said, "I'm betting we have time to fix things up before anyone comes, if anyone comes. If they were going to continue the engagement from yesterday they would have done something by now. Unless, they are waiting for reinforcements to arrive before they launch an attack. The tactical thing for them to do would have been to wait for our adrenaline to subside and fatigue to set in before they come for us. They should have attacked around three or four in the morning when our circadian rhythms are lowest. They didn't. That doesn't mean they won't attempt a daylight attack. It simply means they didn't think tactically, or they're waiting on something, or they fled and are hoping we don't come looking for them. Us not knowing is always an advantage for them, but them waiting is an advantage for us."

Kit said, "How do we prepare?"

Charles said, "Yes, how do you prepare?"

Alex looked around the cabin. He turned to Garrett. "What did you come up with?"

"I defer. If you miss something we thought of, I'll let you know. Otherwise your experience is broader than mine."

Alex said, "Okay, the front door and back door both have impressive locks and hinges and cross pieces that appears to have been forged sometime in the early Iron Age. Both doors are rock solid. The roof is probably impenetrable between the original log roof and the newer metal roof they laid over top of the wooden one. The windows all have tornado shutters and they have what appears to be a gun port cut into them. The storm shutters can be locked from inside and seem to have the same iron-age hinges and hardware as the front door. The walls are over a foot thick. We seem to have good craftsmanship working for us."

Kit looked at Alex, "What do you suggest?"

"Close the fireplace flue and use the grate to jam it closed. Don't give them a chance to gain a surprise entry through the giant chimney."

Charles laughed derisively. "Now you're saying whoever is out there is an evil version of Santa Claus. You guys are unbelievable."

Kit looked at the fireplace's oversized firebox. "You think somebody will try to slide down the chimney? Or drop a bomb down it?"

Ethan said, "A bomb?"

Charles said, "How could they get on the roof without us hearing them? And, I saw a spark arrestor on the top of the chimney."

Alex said, "Anything is possible, and should be expected, from an enemy you don't know anything about. War is like hunting in that the more you know about your prey and territory the better your chance of being victorious. A bomb or a Molotov Cocktail dropped into the interior here would do a great deal of damage and force us outside right into a killing crossfire."

Kit hesitantly said, "Well, the fireplace is pretty large and it was built to heat the entire lodge. So, yeah, the chimney is actually big enough for a man to come down it if motivated. It is at least big enough to drop a few Molotov Cocktails down into here."

Alex said, "Better safe and secure than sorry and sad."

Ethan slapped the table and shouted, "Yeah. What he said!"

Kit glanced at the fireplace and said, "Okay that's easy enough to do. What about the perimeter?"

Charles said, "That means you've got to go outside to look around. That maniac might be out there."

Garrett said, "Or, we are working ourselves up over nothing. No one has come after us. It could have been some asshole taking a wild shot that connected. He high-tailed it home and is having a good laugh with his meth head buddies. And we're here growing more paranoid by the moment."

Charles said, "Yeah. Maybe. But, I'm still leaving. You guys are unbelievable that you didn't drive straight to the hospital then to sheriff's office."

Kit snapped at his friend. "You've got to go outside to get to your truck to leave us. How did you expect to get to your truck to leave? Your ATV isn't even trailered. Are you leaving it here? You're the unbelievable one."

Ethan sneered with evil delight in his voice. "You don't want that big, showy, Escalade to get shot up. What would your boys think? How would their straight-laced daddy explain bullet holes in his car?"

Charles turned bright red and puffed out staccato breaths. Unable to think of anything else to say he stomped off to the bunkroom to end the conversation.

Kit said, "Let's look around outside and see what we can do." He grabbed his Winchester and checked the safety.

"Okay."

Alex grabbed his Browning and adjusted his well-worn Boonie hat. Garrett took his bow and notched an arrow. The men paused by the front door before stepping out into the open yard. Unaware of it, the men were holding their breaths as they moved cautiously away from the safety of the cabin's interior.

Insects swarmed the men as a gentle, but hot, breeze flowed through the clearing surrounding the cabin. A hawk cried overhead in the cloudless sky sending small animals scampering for cover in the remaining weeds.

Kit said to the group, "I'm sorry this weekend turned out this way."

Garrett said, "Don't apologize for fools and strangers."

Kit sighed, "I just don't see this ending well for my plans. I never seem to catch a lucky break."

Alex changed the subject by saying, "We should find things to use in the barn then we need to secure the barn. We don't want them to hole up in here. They could use the hayloft as high ground to oversee the cabin. I don't think they'll focus on the barn. There's more open space between the cabin and the barn than the cabin and woods. The cars and trailers work as both a barrier or as cover on the rear side of the cabin. The side of the cabin facing the barn has no windows. So that leaves the front, back, and the garden side open and vulnerable. We need to search the barn for anything we can use for our advantage."

Garrett said, "Alex, do you really think we might be attacked?"

Alex said, "Hard to say without knowing more about whoever shot Ethan. And, why they shot him."

Garrett said, "It was one guy that I saw climb down out of the tree and he left without looking around the clearing. I give him props for his tree skills. He seemed disinterested after you all left."

Kit said, "I hate not knowing."

Alex said, "Every soldier does."

Kit looked at Alex and said, "So, are you our force multiplier?"

Alex shook his head and said, "Just an advisor."

The hungry hawk screeched from high above the forest canopy. Squirrels shook tree branches as they raced for cover.

Alex said, "The predators are out today."

Garrett said, "I feel a change in the weather. Maybe the barometer is dropping. Critters tend to become active when the air pressure changes."

Kit said, "Of all the animals I thought I would have to deal with, I didn't think crazy people would be my worst predators to contend with."

Alex said, "The circle of life. Predators and prey all have to eat. It's a shame so many predators are human; they tarnish the term."

Garrett said, "Remember the term 'thrill killer'?" I bet that's what we nearly saw with Ethan. Some rancid asshole wanted to see what it was like to kill another human being and Ethan got lucky the asshole didn't succeed. I remember thrill killing was a thing for a while when I was a new cop. Cops know the world has always been violent but now it seems there is a lot more bad brain wiring in the general population these days or there is way more news coverage of incidents so more people are aware of it.

"Then, all I saw as a school resource officer was kids wanting to be all grown up before they even hit puberty, so they did all kinds of stupid and criminal things to get street cred or be on the internet. The lust for money or fame makes teens and others do crazy shit. Most high school kids haven't been taught there is a long view to look at; they're fixated on the here and now only.

"I'm so damn glad I'm not a cop or a security guard now what with all the black people getting shot by cops. I will opine that none of those deaths should have happened, but the black community has got to realize that their bad behavior and unwillingness to fit in a little more civilly has played a major role in people's perception and tolerance. People can protest and use rioting and looting or social media all they want, but the key to positive change is to show change in action. Look at Detroit and Chicago and other cities' murder rates and the breakdown of perps and victims. Facts are facts, people have to change and that change has got to be widespread, evident, and real. It has got to be a visible change that the majority of people see enough of to believe in. Race baiting and political bullshit has turned a lot of Americans' hearts dark and cynical, and not without merit. I'm just saying that from a cop and taxpayers point of view."

"Everyone thinks their point of view is the correct one."

"That is simply human nature."

"We are a country of relatively smart people and we can identify problems clearly, yet we cannot collectively come together to fix said problem even when it affects everyone equally. Go figure."

Kit said, "We've all seen overwhelming evidence that insanity and criminality are inescapable. It seems that Ethan was a victim of the equivalent of a forest drive-by shooting. There are a lot of dark hearts in the forest but the darkest heart of all belongs to man no matter where he lives. Most wild creatures are simply acting on instinct and for survival. Man acts on selfish motives for gratuitous gain or worse and that will be all mankind's undoing. I thought the darkest hearts were in the inner cities and Congress, but, even in these beautiful natural forests we find the dark heart of man lurks. It just sucks the optimism right out of you."

Garrett said, "You are preaching to the choir about dark hearts and the evil that men do to one another."

Alex said, "Amen. Even a simple, innocuous, thing can turn a person's heart dark and that is a frightening fact. Most times darkness creeps in more than pounces. It is an insidious takeover of the heart and mind. One day you wake up and are different; you don't know why, but you know you have changed. The final straw that breaks the camel's back just floats in and lands without a sound. Then you hear the sound of the camel's spine snapping and the pile of straw you so carefully compiled is scattered into a mess you no longer recognize, but it doesn't bother you and you accept it as the new normal. What is that Pink Floyd song? Comfortably Numb? That is how the darkness takes root and grows."

Kit said, "Damn, it sounds like we're the ones who need time at a resort."

Garrett said, "I thought that is where we are now."

Alex said, "Resorts usually aren't dangerous."

Garrett said, "There's nothing to worry about or we'd be dead by now." He waved his arm to indicate they had paused to talk in an open space, unprotected, and very exposed.

Kit looked at Garrett as Alex resumed rushing to the barn. The men huddled in the barn, looked at each other, and laughed.

Garrett said, "Well, that was a dangerously ill-timed therapy session."

Alex said, "And a damn foolish time for a leisurely pause and a deep talk."

Alex kept watch moving between the open doors of the barn as Kit and Garrett searched for something to use during a possible upcoming attack. Alex studied the surrounding trees placing himself in the position of an attacker. Only a few lines of sight allowed visibility into the barn's interior. Garrett and Kit were banging and thumping loudly as they hurriedly rummaged through the barn's vast collection of junk looking for any item that could be useful.

Alex drifted out of the back of the barn and disappeared into the woods. It was several minutes before either man noticed Alex was gone. Garrett and Kit continued to pile items in the middle of the floor.

Preston completed his chores at the family compound then packed a wooden crate with weapons without encountering other family members. The process took longer than Preston had anticipated. Inside the sinkhole John Lee had lost track of time but knew his new partner had been gone for an extended period.

Preston finally returned to the clearing riding an ATV with a large rectangular wooden crate strapped to the rear cargo carrier. The return trip to the sinkhole had gone slowly as Preston stayed in first gear to avoid overly jostling the contents of the crate.

Preston parked near the sinkhole then called down into the darkness. John Lee answered with obvious relief in his voice. Spending time in the sinkhole with the dead bodies, four dead bodies, had begun to creep John Lee out. Preston's voice calling down into the hole was the best sound he had heard in hours. John Lee yelled back in reply then hurried to the metal ladder.

John Lee struggled to climb up the chain ladder as he favored his injured arm; he was sweating profusely by the time he reached the surface. John Lee pulled himself over the lip of the sinkhole and lay on the grass looking up at the sky breathing hard and trying to speak through greatly parched lips. The wind brushing his face had never felt so welcomed. Preston tossed John Lee a bottle of water before dismounting from the ATV and telling him he looked like a zombie emerging from an underground crypt.

John Lee sat up and drained the bottle before replying. Ignoring the zombie remark he said, "Took you long enough to get back here!"

Preston grunted, "Had to do my chores and get my toys. Some of us have real jobs."

"Hey, my job is just as real as a legitimate factory job."

"Hmm."

"More water!"

Preston thought about drug dealing as a real job as John Lee downed a second bottle of water. John Lee tossed the empty plastic bottles down into the sinkhole then turned to watch Preston.

Preston carefully unstrapped the weapons crate and lifted the lid revealing his choices for the attack on the Carson cabin. Most of the weapons were readily available at sporting goods stores; Preston didn't want the attack to look too sophisticated or it would certainly bring in the BATF in addition to the local cops. He understood the details of the presentation made or broke the scam. Once the family had used Bigfoot as a ruse to scare off and murder intruders but now the boogey man was a meth head; so, emphasize what the cops already suspected and half the work was done for you.

The rifles Preston had chosen had never been used in a criminal manner so there would be no ballistic evidence of consequence. The attack had to appear as if a rival gang had shot up the cabin and men. The attack must divert attention from his family. He didn't care which local gang took the heat for the attack; maybe the different gangs would think the others were trying to frame them for the attack and then a gang war would reduce the competition even more. Preston thought he was devising a win-win situation.

Smiling, Preston tossed John Lee camouflage clothing and told him to change out of his blood stained denim jeans and T-shirt. As John Lee struggled to change clothes Preston painted his face with dark streaks. John Lee, favoring his arm, laboriously changed into the camouflage clothing Preston had thrown to him. John Lee then smeared dark paint over his face to match Preston's.

Preston said, "How is everything in the lab?"

"Fine." John Lee did not want to think about the lab and the pile of bodies in it.

Preston said, "I think I dropped my pocket knife into one of the beanbags. I need to go and try to find it. It's my lucky knife."

John Lee said, "Knock yourself out. I'm not going down then up that ladder again today." He held his injured arm out as reason for his statement.

"Back in a sec."

Preston lowered himself onto the ladder and descended into the sinkhole. The moment Preston's head disappeared from view John Lee began a close examination of Preston's crate of weapons. He felt like a child getting a sneak peek of presents before Christmas morning. He wondered which rifle Preston was giving him to use in the attack; and he hoped he would get some of the grenades. The grenades excited him; he hand never used a grenade before. He downed another bottle of water as he waited on Preston to return.

Inside the sinkhole Preston made a beeline for the plastic tub full of John Lee's designer drug. Preston had not felt this good, physically or mentally, for at least a year now. The aches, malaise, and unfairness of life seemed to fall away under the influence of the magic pill. He looked around at the jugs and bottles of chemicals and wondered how some dumbass like John Lee had found a chemist with the brains to concoct such a wonderful drug.

Preston grabbed a pill from the tub and swallowed it using only his saliva. Preston pocketed a few more pills after looking over his shoulder to make sure John Lee hadn't followed him down into the depths of the sinkhole. To kill a few more moments to feign searching for a pocketknife Preston walked to the back chamber and checked on the four bodies piled in the corner. The bodies were exactly as they had been left. It was cool enough in the chamber to maintain the bodies until the cabin was secure and ready to burn. Preston was relieved to know that John Lee had not committed any kinky acts with the blonde's body. Preston returned to the ladder and climbed his way toward daylight.

As Kit, Alex, and Garrett searched the barn Charles trailered his ATV. After securing it to the trailer he returned to the cabin and packed his luggage. After stowing his luggage in the Escalade, Charles loitered in the great room fuming silently, impatiently waiting to say one last thing before leaving. As he waited for the others to return from the barn, Ethan emerged from the bunkroom and silently stared at Charles.

Charles said, "I can't talk any sense into any of you?"
Ethan went to the kitchen and made a drink ignoring Charles.
Charles stared out of a window, "What has happened to us?"
Ethan said, "Chas, I understand you've got motherless kids to worry over. I, none of us, will think any less of you. Just leave us your gun and all of your ammo."

"What?"

Ethan said, "At least show your support by helping to arm us. If you leave we're down one gun. Even if all you have is a peashooter. I wouldn't mind the archer leaving, what use is a bow and arrow in a gunfight? That's just bringing a throwing knife to a gunfight, and it's still just a blade versus bullets. I don't know why he just doesn't use his sidearm. Maybe it's a retired cop thing?"

"I'm not leaving my gun behind. I'll never see it again."

Ethan said, "Dude, show your support even if you can't show us your spine."

Charles snapped, "Says the man who married his mother."

Ethan lunged at Charles, his single good arm outstretched with splayed fingers reaching for a chokehold on Charles's neck; but Ethan's lunge came up short as intense stabbing pain stopped him in mid attack. Ethan stopped, stared at Charles, then slowly took a bottle of pills from his pocket and swallowed two. He chased the pills with another Bloody Mary.

Charles stared at Ethan, disapproval clearly evident on his face. The men stared at each other as Ethan slowly took a long, deliberate gulp from the fresh drink.

Ethan set the drink on the table then glared at Charles as he said, "You are so lucky I'm hurt or I'd kick your ass so bad. And for the record I didn't marry my mother. I married a woman who was one way when we dated but changed a year or so into the marriage. She can't, or doesn't want to, help herself; it's her hormones or something psychological. I've mentioned the change to her but she is in denial. There's nothing I can do in this situation and she simply does not see herself as having a problem. Denial or obliviousness, the result is the same. I can't break through her resistance to hearing she might have a problem. Case closed. I live with it. Don't judge me by how I cope with it."

Charles said, "At least you've got a wife to go home to."

Ethan said, "And I am sorry you do not. I really am. I know you loved her with all of your heart. Now, you've only got your boys. But, Charles you'd better go now or you might get caught by the psychopath who shot me for no good fucking reason. But leave your gun and ammo like you're a real friend."

Charles said, "I don't know."

"When was the last time you actually shot it? Before today?"

"I don't remember."

Ethan said, "I'll follow you out to your truck and collect it. Then you can be on your merry way. No hard feelings. You've got family obligations. Kit will ship your gun home to you after this is over."

"And what if none of you are still alive after this is over?"

Ethan paused before answering, "Well, then, you will know that your gun and your bullets helped us hold out that much longer."

17

> No, I don't want to battle from beginning to end
> I don't want a cycle of recycled revenge
> I don't want to follow Death and all of his friends
>
> -Coldplay

Preston returned to the surface to find John Lee admiring the contents of the wooden crate. Preston had been torn between choosing combat weapons or common weapons to support the charade he had planned. Military grade weapons would bring in the Bureau of Alcohol, Tobacco and Firearms which would mean a more thorough investigation. But on the other hand, that kind of weapons usage could strongly suggest an organized gang attack. A violent meth related dispute could be the answer to a lot of questions and conveniently misdirect the investigators.

Preston was counting on the past affecting the future and the long Chickasaw County history of upstart rivals attempting to carve out a piece of the drug or moonshine trade for themselves. Three local gangs frequently fought each other but local gangs did not target the LaHarpe clan more than one time. Following an attempted power play, once the smoke cleared, either a deal was made with the LaHarpe clan or the LaHarpe's left no one alive to deal with. The LaHarpe clan had established their reputation over a century ago, but it was violently reaffirmed, when required, to upstarts who tried to muscle in on LaHarpe territory.

Preston patted John Lee on the shoulder and said, "Do you like what you see?"

"Hell, yes!"

"Do you know what all of it is?"

"Hell, no."

"Then let me show you and show you how it works." Preston pointed to the grenades and said, "These are mine. Period. Now let me show you what I have for you."

Preston instructed John Lee on the operation of his AR-15. The men drank beer under a blazing sun as John Lee practiced firing his military style rifle. During a break John Lee secretly took a pill while Preston stood off to the side and urinated. After John Lee had gone through three magazines of ammunition Preston felt that he had the basics down.

Preston placed the wooden crate on the ground between the sinkhole and the ATV. He opened two beers and handed one to John Lee.

Preston lifted his beer and said, "Don't trip over that, you might fall down into the sinkhole." He waited for John Lee to acknowledge what he just said. John Lee nodded. Preston said, "For our family. For our future."

John Lee touched his can to Preston's then drank his beer in one long slow draw. Preston downed his in two mighty gulps.

Preston said, "Time has gotten away from us. I wanted to do this before nightfall but it don't look like we'll make it in time. We can only drive so far then we'll walk in the rest of the way. I don't want them to hear the four-wheeler and lose our element of surprise. We park and walk in, nice and quiet. We pick our spots then we pick them off. If we see cops or reinforcements we bounce, got it?"

"Solid. Just let me get my ATV out of the woods and I'm ready."

Preston used a booted toe to tap the crate of weapons. "Let's get this show on the road."

Alex returned from the woods to find Garrett and Kit chatting quietly near the front door of the barn. He silently studied the pile of items the two men had gathered. Garrett noticed Alex first and nodded a greeting. Kit looked around and nodded a greeting to Alex as well. In the background the men heard Charles's truck leaving as it drove down the gravel driveway leading to the highway.

Kit stared toward the sound of tires on gravel and said, "You guys can leave if you want, and you probably should, but this place is mine now and I have to stay. I have to see this through for good or bad. I'd rather see this through, even if it ends badly, than go back to my job without knowing for sure that I at least fought for a chance to turn this place into something good. Yeah, I make good money but right now peace of mind is my treasure quest."

Garrett sighed, "Often peace of mind comes with a great price."

Kit said, "You get what you pay for."

Garrett said, "You need to live through this to enjoy the peace of mind that follows."

Alex said, "You can't do anything by yourself if someone actually comes for you."

Garrett said, "I'm really not looking forward to driving that food truck and trailer again so soon. I'll procrastinate that chore another day. If that's okay with you."

Kit smiled then said, "Charles is right, you all have responsibilities, family. You should go. If the bad guys don't come by tomorrow morning I'll drive into town and report everything to the sheriff. I cannot live in this paradise always looking over my shoulder wondering if someone is out to get the city boy." Kit sounded defeated as his dreams of a better life in a peaceful setting teetered on the verge of falling apart.

Alex and Garrett said in unison, "We'll stay."

Alex said, "What about Ethan?"

Kit said, "He's wounded. It normally wouldn't be hard to get him to leave in a situation like this. But if he's afraid to go home and face Martha, we'll need to tie him into his bunk to keep him out of the way if something bad actually happens."

Garrett said, "Good. That boy is a liability."

Preston was forced to slow to his ATV's speed to a crawl as the four-wheeler powered over the rough terrain. John Lee, lagging behind, could not get his mind off of exploding jolts of pain every time his ATV rolled over a root, or limb, or bounced through a leaf hidden hole. John Lee ignored low limbs smacking him in the face as he drove with tears of pain blinding his eyes.

Their progress was agonizingly slow but the upside of remaining slow was reduced noise. Both of the ATVs had mufflers modified to be as quiet as possible for hunting the deep woods, but Preston wished that John Lee had spent a few more dollars on his modifications. The slightly noisier engine of John Lee's ATV would require them to park further away and endure a longer walk to the cabin to maintain the element of surprise.

Their travel time over the rough and unfamiliar terrain forced the two killers to accept the fact that they would arrive at the cabin much later than originally planned. Although they were making progress their slow, bumpy, ride grew more uncomfortable by the minute.

The three men stood pondering the items Garrett and Kit had gathered. As Kit stared at the collection, his thoughts bounced between fond remembrances of times past and wondering if anything they had collected would actually be useful in case of an attack.

Garrett asked Kit point blank, "What did you really want at the end of all of this?"

Alex turned and looked at Kit waiting for him to answer. Alex said, "Yes, what precisely is your goal?"

Kit thought before answering; he glanced at Alex then Garrett before he replied. "The opportunity to enjoy the rest of my life with less stress away from the bullshit of the city. I thought I had a better chance at that through this opportunity than buying lottery tickets every week. I hate my job managing people collecting money from sheeple who are living hand to mouth but feel it is imperative to put on a front for others to see. It's seeing children suffer that really makes me sick when I have to make the tough decisions about repos and credit and making sales quotas. I hate looking into the entitled eyes of stupid, selfish, parents who are ruining young and innocent lives because they put their wants over legitimate needs. Kinda like Garrett said, it takes a toll on you after a while. I'll admit, back in college, I never saw my career path turning out like this."

As Kit spoke Alex paced the barn's floor in a random pattern. He did not join the conversation.

Garrett said, "I see. I didn't know you were harboring all that."

Kit said, "I don't want to be one of those people who bitch and moan all of the fucking time. I don't want to be seen as a downer. On to a new subject. Period."

Garrett leaned on a stall wall looking compassionately at Kit. "We need to think more positively. First, we need to think of how to increase our chances of survival if someone attacks. We've got to be ready to defend ourselves if we need to do so. Or, we can take the fight to them."

Kit looked up, "What?"

Alex said, "No. Absolutely not. We don't know with certainty if anyone is coming to do us harm. We don't have enough intel to go after them. Where are they? What is the lay of the land? What is their strength? What kind of weapons do they have? Did some asshole shoot at us just for kicks or was it a warning? We don't know enough for an informed decision."

Kit said, "Okay, I hear you. I agree. I say we make our stand in the fortified lodge and if we have to fight, we fight on our home turf."

Garrett said. "First of all we need to make use of this binary explosive compound. Alex can make some pipe bombs or IEDs or something."

Alex said, "No." His tone was adamant.

Kit said, "I thought you were trained in all that kind of stuff."

Alex said, "I won't do it."

Kit asked, "Why?"

Alex said, "IEDs, pipe bombs, and landmines are evil. I refuse to be a part of it."

Kit said, "Hey, all is fair in love and war. Right?"

Alex turned and glared at Kit. The glare and look of determination made Kit realize he had misspoke and the veteran's hatred of Improvised Explosive Devices was deeply ingrained and resided near the surface. Kit knew the story of Alex's head scar, but now he wondered about what he didn't know; Alex obviously had experiences he was not sharing with anyone.

Alex said, "Only people who haven't seen what an IED can do to a person say that. IEDs, pipe bombs, and landmines are for cowards. I will not use or make one and I will not support you using them either."

Kit looked away, his face burning under Alex's admonishment. Garrett moved silently toward the rear of the barn. Alex continued to stare at Kit for another minute before he turned his attention to the woods. Kit took a breath and prepared to apologize but Alex's tense posture told Kit to remain silent. Garrett studied Alex from across the barn.

Kit knew they needed some type of explosive but worried making one would alienate Alex. Kit wondered what experiences Alex had with IEDs but would never ask outright respecting Alex's privacy.

Preston parked his ATV behind a holly bush thicket and dismounted. John Lee parked then gingerly dismounted from his ATV and urinated as Preston listened to the forest. John Lee finished and took one of his pills as Preston stretched and refreshed from the tedious ride.

John Lee shifted impatiently and cracked a fallen stick. Preston glanced at the ground around him recalling his recent experience with the copperhead snake. Preston saw no danger and turned his attention to his rifle. After several minutes he turned to John Lee and pointed at the AR-15 he had given him.

Preston said, "Check your weapon."

John Lee checked his rifle then placed extra magazines in his cargo pockets. The fully loaded magazines forced John Lee to retighten his belt to support the added weight. Preston smirked at John Lee but said nothing.

Preston put on upper body armor then armed himself.

John Lee watched, waiting for his armor. Preston ignored him until John Lee said, "Hey, wait a minute! Where's my body armor?"

Preston put his hand on John Lee's shoulder, "I only have one."

"This isn't fair!"

"John Lee, it will be okay. Just keep hidden and move around after you've fired from one spot. Don't let them zero in on you."

John Lee was visibly upset, "Preston, I don't know about this."

Preston kept his hand on John Lee's shoulder, "Look, we have the element of surprise on our side. I'll lead the attack and you just keep hidden and look for targets of opportunity. Their fire will be focused on me. They'll never see you coming so they won't be shooting at you. You won't need body armor."

John Lee brushed Preston's hand off of his shoulder. "I'm not happy about this."

"I'm not happy about the situation either, but you don't hear me bitching about it."

"Because you have body armor."

Preston said, "I will make it right with you after this is done. The cabin is that way. I don't remember exactly where but I'm sure we can't drive any closer without being heard. We walk from here so search for any recent trails or paths they've made. We'll follow that if we find one; it should lead us directly to the Carson cabin."

John Lee said, "I need a drink first."

Preston said, "Yeah, me too. Got no room to take drinks with us. We might as well hydrate here."

"Here, here."

Preston pulled cold bottled waters from the cooler on the front of the ATV; he handed a bottle to John Lee then opened one for himself. The men enjoyed the cool, refreshing, rehydrating water in the shade of the dense forest.

The long, slow, bumpy ride with an aching jaw had been torturous for John Lee so he swallowed another pill. Preston noticed and held out his hand for a pill. John Lee dropped one of the tiny white pills into Preston's massive palm. Preston popped the pill with a wink at John Lee.

Garrett said, "Kit and I will begin mixing the binary compound. It's hard to say if the stuff is even active after all this time in the barn. Alex, will you at least stay here and act as a lookout to give us a heads up if needed."

"Yes." Alex was clearly displeased at what the men were planning to make. He climbed the wooden ladder into the hayloft and moved between the front and rear loft doors keeping watch. As he paced across the hayloft dust and desiccated straw gently rained down onto Kit and Garrett.

Garrett began reading the instructions for the binary explosive compound as Kit gathered containers to use. The men mixed the components together then packed several small cans and glass jars with the mixture. Kit thought of asking Alex about strategic spots for the containers to be placed, but consulted with Garrett instead.

Other than the homemade bombs there was nothing else in the pile that seemed useful for defending the cabin. Kit looked at the row of improvised explosive devices before him.

Kit said, "We should try one of these so see if it works."

Garrett said, "Good idea."

Alex said, "No. If you detonate one now, you will give away info to the bad guys."

"We don't even know if this stuff works anymore."

Alex said, "Do what you want."

Garrett looked at Kit. Kit asked Alex, "Okay. Do you at least want to suggest some places to put them?"

"No."

Garrett shrugged.

Alex said, "I told you. IEDs are evil and I will not be a part of using them."

Garrett said, "Just think like the bad guys and determine where a good ambush or sniper spot would be, then put one there."

Kit nodded. "Okay, I say we put one near the outhouse, one in the tree line dead ahead, and the rest wherever we think would be a good position for the bad guys to use against us. All we need is a clear line of fire to shoot the containers and conceal them enough for us to see but not for them to see. I'll place them while you two keep me covered. Alex, are you good with that, at least?"

"Yes."

Alex remained in the hayloft and Garrett followed Kit. Kit had his rifle slung over his shoulder and carried the bombs in five-gallon plastic buckets. He strategically placed each container lightly covering them with leaves. Kit placed all of the IEDs in twenty minutes. The men returned to the cabin for planning and food.

Preston hated to admit it to John Lee but he had to stop to have a bowel movement. John Lee wandered nearby as Preston took care of business. John Lee felt the day slipping away as he tried to find the setting sun through the thick leafy canopy.

Upon his return to the family compound that morning, Preston had found hot coffee and bacon and eggs waiting for him. After eating breakfast Preston tended to his chores so nothing would seem amiss to Eugenia. Afterwards he drank four cups of coffee as he packed the crate with the weapons he chose for the attack. Now, the coffee had worked its way through him and he had to answer the call of nature in the middle of nature. John Lee, waiting patiently while fighting hunger, took another pill washing it down with the little bit of saliva he could generate.

The aroma of griddle burgers filled the cabin; Ethan had done a good job of cooking the patties with only one useful arm eliciting compliments from the others. Ethan struggled to eat the burger with only one good arm but refrained from complaining. Kit was concerned that Ethan wasn't going on and on about Charles abandoning them, but he kept his concerns to himself, knowing Garrett and Alex were happy for the silence. As each man finished eating he moved to a window and looked out, lost in private thoughts.

Around the clearing night birds called as a strengthening breeze made the leaves whisper. Kit stared out the window relishing a beer. Despite the delicious dinner and beautiful environment it was hard to escape the feeling that they could find themselves in a life and death battle at any moment. Kit glanced at the group and wondered if this was how Alex constantly felt while deployed.

Pushing aside the negative thoughts Kit broke the silence and said, "Griddle cooked burgers always seem to smell better and taste better the further you are from home."

Suddenly the sound of a vehicle on the gravel drive intruded upon the woodland sounds. Alex raced to the rear window and looked out. The other men took up weapons and positions at the other windows.

Ethan said, "Is the sheriff?"

Alex said, "No."

Brakes squealed to a stop. A door opened and closed under the sound of bent metal and damaged hinges protesting the action.

Kit asked, "Who is it?"

Ethan called out, "What the fuck is all that?"

Kit said, "Decoy?"

Alex chuckled softly.

Ethan said, "What?"

Before Alex could reply, a knock on the back door stopped the men cold. Kit and Ethan brought their guns up, aiming at the door. Alex waved for the men to put their guns down before moving toward the door. Alex grabbed the doorknob. Kit held up his hand signaling Alex to wait before opening the door.

Kit crept, walking as quietly as he could across the plank floor, to the door and called out, "Who is it?" Kit stood to the side of the door across from Alex.

A muffled voice replied from the other side of the thick wooden door planks. Kit could not understand the reply so he asked for identification again. Alex laughed lightly.

"Who is it?"

A third knock, this time it was more of a desperate pounding, forced Kit to shout, "Who is it?"

Alex opened the door. Standing in the doorway Charles said, "It's me, Charles. Let me in! Don't leave me exposed like that!"

Ethan laughed aloud at the sight of a disheveled Charles.

The men looked at each other in shock over Charles's return.

Charles staggered in to the cabin bleeding from a broken nose, dragging a suitcase behind him. Wiping his watering eyes, Charles staggered to the sofa where he collapsed leaving his suitcase in the middle of the floor. Once on the couch, all of the energy drained from his body causing him to look like a discarded plump rag doll. He slowly raised a hand gingerly dabbing his bloody nose with a wad of blood soaked tissues.

Alex closed and locked the door as soon as Charles crossed the threshold. The men gathered around the fat man who looked up at them with a look of hopelessness and pain.

Kit simply said, "Well?"

Ethan said, "Nice to see you again, so soon."

Alex returned to the rear window and looked out.

Charles wiped sweat from his chin using the tail of his brightly colored island shirt before speaking. "I ran over an armadillo. Then hit a tree."

Ethan laughed as the others exchanged looks.

Kit said, "You were texting and driving weren't you?"

Ethan said, "Some folks just never learn."

Charles said, "I simply glanced at my phone to see if there was cell reception yet and wasn't paying attention. I may have been speeding a bit. Damn, I was less than twenty minutes from here. The airbag got me. The door is crunched in. My front tire is rubbing on the wheel well. The grill is smashed. The engine sounds funny. So, now I'm stuck here with you."

Ethan said, "Damn. How fast were you going?"

Alex studied the Escalade's damage from the safety of the cabin and said, "You could have driven on."

Charles said, "You don't know that! I don't know how badly my car is damaged. I didn't want to stay on the side of that narrow ass highway. They forgot to build shoulders for the road down here. It's pavement then ditch or tree."

Ethan said, "You are fated to be with us until the end."

Charles spat out, "Fuck you."

Kit said, "Welcome back."

Alex and Garrett remained silent.

Kit sighed in resignation then sat at the dining table.

Charles said, "I think I might have a concussion."

Ethan said, "At least air bag shrapnel didn't kill you."

Alex and Garret joined Kit at the table.

Alex said, "Naw, you're still talking way too much for that".

Garrett looked at Kit. "I guess I need to be in the barn in case something happens." Kit wondered if Garrett's motivation for saying that was to get away from Charles and Ethan.

Charles looked bewildered. "Wouldn't it be safer in here?"

Ethan said, "See! You don't have a concussion. That was a good question."

Kit nodded at Garrett, "Better sooner than later. Chas can stay in the lodge. Three of us might have a better chance of succeeding against whatever we come up against. Ethan you don't have to go anywhere, just watch our backs and protect the lodge."

Charles snorted a spray of blood out of his nose. "There's a possible maniac wanting to rub us out and now you want to leave the safety of the cabin to run out to the barn? To do what? Shoot some pool?"

The men ignored him.

Charles said, "So, what have you decided to do?"

Alex said, "You two go first, I'll follow and keep my eyes out. I've got our six. I've identified several spots where the bad guys have good cover. The main thing is we can't get pinned down in here. Plus, we have no idea if they have any training, think like hunters, or just want to come at us with brute force. If they're drug dealers, I would bet on a brute force attack."

Charles said, "But this is so late in the day and there hasn't been an attack, so either they've moved on or they're waiting for night. Or you've just worked yourselves up over nothing. I don't think they would have given us all this time to prepare if they were coming after you. I didn't see any redneck reinforcements on the road. I don't know what to think!"

Ethan shouted, "No one knows what to think!"

Alex said, "It could be strategy to lull us into complacency."

Ethan said, "I think I just spooked some punk kid spying on us from the tree. My shot came close and he reacted then got the hell as far away from here as possible. He had a lucky shot. Maybe he's all fucked up inside because he thinks he killed a man. Karma. I say let's keep it that way."

Garrett said, "Then we were lucky it was only a kid and he only had a handgun. But it was the biggest kid I've ever seen."

Alex said, "We may never know who it was or why he took such a shot."

Kit turned to Charles who was slouching on the couch using a paper towel to soak up the blood flowing from his smashed nose.

Kit said, "Chas, your job is to help Ethan keep the lodge secure. Lock the doors after we all leave. Then let us back in when we return. Can you handle that?"

"Of course."

Kit turned to Ethan, "Can you two get along while the adults are gone?"

Ethan looked at Charles, "It's all in good fun. Right? You know, it's all in good fun."

Charles said, with no conviction at all in his voice, "Whatever you say."

Kit summarized the first part of the plan, "Okay, we're going to make a beeline for the barn. If we make it, Alex will follow us a minute or two later. Right?"

Charles shouted, "Do you hear yourself? If we make it. If?"

Kit said, "What are you shouting about? You don't even think there's anything going on. I hope you're right, but for now I choose to err on the side of caution. Ever seen the movie Southern Comfort?"

Charles continued to shout, "This isn't a movie! You are erring on the side of paranoia which is a bastard cousin of caution."

Alex said, "Roger that."

Kit grabbed his Winchester Model 94 and chambered a hollow point round. He dropped a box of shells into a cargo pocket on his pants.

Kit turned to the group and said, "I kind of wish we hadn't replicated the Predator movie gun orgy now. I hope we don't regret wasting all of those shells."

Charles sighed, "Thanks for that thought."

Ethan said, "No matter how this turns out. That, my friends, was not a wasting of shells."

Charles said, "Time will tell."

Kit said, "This hasn't turned out like I had envisioned."

Alex said, "I'm with Ethan on that one thing."

Ethan said, "I always win people over. That's why I'm king of the sales department. Plus, I'm there all of the time so I don't have to be at home. Escape disguised as work ethic. Martha's so very proud of my work ethic and the commission I produce. She loves our European beach vacations twice a year. I am the king!"

Kit said, "Except you are going to work yourself to death in the long run."

"Didn't you always say that the long run is made up of short sweet sprints with mind numbing slogs between them? Or, something like that?"

Kit said, "Something like that. I never encountered the headwinds back then that I do now."

Alex said, "You two are off topic."

Garrett said, "Time to go."

Kit and Garrett paused near the front door. Kit had to take a few deep breaths to prepare for the long unprotected dash to the barn. He felt foolish thinking they were about to be attacked since there was no evidence to indicate an attack was going to happen.

Kit attributed his indecision and confusion to needing a break from his soul crushing job combined with a nostalgic longing for the adventurous days of his youth. Maybe it was his imagination on overdrive in a strange environment or simply his brain's method of processing accumulated stress. Whatever the source, the incongruous mix of possible doom and fresh start created a churning whirlpool in Kit's stomach and a tornado of uncertainty in his mind that unexpectedly leaned more toward exhilaration than fear.

Kit glanced around to try to determine if the others felt as unsettled as well. Whatever was causing him to feel this way would, someday in the future, be the genesis of an unbelievable, but true, story that would be shared until dementia erased all of their memories or greatly altered the way they remembered the facts.

Kit lingered looking at each man. The camaraderie was unmistakable and felt good. Alex patted Kit on the shoulder breaking his reverie. Kit opened the front door a crack and listened. The cacophony of forest sounds gave him a sense of security. He recalled that in the movies it was when the local fauna grew quiet or fled the area that it was time to worry.

Kit took one last deep breath then nodded. He and Garrett broke from the safety of the cabin and raced toward barn. The open space between the cabin and barn felt like a mile, but they made it into the barn without encountering resistance.

Once inside the barn the two men hurriedly checked all of the ground floor nooks and horse stalls for anyone that might have hidden in there while they ate burgers. Once they felt the barn was secure they leaned on support beams and caught their breath.

Alex joined them then took up a position in the hayloft. He had a wide field of vision out of the front of the barn through of the hayloft loading door.

Kit said, "Please reassure me this will work."

Garrett said, "I don't know."

Kit said softly, "I don't know what Alex experienced over there but I know he must have friends with PTSD or TBI. I won't even pretend to understand what soldiers go through or live with. You at least have an understanding of being shot and living with trauma. I just don't know what that is like."

Garrett looked at Kit, "Focus on the present moment."

Kit said, "Easier said than done."

Alex called down, "Situational awareness. Look for anything amiss. Look for odd movements among the trees. That type of stuff."

Preston and John Lee took their second breather after leaving the ATVs. The two men leaned against trees breathing hard and dripping odorous sweat. The sense of irritation lingering from the painfully slow ATV ride was growing stronger with each difficult step they took toward the yet unseen cabin. The weapons they carried were heavy and ungainly and Preston's body armor seemed to gain weight with each step. He considered giving it to John Lee.

Gulping air, John Lee said, "After we kill them, let's raid their coolers before we burn the cabin."

Preston said, "Good idea."

"I do have those from time to time."

"I didn't say you didn't"

"I don't want to do this in the dark."

Preston said, "Maybe we should just walk up to their front door posing as neighbors. They don't know us from Adam. We could be all friendly, meet and greet, get invited into the cabin, slake our thirst then kill them. We don't really need to ambush them."

John Lee wiped his face with the tail of his shirt. "I don't care how we kill them; I just want to get a cold drink out of the deal."

"I hear ya, brother."

John Lee said, "You know I've never done anything like this before."

"Yeah."

Time passed and Kit admitted his lack of confidence in being attacked, "I get the feeling we're doing this for nothing. Something should have happened by now, if anything was going to happen, that is."

Alex said, "Hard to say without more information."

Garrett said, "How so?"

Kit said, "It's late. Surely they would have come before now. Why wait? Why wait so long?"

"You can't predict what any human will do."

"Yeah." Kit shook his head in despair.

"Garrett said, "Or they could be waiting for full on darkness."

"Or it could have been what Ethan said."

"Great. Thanks for clearing everything up."

Alex joined Kit and Garrett on the dirt floor of the barn. He looked out at the forest. Alex said, "Kit has a point. But if they do come there are only three of us. I don't think we can count on Chas or Ethan to be of any use in a real fight of any kind."

Kit said, "But the bad guys don't know that. We have limited choices on who positions himself where."

Garrett said, "Kit, you should stay in the cabin. Alex and I will take positions in the barn and in the woods."

Kit said, "Okay, I could take the lodge, but even with those two wounded they should be enough to protect the lodge. Ethan has his shotgun. Charles might man up under fire. Why can't you guys start calling it a lodge? But, after deeper thought, I think I'd rather face the mosquitos and heat out here than listen to Chas's whining and Ethan's bullshit."

Alex said, "The cabin is the sturdiest structure. You can have Charles watch the front and Ethan can keep watch out of the back. He doesn't have to shoot, only shout. Prop him up against the wall. If nothing else you'll look fortified. Garrett and I can use the barn and trees as cover. One of us can use the hayloft as high ground."

Garrett said, "Now for the fun part. We need to make it back to the cabin without incident and really prepare better. Now that we have an actual plan we should regroup, fill the others in on the plan, and do a weapons check. Afterwards, I'll take the hayloft and Alex can have the woods."

Alex nodded, and said, "I concur. Good plan."

Kit said, "Garrett, why don't you switch to your gun?"

Garrett said, "I have the element of silence with an arrow. Handguns are only good for close range. Plus, using my bow may give an element of surprise; they won't know where to look."

Kit said, "Okay."

All three men took a deep breath and exhaled slowly. On the next breath Alex bolted from the wide doorway dashing toward the cabin. Kit nodded at Garrett and followed. The men sprinted past the horse corral and made it safely to the cabin. Garrett, last man in the door, slammed it close without looking back. Alex was already at the cooler counting remaining water bottles.

Garrett said, with some wincing, "That sprint wasn't good for my back."

Kit, breathing hard, labored to say, "Alex, have you gotten faster? We're the same age and that little run of fifty yards or so from there to here nearly did me in!"

Garrett, also breathing hard, said, "And Kit runs the neighborhood most every day. And, believe you me, our neighborhood streets are not all level, let me testify to that. I think we're the hilliest neighborhood in the entire city."

Eventually the two men's breathing returned to normal. Alex, Garrett, and Kit outlined the plan to Ethan and Charles. Garrett gathered water bottles and gave each man two bottles.

Suddenly Kit shouted, "Shit! Damn it! Fuck!"

Ethan said, "Pussy. The bottles are not that cold to hold."

Alex said, "Excuse me?"

Garrett acted offended, "My! What salty language!"

Kit said, "The twins. Maybe whoever shot at Ethan thought he was one of the twins' crew. Both of them have been guilty of sky busting clouds and shooting at anything that moves without identifying it. And the whole county knew they were shotgun fanatics. Ethan made a boneheaded twins move and got mistaken for one of them or one of their crew. If this is someone gunning for the twins because of something they did we could be in serious trouble."

Garrett said, "I thought the twins were a year plus dead?"

"Maybe not everyone knows that. Maybe somebody just got out of prison and came looking for payback?"

Garrett said, "Really?"

Ethan chipped in, "Yes. Really. Good odds of that happening. The twins were not the best of people. They had a knack for pissing off, well, everybody."

Kit said, "That is true. The burned spot in the clearing may have been some of the twins' remaining crew keeping business alive. They crossed someone, evidenced by the firefight scene, and now with us here at the cabin, they, whoever they are, think we are part of the twins' crew or legacy and are targets for revenge."

Ethan said, "So the delay means they are gathering forces for a big all-out assault. The twins were not the simple neer-do-wells they portrayed themselves as. They did business with some very bad and ruthless people. We could be in trouble for real."

Charles groaned theatrically. No one would turn to look at him. He moaned again then grew quiet, resigned to his fate.

Kit said, "Never thought the twins would ever bother me let alone come back to haunt me. Hell, I never socialized with that side of the family except during big special occasions. That whole side of the family was like the black sheep side. Not fun to be around."

Ethan said, "I'll take my chances with my shotgun. If the asshole that shot me actually comes back, I think I owe him some steel. Just prop me up by one of the windows. I can handle recoil if it means shooting back at the ass that shot me."

Garrett and Kit exchanged glances.

Alex looked at Ethan then at the other men and said, "It's getting late. We've burned a lot of daylight and nighttime may not be our friend. Are we ready? Heads in the game? Heads in the moment at hand? Focused?"

Kit said, "Fate rarely gives anyone an option about when or where or how it interacts with us. Fate is like the Borg; resistance is futile and you will be assimilated. I'm as ready as I'll ever be."

"Well, that's fatalistic, or is it deterministic?"

"Good. Here we go."

"Not the best pep talk to end getting ready with."

Charles snapped his fingers looking around with a wide smile. The others jumped at the snapping sound then stared at Charles. Charles pushed himself off the sofa and wobbled to his suitcase. Kit watched as Charles fumbled through the densely packed suitcase's contents. A wide, victorious smile spread across Charles's swollen face as he lifted a satellite phone in triumph.

Ethan asked, "What the hell? We need your attention on the problem at hand."

Kit said, "Focus on the present. If there's not cell service you're not going to get wireless either."

Alex said, "I could use a sports update."

Charles smiled smugly ignoring the men while he studied the phone's menu screen. Kit moved around to look down at the device. The other men kept watch out of the windows. Kit leaned down for a closer look at the menu screen.

"A satellite phone?"

Ethan said, "You're just now remembering that you had a satellite phone?"

Charles tapped a key on the keypad and the screen came to life. Then he paused, not sure what to do next.

Ethan noticed the hesitation. "Great, but who are you going to contact?"

Kit said, "Don't you know, Charles owns a big computer security company. He must have all sorts of gadgets. Especially devices with satellite connections."

Charles said, "Yes, this is satellite linked, but it's not a programmed phone. I haven't put any information in it or given it an ID yet. Anyone who sees the unfamiliar number will ignore it or think it's a robocaller and ignore the call."

Kit said, "Use your social media accounts to get help."

Charles shook his head, "I let them all go after the funeral."

Ethan said, "Contact one of your worker bees."

Kit said, "Or one of Alex's friends. If one is close to here."

Alex said, "No go on that. No one will answer an unknown number."

Charles shook his head again, "I know the people who work for me, I'm sure they will think I'm punking them. We had a big discussion on me coming down to the boonies. No one believed I was spending a week in the woods. They thought I was actually headed for Vegas to blow off some steam but that I was too embarrassed to admit I was going to Vegas. They even gave me a box of condoms and two hundred dollars in singles. They'll think I'm shining them on if I call with this story."

Kit said, "I know I don't answer unfamiliar numbers on my personal phone. And good going for your staff!"

Garrett said, "Only two hundred dollars?"

Ethan said, "I bet you wish you really were in Vegas."

Alex said, "What about the sunspots interrupting communications signals. It was on the news, a big solar storm. Biggest solar blast of the century is what they are reporting."

Kit said, "Chas only uses state of the art equipment. Satellite linked and all that jazz; Chas is always prepared! Don't you know he owns a cybersecurity business?"

Alex said, "Let's hope the solar activity doesn't interfere with the transmission."

Garrett said, "What about a timber and metal roof?"

Ethan said, "Who keeps up with solar flares? Who cares about that stuff? Why do you know that stuff?"

Charles said, as he lightly fingered the keypad, "If there's a God, He'll give us a window in the solar flares to get a message out."

Garrett asked, "Who do you contact? Who will believe this? I can't call my wife because she's on a weeklong cruise and my son and daughter-in-law are probably holed up somewhere arguing it out over the food truck. Kit?"

Kit said, "No one comes to mind. Garrett is already here. My employees won't answer unknown numbers. Ex-wives? Ha!"

Charles looked up from the menu screen toward the cabin's ceiling. "I'm open for any suggestions."

Kit looked at Alex and then at Garrett. Garrett shrugged.

Ethan said, "No one comes to mind for me either."

Kit said, "Your wife."

Ethan shook his head, "No go on that, good buddy."

Kit said, "Side girlfriend? Sales associate?"

Ethan said, "Ain't got the energy for an affair and all of the sales associates hate me."

Alex said, "This is truly sad. We were not like this in college. What the fuck happened to us all?"

Kit said, "Yeah, how did we come to this point? We've got no one to call for help. This is sad and depressing."

Garrett said, "If you get a signal, contact the sheriff's office. They know our name. We talked to the sheriff. That will give us credibility."

Kit and Alex said in unison, "That's a great idea."

Charles said, "Does anyone know the sheriff's phone number? Didn't he give us his business card? Is it lost already?"

Alex said, "You will need to go outside. The signal won't go through a roof like this one."

Ethan said, "Doesn't satellite phone service have an information feature?"

Charles said, "No matter who I call it will be an unfamiliar number and no one is going to answer it. I was going to program it while I was down here but forgot about it until now."

Ethan snorted, "And you call yourself a professional."

Garrett began to pace from the back window to the garden window. Alex returned to the front window and stared out at the edge of the forest. Kit circled the room finishing his circuit at the dining table looking down at Charles and the satellite phone.

Garrett said, "I feel a weather change coming."

Ethan said, "In your knees?"

Garrett said, "And my back."

Preston and John Lee finally saw a lighter space through the trees a hundred yards ahead. Preston was sure it had to be the clearing that surrounded the Carson cabin. Preston had never visited old man Carson but he had done business with the twins. He thought it was a shame to kill neighbors you had never met but this was not personal, it was business; and there was no shame in being a ruthless businessman.

Finally the cabin was in sight. One hundred feet from the clearing Preston stopped in his tracks and John Lee blindly plowed into him. John Lee's jaw surged in pain, chasing his inattention away for a moment, as the collision with the plates in Preston's body armor jolted him from head to toe.

Preston ignored the impact but hushed John Lee's grunt of pain. He surveyed the cabin, the barn, the corral, and trees surrounding the homestead until he fixated on the colorful food truck parked amongst the trucks and trailers. Unexpectedly he found himself lusting over what he imagined were coolers full of cold water and beer.

As Preston stared at the food truck an annoying buzzing sound overpowered his brain disrupting his thoughts. His lips were parched and licking them with a dry tongue did not help at all. Preston's goal faltered for a moment. The promise of food and drink in the food truck called to him.

The paint on the truck mesmerized John Lee who saw the paint as swirling pools of liquid color rippling on the side of the truck. For a moment he forgot about his pain as he envisioned the truck to be full of burgers, sodas, and cold, clear, water.

The setting sun illuminated the food truck with a light ray coming through the treetops. The beam of light made the bright paint glow with an unnatural beauty. The men began to smell phantom burgers and hear ice cubes clinking in tall glasses.

John Lee said, "Let's check out the food truck first."

Preston thought about it for several minutes then said, "No. We take care of business first."

John Lee said, "I didn't expect to see a food truck."

A thought clicked in Preston's addled mind. He reasoned that the truck might not be for feeding the men and his assumption must be correct; the men were rival drug dealers and the food truck was their distribution method. Preston viewed the interlopers with a new perspective, almost respect, as his inner businessman momentarily overcame the thirsty man.

Preston said, "They might be savvier than we thought."

John Lee said, "What are we waiting for? We're here; let's get this show on the road. Are you still thinking walk up close encounter ambush?"

Preston wanted a closer look at the food truck. He paused then said, "First, we creep in closer and see what's what. Just like stalking a deer or a bear."

"I thought you said we were going to walk up like we're lost and get all friendly and refreshed before we kill them."

"Well, I said that was an option. I may have changed my mind. You got a problem with that? New information coming to light and all that."

"What new information? I've been with you the whole time."

Preston said, "The food truck is making me think. Do we have a problem?"

"No, I just want to get his over with, have my jaw looked at by a real doctor and drink a gallon of cold water. I bet that food truck has water, maybe sodas, too."

"Look, listen; there may be more men in there than we know about. I don't want to walk in to their base and find out we're way outnumbered. You don't win battles without intel and a strategy."

John Lee said, "Okay."

"This will all be over soon." Preston stared at the cabin not really believing his own words.

"How soon?" John Lee was licking his lips as he stared at the food truck imagining all of the goodies stockpiled inside it.

"I don't know. I don't think you can kill people on a schedule. Unless you're the government's prison system. That's the only place I know of where people get killed on a schedule in front of an audience. If prisons charged admission to view executions I bet their budget worries would be over quick enough." Preston failed to see the nasty glare John Lee shot him following his last comment.

John Lee angrily said, "Don't get me started on prisons. They killed cousins. First they locked 'em up in solitary for fifteen years of appeals then poisoned them in front of an audience. How fucked up is that?" John Lee's hands were balled into tight, hard, fists.

Preston put his hand on John Lee's shoulder and said, "So if we don't want to end up like your cousins we've got to do this smart and clean. Do what I say and everything will be okay."

"Okay. What do you want me to do?" John Lee exhaled and relaxed his hands.

Preston wiped his face on the sleeve of his shirt. He silently stared ahead.

John Lee said, "Can we search the food truck first?"

"Be quiet and follow me. We need to observe our prey up close. We don't how many people there are in that cabin."

John Lee said, "It is getting so dark. I thought this was going to be a daylight job. What if they don't come out?"

Preston stared at the food truck as he answered, "One problem at a time. Hey, you got any more of those pills on you? This might take longer than I thought."

Charles stared at the satellite phone's menu screen. He said, "I don't know what to do. The battery is showing only five percent capacity."

Kit said, "Just call all the numbers you know until someone answers."

Charles said, "If someone answers I'll have them call the Chickasaw County sheriff and relay a message."

Ethan said, "Don't call anyone you've ever punked before."

"I don't do that to people."

"Good."

Kit said, "Start dialing."

The men took seats and watched Charles as he begin inputting phone numbers. Charles stared at the phone praying at least one call would make a connection.

18

> I like driving backwards in the fog
> Cause it doesn't remind me of anything
> I don't want to learn what I'll need to forget
> - Soundgarden

Kit's first thought upon waking was, 'Yeah, still alive.'

He jumped up from the sofa where he had fallen asleep frantically looking around the room as the others began to stir; it was clear nothing had happened and he breathed an audible sigh of relief. Charles, snoring away, slept at the table next to the phone. Ethan slept on the floor next to the massive fireplace. The last thing Kit remembered was sitting next to Charles as he stared at the phone's keypad, but he had found himself sprawled out on the sofa upon waking with a start.

Garrett stood watch at the window drinking coffee from his thermos cup. He turned to look at Kit and nodded a greeting. Kit acknowledged the nod then looked around the room again. He noticed Alex was missing from the group.

Garrett turned back to the window as he sipped coffee. Kit stretched before speaking.

Kit said, "Garrett, where's Alex?"

"Out."

"You were up all night?"

"Yeah."

"Thanks. Seriously. But, you could have woke me up for a shift."

"Alex and I talked. We think you got yourself worked up over nothing. Whoever shot Ethan got their shot in, and then got the hell out. They did their thing and made a clean get-away. I couldn't sleep anyway so I just stayed up. When was the last time you watched an entire night's life cycle from dusk to dawn? It was a beautiful experience. Lots of coyotes over to the south from the sounds of them. You need a good telescope down here. There's coffee in the pot."

Kit smiled, "You sound wired."

"Been drinking coffee since midnight. Standing right here watching the heavens. I almost took Alex up on a cigar. Seemed like the time and place to try one. But didn't. Stayed with coffee."

Once fully awake Kit heard birds singing and could see faint light in the clearing surrounding the cabin. Kit stretched for another two minutes, filled a cup with coffee, and joined Garrett at the window.

Garrett pointed to a small rabbit he had been watching for a while. The rabbit calmly looked around as it fed on grass growing near the bonfire pit. Kit enjoyed watching the rabbit; all he had back home to entertain, but more frequently annoy, him were squirrels.

After thanking Garrett a second time for standing watch all night Kit reluctantly moved away from the window and nudged Charles to wake him. "Chas, check to see if you have a reply to any of your calls."

Charles took a sharp intake of breath and put a hand over his eyes. "The battery died."

Garrett, who was in the kitchen looking at the coffee pot called across the room, "Yeah, I was afraid of something like that. At least the battery let us get some messages out. We should be thankful for that. Put it on the charger now! We need to see if you got any replies."

Charles said, "I don't think I brought the charger."

Ethan coming slowly awake said, "Dumbass."

Kit said, "I think we made much ado about nothing."

Charles perked up. "Then let's make a run for town. I need a mechanic."

Ethan said, "Be my guest. Don't hit an armadillo this time." Smiling at Charles he silently added, 'and good riddance'.

Charles gently placed the satellite phone on the table and said, "I said, 'let's, as in let us, not just me."

Kit said, "No one's stopping you. If the nut job wanted us to stay put, we'd all have flat tires or worse."

Charles said, "Yes, that's it. No harm, no foul."

Kit said, "Right. So, go."

Charles glared at Kit. "What is your problem? And where is Alex?"

Garrett interrupted, "Enough. We'll all be at each other's throats if we have to stay in this sweat lodge very long. We need to relax and get on with what we came down here for."

Kit nodded, "Yes. I've got reports to make and photos to send.

Ethan said, "I'll do as much as I can with my bad arm."

Kit looked at each man in turn. The daylight outside the cabin's walls filled him with hope but the uncertainty of what might wait inside the dark woods lurked ominously at the edge of his thoughts, tempering the hope with nagging dread.

Kit said, "Well, I don't know where Alex is but I'm sure he's watching our backs."

Garrett said, "At least Alex is doing what he has been trained to do and he has situational awareness. I hope he comes back and gives us a report soon."

As if on cue Alex stuck his head inside through the open kitchen window said, "And that report is that there was no activity in the compound overnight." Alex entered the cabin and walked straight to the coffee pot.

Charles nearly screamed the words, "You mean that door has been unlocked all night!"

Garrett said, "I was on watch."

Charles snorted and said, "Thanks." He turned and walked into the bathroom.

Garrett turned to Alex, "Thanks."

Alex said, "I couldn't sleep and after all of you except Garrett drifted off, I was antsy and decided to keep watch outside."

Garrett fired up the gas stove and began cracking eggs. Kit said, "I'll help after I visit the outdoor reading room."

Ethan said, "I thought it was a throne room."

Kit said, "Only for shit-heads of state."

Kit tried to open the cabin's back door but found it stuck. He pulled on the heavy iron handle but the door remained closed. Kit looked around to see if anyone noticed he was having difficulty opening the door. They all noticed; it was unavoidable.

Alex said, "You'll have to get that fixed."

Kit sighed, used two hands to try and pull open the door. The door would not budge. Shrugging in defeat Kit gave up trying to open the door.

Garrett called out, "Get a move on."

Ethan cried out merrily, "Bloody Marys' for all!"

Kit said, "Make mine spicy. And who knows carpentry?"

Alex said, "I might have a rasp in the Jeep!"

Charles called out from behind the closed bathroom door, "So everything is back to normal? Just like that?"

Ethan said, "So far, so good."

Kit said, "Yeah, maybe breakfast drinks aren't a good idea until we know for sure."

Ethan said, "Call mine a medicinal drink. I've been shot."

Garrett said, "Make your own, I drink coffee for breakfast."

Kit peered out the window on the back of the cabin toward the parking area. The vehicles were unmolested and there was no sign to indicate anything was amiss but the outhouse seemed dangerously far away under the circumstances. He turned to look at the bathroom door willing Charles to hurry and finish.

Charles exited the bathroom with his standard cell phone in his hand. Ethan said, "Everything come out okay?"

Charles glared wordlessly at Ethan. Kit suppressed a snicker as he cautiously entered the unvented bathroom.

Ethan said, "Breakfast. It's hard to think on an empty stomach. We need breakfast."

Charles said, "Breakfast food would not be my choice of last meal fare."

Ethan said, "Even with a plate full of bacon?"

Garrett said, "I'm on it." He lit a second burner on the stove and opened a new carton of eggs and a package of bacon.

Garrett continued to cook bacon and eggs then fried cubed potatoes in bacon drippings. Ethan slowly moved from window to window scanning the woods for movement as he massaged his injured shoulder.

For several aroma-filled minutes the only sounds in the cabin were the sound of breakfast foods cooking and coffee percolating. The aroma was a siren like call to the hungry men. One by one the men gathered behind Garrett as he cooked. Garrett moved like a master chef working black pepper slabs of bacon, frying up Geotta, scrambling eggs, and turning hash in cast iron skillets. After several minutes he turned and chased off his audience.

The cabin filled with heavenly breakfast aromas. To a man the smells invoked happy memories of family camping, of hunting camps, and of leisurely breakfasts at home on lazy weekends.

Twenty minutes later breakfast was served. The men applauded as Garrett removed an apron he had taken from the food truck. Everyone grabbed plates and utensils and began enjoying the fruits of Garrett's labors. Once the paper plates were piled high with food the men dug into the delicious fare consciously delaying discussing what to do next.

Kit set his plate on the table to cool and went to the back door where he pulled on the iron handle one more time. The door still refused to open. Sighing over the unexpected structural issue Kit turned from the door and returned to the table.

Alex said, "Look, you'll probably need to hire a carpenter for some wood work. I know just enough to take a look at the door, but you'll need to start a list of projects for a professional to fix."

Kit nodded and eyed a piece of Geotta before eating it.

The men stole glances at the back door as they ate in silence. Each man chewed in silent thought preoccupied with what the day ahead might hold. Despite the sunny morning and delicious breakfast everything felt slightly off. Ignoring the oppressive apprehension no man would admit to being besieged by an undefined uneasiness.

Earlier the previous evening, Preston had shadowed Alex's movements wishing more than once that he had brought his prototype night vision helmet. Preston followed a generous ten yards behind the man in the Boonie hat. To Preston, it seemed that the man was alternating between patrolling and stargazing for extended periods. It worried Preston that the man's movements clearly indicated he was moving around the grounds at night for more than a case of insomnia. Preston recognized the athletic man had military training and targeted him for a quick and silent kill during one of the man's stargazing episodes.

Then a primal urge overcame all other imperatives. Preston had to urinate. It was impossible to hold it in any longer. He stopped behind a large pine tree and scrapped the leaves away from the ground. He urinated into the soft, quiet, earth. Preston glanced over his shoulder twice but could not reacquire the man in the Boonie hat.

Frustrated over allowing his target to escape Preston forced himself to remain in place, quietly waiting and watching until the man's next movement gave his location away. Time passed and none of the shadows Preston thought was his target moved. He cursed himself for such a rookie mistake yet he refused to go blindly wandering through the forest trying to find him. He tried to convince himself that he had not spent that much time urinating to completely lose his target as uneventful minutes passed. He continued scanning the darkness waiting for a man-shaped shadow to move.

The smell of breakfast foods wafted out of the cabin filling the forest as a breeze spread the aroma. John Lee began to salivate at the wonderful aroma of bacon. Tantalized by the wafting breakfast smells John Lee thought it odd the men were not using the fancy food truck to cook their breakfast meal. The fact the men were not using the food truck could only mean that the truck in fact was the men's drug distribution method. Preston was right!

John Lee looked around for Preston. The big man had been gone all night and John Lee was concerned. During the long night, waiting for Preston to return, John Lee had grown bored and vandalized the cabin's back door with a horseshoe nail. Upon returning to his hiding spot he must have fallen asleep because it was now dawn. John Lee was relieved Preston had not caught him sleeping; he felt there would have been hell to pay for that. Still, it was morning and there was no sign of Preston or activity other than breakfast aromas drifting from the cabin.

John Lee began to stretch cramped muscles. He felt his swollen jaw and checked the gashes on his arm and face. Everything still hurt like hell but he had pills for that. He took one of his pills forcing it down with saliva.

Preston crept up behind John Lee and softly whistled like a bird in his ear. John Lee jumped but Preston covered the man's mouth before he shouted. A muffled John Lee whispered, "Man, where the hell have you been all night?" Preston released his grip on the smaller man.

"Watching and waiting and planning."

"Okay, I just wish you hadn't left me hanging like that. I got bored."

Preston said, "I was in a situation and couldn't return. Let's go over what we know."

"I jammed the back door closed."

"You did what?"

"I jammed it shut with an old horseshoe nail."

Around midnight Alex had settled down on the trailer behind his Jeep. He lay on tarps watching the stars and letting his stress float away to burn up in some distant star. At some point fatigue had overcome him and he had fallen asleep. Then the sun rose waking him forcing him to think about what might lie ahead.

Alex knew his non-veteran friends did not tense up or begin evasive action when someone tossed a glowing, cherry red, cigarette butt from the car in front or veer away from every bag of trash or car abandoned on the side of the road. Alex was certain that the other men didn't smell blood in their dreams or hear garbled radio traffic in the sound of flowing shower water. Their troubles weren't insignificant, they just weren't combat born and they surely could not be as dark or as intrusive and debilitating as his. But Alex Bobo would not wish his burden on anyone else; it was his alone to bear.

Following breakfast Alex excused himself and exited the cabin in an attempt to shake off persistent anxiety. Ethan shouted a joke about Alex using the outhouse but Alex did not react to the taunt. Garrett looked at Kit with obvious concern for Alex written on his face. Kit shrugged in reply. Garrett shook his head lightly clearly indicating Kit should speak to Alex. Kit mouthed, 'He'll be okay.' Garrett looked skeptical letting the moment pass without replying.

After losing the man in the Boonie hat Preston held his position unwilling to give himself away first. Hiding in the darkness, waiting for his target to reveal himself, Preston imagined a scenario that would seem like drunken hunters had died in an accidental fire. The empty beer cans and liquor bottles littering the bonfire pit would convincingly support a drunken party weekend gone bad scenario.

The weak link in Preston's plan was if some of the men attempted to escape he would have to shoot them. Bullet wounds would be difficult to explain in the context of an accidental cabin fire. So would artificially jammed windows and doors needed to prevent their escape and eliminate the need for bullets in the mix.

Warring ideas fought for dominance in his addled mind. He hated being pinned down, trapped, alone with the cacophony of voices in his head. The night passed in tedious misery as a parade of conflicting emotions tormented his fatigue stressed thoughts.

In Preston's mind it became clear that the food truck was their distribution method; what other reason could there be for a brand new food truck to be way out here in the middle of nowhere? These city dealers probably had a fleet of food trucks so they could deal drugs in plain sight. Preston thought it was a brilliant idea and a great cover for bringing the product to the consumer.

Although Preston had never set a foot in a food truck he was certain there were lots of nooks in which to stash drugs. The food truck was proof the men were dealers; and any competition had to be stopped. Preston visualized the shiny truck pulling up at festivals, swap meets, and race tracks stealing LaHarpe customers with each stop. Stopping them was the thought that persisted through the night.

John Lee moved to sit beside Preston. "What is the plan?"
Preston put his index finger to his lips and said, "Shush."
John Lee took a pill and forced it down his throat. Preston held his hand out and John Lee gave him a pill. It was difficult to swallow the pill with only saliva, but the result was worth it.

Ignoring John Lee's impatience, Preston continued to silently evaluate his foes assigning them roles. The Escalade driver must be the money man, the man that patrolled all night was security, the ass that shot up the trees must be the trigger man, and the others had to be the logistics man, and a chemist. He was certain if he could prevent the establishment of a new rival in town his value to the family would rise. Then the paradox hit him; if he took credit for the action he would be further reprimanded for acting unilaterally, and if he didn't tell anyone he wouldn't get credit. And how would he explain suddenly owning a big city food truck to everyone?

The paradox bothered him greatly. The ache in his head returned and this time it was more of a stabbing pain than a thumping pain. Preston decided that acting unilaterally, without expecting appreciation from the family, seemed to be the only course of action. But if he were to do this alone he wanted something out of it.

Preston considered the food truck desperately trying to think of a way to incorporate the truck for his own uses; to either sell at the chop shop or use it to distribute John Lee's wonderful pills. As much as Preston wanted the food truck for his own purpose, he decided it was too much of a risky attention getter. A food truck in Chickasaw County, even at festivals and fairs would be out of place and bring unwanted attention if it were operated by locals with any criminal history. Unfortunately, the food truck would need to play a key element of the plan to convince the cops that the bodies in the cabin were drug dealers and the food truck was their distribution vehicle. Regrettably the brand new food truck had to burn.

Preston sighed, resigned to losing the food truck; but he could profit from some of the ATVs. He'd have to leave the one or two ATVs to account for all of the tire tracks in the woods. But the better ones he could sell to a chop shop or to local kids and still make some cash; after all, he would need to purchase more ammo when this situation was resolved.

Preston remained silent, lost in thought, for an extended time. John Lee fidgeted noisily on the dry litter of the forest floor. Preston turned and glared at the smaller man who smiled lamely then settled down.

After another long period of silence John Lee cleared his throat but after a second harsh glare from Preston he leaned against a tree and remained silent. He began plucking green leaves from low hanging limbs to burn off nervous energy. Preston was only five feet away from John Lee but seemed more like a mile away.

Long, silent minutes later Preston came to the decision his original scenario was the best and that an apparent turf battle between rival drug gangs would be most believable to the local cops. The food truck and whatever evidence he and John Lee would plant after the dirty work was over would assure that the cops would pursue that line of investigation first.

John Lee suddenly grabbed Preston's arm and pointed at the cabin as Alex rounded the far side of the old cabin and walked into view. Preston pried John Lee's hand off his bicep. Preston watched Alex enter the cabin hoping to get a head count by seeing through the open door.

John Lee said, "We've got them now!"

Alex met the men with a grim look on his face. "The door was purposely jammed with an old horseshoe nail." The statement was met with stunned silence.

The fact that someone had intentionally jammed the door closed changed everything. The men looked at one another as everyone digested the alarming news.

Charles voiced the common thought as he said, "Oh, shit, so this is real? We really have someone trying to trap us in here?"

Alex said, "It was jammed with a horseshoe nail. But none of the vehicles are molested, no flat tires and nothing seems molested."

Garrett snorted. "Why would anyone jam the back door but not do anything else?"

Charles said, "Maybe Alex on patrol scared him away during the night. Thanks for staying up all night to patrol."

Reluctant to admit he had fallen asleep Alex said, "It should have never happened. Whoever did it is good and stealthy."

Ethan talking with a mouth full of food said, "Yeah. That's a pretty lame thing for a would-be attacker to do. Sounds like a kid."

Kit said, "I would say, from my experience, a single prank indicates kids. I scared off some kids on ATVs the day I arrived. And there was a lot of trash by the fire pit. I bet we pissed off some teenagers by disrupting their private party spot. Maybe one of us made a noise or got up to pee and scared them off before they could do any other vandalism. For all we know whoever jammed the door is the person who stole the copper wire and electronics from the cell phone tower complex or they're simply pissed off teenage vandals."

Garrett shook his head, "You're reaching. Again."

Ethan said, "I think the teenagers around here need a good ass kicking."

Charles said, "Whether it be punk kids or psychopaths let's get the hell out of here while the getting is good."

Ethan asked, "If it was just one door and nothing else is amiss that indicates teenagers, right?"

Alex said, "If it were me, I'd jam shut one door, blow up that big propane tank next to the cabin, then shoot everyone who ran out the unjammed door."

Ethan sarcastically said, "Now that's thinking like a mercenary."

Alex glared at Ethan who realized he had crossed a line.

Kit said, "But, good news for us, the propane tank is as good as empty. So what would his Plan B be?"

Alex said, "Hide in the woods and shoot anyone who comes out of the cabin. Everyone in this part of the county must know the cell service is out. We're isolated and facing unknown numbers with no way to call for backup."

Charles said, "You were just outside and nobody shot at you!"

Alex said, "Unless you've got a silenced weapon, you don't shoot one guy thereby alerting the rest."

Charles said, "Look, there was one door jammed, no cars vandalized, and Alex is safe. I think the teenagers are gone. Let's just go and report all of this to the sheriff!"

Ethan said, "Dude, you're one of those people who just can't face the facts even with overwhelming evidence. You're one of those bleeding hearts who wants to give a murderer a trial even if his crime is caught on camera in high definition. What does it take for you to believe?"

Charles said, "Believe what? That our nice little get-away turned into another disaster! I believe that, believe you me. I remember some epic fails during college, even if you don't!"

Garrett said, "This is far worse than some keg party fail."

Charles shouted, "You didn't see some of the fails. You don't know; you weren't there. This group can fuck things up with the best of them. Get Kit to tell you some of the stories from back then."

Kit said, "Yes, and I accept this situation is all my fault. I saw a viable job exit strategy and dollar signs and didn't think this through. I am sorry I got all of you into this mess."

Alex said, "You can't hold yourself responsible. You are minding your own business. Ethan got this whole mess started."

Charles slapped the dining table, "Yeah, Kit isn't responsible because, Ethan 'Asshole' Boone started this whole nightmare by blasting at that damn buzzard and pissing off some psychopath hiding in a tree."

Garrett said, "It was the person in the tree who started this. He did not need to shoot back."

Charles said, "Ethan didn't need to shoot up the forest and innocent birds either. But he did. That was what started all of this!"

Kit said, "Point taken, but why was someone hiding in a tree spying on us?"

Ethan said, "Hey, maybe it was my fault. I'm sorry if it is my fault. Who knew that shooting a damn bird would cause all of this?"

Charles said, "Yeah, who knew?" Sarcasm and unconcealed anger colored his words making his position crystal clear.

Ethan slammed his plastic spork onto the table top, "Hey, some ass was in a tree spying on us. He shouldn't have been there. Some ass was in the wrong place at the wrong time and you're blaming me? These country folk are crazy. They abide by their own laws and codes. I've seen all those reality TV shows. So, get-the-fuck-off-of-my-ass." Ethan glared at Charles then took a pill and chased it with a Bloody Mary.

Alex returned to the group, "We've got to get outside and look around."

Charles waved his arms, "How do you expect to get out of here with the back door jammed and maybe a whole bunch of guns waiting for us like we're Butch and Sundance?"

Kit said, "The windows."

Alex looked at Kit then shook his head.

Charles looked at the windows then the three men in turn. "Struggling through those windows would make you a sitting target, don't you think? What if it is the twins' enemies and they called in reinforcements?"

Kit picked up his .30/30 and a box of shells. "Yippee-ki-yaa, motherfuckers."

Charles said, "No. You need to get real. Only two of us are trained for this shit. You are not one of them."

Kit said, "It's my property. I've got to make a statement now or all is lost. I'd rather die defending a dream than go back to work defeated and second guessing myself all the way to retirement or an early death at my desk."

Charles said, "You may not live till retirement."

Garrett said, "Kit, Alex and I have training. You don't. You should stay in here and keep the cabin secure."

Kit looked at each man in turn before answering. "I can't be passive. This is my property. This property was to be my ticket out of the shithole I'm in now. I don't think I could sleep at night knowing that I passed off the defense of the lodge to you guys while I sat in here doing nothing. Plus, each of you are here at my invitation. It's all of you that should get the hell out now."

Garrett said, "That's noble, but let Alex and me do the dangerous work. Someone will need to live to tell the tale to the police once this is over."

Charles said, "I volunteer for that job."

Ethan snorted, "At least you're able bodied. I'm wounded."

Kit glanced at Charles and Ethan but stood his ground. Facing Garrett Kit stated, "I appreciate what you're doing. We don't know how many of them there are out there. Whether it's one or more, let's give them multiple targets to shoot at. None of you can talk me out of staying and defending my property. We don't know who jammed the door, but I'm hoping it's just pissed off teenagers that just lost their party spot."

Ethan said, "Hope they don't have full autos. That's a lot of bullets to dodge even from only one or two shooters."

Charles became agitated at the thought of being left all alone with Ethan in the stifling hot cabin. "So, what am I supposed to do? It's clear the bad guys have a plan. Kit, buddy, let the cops handle this then we can all go home safe and sound."

Kit said, "You tried to make it out and got turned around by Fate. And, we have a phone but no power to call. What does that tell you?"

Ethan said, "It tells a story that is bad for Chas." After rubbing his shoulder he took a pill and washed it down with coffee. "What does that tell you? It tells me we are all in this together. One for all and all for one."

Charles said, "That's not Fate telling me anything. It's simply the luck of the draw. Shit happens, pure and simple. I glanced at my phone and hit an animal. That happens all of the time."

Garrett turned to Kit. "You're sure about this?"

Charles echoed Garrett but with more of a forceful tone, "You're sure about this? Really sure?"

"I'm really sure, but I'm certainly not enthusiastic. This is unlike anything I've ever done, that's for sure. This situation gives a whole new meaning to the term 'sweat equity'."

That brought laughter from both Alex and Garrett breaking the tension and allowing the men to relax a little. Kit smiled for the first time in a day and a half.

Garrett said, "If we all go out different windows at the same time we will at least momentarily confuse anyone waiting to ambush us."

Ethan said, "Have you actually looked at the windows? None of you can climb through those things. And if you tried it would be like shooting fish in a barrel."

Kit glanced at the windows loathe to give Ethan credit for stating the obvious. Alex shook his head when Kit looked at him.

Charles said, "How do you even know anyone is waiting for us? Maybe they tried locking us down, got scared away by Alex on patrol."

Kit said, "We should be so lucky."

Garrett said, "We won't know until we go outside."

Alex said, "The only reason to block one door is to force people to use a different door."

Charles moaned reburying his face in his hands. Ethan sat at the table and patted his shotgun.

Alex stated firmly, "Ethan and Charles will stay in the cabin. One of you watch out the garden and kitchen windows and the other keep an eye out the back. Or just shutter the back window and each of you can take one of the other windows. Ethan is injured and Charles only has a .22 rifle so your duty stations are in the cabin. The three of us will go out and deal with things outside."

The plan, as outlined by Alex, was for him and Garrett to make it to the barn where Garrett would take the hayloft with his bow and arrows. Garrett would provide cover from an elevated perch allowing Alex and Kit to move freely as needed. Kit was to find cover just inside the tree line where he could reposition, as needed, using trees as cover once any shooting started. With the plan outlined, it was time to move.

Kit peered out the garden window. It opened with effort and noise, but no one shot at the activity. Kit cautiously peeked out and looked around. Seeing nothing amiss he turned to look at the others.

Charles said, "How do you expect to get out of here without being picked off?"

Kit said, "Jail break. None of us can fit through the windows. So the jammed back door is forcing us to do exactly what they want us to do. We can't stay trapped in here all day."

"We need to turn their own stratagem against them."

"Easier said than accomplished."

"You could bust out the front door shooting in all directions to confuse them and drive them to cover giving us time to get to safety."

Alex said, "It is time to be serious."

Charles said, "This is deadly serious and you guys are acting like this is a paintball game."

Kit snapped at Charles, "If you have an idea to contribute then spill it. If not, shut the fuck up!"

Charles moved away from Ethan and said, "I'm just the voice of caution and reason, not tactics."

Garrett said, "We don't know where they are positioned so shooting blindly is stupid and wastes ammo."

Alex said, "Right, one of them can cover us from the kitchen window."

Charles said, "I thought it was a jail break situation, all at once from multiple exits so no one knows who to shoot at? Won't the first man out the door be an easy target?"

Ethan called out, "I wanted to see all of you climb through the windows. It'd be like when you had to scamper out the window when your girl's dad came home early and you had to escape before he got to her bedroom." Ethan laughed heartily.

"Good thing you never dated a cop's daughter."

Garrett glared at Ethan then moved to the front door. Ethan nodded and moved to the garden window. Charles moved to the kitchen window. On a signal from Alex, Garrett burst through the front door hugging the wall of the cabin, moving quickly toward the rear of the cabin where he disappeared from view without being shot at.

Kit burst through the door next racing straight to the nearest large tree taking cover behind it. He glanced at the outhouse making sure no one was hiding inside it then he looked for Garrett.

Garrett crept toward the row of parked cars behind the cabin. He knelt next to one of the SUVs and rubbed the nagging injury in his lower back. After searching among the cars for lurking intruders he carefully continued toward the barn.

Kit saw Garrett as he left the parking are then turned his attention to the forest spreading around him. Finding a downed tree he took cover behind its long trunk and listened to the forest.

Alex exited the cabin last and took cover behind the wall of railroad ties shielding the cabin from the large propane tank; he studied the tree line surrounding the clearing while waiting to make his final dash to the barn. Alex saw Garrett safely cross the open space and disappear beyond the corner of the barn. Alex counted off five minutes to give Garrett time to get to his elevated perch before beginning his dash to the back of the barn. The beautiful day seemed incongruous with the danger, real or imagined, he was feeling.

John Lee had moved away to relieve himself during which time Preston watched the three men burst from the cabin. He watched them scatter like windblown leaves to different positions around the cabin and barn. The short man in the woods would be the most mobile so he would put John Lee on him. Preston felt there were only two men left in the cabin; certain no reinforcements had joined them during the night. Preston mentally began to finalize his new attack plan now that he knew for certain where his enemies were located.

Ethan and Charles stared at the forest from the kitchen window. Each man's heart was beating fiercely, pounding as if trying to escape to freedom through their ears; they may not have heard a gunshot had one been fired.

Ethan said, "See, it's going to be okay." He moved to the window overlooking the overgrown garden.

Charles grunted in reply and focused on the forest in front of him.

Watching the peaceful clearing from behind the fallen tree's rotting trunk, Kit began to convince himself that he had over reacted to an ambiguous threat. Surely whoever had shot Ethan would do more than jam one door closed; Kit felt the simple prank of jamming a single door indicted skittish teens and impotent childish revenge. He wanted the culprits to be the kids he scared off the first day, angry over losing their private party spot. Kit peered over the fallen trunk wishing something would happen just to know what, if anything, they were actually facing. Peeved teens were one thing, but drug dealers or psychopaths were another level of problems all together.

Garrett moved cautiously in the hayloft, his hesitant and light steps still made the old floor creak and pop. Each step rained desiccated straw bits to the floor below. Garrett looked around the empty loft wishing there was a bale of hay to sit on as he massaged his aching lower back.

Alex took a breath and prepared to make his move. He surveyed the area from behind the railroad tie blast wall. The birds and squirrels were still and the breeze carried the aroma of forest potpourri throughout the clearing. The day was already hot and sweat beads dampened his forehead just under his Boonie hat. The forest was quiet except for the breeze making the leaves whisper. White clouds dotted the blue sky as a hawk flew overhead.

19

> It was a wild weekend,
> It happens every now and then
> It was a wild weekend
> I don't know why and I can't remember where or when
> -Hank Williams, Jr.

Preston both rued and appreciated the fact that John Lee had jammed the back door closed. He wished he had thought of it but he would have had a better end game and he silently cursed John Lee for not telling him of his plan in advance. Now the men in the cabin knew something was up ruining the element of surprise. Watching the men exit the cabin and take up obviously strategic positions confirmed they were aware something was up and were trying to prepare.

Preston exhaled and stated the obvious. "Well, it looks like they know we're here."

John Lee said, "Yeah. Sorry, I couldn't find you at the time."

"Water under the bridge. You ruined our element of surprise."

John Lee patted his AR-15. "Not entirely."

Preston said, "If you had let me know about jamming the door earlier we could have mowed them down when they made their jailbreak. Now it's a war of hide and seek."

John Lee silently nodded patting the extra magazines in his pockets.

Preston said, "Okay, we're going to need to be smarter than them to win. I'm certain they're a rival drug operation and these guys are the brain trust of the outfit. The brain trust is rarely warriors and that gives us the edge. Based on the cars and the men I've seen, I bet we are seeing the moneyman, logistics man, and maybe the chemist. If we're up against mostly paper pushers this should be a piece of cake. The only man I'm worried about is the man in the Boonie hat. He looks like an ex-solider to me, but he's the only one that looks worrisome." Preston licked his parched lips. "We can get as nasty as we want so it looks like a drug war took place."

John Lee smiled, "Yeah. That sounds righteous."

"You ever kill a man before?"

"Sure."

Preston looked John Lee in the eye. "Are you ready for this?"
"You bet."

Preston said, "Okay, we need to move. They are ready for us. There's a man in the woods over there. He is your first target. He is short but stocky so he shouldn't be too hard to hit. Take him out and wait to see if anyone comes out of the cabin to come to his aid. Then, take them out. I'll engage the men in the barn. Keep moving so they can't pinpoint your location. And stay behind cover."

"No problem, brother, you're the only one with body armor."

"Hey, I've been lugging around forty pounds of armor plus weapons and ammo. You can carry all of the shit back to the ATVs when this over."

John Lee grabbed Preston's arm. "Here, take this. It'll perk you up." John Lee offered a pill in the palm of his hand.

Preston took the pill chasing it with the little bit of saliva he could create. He nodded at John Lee then turned toward the cabin. Preston watched the man by the propane tank study the forest as John Lee cautiously moved closer to the cabin.

Kit crept from tree to tree until he found concealment that he liked allowing him good shooting lanes and a stump he could use as both a gun rest and protection. He calmed his breathing and searched the forest for anything out of place. Anxious minutes passed in incongruous peace and quiet; Kit relaxed as he began to actually believe the situation had become overblown in his mind. Yes, the door had been purposely jammed but surely such a harmless prank must have been the kids he passed on the road during his arrival. Despite the scant evidence and annoying feeling of uncertainty Kit began to believe he was over thinking the twin's legacy and role in the situation.

Alex kept patient watch from behind the propane tank's blast wall as his training had taught him to do. He trusted his training and combat honed instinct, but he was facing a situation without any intelligence, with untrained personnel against unknown forces and weapons, and no trained unit for back up. In the silence Alex felt the anxiety moths fluttering next to his ears and a vacuum beginning to form in his chest.

Alex recalled lines from The Desiderata to chase the anxiety away. Keeping his eyes moving and ears alert he silently repeated a few familiar lines to center himself.

Alex mentally recited: 'Go placidly amid the noise and haste, and remember what peace there may be in silence. As far as possible, without surrender, be on good terms with all persons. Speak your truth quietly and clearly; and listen to others, even the dull and ignorant; they too have their story. Avoid loud and aggressive persons; they are vexations to the spirit. If you compare yourself with others, you may become vain and bitter; for always there will be greater and lesser persons than yourself.'

The familiar lines had a calming effect. His mind and body were back under control and he felt like a well-trained soldier again. Taking a deep breath, Alex squatted behind the railroad ties rocking on the balls of his feet readying himself for an exposed sprint to the barn. Alex patted the thick creosote soaked railroad ties and gave thanks that the large tank was empty since the unprotected side of the tank was exposed to possible attackers.

Kit inhaled forest potpourri aroma as he stared into the shadows searching for danger. The scent calmed his mind as he recalled what he had learned hunting with Ulysses. Kit pondered the current juxtaposition of danger and beauty and it seemed natural despite the fact this situation was closer to danger and death than he had ever experienced; it was a situation that only Alex and Garrett could actually relate to. Kit knew no man fully understood what he was capable of until such a moment to call upon one's true grit occurred. He also realized his friend's lives were on the line as well and that placed a burden of responsibility on Kit that he physically felt. He took a breath then slowly exhaled and pushed the anxiety away, for a moment, the stress he felt was replaced with a sense of nostalgia.

The hunter in Kit fondly recalled the excitement of seeing fresh tracks crossing a dewy hay field first thing in the morning indicating deer were moving. Kit smiled as he replayed in his mind the seemingly magical appearance of a deer as it stepped through a tree line into view, or simply appearing in a spot he had just looked at a moment ago, or a buck working a doe. Kit missed Ulysses and the bawdy banter at the skinning tree.

Kit remembered watching deer just out of shot range but in clear sight and watching other forest animals engage in their natural activities as he impatiently waited for a deer to wander by his stand. He fondly lingered on reliving the shot that had earned him Ulysses' respect and his nickname Killer.

Kit recalled many hunts of waiting in a deer stand with no deer movement as well as times of getting busted by an unseen deer as he crept to his stand in the pre-dawn darkness. The current situation was a bizarre combination of hunting and being hunted. The biggest difference was getting busted this time would mean getting killed. Kit prayed the skills of stalking deer and waiting patiently that Ulysses had taught him would be useful as he scanned the forest trying to find an intruder with bad intentions.

All of the beauty and mystery of the forest made Kit realize how much he wanted his plans for his new property to succeed; but despite the stillness of the moment, there could be hidden men who meant to do him and his friends harm. Kit's thought train brought him back to the reality at hand and he checked his Winchester's safety.

The forest around the cabin was quiet. Even the birds seemed to know something was amiss with their part of the forest full of intruders. The sun shining in the clearing around the cabin highlighted the colorful weeds, butterflies, and inviting openness that seemed more suited for a family picnic or a game of horseshoes than an impending battle. Kit shook his head in frustration as squirrels scampered among the treetops.

Alex felt Garrett had been given enough time to get into position in the hayloft. Alex exhaled and pushed off, sprinting toward the back corner of the barn. Ten yards from the barn, he came upon a fat timber rattlesnake directly in his path. Concentrating on reaching the safety of the barn Alex had not seen the snake until the last moment.

Both Alex and the snake shared surprise and alarm at the sudden meeting. Instinctively, Alex pivoted away from the reptile, sliding on loose, dry dirt as he abruptly changed direction to put distance between himself and the large snake. The surprised rattlesnake reacted to the intrusion with loud rattling that seemed to drown out all other sounds. The snake coiled to strike.

Losing his footing as he abruptly changed direction Alex put one hand on the ground to keep his balance but his boots lost traction and one knee hit the ground hard. Alex grunted at the bone jarring impact. The rattler lunged striking Alex's booted foot. It was a hard impact that unnerved Alex but the snake's fangs could not penetrate the thick leather boot. As the rattler recoiled Alex used his free hand to throw a handful of dirt at the snake's head.

Recovering his balance, Alex flung his body away from the large rattlesnake. The snake's head tracked him poised to strike again. Time seemed to stop as Alex involuntarily paused mesmerized by the noisy snake. The snake's distinctive rattle made his entire body tingle from primal fear.

The snake was stunned after striking the thick military boot. Alex used the pause to back away from the snake. The snake grew still as Alex retreated out of striking distance. The snake turned; Alex stared at the snake as it slithered toward the forest. Alex watched until it disappeared into the leaves.

Moving cautiously through the trees John Lee thought the saw the short man kneeling behind an enormous stump. John Lee took cover behind a tree and peered around its trunk watching for the stocky man to expose himself.

Inside the cabin Ethan saw John Lee hiding beside a tree. The man in the forest raised his assault rifle and moved his head searching for a clear shooting lane. Ethan aimed his shotgun and pulled the trigger.

The blast of the shotgun got everyone's attention. With the single shotgun blast everything changed. The shot was like a starter's pistol giving permission for everyone to act. Kit, Alex, and Garrett hesitated for a moment as they each wondered if the blast was Ethan being diligent or careless. Preston and John Lee showed no hesitation.

Preston reacted to the sound by quickly shouldering his AR-15 and firing at the man staring at the dirt by the corner of the barn. Off-hand Preston fired a single shot narrowly missing Alex's head. Alex sensed the bullet whizz past him before thudding into a pine tree beyond the barn.

Alex dove behind the barn and rolled away from both the retreating snake and the unseen shooter taking cover behind the safety of the barn. A second shot punctured old barn wood above his head.

Alex instinctively felt a small amount of relief that the bullets had been single fire; he hoped that meant they were not facing attackers with automatic weapons. A crushing wave of responsibility overwhelmed him as he realized there was actually someone out to do him and his friends harm. He berated himself for forgetting his training and standing like a newbie in the open. A third shot punching through the old wood just above him brought focus back to the moment.

After the three shots at the man in the Boonie hat, Preston quickly moved to a new position. The man behind the barn was not returning fire giving Preston a moment to wonder what had caused the man's pause out in the open. He blamed needless haste and John Lee's pills for missing a stationary target. Preston remembered some adage about best laid plans falling apart but until now never believed that would apply to him. Preston sighed in resignation and focused on the barn ruing the fact he had blown his chance to kill the only man of the group who seemed worthy of concern.

Inside the cabin a very startled Charles was shouting questions at Ethan who was shouting back at Charles. Ethan was looking out the window toward where he had shot as Charles continued shouting at Ethan's back. Neither man could hear what the other was shouting over the ringing in their ears. Ethan dared a quick look at Charles giving him the harshest glare he could manage. Charles joined Ethan at the garden window and looked toward the forest searching for what Ethan had shot at.

John Lee heard the shotgun shell pellets pepper the leaves and tree trunks around him. The impact of pellets so close gave him a surge of adrenaline making his mind explode with release that the fight was finally beginning. Trying to steady his shaking, John Lee fired at Kit who peered over the stump searching for what Ethan had shot at. John Lee's shot thudded into the old stump trunk forcing Kit to drop to the ground and hug the forest floor. After a moment Kit crawled into darker cover beneath thick holly greenery.

Ethan's second blast from his shotgun shredded the leaves concealing John Lee. John Lee returned fire from behind the tree peppering the cabin wall chipping exterior logs and sending several rounds through the open window cratering an interior wall. After firing half a magazine at the cabin John Lee ducked behind low growing brush and crab crawled to a new location remembering Preston's instructions to fire then move to a new location.

Kit peered through the shrubbery toward rustling leaves from the shooter crawling through the undergrowth. Kit was thankful that Ethan had been on watch and able to shoot a warning shot or two. After glancing at the cabin Kit turned his focus toward finding the unseen man crawling over dry leaves.

Preston could see through the barn, front to back, but the interior was dark concealing the men inside. Confirming his math he counted two men in the barn, one in the woods, and two or more in the cabin. That made it at least five men with limited weapons and unknown training against two men who had military weapons and deep motivation. The enemy had divided their force and he was sure they could be taken out group by group.

Preston decided, in hindsight, that he and John Lee should have walked up to the cabin all friendly like then ambushed the men; but now that shots had been fired, the engagement was fully underway and there was no going back. Part of Preston's mind blamed the pills for his lack of judgment, but another part of his mind loved the way the pills made him feel. Annoyed by feeling conflicted he forced aside the distractions to focus on the engagement with the interlopers.

Alex glanced at the bullet holes in the corner of the barn then hurried into the structure. He took a knee just inside the rear door steadying his breathing.

From the hayloft, Garrett called out to his friend, "You okay?"

Alex said, "Yeah, missed me by a country mile. Did you see where the shots came from?"

"No."

"Okay. At least Ethan is armed and on point in the cabin. And, we know there are at least two of them."

"Well, what now?" Garrett had an arrow notched as he studied the forest searching for the unseen shooter.

"Knowing there are two of them is more than we knew before. And we know one is not patient enough to hold fire until he gets a golden moment to take a sure shot."

"Lucky for you."

"No shit."

"I was looking in the wrong direction when the bad guy fired on you. Sorry, but I didn't see his position."

Alex said, "I didn't get a fix either." He decided not to mention the encounter with the rattlesnake.

Garrett said, "I've got a limited field of view without exposing myself in the doorway."

Alex said, "Keep your cover and be safe." After a moment he added, "You looked like you had a little problem moving fast."

Garrett said, "Yeah, Sometimes my old back problem flares up at the worst possible moment."

"Like running for cover so you don't get shot?"

"I was thinking more like having sex."

Alex laughed.

Garrett said, "You think anyone is out back?"

"I don't think there is anyone out back. I had a brief delay and the only shots at me came from the front."

Garrett said, "Okay."

Alex said, "I think your high ground is still our secret."

Garrett glanced out the front hayloft door then moved to look out the back one. Alex heard the older man limping slowly in the loft. Under a gentle rain of dust and ancient straw sent down by Garrett's movement Alex hoped the upper flooring would hold. Pieces of old straw continued to rain gently down from the loft causing Alex to sneeze.

Struggling to stifle more sneezes Alex moved quickly toward the front door but stopped by the pile of items Kit had assembled earlier. A wooden box of rusty metal globes with wicks sticking out of the top caught his eye. Sneezing uncontrollably, he lifted a rusty smudge pot and oil inside the globe sloshed around.

Alex called up to Garrett. "I'm going to start some smudge pots burning. The wind is in our favor and should blow the smoke into the clearing to give us some cover or even smoke out the shooters in the woods."

Garrett said, "Good idea. Maybe the smoke will attract some attention and the sheriff or VFD will come to investigate."

"We should be so lucky."

"I just hope they don't think it's some farmer simply burning off their field."

Alex lit the wicks on five oil-burning smudge pots intending to fill the air in front of the barn with thick black smoke. He used a long pole saw handle to push the smudge pots out the front door of the barn. The wind took the thick, oily, black smoke and made it swirl in the large clearing between the barn and woods.

Garrett said, "All we can do now is wait."

"Yeah, hurry up and wait."

"Yeah. Copy, that."

In the stifling hot cabin, Charles wiped sweat out of his eyes and worried. Certain that there were actual attackers, Charles re-checked the locks on the back window and back door. Next he confirmed that the giant fireplace's flue was closed so no one could drop a Molotov Cocktail down the chimney. He returned to the kitchen window and stared out silently.

Ethan looked over Charles's shoulder. Black smoke drifted throughout the clearing. He patted Charles on the shoulder and said, "Looks like something is going on. I hoped it's planned."

Charles said, "Maybe the smoke will draw in help?" The comment sparked an idea in Ethan's mind.

Charles kept his gaze on the yard, rifle in hand. He was determined not to let his friends down now that he had no escape. Realizing he had no choice in the matter Charles grew determined to make the best of the bad situation, which included ignoring Ethan.

Ethan disappeared into the bunkroom and Charles fumed silently as his responsibility grew to covering two windows. Fearful of the unguarded garden window Charles moved between the two silently cursing Ethan for leaving his post.

After a moment Charles heard water running in the master bathroom but gave the sound little thought. A minute later Ethan returned to the great room dumping a damp sleeping bag into the fireplace.

Ethan opened the flue then lit the dry corner of the bag fanning the flame until the sleeping bag was blazing away. The damp bag began to send white, acrid, smoke up the chimney into the sky.

Charles turned to look at the commotion and the source of the horrible smell. A moment later he ran toward Ethan and shouted, "That's my sleeping bag! What the hell?"

Ethan used an iron poker to arrange the smoldering sleeping bag. Ethan shrugged and gave Charles a 'oh' look. Charles flipped Ethan the bird and turned back to the window. He muttered loudly under his breath, "You're an ass."

Ethan said, "Sorry, they all look alike in the dark and I was in a hurry. But, it's going for a good purpose, with all of the smoke maybe the sheriff or local fire spotter will see the smoke and respond and put an end to all of this nonsense."

Charles glared at Ethan but said nothing, reluctantly admitting Ethan had good idea; but he did not for one moment believe Ethan's act of choosing his sleeping bag had been an accident. Ethan continued to poke at the smoldering bag.

Charles shook his head without responding or admitting Ethan had a great idea. He returned to the kitchen window as thick white smoke rose through the chimney. Satisfied with the blazing sleeping bag Ethan shouldered his shotgun and stood beside Charles.

Charles icily said, "Why don't you go cover the garden window?"

Ethan said, "Well, at least by this window it's cool."

Charles ignored him for a minute before saying, "You may have a good idea, but you are still an ass."

Ethan shrugged, "It was an honest mistake; I'll buy you a new sleeping bag."

Charles said, "Why don't you go back to the garden window? We both can't shoot out the same window. Keep an eye out for Kit."

Ethan said, "We're here to lend support and make sure none of the bad guys come through these doors. Between my scattergun and your peashooter, we've got the cabin locked down. Just chill."

Charles looked nervously at the shuttered rear window then returned his gaze to the mix of black and white smoke mingling in the clearing outside. Ethan cradled his shotgun and watched through the window as well. He said, "Looks like a Fourth of July party gone bad." Charles took a small side step away from Ethan.

In the barn, Garrett coughed and waved black smoke out of his face as he called down from the hayloft. "I see the wind is shifting, I guess the flow into the clearing wasn't the prevailing wind direction. This could have gone better for us. What do you think the bad guy is doing?"

Alex wiped watery eyes and coughed before he answered, "Oh, he's waiting for the smoke to fill the barn and force us out into the open while laughing his ass off. You know, best laid plans and all of that."

Garrett said, "Or, he's waiting for us to suffocate in our own smoke."

"While laughing his ass off."

Garrett said, "What now?"

Alex said, "Maybe it is time for Plan B or C?"

"What do you think Sun Tzu would say about this situation?"

Alex waved smoke out of his face. "Hmmm."

Garrett gagged as he said, "We are going to need to bug out soon if the barn keeps filling up with smoke."

"Yeah, it seemed like a good idea at the time."

"We will need to go into the woods behind the barn here and circle the long way back to the cabin."

"Give the wind a minute, it may change direction again."

"I'm not sure how much more of this I can take. Let's hope the wind shifts soon. I'm having a hard time breathing."

Ethan was surprised at how fast the sleeping bag burned. Still believing his idea to summon help by adding to the smoke was sound; he gathered the remaining sleeping bags and wetted them before tossing a second bag on top of the first one.

Most of the smoke flowed up the chimney but the noxious smell of burning sleeping bag material filled the cabin. Ethan waved his hand in front of his nose to disperse the odor. Charles tried to wave the odor out through the window while remaining silent, loath to admit he believed that Ethan's idea had merit.

As Charles stared out of the window he felt better knowing other sleeping bags were being burned in the name of summoning help. Ethan poked the burning sleeping bag with an iron poker and got the flames eating at the damp material. Charles looked back at the fire and wondered what carcinogens were in the fumes they were inhaling.

Preston watched the thick black smoke envelope the barn. Preston had seen the man in the Boonie hat push the ancient smudge pots past the threshold of the barn's main door wondering what the man was thinking. The wind was intermittent and when blowing did not keep to a single direction. Preston was certain the smoke was cover for some kind of offensive attack, but what that might look like he could not imagine; he also knew better than to waste ammo shooting into the smoke blindly hoping to hit someone.

Kit studied the black smoke also wondering what the men in the barn were thinking. He wiped his brow then looked up at the sky to see how high the black smoke was rising. That was when he noticed thick white smoke billowing out of the cabin's stone chimney.

John Lee wasn't confused by the thick oily smoke. He assumed the men inside the barn had tried something that went horribly wrong. He kept one eye out for the man in the woods and the other eye out for the men in the barn to come rushing outside to escape the black, noxious, smoke. John Lee hoped activity from the barn might draw the short man out into the open for a shot.

Preston began to feel as if an army of ants were crawling on his skin. He lifted his pants legs just to be certain fire ants weren't swarming him. It was then he remembered the grenades in his cargo pockets. Frustrated by the wait, angry at himself for prematurely attacking and giving away their position, and annoyed by the black, acrid, smoke that would occasionally drift over his position, he took a grenade from his pocket, pulled the pin, and hurled it toward the front of the barn. The grenade landed yards in front of the door and blew a large crater in the earth that got everyone's attention; but otherwise it was ineffective.

The explosion startled everyone except Preston. Alex and Garrett took cover behind the barn's thick vertical support posts. Kit instinctively hit the ground. John Lee dropped like a rock to the leaf covered forest floor then popped right back up looking around for what Preston had blown up. Ethan and Charles ducked below the open kitchen window looking at each other with wide, frightened eyes.

Preston readied his rifle and waited for a reaction from the men while trying and failing to ignore the sensation of ants biting his bare skin. Grudgingly he concluded the men in the barn must have some training since there was no wild return fire or panic after the explosion. Preston suddenly felt he might have worthy adversaries and that thought distracted him from the sensation of biting insects swarming his body. Body armor could protect him from bullets but not out of control nerve sensations.

Cowering below the cabin window Ethan said, "Well, that was unexpected." Charles glared at him. Ethan shrugged and leaned against the wall. The men stared at the bullet damage in the back wall.

Garrett called down to Alex, "Was that what I thought it was?"

Alex said, "A grenade."

Garrett said, "Time to show them we have explosives too."

Alex remained silent.

The wind had shifted and was finally blowing in one direction, although it was an inconvenient direction for the two men in the barn. The blinding smoke from the smudge pots began collecting in the barn, filling every nook and cranny in the aged structure. The smoke thickened making Alex and Garrett cough and fight for breath. Garrett risked poking his head out of the loft's back door for a lung full of fresh air. Coughing between rasped words Garrett called down to Alex.

"What do you think we should do? This oil smoke may kill us before the enemy has a chance to do it first."

"Keep an eye out. I'm going to improvise."

"What?"

"I'm going to create a diversion. Keep an eye out for the shooter's position if he fires on my diversion."

"I can't see though the smoke. If he sees the smoke move oddly he'll just shoot at the movement and hope for a hit."

"Roger that. Just stay protected and wait on my decoy to make whatever move you need to do."

The conversation was interrupted by a coughing fit by both men. Once the coughing subsided the conversation resumed.

"Okay. What is your diversion? I can't see anything to make any kind of move. I've got to get out of the smoke!'"

"Can't talk. Too much smoke. Stay alert, I'm moving to the horse stalls."

Alex fanned his way through the smoke to the aged farm tractor parked in the endmost horse stall. According to Kit, Ulysses had paid people to maintain the farm once he had entered the nursing home, but he'd been dead a year plus; Alex hoped the idle time had not been detrimental to the fuel or machine. The large rubber tires still held air and that gave Alex hope for the rest of the tractor. He checked that the key was in the ignition and that the tank had fuel in it. Alex ran his hand over the tractor's engine saying a silent thank you to the tractor for what it was about to do.

Blinking back a steady stream of tears caused by the caustic smoke, Alex grabbed a discarded scarecrow he had seen earlier and placed it on the tractor's metal seat. Ripping pounds of old, filthy shop rags out of the scarecrow's torso he filled the gaping hole with a gallon glass jug of gasoline capped by a rag. Alex stuffed more rags into the cavity surrounding the gas filled jug then re-buttoned the scarecrow's tattered, red and black checkered, flannel shirt. He secured the scarecrow into the driver's seat by running two bungee cords around both to hold the scarecrow in place. Putting the tractor in neutral, to keep the shooters from hearing engine noise, he laboriously pushed the tractor toward the barn's front door.

After aligning the tractor with the center of the front door Alex tied a rope around the steering wheel to keep it moving straight once he started the machine moving forward. The engine started easily but coughed out diesel smoke adding to the noxious mix already filling the inside of the barn.

After pausing until he was confident the engine would continue to run Alex lit the rag coming out of the top of the gallon jug. He hoped the fuse wouldn't catch the scarecrow on fire too early. After igniting the rag fuse Alex placed an iron log splitting wedge on the accelerator pedal. Once in gear the tractor chugged forward bursting through the black smoke obscuring the barn door into the less smoky clearing. The chug of the diesel engine tractor driven by a burning scarecrow riveted everyone's attention.

Garrett caught the tractor's movement out of the corner of his eye but said nothing. For a moment he considered that he might be hallucinating from the fumes.

From his vantage point in the woods, Kit looked on in disbelief as Ulysses' favorite tractor, driven by a flaming garden scarecrow, emerged from the thick black cloud obscuring the barn's front door. As Kit tried to make sense of what he was seeing a loose rag caught fire, flamed up brightly, then floated to the ground. A small patch of dry grass clippings caught fire. The tractor slowly chugged onward.

Preston evaluated the fiery tractor but, seeing no life signs in the humanoid figure sitting on it, refrained from firing on it. Even as his mind laughed at the foolish ploy his heart was pounding in his chest and a bass line thumped in his ears. The loathing he felt over his adversary using such a juvenile distraction, and invisible stinging ants, caused Preston to understand what civilians meant when they used the phrase 'itchy trigger finger'.

The Farmall tractor slowly chugged across the clearing until its front right tire struck one of the logs intended for the next big bonfire. The tractor's forward movement stalled as the tractor struggled to roll over the log. The engine strained trying to drive the tractor forward but the log refused to let the tractor advance. After a few minutes it was clear the tractor would not overcome the log. The large back tires began digging into the earth gouging deepening ruts.

Alex shook his head and decided to make things happen. He crept to the edge of the cloud of black smudge pot smoke and aimed his .308 at the scarecrow's back. He fired. The bullet shattered the glass jug and the blazing fuse ignited the fuel. The explosion was surprisingly loud and shook the cabin and barn. The resulting eruption of flames engulfed the scarecrow and tractor in a magnificent conflagration. Alex retreated toward the rear door, startled, but pleased with his distraction attempt.

John Lee, startled by the explosion, stood and gaped at the flaming tractor in wonderment. Things were exploding making him feel as if he was in an action movie. He was sure explosions were not part of the plan; but, there was chaos afoot and the attack was finally underway. He had never felt so alive and terrified at the same time; he wanted to coordinate with Preston, but now that bullets were flying he was on his own.

Kit saw John Lee standing mesmerized by the burning tractor. He raised his Winchester and took aim placing the crosshairs of his Bushnell scope directly on the man's center mass as he quartered away. The man was standing perfectly still providing an easy shot. Kit moved his finger to the trigger and applied a small amount of pressure but Kit's mind wouldn't let him pull the trigger on the unsuspecting man.

Survival instinct, anger, compassion, and his parent's teachings all fought for dominance inside Kit's mind as his finger rested on the trigger. Kit's heart was beating hard enough to deafen him. The man wasn't even aiming his gun at anyone so the thought of killing him filled Kit with disgust. Despite the fact the man and one of his companions wanted him dead, and Kit had a perfect kill shot available, he could not pull the trigger and kill the unaware man. Kit waited for the man to lift his weapon.

Garrett waved away the smoke stinging his eyes and saw John Lee staring at the burning tractor. Even though he had a clear shooting lane to his target the man was out of effective range for Garrett's bow. Unable to take a shot he moved toward the ladder hoping Alex had a shot at the exposed attacker.

Alex tried to call to Garrett but the smoke constricted his throat making him unable to speak. He had not seen a reaction from their attackers when the scarecrow exploded and caught fire so he began to suspect that their adversaries was more disciplined than he originally thought and wanted to warn Garrett.

Charles stared out of the kitchen window at the towering flames rising from the blazing tractor. Despite his ire toward Ethan he turned to his friend and said, "What the hell are they doing?" Ethan ignored the question as he moved to watch the spectacle alongside Charles. Shoulder to shoulder the friends watched the fire spread across the grass and weeds and worried about the rest of their group.

Preston grew irritated at the seemingly stalemated situation. Waiting, while attempting to stay out of the drifting smoke, gave Preston time to revisit his plan of attack. He wondered how John Lee was holding up and where he was stationed.

Smoke from the oil filled smudge pots, burning sleeping bags, grass, and the blazing tractor filled the clearing and rose into sky. The acrid, noxious, chemical smell of everything that was burning ruined the air. The sound of crackling flames filled the clearing. A rear tractor tire exploded. White hot metal expanded and groaned under the heat. The grass fire spread in an expanding circle. The kindling remains of the corral and plywood sheet began to burn.

Ethan leaned on the wall next to Charles and shook his head in disbelief. Charles could not take his eyes off of the fire.

Charles said, "Find your own window."

Ethan looked at Charles and softly said, "Are you going to be able to actually pull the trigger on the bad guy if you see one?"

Charles said, "I trust you and your scattergun."

Ethan said, "Like Bob Dylan sang, 'If you want someone you can trust, trust yourself.'"

Charles said, "I though Kit was the only Dylan fan."

Ethan said, "If you hang out with someone long enough sometimes things rub off on you."

Charles said, "I don't want you rubbing off on me; go to your own window."

"You've got the best view of the action."

"And you need to cover the side. Cover our asses!"

"I've got your fat ass covered! Do you really think I'd let any of you guys down? No one else came up with the idea of sending up a smoke signal for help. Don't sell me short! Chas!"

Preston thought he saw movement in the barn through the swirling smoke. Giving into frustration he fired two short bursts into the doorway in the front of the barn. The rounds passed through the long open ground floor impacting a tree behind the barn. Alex jumped behind a support post but refrained from returning fire.

John Lee raised his rifle as Preston's shots rang out thudding into the trees behind the smoke filled barn. Kit thumbed the safety off as John Lee searched for a target. John Lee thought he saw a man standing in the hayloft as a gust of wind created a swirling hole in the low hanging cloud of black smoke. John Lee chuckled aloud over the turn of events. With an evil smile John Lee braced his AR-15 against a tree and aimed toward the hayloft.

Kit took a breath and held it. He let the breath out nice and slow. But he couldn't pull the trigger even though he had a clear shooting lane all the way to the stranger. Kit's finger lightly tapped the trigger of his Winchester. He had an easy shot at the man's head and upper torso, but it was from behind and he couldn't pull the trigger. Kit had never shot a person, let alone killed a person, and even under the dire situation he was conflicted about the shot. His mind told him something had to be done now, but the man was turned away from him. For reasons he could not overcome, even in the face of mortal danger, Kit could not shoot him in the back.

Kit glanced in the direction the man was aiming and saw Garrett retreating toward the back of the loft and made his decision. Kit put his scope's crosshairs where the man's hand gripped the AR-15 and pulled the trigger hoping the bullet would destroy the gun or at least the man's ability to fight.

Kit's bullet hit the rifle's extended magazine. The impact knocked the weapon from John Lee's hands and he fell backwards into the brush with a loud curse. Kit could see brush and small saplings moving as John Lee retrieved his gun then scrambled toward a new location. John Lee ejected the damaged magazine then slammed a new one home before belly crawling to a safer spot.

Kit raced forward, using trees as cover, until he was near John Lee's last known position. Gasping for air, Kit knelt by a tree and tried to relocate the shooter. A disturbance in the leaves and twigs led from the tree where John Lee had been but the trail was quickly lost in the thicker undergrowth. Kit knelt and listened for movement. He grew afraid knowing he had lost his quarry.

Standing just inside the barn's rear door, the thick, black, oily smoke had become unbearable sending Garrett into a prolonged coughing fit. He waved his hands in front of his face trying to clear the noxious cloud. Alex moved to peer out the front door.

Preston noticed unnatural movement by the smoke and fired two three round bursts into the hayloft. The bullets punched holes in the old wood narrowly missing Garrett who dropped to his knees then crawled toward daylight. The retired cop's body burned with agony reminding him he was far too old for this kind of adventure. Tears of pain flowed from his eyes mixing with the oily smoke giving him a distorted raccoon mask.

Alex saw Preston's muzzle flash under the dark forest canopy and returned fired. There was no answering fire from the unseen shooter. Preston was already on the move to a new location as Alex fired. Smoke from the burning tractor was filling the woods near the shooter's last known location. The cloud of smoke hovering above the conflagration filtered the sun so deeply the clearing darkened to late dusk level brightness.

Kit reacquired John Lee as the man raised his head from cover searching for who had shot at him. The man was shaking his arms trying to offset the stinging sensation that lingered from Kit's bullet impact. John Lee occasionally looked around for Preston but he was primarily focused on locating his assailant. Kit waited for an opportunity to slowly and quietly advance on the man's position.

Suddenly the tractor's other large rear tire exploded grabbing Kit's attention. John Lee, unable to locate Preston or the short man, decided to creep back toward the cabin using the smoky darkness as additional cover. In the unnatural dimness he passed within twenty feet of Kit but neither man noticed the other. John Lee used his hunting skills to conceal his movement through the underbrush as Kit, momentarily distracted, watched the fire grow larger, slowly consuming the dry debris littering the clearing's floor.

20

>There were demons with guns
>Who marched through this place
>Killing everything that breathed
>They're an inhuman race
>
>-Alice Cooper

Garrett rested on floor near the door and called to Alex. The black smoke obscured his vision and burned his vocal cords as he spoke.

"Alex, I've got to get out of here, I can't breathe."

"Go out the back. Be wary but I think it's clear. I'm right behind you."

Garrett grimaced with pain as he crept toward clear air just outside the back door. He turned for a last look for Alex but a violent coughing fit drove him out the back door into fresher air.

Alex remained at the front door, primarily to provide cover for Garrett's escape but also looking for their attacker. As Alex lingered by the door his mind desperately sought a different plan. He took a step back further into the barn using his hand to wave away the smoke stinging his eyes. The movement of his hand caused swirls in the thick smoke.

Preston saw an area of smoke moving oddly and fired a strafing line across the door of the barn missing Alex but sending bullets whizzing over Garrett who had taken a knee outside the door. Garrett collapsed, staying on his stomach, waiting for the bullets and pain to stop.

The strafing fire ended giving Alex time to race to the back of the barn. Alex saw Garrett on his back and shouted, caught up in the moment, "Man down!"

Kit saw the big man blindly fire into open door. Preston ejected the empty magazine and shoved a new one home then wait patiently behind a pine tree waiting for a reaction from the men in the barn. Kit waited for Alex or Garret to return fire. When no answering fire occurred Kit moved trying to find a clear shot at the shooter.

Garrett crawled away from the door taking refuge at the corner of the barn. He studied the forest intending to move into the trees to circle around behind the shooter across the clearing. The retired police officer started to stand but a back spasm drove him to his knees.

Charles forced Ethan to return to the garden window. Ethan muttered about not being able to see anything from that vantage point but remained at the window. Charles ignored Ethan's complaints and continued to watch the spreading fire consume the bonfire wood.

John Lee knelt behind a thick privet patch a dozen yards beyond the neglected vegetable garden. The outhouse was to his left and beyond the outhouse were the men's trucks and trailers. John Lee looked at the unguarded food truck wondering if he could get away with a quick search for a cold drink.

From a distance Kit studied Preston, the man was big, wore camouflage clothing and face paint; he was a stark contrast to the other thinner, wiry, man. Suddenly Kit realized that the big man was standing behind a dead pine tree where one of the IEDs made from the binary compound had been placed. Kit found a clear shooting lane, took aim, and fired at the partially concealed bomb. The IED exploded but the pine tree shielded the big man from harm but not heart jolting surprise. A large section of the trunk vanished in the explosion. Preston jumped away from the tree falling to the ground disappearing into the thick, tangled, undergrowth.

A moment later a loud crack offered up a second surprise and the damaged pine tree began to slowly topple. The trunk had been severely weakened by the blast and the tree fell with a crash, landing in the clearing narrowly missing the burning tractor. A section of the dry wood began to burn as the raging grass fire enveloped the new fuel. Kit squeezed his eyes closed and shook his head surprised at the power of the explosion. The spreading fire worried Kit; it was bad enough they were under attack, but a forest fire would be catastrophic and unstoppable.

A long moment after the tree crashed to the earth Preston reacted to the IED explosion by lobbing a grenade in Kit's direction. A tree limb deflected the grenade into the clearing where it landed in the middle of the men's ATVs. The grenade exploded and Kit's ATV became air born, flipped once, and landed in a blazing heap. Flames spread across the spilled gasoline and began licking at the remains of the other damaged ATVs. Kit searched for the man who had thrown the grenade forgetting about the thin man. Grenades changed everything and Kit suddenly wished they had created more improvised explosive devices.

Preston moved quickly using the chaos as distraction. He raced across the smoke obscured yard taking a position at the front corner of the barn furthest from the cabin. Preston's heart was filled with joy; even the relentless sensation of biting ants couldn't dampen his sense of impending victory. It seemed that he was battling fools, luck was on his side, and everything was going his way.

Inside the cabin Ethan joined Charles at the kitchen window ignoring the danger of being so exposed. They stared at the burning ATVs. A second ATV erupted in fresh flames as its gas tank exploded. Charles pulled his head back into the cabin and wiped his hand across his eyes groaning softly. Ethan looked at Charles, but said nothing. His only thought was, 'this is our biggest fuckup ever' but softly said, hoping to ease the tension, "Hey, at least your ATV isn't blowing up."

Charles glared at Ethan but remained silent. Ethan moved away and stared out the garden window.

Alex could not see what the results of the explosions were, but he knew one had come from a grenade and the other from the binary compound device. Unable to see through the smoke he turned his attention to Garrett thankful and relieved the man was still alive.

Alex asked gently, "Are you okay?'

Garrett asked, "What the hell happened out front?"

Alex replied, "I couldn't see. After he strafed the front of the barn I ducked for cover. We might be in trouble; none of my plans are working the way I intended them to."

"No shit."

Alex said, "Seems I'm having an off day."

"Who are these guys that the twins pissed off? Fully automatic weapons, ARs most likely, and grenades; these guys came prepared."

"So it seems."

"So they wanted to jam the back door of the cabin and pick us off as we came out the front?"

"That's sound strategy. Lucky something prevented that."

"Do you think Kit is okay?" Garrett looked at Alex.

"I don't know where he was when the grenade exploded."

Garrett said, "I don't know. We need to do something. What do you suggest?"

Alex sighed and joined Garret sitting in the dirt. He patted Garrett on the shoulder offering unspoken support then peeked around the corner of the barn. Alex whistled aloud. "Damn, that last explosion took out our ATVs."

"What?" Garrett grimaced then peered around the corner of the old barn.

Alex leaned against the old wood of the barn with his eyes closed thinking about what to do next. His foot tapped the dirt as his mind raced.

Garrett stared at the blazing conflagration and said, "What are we going to do?"

Alex said, "I'm thinking. The problem is that we can't communicate with anyone nor do we know where anyone, friend or foe, is at the moment. Give me a minute."

Garrett said, "Okay. I'll go to the other corner over there and see what there is to see."

"Good. Be careful. I'll have a plan in a minute."

Garrett studied the forest on the far side of the barn. Other than clouds of black smoke hovering in the air, that side of the clearing seemed free of attackers and carnage.

Garrett planned to enter the woods then cautiously make his way around the clearing to surprise their attackers from the rear. As he turned to tell Alex his plan his back seized up freezing him in place. He hoped Alex would devise a plan as he waited for the pain to subside.

Alex looked at Garrett sitting on the dirt and said, "Did you come up with something?"

Through clenched teeth Garrett said, "Back spasm."

Alex said, "Okay. Just stay put."

John Lee watched the open cabin window facing the garden plot. He observed it for several minutes searching for any signs of movement inside the darkened cabin. He knew there were at least two other men still in the cabin. John Lee felt emboldened believing the two men in the cabin must be softies because they remained in the safety of the cabin rather than being out in the fray like the other men. He wished Preston had given him a grenade that he could lob into the cabin. Inside the cabin, movement in the semi-darkened room caught his attention. John Lee began to move from tree to tree creeping toward the unguarded garden window.

Inside the cabin it was growing hotter from the smoldering sleeping bags. The smell was nauseating. Charles cradled his .22 and stared at the burning ATVs. He said, without looking at Ethan, "Things are getting out of hand."

From across the room Ethan said, "No kidding. I have to shit. Can you handle things while I'm occupied?"

"Now? I thought those pills stopped you up." Charles snorted dismissively.

"When you gotta go, you gotta go."

Ethan winked at Charles then hurried toward the bathroom with his shotgun slung over his good shoulder. Charles turned and watched Ethan disappear into the bathroom. Charles divided his attention between the kitchen window and the garden plot window. Nervous sweat mingled with heat sweat. Wiping his eyes he snuck a look at his cell phone. There were still no signal bars. Charles looked toward the satellite phone cursing himself for the oversight of forgetting to charge the battery or program it before leaving the office. Despair overcame him as he thought of his sons.

The big man had vanished and Kit began to suspect the thin man had gotten past him unseen. Kit slowly crept past the burning ATVs searching for the thin man. It was difficult to see too far ahead. The clearing was eerily dark from the cabin's chimney pumping its own white smoke into the column of smoke rising from the ATVs, the tractor, the bonfire fuel, pine tree, and grass clippings. The fire was moving away from the cabin but slowly eating its way toward the edge of the forest. The scene made Kit feel like he was in a waking nightmare watching his hopes and dreams turn to ash in front of his astonished eyes.

John Lee crouched behind tall weeds growing in the abandoned garden plot. He watched the cabin window for more movement. More than ever he wished he had a grenade to use.

Alex turned to find Garrett grimacing as he struggled to stand. Alex raised an eyebrow, "Can you make it in your condition?"
Garrett nodded unable to speak.

Preston saw an unnatural swirl at the barn's front door as a gust of wind manipulated the smoke. The odd swirl looked man made to Preston so he fired two short bursts into the barn.

John Lee emerged from the weedy garden hoping Preston's bursts of gunfire and growing fires would distract anyone in the cabin who might have been guarding the garden window.

Kit saw the thin man's movement in his peripheral vision. Immediately Kit realized that the man was moving in for an assault on the cabin and envisioned Ethan and Charles bickering or fixating on the ruined ATVs, unaware of the thin man's advance.
When no one from the cabin fired at the thin man Kit broke cover and raced through the trees. He ignored branches slapping his face as he ran to get to the thin man before he could fire through the open window. Kit's foot caught on an exposed root and he tripped landing face first in the leaves. Kit rolled behind a tree expecting a barrage of bullets to come his way. Nothing happened and he was grateful the thin man's attention was focused elsewhere.

John Lee crouched below the cabin window listening for voices. The cabin was quiet. John Lee grew confident that the men were either securing their drug making equipment and supplies or were fixated on the chaotic action in the clearing. He smiled, knowing the element of surprise was his.

Kit rose to his feet and began running again keeping one eye on the thin man who was crouched beneath the window, listening. Kit made his way to the outhouse undetected. He knelt next to the outhouse where he found a clear sight line to the thin man lurking below the open window.
In the clearing another ATV tire exploded.

Charles considered recording a last message to his sons on his cell phone's voice recorder app. Ethan made an indistinguishable noise from the bathroom. Charles sighed and reached for his phone.

The exploding tire emboldened John Lee to make his move. He rose quickly for a sneak peek into the cabin. He saw at least one man in a Hawaiian shirt standing at the front window. Ducking back down, keeping his head below the window ledge, John Lee slid the barrel of his rifle through the open window.

Inside the cabin Ethan emerged from the bathroom in time to see the barrel of John Lee's rifle cross the windowsill. He shouted for Charles to take cover but his warning came too late. At the sound of Ethan's warning shout John Lee pulled the trigger.

The AR's rounds dug into the furniture, the walls, and ricocheted off the cast iron cooking stove. Charles tried to find cover but tripped over the trashcan. He fell onto his hands and knees and screamed as bullet fragments ricocheted off the cast iron stove ripping flesh from his butt cheeks. Charles screamed at the searing pain.

Ethan felt no shoulder pain as he reacted to the attack. He shouldered his shotgun and fired at the window. Outside, John Lee felt the buckshot whiz past him peppering the trees at the forest edge. John Lee, fueled by adrenaline, pushed his rifle barrel through the window and fired blindly keeping the trigger down until the magazine was empty. The bullets chipped away at the upper wall and ceiling, missing Charles and Ethan. Ethan struggled to reload with only one good arm. Charles continued to scream in pain. Kit shouldered his Winchester.

John Lee pulled the muzzle back below the window and ejected the empty magazine. He pulled a fresh magazine from his pocket replacing the empty one. He heard shouting and screams of pain from inside the cabin but was unable to make out any words; but the tone of the shouting told him he had done some damage. For the last time he wished Preston had given him a grenade.

Ethan aimed his shotgun at the window and waited. Daring to take his eyes from the window, Ethan cast a glance in Charles's direction. Charles was writhing, bloody, and slapping at his ass.

From his position by the outhouse Kit fired hitting John Lee in the ribs. John Lee screamed, slumped down on the dirt next to the cabin's wall, swung his rifle in Kit's direction, and pulled the trigger emptying the fresh magazine. Kit dove into the outhouse as bullets flew his direction. One of the last bullets in John Lee's magazine hit the IED Kit had placed next to a tree near the outhouse. The IED exploded, its shock wave knocking the outhouse off its foundation and pushing Kit into the collection hole below it. Kit vanished from view as the structure collapsed into a heap.

John Lee watched Kit disappear down the sinkhole as the outhouse collapsed into a pile of splintered kindling. John Lee had difficulty breathing; he knew the rifle round had done major damage. He put a hand over the bullet hole frantically trying to stop the bleeding. Panic set in and the world grew blurry but John Lee forced himself to his feet fighting the pain, weakness, and shock. The thin man struggled to stand using the wall for support then forced himself to stagger toward the forest. He did not waste energy looking back at the cabin or destroyed outhouse.

Ethan was at the garden window and fired at the retreating man. The buckshot peppered the man's back and he stumbled forward. The thin man used his rifle as support as his feet faltered. Ethan fired twice more and the thin man fell face first to the ground and died. Ethan watched making sure the man was dead; then unaware that Kit had been blown into the outhouse sinkhole, turned his attention to Charles.

Garrett said, "I wish I had one of Ethan's pain pills right now."
Alex said, "Garrett, are you going to be okay?"
"Yeah. This is just a real inopportune time for my back to go out on me."
"Is there ever a good time?"
"Not really."
The men looked at each other conveying their concern without speaking. For a few moments following the gunfire and explosion the only sound was that of the fire raging in the clearing.
Alex said, "I've got to get a better vantage point. Why don't you find a comfortable spot to stay safe?"

"The pain is less. I'll be okay in a moment."

"So you say. But will you be able to draw your bowstring?"

"Yes."

Alex did not believe Garrett but admired his determination. "How far can you move?"

"I can make it to the rain barrel on that side of the barn."

"That's not any type of protection if they shoot at you."

"I'll try to get them first."

"I don't know about this."

Garrett grimaced from the pain, "Look I've got to do something. I don't think we can afford to lose a man."

Alex said, "In your condition, you're a liability. No offense but the fewer people I have to worry about the better."

"Look, Alex, I know you have experience none of us have. With me limited, all you have is Kit. At least I was a cop and I do have training. Kit means well but he's never had anything shoot back at him. And, those two in the cabin are probably worthless. I'm only half worthless; at least until the spasms stop. Go. Use your training and experience to save us all. I'll be okay in a few, the pain is already less." Garrett lifted his bow and gently pumped it up and down as if to prove to Alex he was improving. Alex saw tears of pain swell in the old man's eyes but nodded and patted him on the shoulder.

"Okay." Alex winked at the old man then moved to the opposite side of the barn and surveyed the area. Alex returned and gave Garrett his sidearm, "I know you can't pull your bowstring so take this. Don't argue. It has a full magazine. Don't argue. Take it!"

Garrett took Alex's sidearm and said, "Thanks."

Alex dashed away through the smoke. Garrett turned toward the old rain barrel considering his options. He crawled to the barrel breathing hard and fighting back blinding tears from the pain. Behind him, in the woods, Garrett heard a noise and turned to see who was making it. The twisting movement sent needles of searing pain through him. Garrett placed one hand on the barrel for support, the other holding Alex's Glock in a white knuckle grip.

Preston, annoyed by the smoke surrounding the barn, retreated into the forest. Impatiently he waited, looking for targets of opportunity, while considering what to do next. He risked taking his attention from the barn to look for John Lee.

Widespread fire roared over all other sounds. The fallen pine tree was fully engulfed by flames adding the acrid smell of burning pine to the mix. Another ATV tire exploded. The bonfire wood fueled tall, bright, dancing flames.

Kit woke painfully contorted but alive. He was halfway down the outhouse collection hole. Rocks dug into his back and wooden splinters pierced his arms, shoulders, and face. Kit's hearing came back slowly as he stared upward into a smoky sky. Sound came to him as if he had his ears stuffed with cotton while sitting in a barrel. With a deep breath of determination and bad expectations Kit slowly began to climb out of the sinkhole using jutting rocks and gnarled roots for handholds as he inched toward the sky. The stench of unseen refuse at the bottom of the hole motivated him upward.

Taking a rest Kit looked down into the ominous sinkhole and saw only darkness, fortunately no noxious pile of refuse was visible, only an empty void. Kit should have been happy he was still alive but he hurt too much to be anything more than thankful. His head throbbed and his body pulsed with shots of pain each time he pulled himself higher. During another rest Kit looked up expecting to see his executioner pointing a gun down at him but the opening was clear and he could see sky.

It was at that moment an earworm began and jumbled lyrics from a song looped in Kit's mind. He grabbed a root and grimaced as he looked up toward the opening. He shook his head to clear the song but pain from the movement overpowered his ability to focus and he knew he had to let the earworm run its course. He tried to ignore the pain wracking his body as the lyrics gave him hope.

> *'Ain't found a way to kill me yet,*
> *Eyes burn with stinging sweat,*
> *Every path seems to lead me nowhere,*
> *The bullets scream at me from somewhere,*
> *Here they come to snuff the rooster,*
> *You know I ain't gonna die.'*

Giving into the unstoppable earworm he turned it into motivation. Kit slowly climbed upward more determined than ever to end his waking nightmare.

The combination of smells, smoke, sweat, sticky blood, and pain nearly overloaded Kit's senses. He knew he might be climbing to his death but the smell of shit below and promise of escape above drove him relentlessly upward. He kept glancing at the opening expecting to see his executioner block out the light just before pulling the trigger. Each foot he gained without getting killed lifted his spirit as well as his body.

Inevitability, anger, and acceptance slightly tempered the constant pain that challenged his effort to climb out of the sinkhole. Just below the lip of the sinkhole, hanging by its tattered shoulder strap on a thick root, was his beloved lever action Winchester. Unfortunately the Winchester was a total loss, the scope was ripped from its mounts and the barrel had a life ending bend in it.

Kit took a moment to rest and mourn the loss of his Winchester rifle. Kit touched the shattered stock angry over the loss of his Winchester. Turning his thoughts away from the destruction of his rifle he was grateful he had no broken bones but his muscles felt tight and were slow to respond. Blood seeped from multiple puncture wounds and scrapes inflicted by rocks and glass and wood splinters; tears of loss mingled with stinging sweat. Ignoring the pain Kit resumed his climb toward the surface.

Garrett was unwillingly frozen in place, unable to move because of the back spasm. He forced his eyes to turn toward the source of soft leaf rustling sound. A large red squirrel rooted through the leaves at the wood line unconcerned about the chaos unfolding around it. Garrett tried to smile at the situation but couldn't. He wiped a tear from his eye and forced himself to peek around the rain barrel.

Kit raised his head above the edge of the sinkhole and glanced around. Smoke filled the sky beyond and above the cabin. Pieces of the outhouse burned and smoldered around him. He heard the crackling of the raging fire and another ATV tire blow out.

The fire roared in the clearing. The fires closest to the barn and cabin died as the grass clippings were consumed and the blaze reached bare dirt surrounding the structures. A shift in the breeze delayed the flames from reaching the forest, but a change of direction could undo that in a heartbeat.

Kit clawed his way onto the surface ignoring the pain and wet, sticky, blood. He pulled himself to his knees and looked around fearful of finding himself looking at the muzzle of his attacker's weapon. Once his eyes focused, Kit saw the thin man's body lying beyond the garden plot, almost to the woods. It was obvious the man was dead. Kit felt a wave of relief at the sight.

Kit glanced toward the cabin window overlooking the garden and saw no movement but did hear loud, agitated, voices coming from inside the cabin. The voices of his friends ended the earworm and brought a wave of relief to Kit. He rolled onto his back then lay staring at the sky waiting for the world to stop spinning madly around him.

Preston used the lull in the fight to move to a new position wishing he had remembered to pack walkie-talkies; he really needed to coordinate with John Lee as he became more concerned about the attack becoming a siege and the massive amount of smoke drawing unwanted attention before they could finish off the intruders. The heat and smoke intensified Preston's thirst challenging his concentration.

Kit, wobbly on his feet, walked to the dead man and knelt beside him. Kit noticed the buckshot wounds in addition to his shot. Preston saw movement and ducked behind a tree where he watched the short stocky man moving toward the woods, seemingly without concern. Preston watched, frustrated that he was unable to draw a bead on the man from his current position. The short man stopped then knelt down. Preston then saw John Lee lifeless on the ground. He saw the short man check John Lee's body then take his weapon and check John Lee's pockets. Realizing the situation had taken a bad turn Preston began a strategic withdrawal back to his ATV.

Kneeling beside the thin man Kit felt for a pulse to make sure he was dead, although the visible amount of blood loss and wounds assured he was. Kit took the dead man's rifle, ejected the spent magazine, loaded a new magazine he took from the dead man's cargo pocket and secured the magazine in the gun. He chambered a round and made sure the firing selector was on full automatic. He also pocketed the last full magazine John Lee had on him.

Kit smiled as he held the new weapon then looked at the enormous cloud of smoke rising into the sky. Anger, resolve, and the desire for revenge coalesced in Kit as he turned his attention from his own pain to his friends. A wave of guilt over getting them into this situation washed over him adding to his physical pain.

Leaving John Lee's body, Kit staggered to the cabin's front door and hugged the wall next to it before announcing himself. He did not want a face full of buckshot. He heard raised, distressed, voices coming from the dark interior of the cabin.

Kit yelled as loudly as he could. The effort hurt. "It's Kit. You guys okay in there?"

Ethan answered, "We're alive. Chas took some shrapnel to his ass. But no vitals were hit. Unless you believe his brains are in his ass."

Charles said, "Shut the fuck up and fix me, damn it!"

Kit yelled, "I'm coming in!"

Kit stuck his head in the door. Charles was lying on the dining table with his pants down around his ankles. Both ass cheeks were a bloody mess. Ethan was soaking up blood and using hemostats from the first aid kit to pick out metal fragments from Charles's damaged ass.

Charles was in obvious pain, gripping the edge of the table in a vise like grip. Ethan seemed delighted to be administering medical help to Charles. Kit watched and wondered if Ethan was enjoying inflicting pain in the name of helping a little too much.

Kit said, "I'm going after the other guy. I don't know anything about Alex or Garrett. Do you?"

Charles said through gritted teeth, "Probably better off than me right now." His voice was an octave higher than normal as he spoke through the pain.

Kit looked Charles's bloody ass and said, "Yeah."

Charles said through clenched teeth, "I'm sure they're okay."

Ethan looked at Kit for the first time and exclaimed, "What the hell happened to you? Are you okay? You look like shit."

Kit said, "Later. What is his condition?"

Ethan said, "Kit you are the epitome of 'walking wounded'. Charles is lucky a piece of shrapnel didn't nick his actual asshole or he'd be in for a bad time. He's going to have to stay off of his ass for a while."

Kit asked again, "What about the Alex and Garrett?"

Alex stuck his head through the kitchen, window. "We're both okay. Garrett's back went out on him and he's out by the rain barrel on the far side of the barn. Maybe after you finish working on Charles you can help get him back inside the cabin. I'm going after the big guy. I saw him retreating."

Kit said, "I'm coming with you."

"No."

Charles said, "Just let him go. Let's go get the cops."

Kit lifted John Lee's weapon so Alex could see it. "You don't have a say. This is my land and my mess. My responsibility. We're sending up enough smoke for the whole county to see and no one has come to check it out. I say that puts the responsibility squarely on us. And, I am not going to spend the rest of my time down here worrying and watching over my shoulder, never able to enjoy a hike in the woods or a peaceful night's sleep thinking someone is after me, or worse yet, live in fear over a case of mistaken identity because of the fucking twins. They blew me down a literal shit hole and I am fucking mad as hell. I'll do it alone if I have to, but this is my battle to finish!"

Alex said "No!" as firmly as he could.

Kit said, "We either work together or separately, but we will be working toward the same end. United we stand, divided we fall and all that. They tried to kill us, kill my dream! I'm finishing this with or without help. Period."

Alex thought it over for several long seconds. "I'm trained you are not. That makes you a liability. I can't do my job if I'm worrying about you."

"Okay. Stay here and tend to the wounded. You're trained in that too. I'll take on the other guy."

Ethan said, "I could use some help here. I'm just winging it on this."

Charles said, "Great. Yes, someone trained please take over!"

Alex glanced half-heartedly at Charles's bare bloody ass, "It doesn't look too bad. Just hope it didn't sever any muscles. You're doing fine, Ethan. Try to use that super glue stuff to close the wounds if you have to."

Ethan said, "I thought you couldn't find any to use on me?"

Charles said, "Glue?"

Alex said, "Yes. Look again!"

Ethan sighed, "Okay. Charles, take two of these pills." Ethan pulled a pill bottle from his pocket, opened it and handed two pills to Charles.

Charles hesitated, looking at the offered pills, then grabbed them both. Ethan grabbed a half-empty bottle of warm water and handed it to Charles. Charles swallowed the pills without question.

Alex said, "Good."

Charles asked, "How long until they kick in?"

Kit said, "I could use one of those too."

Ethan gave two pills to Kit then said, "Right you go. I'm going to find some kind of glue, anybody know where to find some? I'll look harder than any of you looked for me."

Kit said, "Look in the glove compartment of my truck. Maybe you should give Garrett one of your pain pills while you're out there."

Ethan said, "Okay" and moved toward the back door of the cabin. No one had removed the nail so after a few tugs Ethan turned around, gave everyone a sheepish grin, and exited out the front without a word. Charles rested his forehead on his forearms and groaned loudly into the tabletop.

Alex stared at Kit. Kit met his gaze. Alex, with obvious resignation in his voice, said, "Come on, he's already got a head start."

Kit called out to Ethan as he reached the edge of the cabin, "Ethan! After you take care of Charles and Garrett check on the fires out front. We cannot let them reach the forest. Do not let this turn into a forest fire. We cannot be responsible for a forest fire. Do you understand?"

"Yes, take care of the injured then try to douse the fires. No problem. Go on and put an end to all of this insanity."

Kit glared at Ethan, "Take care of the damn fires. Don't let me down. Do not let the flames get into the forest!"

Ethan nodded.

21

> Clip the wings that get you high,
> Just leave them where they lie
> And tell yourself, "You'll be the death of me"
>
> -Seether

Kit carried John Lee's AR-15 in a firm grip ready to shoulder it and fire at a moment's notice. Alex carried his .308 as well, growing more nervous with every step, expecting an ambush as Kit bulled his way through the forest.

Alex said, "Trade guns with me."

Kit said, "No."

"I've got more experience with that type of weapon."

"You might be a better marksman than me, but my Winchester is destroyed, they blew me into a shithole, and set fire to my dreams. This is the gun I want when I face the asshole who started this."

"You mean Ethan?"

"No. I mean the guy who shot back at Ethan and wouldn't let it go. The maniac didn't even try to talk it out. And this feud shit must be more common place than I thought. Plus, we're sending up enough smoke to simulate a forest fire and they haven't even sent a plane up to check it out. I think this is what people mean when they use the term Southern Justice."

Alex said, "Okay. I just don't think this is a good idea."

Kit spit out, "Noted." Alex chose not to pursue the subject.

Preston took a circuitous through the forest winding his way back to the ATV. He did not want to leave an obvious trail for his enemies to follow. Once on his four-wheeler he could put distance between himself and the cabin and have time to think about his next action now that John Lee was dead.

Alex and Kit moved with single minded purpose trying to catch the big man from behind. They followed the ATV trail believing that was how the attackers had found the cabin. As sticks cracked under Kit's feet and his relentless, determined, pace Alex felt the familiar anxiety of patrolling unknown terrain come flooding back to him, but he kept it to himself.

Ethan had given Garrett one of his pain pills and a bottle of water then knelt beside him giving Garrett an update. Afterwards Garrett tried to stand but failed. Leaning against the rain barrel he gave an involuntary groan then looked at Ethan.

Garrett grimaced as he said, "I'll catch up with you. Go on. You should try to contain those fires before the forest catches on."

"That's where I'm headed next. Then I'll finish fixing Charles's ass."

Ethan got the flames nearest the tree line under control then turned his attention back to Charles. After retrieving a squeeze tube of glue from Kit's glovebox Ethan sealed Charles's wounds. Ethan had dropped all of the recovered bullet fragments onto a paper plate; intending it to be show and tell material for Charles's two sons. There was no way Charles could hide his injury from his sons, so why not have something to show for it. A story like this would cause his sons to see their dad in a whole new manly way, or so Ethan imagined.

On the other hand, Ethan dreaded going home to face his wife, Martha. The whole menopause thing she was going through, putting him through, was his reason for joining Kit's extended get-away adventure in the woods. Now, a bullet wound in his shoulder would give her innumerable reasons to squash any plan the next time Ethan wanted a guy's weekend away from home. For a long minute he thought about rushing after Alex and Kit for the final showdown. His thoughts were interrupted by Garrett who hobbled into the cabin and eased down onto the sofa.

Alex heard an ATV start up despite the custom muffler that made the engine quieter for stealthy hunting. Alex increased his pace knowing the sound meant a lesser chance of an ambush. Kit finally heard the ATV, but his muddled hearing kept him from determining how far away it was. Kit increased his pace to catch up to Alex.

The two men arrived at John Lee's ATV. The motor noise from the other ATV indicated their quarry was not too far ahead. The men noticed the body armor vest Preston had dumped in favor of lightening the load and feeling cool wind hit his sweaty skin.

Alex said, "He had body armor. We're not facing amateurs; I really think you should turn back now."

"No. I need to see this through."

"Not a good idea."

"Damn it. Okay. Don't waste time trying to talk me out of this."

Alex realized there was more to the enemy than any of them had imagined; but he was retreating which gave them the upper hand. Kit slung the rifle over his shoulder and jumped on John Lee's ATV. He turned the key starting it.

Alex grabbed Kit's arm. "No. He'll hear it."

Kit shook off Alex's hold on his arm. "Not if he's on his. Listen, these are obviously modified mufflers and damn quiet. And we can't follow him on foot with any speed. Do what you want but I'm using this ATV and hope he can't hear it over the one he's on."

Kit began to drive away from Alex. Alex shouted for Kit to stop and climbed on the back of the ATV. Kit put the ATV in gear and took off in pursuit of the big man.

Ethan returned to the cabin after rechecking the various fires; there was nothing he could do with the burning tree, farm tractor, or ATVs but let them burn out naturally. Charles was beginning to feel the effects of the pain pills although he was still lying face down on the table with his ass exposed. Ethan knew Charles was feeling less pain when he didn't complain upon his return. Garrett was sipping coffee from a large mug as he sat on the sofa.

Wanting to have a little fun Ethan winked at Garrett then sang to Charles, "Is there anybody in there. Just nod if you can hear me. Is there anybody home?"

Charles ignored him but Garrett, also feeling the positive effects of the pain medication said, "I hear you're feeling down. Well Ethan can ease your pain and get you on your feet again."

Ethan smiled at Garrett then walked to door to look at the remaining fires. The fires were contained and slowly dying. Charles groaned in reply. Garrett grunted but feeling less pain as he lifted his thermos of coffee.

Alex tapped Kit on the shoulder and motioned for him to stop. Kit throttled down and idled wondering what Alex had to say that was so important to give the big man a larger lead in their pursuit. Alex reached forward and turned the key to the off position.

Kit said, "What the hell?"

Alex said, "Listen."

There was no motor noise. The forest was eerily quiet. In the distance a bright, open area could be seen through thinning trees.

Kit was relieved they had stopped. The jarring ATV ride had been torturous on his battered body and his bloody clothes were sticky.

Alex said, "I think he went to ground up ahead. We need to go the rest of the way on foot."

Kit worried, "Do you think he heard us?"

"Too late to worry about that now." Kit heard the admonishment in Alex's voice but ignored it.

"Maybe he thought it was his buddy's ATV. I don't know if he knows his friend is dead or not. Do you?"

"I don't know where he was hiding before he fled. He may have seen his buddy or not. There's no way to know."

"Okay, forward on foot it is."

"This is not how I saw this weekend going."

"Me neither, bro, me neither." The men dismounted from the ATV.

Alex and Kit crept toward the clearing pushing low hanging limbs and vines out of their way. Once the men reached the edge of the forest they knelt behind an oak tree and surveyed the clearing. They had arrived at a large treeless area, roughly circular, with a device with solar panels located on the far side. More or less in the middle of the clearing sat an ATV and a wooden crate, but the big man was nowhere in sight.

Alex said, "Damn, he's taken position somewhere to see if it was his buddy or one of us riding in. Look hard and see if you can locate him."

Kit and Alex each took one half of the clearing and surrounding forest and searched high and low for a sign of an ambush. The men diligently looked for the glint of sun on metal, an oddly shaped or out of place shadow, movement, anything that would betray a sniper. Frustrated at not seeing their prey Kit looked at Alex wondering what to do next.

Kit said, "What do you think?"

Alex shook his head, "I don't know."

"Why did he leave the ATV out in the open?"

"I don't know."

"Okay. So, we play a waiting game now?"

"It looks that way."

The tractor had burned itself out but still radiated heat. The acrid smoke from burning material hung heavily in the air. The smudge pots had expended their fuel and sleeping bags in the fireplace had been totally consumed. The fire scarred area around the barn, cabin, and forest resembled a battle field.

Ethan leaned on the rake studying the devastated clearing. He began concocting a story to tell Martha. A minor wound from a freak ricochet was going to be hell to explain; but, losing his ATV on top of a bullet wound was going to make going home most unpleasant.

Outside of himself, Ethan felt deep sorrow for his cousin and his grand plans for Ulysses' property. The cabin was scarred from the bullets John Lee and Ethan had fired. The beautiful handcrafted outhouse was destroyed. Their ATVs were melted heaps of toxic metals and plastic. Two men had bullet wounds and another could barely move because of his previously injured back going out on him. There was no way to put a good spin on any part of this disaster. Ethan decided to use Kit's misfortunes as his benchmark, which put the upcoming confrontation with Martha in a fresh perspective.

Suddenly tires crunching on the gravel driveway made Ethan's heart jump. He raced back to the cabin, grabbed his shotgun and took up watch out of the cabin's rear window. Charles and Garrett watched his frantic movements with silent apprehension.

Alex rested against a tree and stared at Kit. Kit kept his eyes glued to the ATV wondering why it had seemingly been abandoned in the clearing. Impatience was one common thing both men had shared since meeting in college. Alex tempered his impatience with combat experience but Kit's impatience grew, fueled by anger.

Alex softly said, "You look like a bloody porcupine." He carefully picked a piece of glass out of Kit's bicep. Then he picked a splinter of lumber out of Kit's neck. Kit wiped the blood away drying his hand on his pants leg. Now that he was still, Kit felt the sharp pains and dull aches beginning to make themselves known.

Kit said, "Yeah, I'm feeling it all now. The adrenaline has worn off but the pain pill is working some."

"At least Ethan will have practiced on Charles before he gets to you."

Kit said, "Hmmm."

Alex said, "Don't worry, I'll supervise."

"That's reassuring. But, I think I want you as my triage doctor."

Alex said, "I'm going to circle around and get on the far side of the clearing. We'll try to catch him in a crossfire if he gives himself away. You'll have my back right?"

"Of course."

"Do you know how to use that rifle?"

"Aim and pull the trigger. And remember muzzle rise."

"Okay. Are your sure you don't want to trade?"

"Yes, I am sure."

Alex sighed and nodded. "Here I go. I am trusting you to watch my six."

Kit said, "I've got it."

Alex nodded while looking Kit in the eyes. Kit met Alex's gaze with steady, unblinking, resolve. Alex moved away from Kit and in a minute he was lost to sight in the thick undergrowth.

Kit scanned the clearing watching and listening intently for any sign of their enemy. The sky was clear and a light breeze rustled the tall grass in the sunny clearing. Kit stared at the ATV willing the big man to reveal himself.

Suddenly the big man appeared, rising up from behind his ATV. Kit shook his head in confusion; surely the big man had not been hiding behind the ATV all this time.

Preston had descended into the drug laboratory sinkhole to search for a drink and devise a new plan. He found nothing to drink and it made Preston angry. Frustrated and thirsty he loaded a fresh magazine and patted the magazine in his cargo pocket.

Preston opened a tub of product and took another one of John Lee's pills. Without anything to wash the pill down with he swallowed the pill with a cupped palm full of melted ice water from the cooler. Preston reprimanded himself for not arming himself and John Lee more thoroughly and for believing the rivals would be easier to take out. John Lee jamming the cabin door closed had completely ruined the element of surprise. He knew he had to return and finish the job but next time he would be better prepared. He also knew that time was of the essence as the Carson gang might go on the offense or worse, that damn smoke cloud might draw in the volunteer fire department or cops. Fortunately, if things went south, none of the Carson group would be able to identify him.

Fighting the urge to turn to his family for reinforcements Preston stared at the hanging metal ladder. The dark, dank, sinkhole seemed to stifle his thoughts and disrupt his concentration. After downing another palm full of tepid cooler water Preston began to climb up the ladder. He reached the top of the ladder and peered over the lip of the sinkhole. The world above the sinkhole was serene, almost as beautiful of a day in the woods one could hope for. Preston paused at the top of the ladder to wipe sweat out of his eyes. A slight breeze cooled his brow and the silence gave him hope that he had not been followed.

Preston pulled himself onto the grassy surface then stood next to his ATV stretching and enjoying the light breeze cooling his face. He glanced around the clearing and saw nothing out of place.

Kit saw the giant and froze not wanting to give himself away until he thought Alex was in position. Yet, he didn't want the big man to escape. Kit tensed up, ready to shoot the man, but forced himself to wait on Alex. He cut his eyes to the distant edge hoping Alex also saw the big man standing unconcerned in the bright sunshine.

Alex neared the midway point, following the tree line, moving slowly and quietly while fighting rising anxiety. To find himself in such a beautiful setting under such dangerous circumstances was hard to reconcile. That beauty and danger existed side by side was a given; but he had never imagined to experience it in such a setting. Alex rubbed his eyes trying to focus as his mind attempted to grasp the incongruity of the situation.

Kit saw the big man's AR was slung over his shoulder as he stood. Kit brought his rifle to bear on the man his finger resting lightly on the trigger. Where was Alex? Kit glanced at the gun to make sure the firing selector was where he wanted it. He just couldn't pull the trigger on the man, no matter how much he hated the man for causing all of the problems, injuries, and consequences Kit would be facing. Kit hoped the man would unsling his gun to give him a reason to fire without feeling guilty afterwards.

Preston stretched then put his hands on his hips turning his face to the sky now that he was free from the sinkhole. The sun was hot drawing even more moisture from his dehydrated body.

Kit shouted as forcefully as he could, "Drop the gun and drop to your knees. Drop the gun and raise your hands!"

Preston could not conceal the look of surprise on his face as he slowly raised his hands while looking around for the man who had shouted at him. Preston saw the short, stocky, man standing with John Lee's rifle held steady and firm.

Alex heard Kit's shouted commands and rushed to the edge of the clearing. Alex's sudden movement spooked an unnoticed yearling doe deer feeding at the edge of the clearing. The doe bolted into the clearing. The deer's flight made Alex freeze in place.

Kit reacted to the deer and took his eyes off Preston. Thirty yards into the clearing the deer made a hard ninety-degree turn and raced back into the forest. Preston reacted to the distraction first, and in a lightning quick move unslung his rifle and began firing at Kit.

Kit returned fire as he fell backwards into the brush bordering the clearing, his shots harmlessly rocketing skyward as he fell backwards. The burst from Preston ripped leaves and bark as they shredded the foliage just above Kit's falling form. The near miss sent Kit rolling behind cover as Preston continued firing.

Assured the short man was suppressed Preston instinctively spun and fired in the direction the deer had come from correctly assuming a second person had spooked the deer. Preston had his rifle in full auto mode. The trees at the edge of the forest took the brunt of the assault; bark and leaves flew every which way as Preston kept his finger on the trigger.

Alex reacted a second too slow as the arcing trail of bullets peppered the trees marking the edge of the clearing. As Alex fell away from the bullets the muzzle of his .308 was driven into the dirt and the stock took a bullet shattering on impact. Two bullets deeply grazed Alex's outer thigh as he fell to the ground. The pain was nearly overwhelming. Alex rolled behind an exposed tree root ball and looked first at his gun then at his bloody thigh. The gun was useless. He wished he had not given Garrett his Glock. He looked at his thigh and wiped blood away from the wound. Flesh was ripped but no arteries or veins had been torn open.

Preston released the empty magazine and jammed the last one home as he dropped behind his ATV. Preston felt confident that he had the upper hand as the short man could have taken a kill shot but had not. He silently scoffed at the short man's sense of honor knowing that would be the man's downfall.

Alex lay on the ground fighting confusion and pain. His heart raced nearly as fast as his thoughts. Nothing seemed right; he knew he was home but every sensation he was feeling reminded him of being under fire and cut off from his men. He knew the truth but he could not gather his thoughts. Alex looked at the blue sky and began to focus on his breathing. Once his breathing was under control he could take action.

Kit rolled onto this belly and found a sight line under the low growth. He fired at the ATV watching the bullets rip the machine's exposed side. Then Kit's magazine was empty. He had a brief thought of amazement at how quickly he ran out of ammo on the full automatic setting. Kit felt for the second magazine and realized he had lost it. Panic swelled as Kit looked around unable to find the dropped magazine.

Preston rose and fired three short bursts from behind his ATV. He dropped down behind the ATV waiting for return fire. Kit waited for Alex to fire. The silence in the clearing was deafening. The birds had gone silent. Even the breeze seemed to be hiding. Kit continued to wait for Alex to fire praying the big man's random spraying of the forest had not gotten a lucky kill shot on Alex. Unarmed, Kit felt helpless as the unbroken silence lingered.

Preston hugged the far side of the ATV next to the large rear tire. Then he remembered he had two grenades left. Unexpectedly, in the lull of the moment, the need for a drink, anything cool and wet, overcame him. His vision dimmed and there was no moisture in his mouth. He realized that despite the heat and danger he was no longer sweating. Preston remembered vaguely that not sweating was a bad thing but he could not remember exactly why it was a bad thing.

Moving sluggishly Preston repositioned himself where he was able to rest the AR on the seat of his ATV. He pulled the AR's trigger and sprayed the forest in Kit's direction with hot lead until his magazine was empty.

Kit flattened himself as Preston's rounds whizzed above his head. Kit mumbled a quick prayer asking for divine intervention.

Alex, reacting on instinct to the gunfire, reached for his Glock and felt only an empty holster. Remembering giving his sidearm to Garrett, a breathtaking wave of panic washed over him. Weaponless equaled death in his experience. A soldier was naked and vulnerable without a weapon. Alex frowned at his .308 lying useless in the leaves then took his survival knife out of its sheath. Alex sighed and looked at the clearing as he struggled to regain control of his mind.

As Kit waited for Alex to act several moments passed uneventfully as none of the men made a next move. Each second of the wait seemed to last agonizing minutes. A back beetle began to crawl over Kit's bloody body. He flicked the beetle away. The breeze resumed causing the tall grass in the clearing to sway. In the awkward silence another earworm crept into Kit's chaotic thoughts; a single line relentlessly repeating itself: *'The waiting is the hardest part.'*

The sun beat relentlessly down on the ATV and Preston. The ATV was radiating heat while darkness and cool air beckoned from the sinkhole behind him. Thoughts driven by the sun and dry heat convinced Preston that he had simply overlooked a misplaced or obscured water bottle. Surely John Lee had an emergency stash somewhere in the sinkhole. All Preston needed was an unpressured minute or two in the lab to find something to drink then he could continue his mission to kill the interlopers.

In a moment of clarity, a plan came to Preston. The big man patted his trusty Colt revolver and the two grenades remaining in his bag. He shouted through parched lips and dry tongue, "I give up." Preston threw his AR past the ATV into the clearing.

Alex, his mind clearer now, cautiously crawled to a position closer to the big man. He kept one eye on the man by the ATV and the other in Kit's direction.

Preston shouted, "I'm standing up. Don't shoot!" He slowly rose towering above the ATV. With the four-wheeler as comparison it was evident how large the killer was. His large, bald, head gleamed in the sunlight and his thick beard was black and matted.

Preston stood behind the ATV with his hands raised. The ATV's large cargo rack hid the lower part of the big man's body, and his Colt.

Kit rose from cover and stepped into the open pointing the empty gun at the big man. Preston remained motionless as the man advanced. Preston noted the man coming toward him was short but stout; he estimated taking him out would not be too difficult once he was weaponless. Preston was more concerned about the short man's unseen partner.

Preston called out again, "Don't shoot. I am unarmed."

Alex rose from the tall grass and saw the Colt holstered on the man's belt. Alex shouted the warning, "Kit, he's got a gun!"

Preston slowly turned toward Alex quickly profiling the new man. He noticed the limping man was only carrying a hunting knife. Preston felt confident he could win any knife fight.

Kit continued advancing as he shouted, "Drop your gun!"

Preston turned back to face Kit. "Okay. I'm reaching for my sidearm, do not shoot me."

Alex limped closer believing Kit had a loaded weapon and would provide cover fire if the big man made a move. His eyes never left the big man.

Preston kept one hand raised as he pretended to reach obediently for his Colt. Then, in a lightning fast move that surprised both Kit and Alex, he pulled a grenade from his bag, pulled the pin with his thumb and hurled the grenade at Kit. Kit saw something flying through the air coming his way and spun the rifle around grabbing it by its warm barrel. He swung the rifle and hit the grenade with its stock like a baseball batter swinging for the center field fence. The grenade reversed direction and sailed back toward Preston who ducked, hugging the earth between the ATV and the empty weapons crate.

Alex dropped to the ground and covered his head with his arms. Kit stood frozen in place unsure of what was happening.

The grenade dropped past Preston into the sinkhole where it exploded on the dirt floor gouging a crater below the metal ladder and igniting fires. Secondary explosions from exploding chemical vials echoed through the chamber and shot flames into the air. Unpainted wooden shelves burned and plastic melted. Small pops and explosions continued and a mix of black and grey smoke rose from the hole. A piece of flaming paper rose out of the sinkhole and landed on the empty wooden weapons crate.

The series of explosions, smoke, and flame billowing out of the unseen sinkhole startled Kit and Alex as they tried to make sense of what was happening. Preston waved smoke out of his face and pulled his Colt searching for a target.

Kit had thrown himself on the ground when the explosions began. He rolled into a shallow depression in the earth, flattening himself as best as he could.

Six quick shots and the Colt was empty. Preston ducked down behind the ATV and reached into his bag searching for his speed loader. It was gone! He remembered packing it, but now it was gone! He could feel heat rising from the sinkhole and noxious smoke was engulfing him. Preston fought back a wave of debilitating uncertainty.

Kit tried reasoning with the big man calling out from his hidden position. "Give it up. There are more of us than you. Your buddy is dead; there's no reason for you to die too."

Preston, suddenly feeling confident, shouted back, "You're the one who's going to die today."

Kit said, "Give up now. You're outgunned."

Preston guessed the short man was out of ammo or he would have returned fire. He stood up behind the ATV then ducked behind it quickly. No shots came at him. He felt the lack of gunfire confirmed his suspicions. He knew the Boonie Hat man only had a knife and that did not worry Preston.

Alex applied pressure to his wounds five yards from the ATV. There was nothing he could do against a gun or a grenade with just a knife. Kit was on this own for the moment.

Kit called out from his hiding place but this time Preston pinpointed his location. Kit aimed the empty gun at the big man. "Come out and get on your knees. Put your hands on your head with your fingers interlocked. Do it now!"

Preston called Kit's bluff. He was larger, he felt, than both of the men combined. One had a knife and the other a makeshift baseball bat. Preston knew they didn't stand a chance against him. He stood and walked toward the short man, hands outstretched, with the most defeated look he could muster on his red, sweaty, face. Kit stood up and advanced toward the man. Alex stood and awkwardly limped toward the man as well. Kit turned his head to look at Alex. He could not conceal his surprise that Alex was only holding a fixed-blade hunting knife.

The moment Kit's eyes widened in surprise Preston grabbed his last grenade and threw it at Kit. The impromptu action and Preston's adrenaline caused him to throw the grenade well past Kit. Preston realized he had over thrown his target the moment the grenade left his hand. Instinctively Kit dropped to the ground as the grenade sailed beyond him to explode well into the forest. The big man paused, perplexed about what to do next, momentarily frozen by indecision.

Alex limped toward the big man, knife in hand. Kit was slow to rise so Preston turned toward Alex who posed the immediate threat. Preston wrapped the empty canvas gear bag around his forearm to deflect the knife blade. Alex stopped and made a quick stab toward Preston's stomach. The attack backfired as Alex's damaged thigh undermined his thrust. Preston deftly deflected the strike and landed a kick to Alex's bloody thigh. Alex stumbled sideways struggling to retain his balance.

Kit closed in gripping the rifle like a baseball bat one more time. He watched the fight between Alex and the big man maneuvering himself to club the big man with the stock of the rifle. The three men circled each other like competitors in a wrestling match with the blazing sun as the spotlight and trees as rabid fans waving from ringside. Smoke continued to rise from the sinkhole.

Alex and Preston circled each other. Kit stopped and waited for chance to attack. Preston said, "It's a little unfair don't you think? You've got a knife and all I've got is an empty bag."

Ignoring his bullet torn thigh, Alex said, "Then surrender. There's no need to die today."

"It's not me who will die today. You're a skinny runt and junior over there looks like my dog's favorite fireplug. Plus, it looks like both of you are only a minute or two from bleeding out. I figure you two, against me, might last two minutes. Let's see."

Kit shouted, "Hey, asshole, there are two of us and only one of you. Surrender."

"I ain't the surrendering type. Plus, two of you against me only makes it a fair fight.

Kit brought the rifle back over his shoulder and feigned rushing the big man drawing his attention away from Alex. Preston braced for Kit's assault not realizing it was a fake out until it was too late. Alex rushed in low and landed a kick, with the full weight of his body behind it, on Preston's knee.

Roaring with a shout of pain as his knee buckled Preston let his weight fall on top of Alex. The big man knocked the air out of Alex's lungs as he collapsed on top of him. Alex pushed Preston off with effort and gulped in air. Alex's knife, knocked from his hand, lay lost in the tall grass. The two men exchanged punches as they fought on the ground. Punches landed with sickening thuds and the men grunted in response to the blows. Preston got a large hand on Alex's throat and squeezed.

Alex drove a knee into Preston's groin and the men separated as Preston's death grip momentarily weakened. Alex, unsteady on his feet, aimed another kick at the big man's knee but the big man intercepted Alex's foot violently twisting his leg. Alex screamed in pain as his leg turned beyond its normal arc. The big man jumped up surprisingly fast for someone his size. Standing over the fallen man Preston raised his booted foot and stomped on Alex's bullet torn thigh. Alex grunted loudly and his vision dimmed.

Preston was taller than Alex and had thirty pounds of muscle on him. The big man smiled knowing in the end the victory would be his. Then he would take the fight to the short man. The thought that the catfish and turtles would have a lot to eat after he dumped all of the bodies in the murky pond passed through his mind making him smile. He raised his booted foot to smash it down on Alex's neck.

Kit rushed the big man intending to use the empty rifle as a bat but he began his swing too early. Preston sensed Kit's charge and turned before finishing Alex off. Preston blocked Kit's swing with his forearm then landed a glancing punch to Kit's forehead sending him stumbling awkwardly backwards. Kit stopped and regained his balance staring at the big man. The big man smirked and took a step toward Kit before he sensed movement from the fallen man.

Alex was crawling away from Preston searching for his knife in the weeds; he stopped searching when he sensed the big man closing on him. Alex struggled to his feet and faced the big man.

Unarmed, Alex and Preston squared off. Alex was not worried about losing although he knew a hand to hand fight with someone Preston's size would last longer than he wanted it to last, but he was certain he would be the last man standing. Alex lurched forward, trying to ignore his bullet torn thigh; Preston maneuvered to take advantage of the man's bloody injury. The key to victory was going to come down to which man could ignore the pain effectively enough to win a prolonged hand-to-hand fight.

Preston used his hand to signal 'come on'. Alex closed and Preston moved to counter him. Alex feigned a charge but dropped and aimed his booted foot at the big man's knee hoping to topple him by finishing the weakened knee. Alex's extended leg exploded in pain as his foot only grazed Preston's knee. The ineffective kick caused Preston to laugh at the glancing blow. The giant man refused to be brought down.

As Alex rolled away the big man pounced on him. Preston landed two devastating punches to Alex's face, one to his nose breaking it and another to his left eye. As Preston raised his fist for a third punch Alex landed a powerful jab to Preston's exposed throat. The big man fell backwards gagging and gasping for air while his hands sheltered his neck. Alex rolled upright and stood over the gasping man. Blood from Alex's nose dripped to the ground as he watched the man massage his throat.

Alex wiped blood from his face and said, "Surrender?"

Kit watched, poised to act, but let Alex lead.

Preston held up one hand in a gesture of surrender as he massaged his throat with his other hand. Preston struggled to his knees gasping for breath. The big man let his shoulders slump and kept his eyes on the ground. He looked as defeated as a man possibly could look. Alex glanced at Kit moving toward them. Alex nodded at Kit and let his guard down a moment too soon.

In a move so fast it caught Alex completely unprepared Preston leaped up and sucker punched Alex who was caught by surprise as he wiped blood from his face. Preston hit Alex's chin with a rocketing dominant hand uppercut. The blow lifted Alex off of his feet. He dropped to the ground where he lay limp and lifeless looking in the weeds.

Kit looked on horrified as he felt the last straw fall.

Alex remained motionless on the ground. Preston stood over Alex for a moment to make sure the man would stay down. Just as the big man raised his booted foot to bring it down squarely onto Alex's throat Kit roared a primal scream and charged the big man.

The animalistic roar startled Preston and he turned toward the sound. Preston smirked at the sight of the short, stocky, man charging him. He glanced down at the skinny man and knew he was down for the count. Preston turned to face the short man; the sight of the little man charging to his death was amusing. Preston wondered if the little man knew he only had moments left to live.

Kit was running at top speed by the time he closed on the man. Preston's confidence turned to a look of surprise as Kit's determination became alarmingly clear. He braced for Kit's impact.

Kit Carson, bringing all of his weight and momentum to bear, launched himself at the big man's torso driving his shoulder into the man's solar plexus. Preston grunted loudly. Kit slid up the big man's chest; the impact staggered Preston who struggled to keep himself from toppling backwards. The top of Kit's skull collided with Preston's chin shattering his jaw and several teeth. Preston's head jerked backwards as he grunted in surprise and pain.

Kit's impact drove the entangled men stumbling backwards. Preston's heel caught the corner of the heavy wooden weapons crate. Kit's weight and forward momentum was too much and Preston lost his balance. The men teetered toward the edge of the sinkhole. Kit landed two quick punches to Preston's broken jaw shattering more teeth. Preston head butted Kit and Kit slightly loosened his grip. Preston pressed the momentary advantage but Kit blocked the big man's blows. Kit drove the toe of his boot into Preston's knee and the grappling men stumbled closer to the sinkhole. Kit kicked Preston in the same knee again. Preston collapsed at the lip of the sinkhole, rolled once then tumbled into the open maw of the sinkhole with Kit on top. Preston managed to land a blow to Kit's ear as they fell but Kit had found a chokehold on his foe's throat and ignored the pain from his pummeled ear. The men fell into the sinkhole with Kit squeezing the giant's throat with one hand while delivering short jabs to Preston's shattered jaw with his other hand. Preston clawed at Kit's grip on his throat gasping for air.

The men landed with a bone jarring thud amid broken and burning debris. Kit felt and heard the air go out of the big man. He straddled the big man hammering his face landing several before the smoke cleared revealing the big man was dead. A jagged two-by-four piece of lumber protruded through Preston's chest. The board had narrowly missed impaling Kit as well. Kit pushed himself off of the big man and rose to stand above the giant. He waved noxious smoke out of his eyes and stared down at his foe.

Several stunned moments passed before Kit noticed he was surrounded by smoldering plastic, small fires, and smoke. Horrified, he saw the pile of dead, charred bodies. Kit looked down at the dead man wondering what kind of monster he had encountered.

A small explosion shook Kit out of his shocked state. He had difficulty comprehending the scene revealed by the light of the fires; a cold chill of fear and revulsion overtook him despite the heat. Something small exploded in a dark recess of the cavern. It was as if he was in some anteroom of Hell. Kit thought regardless of what good he may have done by stopping a madman there was no upside to having his new property featured on Dateline and the evening national news broadcasts. He looked around at the carnage praying that the hellish sinkhole was on someone else's property.

Kit closed his eyes and stood perfectly still hoping this was a nightmare he was about to wake from. But, it was no dream, physical pain was manifesting itself all over his body, threatening to overload his senses. His lungs were burning and his eyes were watering from the toxic smoke trapped in the sinkhole and the temperature, fueled by burning debris, was topping one-hundred degrees.

Another small explosion jolted Kit back to the moment. He looked around for way to escape the hole and saw the chain ladder hanging down at the edge of a shaft of sunlight beaming down through the smoke. The metal ladder was the way out and up to daylight. Kit suddenly remembered Alex and quickly moved to the ladder and grabbed it intending to escape the hellhole before anything else blew up.

Kit released the ladder as quickly as he had grabbed it and looked at his burned palms. The fires had heated the metal ladder rungs to a searing temperature. Cursing in pain and frustration Kit began shaking his hands. He looked at the sky then back into the darkness surrounding him. Fearing more explosions before the metal ladder cooled enough to touch Kit removed his bloody T- shirt and ripped it in two pieces wrapping his hands with crude makeshift T-shirt mittens. After one last look at the big man, to be sure he didn't rise from the dead, at this point anything seemed possible, Kit began to climb toward daylight hoping Alex was alive.

22

If the wolves are outside howling at your door
Invite them in
And make them beg for more.
-B-52s

It was the fourth day since the Carson Conflict, as Ethan had taken to calling the incident, and the last law enforcement teams were wrapping up their investigation. Four days ago, shortly after Alex and Kit had left to pursue Preston, a deputy sheriff had arrived to investigate the ominous column of hellish smoke.

Deputy Sheriff Donna Jo Crossett could barely believe her eyes or the story the three men were relating despite the men's wounds and the burned evidence. Their tale began to ring true when Ethan led her to John Lee Sherman's body. Crossett identified the body immediately and suspected the unseen accomplice they told her about was one of the LaHarpe clan.

Crosset radioed for backup then sat listening to the men repeat their story as she recorded them on her phone. She also recorded the smoldering carnage on her new, high definition, body camera. She was mesmerized by the story; in fifteen years on the force she had never experienced a case like this. The department was still reeling from the disappearance of Sheriff Carver and Crossett began to suspect what may have happened to him as the men related their experience.

As Ethan and Charles took turns telling what they knew, Garrett, moving stiffly in the kitchen, made a fresh pot of coffee. Their relief that a friendly, law enforcement officer was present allowed a torrent of words to flow from each man. The men found it therapeutic to talk to the deputy; and her facial expressions of horror, disbelief, astonishment, and understanding made it clear she was listening and that she believed them.

As the men concluded relating the attack on the cabin backup arrived including off-duty deputies and the Tallyrand Volunteer Fire Department. Deputy Crossett brought the new arrivals up to speed as they stared past her at the burned ground, melted wreckage, then at the three disheveled men in the cabin. The coroner finally arrived and examined John Lee's body. There was a quiet murmur as the officials discussed the scene and the three strangers in the cabin.

As Garrett began a second pot of coffee Alex and Kit returned to camp riding John Lee's ATV. The two were quickly surrounded by deputies and ushered into the cabin where Alex and Kit related the climatic fight at the sinkhole.

Kit's wounds were cleaned and dressed and he was given a painkiller. Alex had his nose set and thigh bandaged then given shots to alleviate the pain. Alex and Kit were then led to the ranking officer and split up to repeat their stories into audio recorders. The tale of the shootout was interesting but the sinkhole lab captured everyone's attention.

A select group of five officers was tasked to investigate the sinkhole while daylight remained. While the deputies were being outfitted for the task Alex and Kit caught up on the condition of the other men before Kit was called away to lead the group of investigators to the secret drug lab.

The deputies were amazed at the underground laboratory's setup but gravely disappointed so much valuable evidence had been destroyed by the grenade explosion and resultant fires. As the deputies recorded their observations and took photos of the site Kit sadly realized the aftermath of the battle was going to be a long lived annoyance. At least the sinkhole was not on his property; he was thankful for that. Sitting on the ATV Kit said a little prayer asking for a quick resolution to it all. The task force spent an hour examining evidence and securing the scene. The crime scene investigators were amazed by the solar energy system and disturbed by the four charred bodies stacked in a corner like firewood. Kit sat on his ATV impatiently waiting for the investigators to emerge from the sinkhole. Once the investigators returned to the surface they drove green limbs into the earth cordoning off the mouth of the sinkhole with yellow caution tape. They debated stationing a deputy at the hole to protect it overnight, but in the end they simply pulled up the metal ladder and took it with them.

Kit returned to the cabin with the investigators. Kit's friends were seated on the cabin's porch while an army of people searched every square inch of the cabin, barn, the scorched yard, and what remained of the outhouse. An FBI agent arrived and asked to be brought up to speed. Garrett described what happened at the cabin and Kit the events at the sinkhole.

Over the next three days the investigators expanded to include more deputies, firefighters, HAZMAT, Wildlife Officers, State Police, FBI, DEA, and the BATF. The citizens of Tallyrand, outraged at first over the invasion of government minions, came to happily accept the unexpected cash flow from renting every hotel room and spare bedroom there was to be had in the city. Tallyrand's lone diner was overwhelmed with business. Several local competition bar-be-que teams rallied to cook burgers and fixings for the army of investigators and support personnel.

Three days of interviews that felt more like interrogations and three days of dozens of men and women gathering physical evidence were finally over. The collection of evidence supported the men's story confirming the deaths that occurred clearly happened as a result of self-defense from known repeat scofflaws. The investigators finally left on the fourth day and now the property seemed eerily quiet and empty.

On the fifth day following the attack the investigation moved to the LaHarpe property. Ponds were drained revealing their hideous secrets. Fifteen Chickasaw County cold cases were solved by draining three deep, murky, abandoned, stock ponds.
The LaHarpe compound and surrounding forest and fields were thoroughly searched or dug up. The LaHarpe family was in turmoil as they learned of Preston's murder spree. Four LaHarpe family members were taken to jail on obstruction charges before the investigation moved to the Sherman side of the family. The LaHarpe bucolic lifestyle was in chaos but chores continued despite the intrusion of investigators. The LaHarpe clan felt violated by the government and would never fully recover. The defilement, brought on by Preston, deeply affected Louis LaHarpe who spent his days angrily staring at the uniformed men and women.

Eugenia and the children had been banished and disowned for Preston's actions but could not leave the compound until cleared by the sheriff. Billy's branch of the family took his death badly and refused to speak to the others, blaming them for his untimely death. John Lee's branch of the family became persona non grata to the extended family. The LaHarpe's would never be the same again. Louis was beside himself with anger, grief, and impotent rage.

For Kit and his friends the property was quiet once again. The stillness was calming as the men rocked on the cabin's porch. Kit and his friends had been cleared of any wrongdoing and were free to return to their regularly scheduled lives. Ethan pulled one beer after another from an ice chest passing them down the line until every man held a cold beer. Plans were being made to return home to face the aftermath of the event.

Kit pulled the tab on his beer and looked around. The once green clearing was now a black and grey, ash covered, wasteland. The burned, melted, ugly carcasses of the tractor and ATVs could not be ignored. A dozen trees at the edge of the clearing were charred and scarred but would recover with time. The remains of the outhouse littered the ground near the trucks. The exterior of the barn was smoke stained waiting for a hard rain to wash it clean. Kit sighed and drained his beer in one long drink. The others watched silently, understanding the turmoil he must be experiencing.

Ethan broke the silence, "Well, this may be last time we are all together. I know I may never be allowed to leave the house again and Charles will probably never want to leave the house again."

Charles, distracted by his phone, mumbled, "With good reason." Cell service had finally been restored and he was constantly texting his sons with updates on his estimated time of arrival home.

Ethan looked at the other men and said, "You know, I thought Charles was going to cry with joy once the cell service resumed."

Alex said, "Have a bunch of feds that need reliable cell service and repairs happen quickly."

Charles stopped and looked at Ethan, "I hope that someday you have someone you care enough about to miss and want to talk to every day."

"Are you talking to me or Kit?"

Kit snapped, "Leave me out of this. I've got enough problems without taking on a new love interest now. This place went from paradise to hell in less than a week."

Ethan said, "No place to go but up from here!"

Alex said, "A good rain and some heavy lifting will get this place back to good."

Kit said, "It's not worth the effort. Everything went down the tubes."

Garrett mumbled, "Quitter", while smiling at Kit.

Ethan said, "At least you know all of the local cops, firemen, and game wardens now. I think you might be some kind of local hero. That's got to be a good thing."

Garrett said, "Kit, don't lose hope. The cabin is still in great shape. A good rain should wash the barn clean. The weeds will grow back. The sinkhole wasn't on your property so there's no EPA hassle to worry about. You can still do what you want with this place; it simply may take a little longer to get going."

Ethan said, "At least you have a name now: Fort Courage."

Kit glared at Ethan. "This isn't a fortress."

Alex waved his hand at the ash covered yard. He said, "How about Camp Phoenix?"

"Maybe." Kit sounded doubtful

Ethan said, "Call it Rancho Relaxo. After this shit, life down here should be a lot more relaxing. Which is precisely what you were looking for. Am I right?"

Garrett said, "Give it a rest, Ethan."

Ethan nodded and sipped his beer.

Charles finished texting and said, "Time for me to go."

"You trust your truck enough for the trip?"

Charles said, "Yeah, one of the firemen used some tools to pull out the fender and get it road worthy. I'm leaving my ATV for Kit to use since his melted. I only used it when it snowed at home anyway."

Kit sighed heavily, "Yeah, I expect a whole convoy of insurance reps coming out to inspect the damages. At least I've got police reports to show them."

"They will also need VINs for the ATVs and such."

Ethan said, "You'll definitely need the police reports from all of the agencies. No one is going to believe this."

Kit said, "Nothing feels the same now. It's like, well I don't know, I've got nothing to compare this to."

Alex said, "Count that as a blessing."

Ethan said, "At least the food truck is undamaged."

Charles stood and pocketed his cell phone. Looking at the other men he said, "I'm out. Men, it has been an adventure I will remember for the rest of my life. I am too old for this shit. If I never see any of you again, I love you all like brothers. Like brothers I have seen enough of till the next blue moon Christmas."

Ethan said, "You want a pain pill for the road?"

Charles glared at Ethan. "No. The EMTs gave me some."

"Are you going to buy an inflatable donut seat cushion for the ride back? Your ass is going to be a problem for a while!"

Charles gathered the folded blanket he was sitting on as a cushion. "This is good enough for now. I just want to get home and see my boys."

Kit said, "I can understand that."

Garrett said, "But you will be back for the grand opening."

"Grand opening of what?"

"Of whatever Kit decides to do with this place."

Kit waved off the optimism, "Don't hold your breath for a grand opening."

Alex looked at Garrett, "We're gonna have to work on Kit's attitude."

Ethan said, "I've been working on changing Kit's attitude for years and his attitude is consistently stoic."

Charles said, "Not everyone can live in denial and function."

Kit said, "Look around. Everything is ruined. Smoke damage, bullet damage, fire damage, reputation damage. Why try?"

Garrett stood and faced Kit. "Because you aren't a quitter. Realize that all of that is in a hundred plus square yards. You have two hundred and forty acres of prime, beautiful, peaceful, wonderful forests and fields. You even said the TV people were going to use the old hay field that is located dozens of acres from here. The producers will live in trailers and have food brought in from somewhere else. You really don't have a problem. Cancel the pity party and man up. The police gave us all a clean pass and you've got friends in the local cops and firefighters."

Ethan said, "Hell yeah, the locals would love for the local gravy train to keep on rolling. Crews and actors and public relations people mean extra money in everyone's pockets. The holidays aren't that far off and the locals have a taste of living large from the all the new found money suddenly pouring in."

Charles said, "He's right. All of the bad shit must have happened already. You got it all out of the way in one fell weekend."

In unison Kit and Ethan said, "Why did you say that? You just jinxed it all!" The two men looked at each other then glared at Charles.

Charles said, "If more bad shit happens here, you need to run away, far and fast, because this place must be cursed."

Alex said, "Nothing got jinxed. Shit happens all the time in different degrees to different people for all sorts of different reasons, some of which we may understand and some we may not understand. The forces that govern life, whatever you believe those forces to be, are both capricious and simply random and we must learn to accept that fact. You must take control of your life within the limits that you actually have control over. But just because shit happens doesn't mean we can't enjoy life between stepping in unexpected cow patties."

Ethan said, "Damn, that was deep, bro."

Kit said, "Yeah, but looking at the ash heap is a downer."

Charles repeated, "I'm out of here." He moved down the line shaking each man's hand before disappearing around the corner of the cabin. A moment later the big Escalade started and eased down the gravel drive. In a moment silence returned as the men finished their beers in silent reverie.

The day after Charles departed the men again found themselves sitting on the porch but now lamenting the fact that they were down to their last four beers. The burned wreckage of the tractor and ATVs were an eyesore but Kit had no method of moving them so he had covered the remains with a large tarp. Relaxing on the porch Kit, Alex, and Ethan sat on rocking chairs recalling some of their more colorful college experiences while assuring a skeptical Garrett that they were not embellishing a thing.

Kit tossed an empty beer can toward a trashcan and missed left. He stood to retrieve the can and dispose of it properly. As he dropped the empty can into the trash he said, "As long as I'm up I'm going to take a look around. I'll have to do it sometime, why not now?"

Alex said, "I need to stretch my legs; I'll go with you."

Garrett said, "Me too."

Ethan said, "Really? If you all go then I have to as well."

Kit was about to reply when the men heard tires crunching on the gravel drive. He said, "Well, the insurance adjusters were fast." Kit began to walk toward the parking area. The others followed slowly behind.

After a moment Ethan said, "That doesn't look like insurance adjusters to me. I hope we don't need guns."

Kit stopped and said, "Shit, will this nightmare ever end?"

Garrett said, "Stop being so melodramatic." He rested his hand on his sidearm.

Ethan said to Alex and Garrett, "You guys carrying?"

"Yes.

"Yes."

A battered pickup truck slowly approached the cabin. It stopped before it got to where the men's trucks were parked, as if keeping a respectful distance. Three old men in the truck's cab stared at the four men lined up across the gravel drive. The truck's engine stopped and the three octogenarians laboriously exited the cab.

One of the elderly men approached Kit while the other two followed a few steps behind their leader. The patriarch held out his hand, "Hello, friend, I'm Louis LaHarpe." Kit reached out and took the old man's hand.

"Kit Carson."

"Yes, you are. I seen you once when you was only knee high. I knew you'd be spunky when you got older."

Kit's group suppressed snickers at the comment. The old man never took his eyes off Kit. Kit waited for him to continue.

Louis LaHarpe turned to the other two men introducing them. "This is Grant Le Moyne and this is Robert Lee Fordyce."

Hands were shaken all around. Kit said, "Would you like to come in the cabin where we are out of the sun?"

Louis LaHarpe said, "No thank you. I came here to apologize on behalf of my family. I came here to acknowledge my negligence. I just wanted you to know that the family was unaware of the evil things Preston and John Lee were doing. We try to live a peaceful life away from the problems of the city, but sometimes that city evil spreads out here and seduces good people. You can't seem to keep the evil at bay even with constant vigilance. Now, I'm apologizing for dead men's actions.

"Preston was always a little different from the other children. Then he had a growth spurt and grew into a mountain of a man with the disposition of a child. Furthermore he rejected the family's wishes and worked for the government. He joined the Army and was betrayed by Uncle Sam. Preston said he was joining the Army to see the world, improve his outdoor skills, and learn how to defend the family. He came back changed. He was a man-child with a killer's skill. And he had no clear direction in life. That was our undoing.

"War is never good but we all fight wars every day. Each of us fight wars against the government, against rivals, against sin, against our own family. I take responsibility as the patriarch of the family. I apologize that our troubles were brought to your door.

"Preston's inner demons grew like a cancer in him. It affected some and infected others. And I didn't do nothing about none of it after his banishment. I believed that family honor and loyalty meant something to Preston. It did not. I did not see that. The evil that bad men enjoy crept in and took root in Preston. I banished him for a month and left it at that. Thought I had made my point about his behavior. Yet the evil remained in him. I underestimated the influence the outside world wields and all the methods it uses to infect and infiltrate minds too weak to defend against the siege.

"The nameless evil is like the chimera and assumes the form of what a host harbors inside. It is this evil what seems to have taken over Preston and John Lee. Preston and John Lee betrayed our trust and the government violated our lives and homes. Our family will never be the same if we stay in Chickasaw County. The family is moving to unspoiled land, sin free land, farther from the reaches of the evil the media and others spread.

"I came here to apologize face to face and to tell you that the family will be moving within the year and that I have told the realtor to give you first offer at buying the land. I'd hate to see a timber company come in and clear-cut the land or some corporation come in and strip it all down to the ground only to build a factory of some kind that pollutes without any regard for Mother Earth. I told the realtor to offer you a price significantly below the lowest fair price. After the offer you will have thirty days to accept or it goes to public auction. It is my way of apologizing for Preston and John Lee and what they got you into. I'm going to donate some of the sales of the machinery and livestock to the families of the people he killed.

"Don't feel rushed. It will be a while before we find new land and get everything sold off and be ready to move, but I wanted you know all of this. Even after all of this I'd rather the land go to you than some timber company or corporation; or worse, fall into the government's hands."

Louis's companions nodded in silent agreement with every statement. Their eyes never left Kit and men standing beside him.

Kit was stunned but offered a heartfelt "Thank you".

Alex nodded a silent 'thank you' as well.

Louis looked at the men standing beside Kit. They looked back at Louis and solemnly nodded. Louis held his hand out to Kit.

Kit shook his hand and said, "Thank you, again."

Louis moved down the row shaking each man's hand. Garrett stood stiffly, watching silently. Ethan still had his arm in a sling. Alex's black and blue face and bandaged thigh revealed trauma. Kit was a patchwork of ugly wounds from the outhouse exploding. The LaHarpe delegation gave the men their due respect upon seeing the evidence of the battle on their bodies and the land.

The other men followed Louis and wordlessly shook each man's hand as well. After the last hand shake the three elders turned and walked back to the old pickup truck. They slowly got inside and stared straight ahead. Louis put the truck in gear and drove in reverse all the way to the paved highway.

Kit said, "That was odd. I'm not sure what to think."

Ethan said, "They are a fucking cult."

Garrett said, "He said below market price. More land would give you more options."

Alex, Ethan, and Garrett all looked at Kit.

Kit shrugged, "I can't afford to buy his land."

Garrett said, "How do you know? You don't know what he will be asking."

Ethan said, "Hell! I'll invest just to have a reason to come back down here. I'd have to be silent partner. But Martha would have to let me visit to check in on our investment from time to time."

Garrett said, "If my son and daughter-in-law are still speaking to one another I'll see if they want to bring the food truck down to cater special events. I might be able to invest some money. I'd be a silent partner. Unless you start to lose my money then we'll need to rethink the silent part."

Alex said, "Maybe Camp Phoenix can be a reality."

Kit said, "I'm not sold on that name. Yet."

Alex said, "That ash field will be long forgotten after a few rains. Some cosmetic fixes and you're rustic chic. The television people will love it."

Kit said, "That's just the morning beer talking."

Ethan said, "Let's nail down some details about investing in your resort so I can have something to distract Martha from the bullet wound and destroyed ATV."

Alex said, "Always thinking about yourself."

Ethan shook his head, "I bet Charles would invest to help buy that old coots land. He's going to have empty nest syndrome soon and I bet he comes crawling back with too much time on his hands. He'll be putty in our hands."

Alex said, "Yeah, like that's going to happen. I bet Charles doesn't even set foot inside a city park again."

Garrett said, "LaHarpe said he'd offer the land to you below market value, you should at least think about it before simply writing it off as impossible."

Ethan said, "I've never pictured you as a cow farmer or hay grower. But that sounds like an easy life."

Kit looked at Ethan and shook his head. "Don't you remember all that stinky, heat of the summer work and winter visits where we had to break frozen water for the horses and cows to drink and the nasty stench of mucking out the stalls? I want a resort."

Garrett said, "Sure, this scorched earth and shoot out is a setback, but, once the TV people pay you, you may have a different outlook. Look, you are the new owner and in a long weekend you've written the first chapter of the exciting next generation history of this place."

Kit said, "I could call it Camp Ulysses."

Ethan said, "That would honor his memory."

Alex said, "Think of all the blood, sweat, and tears equity you now have in this place."

"If you are going to have seasonal activities you need a neutral or encompassing name."

"Camp Five Brothers. Or, Five Brothers Resort."

"Only the brothers who contribute get counted in the name."

Garrett said, "Camp Grenada. Campers send letters home to say hello mudder, hello fadder." No one got the dated reference.

Ethan said, "Yeah, that and between us we can surely come up with a business plan that will work."

Kit said, "I appreciate your enthusiasm."

Garrett touched Kit's shoulder and said, "You've got support. This might be your dream, but a dream is best shared with friends. How well can you balance buyer's remorse versus never knowing what could have been? You are embracing a direction you've just discovered but don't have a map to follow. That's not a bad thing if you look at it a certain way. You've reached a turning point but the destination may not be known for several months or years."

Kit looked out across the burned clearing and past the covered wreckage of the tractor and ATVs. After a long moment he turned and looked at his three friends. Each man had sweat and blood equity invested in Kit's property. Each friend had shown devoted loyalty to him and he should show his appreciation of that to them. A nagging sense of guilt over their injuries also affected Kit's thinking.

Alex, Ethan, and Garrett remained silent trying to imagine the emotional roller coaster Kit must be experiencing. Kit turned away from the men staring at the ash blanketed yard. The men could not see his face but his posture clearly indicated he was torn by conflicting thoughts.

After several minutes passed in silence Kit turned away from the post-apocalyptic landscape. The bright sun made the ashes shimmer as a slight breeze floated larger pieces of ash above the wasteland scene. Under the bright sun Kit knew that the burned trees would recover and the grass and wildflowers would return. Eventually the twisted and blackened metal wreckage would be removed. A few hard rains would wash the barn and cabin clean. Time would heal the land and in turn the land would heal Kit.

Kit felt hope return and he smiled. Taking a deep breath he turned to his friends. He looked each man in the eye before saying, "So, Camp Phoenix rises from the ashes?" Smiling, he hoisted an imaginary beer can and said, "To Camp Phoenix."

The others nodded, lifted their beers, and then said, in unison, "To Camp Phoenix."

Weekend Playlist:

Don't Drink the Water
Dave Matthews Band

Copperhead Road
Steve Earle

Down South Jukin'
Lynyrd Skynyrd

Fred Bear
Ted Nugent

Road Trippin'
Red Hot Chili Peppers

Nada
The Refreshments

The Boys Are Back in Town
Thin Lizzy

That Smell
Lynyrd Skynyrd

Take a Look Around
A Group Called Smith

Going Up the Country
Canned Heat

A Country Boy Can Survive
Hank Williams, Jr.

Frustration Incorporated
Soul Asylum

Monster
Steppenwolf

You Never Call Me By My Name
David Allen Coe

Most Beautiful World in the World
Harry Nilsson

Bad Company
Bad Company

Hey Man, Nice Shot
Filter

Copper Kettle
Bob Dylan

Red River
Tom Petty

Same Damn Life
Seether

Little Things
Alice Cooper

Trust Yourself
Bob Dylan

Death and All of His Friends
Coldplay

Doesn't Remind Me
Soundgarden

Wild Weekend
Hank Williams, Jr.

Pick Up the Bones
Alice Cooper

Rooster
Alice in Chains

Thrills
Seether

Hallucinating Pluto
B-52s